The Lazarus Chain

The Lazarus Chain

By

J. R. Baude

Printed in The United States of America

ISBN : 978-0-578-66846-8

Edited by Keely Latcham Boeving

Cover design by Nanjar Tri Mukti

J.R. Baude is an author of The Unremarkable Uneventful Life of Harvey Henderson and upcoming novel The Six.

Acknowledgments

My heartfelt thanks to Dr. Edward Weinstein for contributing his scientific expertise and keen insight to this work.

Dr. Weinstein is currently the Co-Founder and CEO of Canopy Biosciences and has earned a Ph.D. in Genetics from Harvard University, a Masters of Medical Science from Harvard Medical School and bachelor degrees in Chemistry and Cellular-Molecular Biology from the University of Michigan.

***

My deepest gratitude to The Reverend Gary Stoddard for his role as a theological resource and sounding board.

***

Many thanks to the stalwart members of the writers group for their guidance, advice, support, frank but gentle criticism and, of course, wine.

Alison, Dan and Sonja

***

One
July 22, 1987

There is a freight elevator, but it hasn't worked in years. Some thought was given to repairing the lift, but that would require a technician, an outsider, someone not to be trusted with knowledge of the location. A working elevator would be a godsend. The equipment could be transported in a fraction of the time and re-calibrating might not even be necessary. But secrecy is paramount; the staircase will have to do. Sturdy black steel built to survive an apocalypse, threaded through a spiraling tube of concrete. A stone sausage casing of a stairwell that amplifies each footfall to levels of ominous doom. Until nearly five months ago, the risers lay dormant and mute, un-tread for nearly a generation. Their silence breaking heralded the genesis of a project the world had never considered.

It had to be covert. No one outside was ready to know about this, certainly not during the conception phase. It was even decided that, when completed, the world should remain unaware. It was in their best interest, really. It was in the best interest of the project, too. The general population would be better off in the dark, or so it was thought.

All the way down. Seven levels separate the light of day from a cadre of experts, each from varied disciplines. In this place, nature is a stranger. Cinderblock walls wear a thick, floor-to-ceiling gloss of light green. But, a color unknown to the natural world, an ironic green. A hue reserved for diarrhea medicine, and millions of gallons of government-surplus, high-gloss latex enamel. Under foot lies battleship linoleum, parchment toned, speckled at random with brown, framed with a black border—chaos, but with a boundary. From above, in the room spaces, fluorescents flicker an anemic pallor. Caged 60-watt bulbs strain to fill the hallways. It is here, in this lifeless burrow, the birthing begins, an endeavor spawned from the nagging poke of uncensored curiosity, the offspring of cavalier impulse to offer open arms to the dark shaded whims of the unknown... to do it just for the hell of it.

"Okay, on to four-seven-one-K-eight-Baker... aaaand... negative," mumbles a weary voice.

"Check."

"Four-seven-one-K-eight-Charlie, results negative."

"Check."

The tech places another sealed petri dish marked "471K8D" under a large microscope.

"Okay, this one is..."

"Let me guess, four-seven-one-K-eight-Delta."

"*However* did you know?" the second tech returns with feigned surprise.

"And results? Guessing again, *negative,*" he drones expecting the same.

The second tech at the microscope arrests the established rhythm pausing an extra beat. "Ah, no. Actually, there is activity, *lots* of activity. One of you two want a look?"

From a shadowed corner two bald men in dark suits approach the microscope. "What am I looking for?" one asks.

"Well, it's kind of obvious. Here, look at the first dish." The tech replaces the dish with the previous one. "See nothing, just dead nothing. Now, the last dish. Look."

"Yes, I see it. What does this mean?" one of the suits asks.

"It means we did it, man. I told you we were goddamned geniuses, but you just think we're punks. There's still a lot of work ahead, but I've looked at thousands of these now and nothing has come anywhere close to this kind of response."

"So, now what?" the other suit asks.

"We grow a few more of this batch to be sure. You know, verify the results, and then we move on to..."— the tech tosses his hands in the air—"well, whatever you guys have planned for this?"

The first suit returns a dismissive smirk, "How long?"

"Probably another eight weeks, give or take."

"You will..."

"We know how to reach you, okay. Hey, where did you get this stuff, anyway? I think we at least deserve to know that, reward for a job well done, a little bit of love our way."

"That knowledge is not required for the completion of your specific duties," the second suit responds stone-faced.

"Yeah, whatever. Just thought you'd softened up a bit, wanted to embrace the spirit of celebration. But, I know you guys are all about *serious*, soooo..." The tech dons a more determined face and looks them both sternly in the eye. "Hey, you should know, I've been working on this kind of thing for a few years now, right on the cutting edge of it. I've never seen a result like this one. It's exploding all over the place in there. There's something different about it. This isn't alien shit, is it?"

The first suit smiles smarmily from one side of his mouth and both leave the room, down the hall, up the stairs, treading thunderous echoes and out through the screw-hatch to the surface. Night has fallen and the world is fast asleep.

Two
Present Day

Center mass and clean through. A second bullet goes astray, the limp victim folding over too quickly. The ensuing scramble of innocents rules out any further attempts. Resolved: the first shot will be enough to accomplish the task. The starburst of red spray painted on the wall behind tells him the impact offered sufficient devastation. The gun barrel wanders, looking down from five stories above, firing at random but away from innocents.

On to act two, double time down the stairs from the roof. With the violence unleashed, the plan is set in motion. Now, answers to unknowns reveal themselves down five flights of stairs. First and foremost, that he possessed the will to send the bullet on its way. A tsunami of *what-ifs* ebb through next. His nimble mind, one uniquely equipped for the task, works out the ensuing tumble of dominoes. The theoretical gives way to actual reality. The shockwaves delivered to the global social order dances before him. Each future move and subsequent reaction unfolds in his imagination with crystal clarity. A task unthinkable for any other brain is delivered to him intuitively like a child reciting their A-B-C's.

He decided long ago, the world had to know. A necessary jolt to the system was required, a disruption to the course of mankind was needed to focus attention more keenly on a brewing situation, one that will impact every soul on the planet. After deft consideration of every possible scenario, he concluded that assassination would be the perfect catalyst. Better still, the shooting would be interpreted as random desperation, the true purpose remaining hidden and unknown. It will be decided, he was just another lunatic pushed to the brink taking out his misguided ire on an unfortunate, wrong place—wrong time target of opportunity. The victim, a relative unknown, will have full attention brought to bear. It became apparent to him over time that the world needed to learn what this man was up to. He reasoned a simple telling of the facts would not be welcomed. They would be dismissed as ramblings of kookery, and very easily so.

Act three, ground level, the finale begins. To his right is a route that will lead him to safety, but a clean escape does not figure into his plan. Instead, he swings a door open to the street. Chaos is in full bloom growing more urgent as he weaves the crowd, his gun brandished wildly for all to see. His pulse saws through him. Hot breaths are rapidly counting down to his last. He spies his final destination. Approaching, he yells over and over a senseless phrase, one spectacularly out of context but certain to multiply the mystery.

"Saint John, Beloved," soars over the cacophony. "SAINT JOHN, BELOVED." Looking the part in military fatigues, the requisite costume of purveyors of mayhem, he approaches his destination. Thirty yards away a S.W.A.T team awaits. He raises his rifle to draw fire. His deliverers oblige. Hot lead rips through. The turmoil he unleashed finding full-circle finality. The full brunt of it returned to its maker. One second, maybe two in hell, then expiring to a merciful end. Into the great, endless darkness. The last box is checked. It is finished.

Three
Present Day

"Did you ever have a sense he was capable of violence?"

"Not at all, but we never really know everything about a person, do we?"

Just minutes before, Alex Traeger's quiet day unraveled when he opened his front door. Three uniformed Maryland State Troopers and a woman, FBI detective Patricia Hamer, now roam his condominium. The serious questions began swiftly and rapid-fire. Traeger's thoughts are struggling to keep up. Just moments before, he was enjoying solitude. Now, his mind spins with incongruous questions.

"Did you sense any instability in him?" Hamer asks, eyes fixed on Traeger's pupils. "Do you remember him speaking unusually about anything? Maybe something that didn't seem out of proportion then, but does now?"

Traeger battles with himself to strike the correct balance between candid and cautious. "Honestly detective, no. He was really just a nice guy. I guess I always felt he had something stirring in the background, though."

"Explain that," she says shifting to lean in closer, her curiosity piqued.

"I mean his take on things was always one of biblical proportion. Not biblical, *literally*, but there was always more consequence to the way he said things, sizing things up with his own impossible, eccentric yardstick. To answer your question, though, I never had any indication he had the capacity for violence."

"Thank you, Mr. Traeger. That's really all for now. You may—probably will— get some follow-up inquiries as we learn more. He didn't have a lot of contacts or acquaintances, no immediate family or close friends, at least that we can determine. So, we will be focusing on the names, like yours, that pop up in his personal effects."

"No problem, Detective Hamer." Gripped with an urgent thought, Traeger asks, "Am I a suspect in any way, Detective?"

Hamer responds with a slight shake of her head that might be a "no," leaving Traeger unrelieved. Nevertheless, he leans back in his living room arm chair, breathes deeply, and unpeels his clenched hands from the armrests.

While entering notes on her phone, with one eye Hamer observes Traeger's posture and eye movements. She notes his breathing and reaction to the troopers roaming his living space. Standing over him, she asks a fresh question.

"There is this one curiosity, though. Of the dozen or so names in his address book, yours is the only one that has this mark beside it." She angles her cell phone down to Traeger, showing him a snapshot of the address book page. "It kind of looks like an asterisk, but then not really. Do you know why that might be there?"

"No earthly idea," Traeger replies, earnestly meeting her gaze trying to ward off any suspicion on her part. "If I spent a grand total of two hours talking to him, I would be surprised. I think our longest conversation was under ten minutes. We sort of had coffee once at the cart in the lobby at the university offices. I just ran into him there. Our conversations were always small talk. If it was anything deeper than that, I would think he would have initiated more between us." Traeger's thoughts stir further, but calming conclusions elude him.

"I'm sure you're right, just needed to ask. Here is my card if you think of *anything* that might be helpful. Please don't hesitate. It's usually the stupidest little thing that can break a case open."

"Sure thing, detective Hamer." She turns and takes a step away. "Oh, Detective? I… I don't know… Well, I guess I'll just go ahead and ask," Traeger posits, rising to his feet. "I know it's way early in your investigation and any information probably has to remain with you. But, it might help me jog my memory if you gave me more details. You know, where he was, who this guy was he shot."

"You're right, Mr. Traeger. I can really just sum up what we have already released in the press briefings. I don't want to assume you have full knowledge, so let me see." She taps her phone a few times and begins reading. "The search of his home and the actual act itself surprisingly doesn't speak of unhinged delusion or derangement. The shot he landed took some skill and training. Your friend, pardon me, *acquaintance*, William Reader apparently had some sort of vendetta against this guy."

"Vendetta? William? He was an academic. He studied cultures. He was an anthropologist of sorts, not a hit man." Sensing a casual trust from the detective, Traeger's concerns relax a bit. He fixes his gaze out the window to nature to remind him of the ordinary, pure and predictable.

"I agree. Everything we have turned up has pointed to a mild-mannered, although quirky, individual until this one incident a few days ago."

"See what I mean?" Traeger strains out in frustration to understand. "It is senseless in every way."

"To your point, the whole vendetta theory still has one glaring flaw in it," Hamer sidles up shoulder to shoulder with Traeger finding common refuge in the landscape outside. She hopes being less aggressive may birth a eureka-moment.

"Yeah, what's that?"

"The victim, the guy he shot, I have interviewed nearly two dozen people and not one of them has said anything bad about him. He is highly revered in his field of study... *fields*, really. By all accounts he's brilliant and spoken of as a sure-thing Nobel winner someday. He's contributing to breakthroughs in medical science, agricultural issues, and cultural conflicts."

"Sounds like the love child of Gandhi and Einstein," Traeger muses.

"Exactly, Mr. Traeger. Hard to figure why there is a shooter in all this. Reader was clearly not taking this lightly, whatever it was. Based on preliminary searches, and I'm dancing on the edge of what I can tell you, but this will all be out in a couple of days anyway. We found his mountain property littered with shells, apparent repeated rehearsals for the shooting. The weapon he used was not off the rack. It was military grade, and even then highly customized, some ceramics involved, custom designed rounds. He was extremely prepared for this, planned to the last detail. Whatever the victim was doing in his life, William Reader determined it needed to come to an end with massive damage."

"And the victim? Um..."

"Carpenter, James Carpenter."

"Right. Why haven't they reported his death yet, or released his name?"

"Because he isn't dead. He survived and is making an amazing recovery. His name hasn't been released at the request of his handlers. He is still in critical condition."

"That's incredible. The initial report was the bullet pierced his heart."

"It did. But he's alive. Someone up there likes him, I guess."

Four
Present Day

"The higher-ups are rapidly encroaching on the investigation. So, I'm not sure how much longer I will be in control of it," Patricia Hamer advises her long-time friend Ivan Myer. "While I'm still central and active, I'd like to borrow you for a bit, if you don't mind." Myer nods, already examining the case data.

Across from each other at a tired wooden desk, they brainstorm after hours in a precinct room. A crippled overhead fixture cradling a dozen or so insect carcasses struggles to illuminate the area beneath. A tablet device belonging to Hamer sits off to the side glowing eagerly in standby mode—a virtual vault bearing several hundred stills and a dozen or so video clips collected from street-cam and security system servers.

"There are some aspects here that seem to go against the grain," she advises her colleague. "But I'm getting the sense the brass want to tie it up quickly. With a deceased perp, and a narrative that just says *random gun violence,* there isn't a lot of motivation to dedicate resources to cast a wide net on this case, one that seemingly will conclude with nothing more than *deranged gunman.*"

"Yeah, and the press is running with that as we speak. I'd say, if there's an alternative, it will be scoffed at and unwelcomed in less than a news cycle or two," Myer adds, stroking two-day salt-and-pepper whiskers poking from his taut jaw. His dark eyes dart from picture to case notes and on to another picture. Almost trance-like, he draws in data. His non-linear process relies on his keen intuition. Myer's credential is not one of letters or attached to anything as mundane as a bureau or agency. He is strictly a freelancer, navigating the seams that join politics, crime, and news reportage. He possesses an intuition surpassing any of her other colleagues and she values his investigative skills as a complement to her own. Together, they catalyze each other.

"Tomorrow is Friday and the short-attention-span media will not be interested in new angles by Monday," Myer continues. "That's just the way these things go these days. Once that happens, neither one of us will be willing to risk our careers or reputation to proffer an alternate theory should it exist. We'd just come off as conspiracy mongers."

Hamer nods in agreement, adjusts by crossing her toned legs, and leans in to the table. Myer reaches to a grouping of coffee mugs, judging the warmest to be his latest pour. He sips, squinting off the tepid bitterness.

"So, you said something about *against the grain*," Myer offers as cue for Hamer to tap her profiling skills.

"Right, well, the most glaring thing is, he didn't leave a note or a manifesto." Her slender features and gentle hazel eyes lend no hint as to sturdiness of her inner mettle. Her abilities are well known to Myer, though, who listens intently. "These guys are always steeped in delusions of grandeur. The violence is merely the macabre attention-grabbing event to lead the masses to their insane ramblings, which are always left on some social media or web presence. William Reader had nothing like that. The only place he can be found in cyberspace is buried in the university's official website and even then it's just a departmental blurb, a paragraph about his credentials and curriculum. He didn't even write it. Of course there are tomes of academic material he left behind, but that's all."

Myer jumps in. "S.W.A.T. found no booby traps in his apartment; that's become a commonplace addition to the random shooter repertoire. A few days ago, he even arranged for his neighbor to take care of his cat, telling her he was going on sabbatical. There just aren't the usual markers here for insane egomaniac."

"What do you make of the other shots he took, Ivan?"

"Clearly designed as some sort of diversion or misdirection. It's almost like he wanted to give the impression he was the classic bell tower guy firing haphazardly into a crowd. If he takes only the one shot, it screams contract hit. The first shot was the only purposeful one, and it was a hell of a shot. The other four are cosmetic to cover his true motivation. He was a good enough marksman to take out many more if he wanted."

"So, you think it was a hit, a contract killing?" she offers with a look of skepticism.

"No, I don't, Pat. This guy was a legitimate academic. He was well published and still taught even though he had enough tenure and clout to be a full time researcher. He simply didn't have time to be a hit man." Myer sips his coffee and resumes without missing a beat. "He did travel a lot, and you're going to want to check that out, see if you can tie it to other killings. But I don't think you're going to find anything. And, by the way, contract killers disappear after they get the job done. Reader did nothing of the sort."

"I'm totally with you so far, Ivan. So, why the obsession with this Carpenter guy? I should have picked up a connection by now, but I'm not. They led completely separate lives. There is no motive, no professional jealousy, no cheating spouses, no spouses period. No money involved, no political animosity; it doesn't make sense."

"Ditto," Myer replies while nodding. "And you know what else doesn't make sense? Reader comes down in plain sight and basically sacrifices himself. Tell me if you think differently, but he could have delivered the one shot, dropped the weapon, and casually strolled down and out of the other side of the building and blended right in. He was right there on his own campus, could have had a seat at the café on the street below and gotten away scot-free. He probably would have had a dozen witnesses to swear he was somewhere else at the time of the shooting. Chances are, he would have made a clean getaway."

"Excellent point," Hamer agrees and sighs at the increase in variables. "The gun was untraceable, the ammo was homemade. But, with his mission apparently completed, he just went out into the street with gun in hand, approached the first uniforms he could find and walked straight at them until he was shot to pieces. He wasn't even wearing a vest. He just committed suicide."

"That part of it is unusual, too, since they usually kill themselves."

"And what do you make of his last words? *Saint John*? *Beloved*?"

Myer runs a hand through his rumpled hair and shakes his head. "It makes no bloody sense."

"I know." She raises her hands in dismay. "I've heard some unusual references uttered by gunmen, but this one is completely baffling." She taps out the phrase on her tablet. "Let's see... Catholic schools... Churches... Encyclopedic references to the apostle, nothing out of sorts." She adds the name "William Reader" to the search phrase. "And," she scans the list quickly, "even more nothing."

"I'll look into it deeper tomorrow, Pat."

"You're not going to find anything, I already know," Hamer answers boldly drawing from her years of experience in investigative fields, forensics, and related sciences. "It's just another mystery. I'm afraid he took that knowledge to the grave."

"You're going to slam the lid on it, just like that?" Myer gives a puzzled look.

"I know that sounds defeatist."

"It must mean something to someone. He made sure a whole bunch of people heard it while he was center stage. He even repeated it four times. If it was some sort of prayer or affirmation with some personal attachment, he would have done it after the shooting in his own private way. Why wait until you are down at street level moments before you die?"

"Maybe that's exactly why," she counters. "You might be on to something. I don't think it was an affirmation and certainly not a prayer. There isn't any indication he had any religious affiliations at all. The search of his home found a few religious items," she pauses to review the list. "Well, *items* is even too much of a word, reference material is more like it. The investigative team found books on religious history, anthropology and early cultural studies from the Holy Land, but nothing reverential or indicating some adherence to a system of beliefs, not even close."

"I still think it means something to someone. We just need to find that someone."

"Good luck with that, Ivan.

Five
August 26, 1988

The forested areas are best. Open spaces allow too many distant objects into the field of view, anchoring the foreground, disappointing the brain as to the actual speed underway. But when trees stand at both sides, blurring and bleeding together, the genuine fury is palpable. It quickens the heart, steels the senses, and for an adrenaline junkie like Anders Kipner, it is pure dope.

Kipner is an uncommon genius, a wunderkind in the fields of biomedical research and genetic modeling. Here, rocketing on four wheels, he finds sanctuary. A place of frenzied solace to contemplate his own brilliance. Deep in self-veneration, he reviews the last few of his brief twenty-eight years on the planet, one globe-hopping assignment after another. Scotland, then to India, Argentina across to New Zealand, and now settled in

Germany. The engine's hum blooms his ego while rehashing the roster of cutting-edge bio-research entities who sought his scientific magic. But the work he treasures most proudly, remains untold. For a nineteen-month period from mid-1986 to late 1987, he was part of an elite team working on an underground project—literally underground. Work of such disrepute, if made known, would irreparably damage his stature and credibility, no matter what value he might bring to a given project. The stain of his dark research in a long-forgotten bomb shelter, seven stories below ground, would disgrace any legitimate achievement he was even slightly associated with. The entirety of the project would be discredited and tarnished, including the reputations of those working with him. Kipner remains fully resolved that it is a matter best left unmentioned.

He wishes he could confess it all, so many monumental breakthroughs he helped nurture that others won't approach for another twenty years. But he knows it would all be sorely misunderstood. He callously dismisses as "common minded" the establishers of the stifling boundaries of scientific ethics, loathing their limited imaginations. If they knew, they would heap ridicule and scorn, banish him to the outskirts, an unforgivable pariah.

But there were other benefits besides bragging rights. The project was financially gainful. Within his hands, he clutches his consolation prize, the tan, kid leather wrapped steering wheel of a blaze-red 1988, Ferrari Testarossa. For the most part, he keeps his expenditures low-key, off the grid, as instructed. But the car is too important to him. He needs one overt symbol, one sublime, egotistical appendage to counter-balance his needling desire to expose his indulgent scientific dalliance. He safely explains off his vehicle as an impulse buy, a cashing in of an inheritance from a wealthy great-aunt.

The whine of the engine whispers sweetness in his ear, a glorifying minion reminding him of his own brilliance. Each vehicle he passes rightly reaffirms his rarefied abilities. When you have the proper tools and the God-given talent to use it, it's expected you should embrace the glory. It is the evolutionary mechanism at work, the superior supplanting the inferior when the moment arrives. He decided anything less would be a sin. The speedometer serves up more validation, displaying the number "168." His nimble brain converts the kilometer reading to miles per hour: 105. Thank God for the Autobahn, or is it the Fuhrer who should be praised?

The car embodies a confirmation of his internal sense. He belongs here. This is his place in the world, galloping alongside the supremely bred, and three-digit speeds externalize his glorious assessment of his own self-importance.

The sound of a bee approaching his ear breaks him from his self-concerned thoughts. He swipes at it only to instantly learn it is not an insect. On his driver's side, a motorcycle passes him. His superiority is questioned. That cannot be allowed. His right foot finds the floor and the car leaps forward. The gap narrows. Fifty meters and gaining, he sees the rider. It is a woman. Straddled above a powerful, four-barrel rocket rides an hourglass figure wrapped in skin-tight black leather. A pink crash helmet fails to completely contain her silky black mane, stirring Kipner's curiosity and libido.

The speedometer has climbed to 208 km/h. He has never gone this fast. He gains until he is side by side, matching her pace. He glances over. She glances back. Through her faintly tinted visor, he sees a sparkle in her eye, and a sly smile of blood-red lipstick. She looks ahead and throttles up, pulling away again. The game is on. Kipner speeds up, disbelieving a motorcycle exists that can reach these speeds. He imagines the raw appetites of a beauty so comfortably embracing velocities of 130 mph while balancing on two wheels. He is intrigued, even aroused.

He feels a stiffness, but not the one he expected. His leg, the one on the accelerator has become frozen. He can't bend it. His other leg soon follows, his hands as well, welding to the wheel, his whole body now. Arousal is furthest from his mind; stopping is first and foremost. But how is this happening? Something he ate? Something he drank? He remembers now ordering one double bock but two arrived, delivered separately. He remembers thinking it a windfall of an overworked server, now not so much. He has been drugged. He is certain of it. The first beer was unusually bitter. Paralyzed, he is a rigid board moving at frightening speeds for someone so lucid in thought. A paralysis so complete he can't even blink.

His foot is glued to the gas and his hands unable to reach the key to kill the engine. The highway remains unbending as far as he can see, but he knows that can't last.

She gazes back purposefully in her rearview mirror, maintaining speed, observing. The car drifts gradually across the inner-shoulder boundary, pulling left towards the center guardrail. Ahead, the road now bends, ever so slightly. It is just a matter of seconds now. Sheer terror races through him. He knows he is going to die. The front panel of the Ferrari eases into the railing, sparking, scraping. For a moment it seems he might be slowed.

A loud ping, and then a bang. The sky spins outside, then the earth below. Blaze red steel flies upside down. It is an unnatural peace, one disturbed only by the solitary whirr of the motor spinning tires that find no traction. He is floating, and tumbling, and spiraling. The car finds a thick, mighty oak trunk. Fine, Italian craftsmanship explodes on impact, but not in a fiery blaze, just a matter of physics. The proverbial unstoppable force meeting the immovable object. Object stands firm as victor. The car litters the forest, a three acre yard sale of Ferrari auto parts. The driver is undetectable anymore as human, parted out in similar fashion.

Three minutes pass. Easing by slowly, after circling back, a performance motorcycle with female rider scans the wreckage strewn deep into the forest. Satisfied, she snaps down her visor, grips the throttle and flicks her wrist. Down the highway she disappears. Her work is done.

Six
Present Day

An envelope slides into view, capturing the somber eyes of a slight, elderly man and interrupting him from his daily devotional reading. The humble, time-worn table before him, now bears considerable weight. There is a single stamp, one of great expense wearing a United States postmark from three weeks previous. The man nods to the deliverer as both absolution for the intrusion and as dismissal. The teen boy, clothed in saffron robes, quietly turns and departs. A tear wells in the man's eye, hanging, ready to fall as if needing permission. It decides on its own, plummeting onto more saffron linen.

"Dear William, my heart breaks, but you are finally at peace, good sir," he emits breathlessly.

It is the first letter the elderly man has received in thirty-one years, one he hoped would never arrive. Without opening the envelope, its meaning is clear. He need not read the sender's name. He knows it. He need not open the letter. He knows it will be empty. Yet, its arrival alone brings an awful news. He rises and paces gingerly to an open window framing a view from on top of the world, before him a sea of Himalayan peaks. The bright morning sun rises upon a day of darkness like none before.

"And so it has begun. The one has been found. Let us hope the extreme price was a wise purchase, William."

They agreed long ago when they parted company that, if the time came to employ this last resort, William Reader would send the letter to his colleague Jonas Kovacs. The letter, more a signal flare, would contain no text. Too much would be at stake to pass along specifics should it find its way into the wrong hands. Upon receiving it, Kovacs would leave his secluded existence in the Tibetan ranges to resurface near Reader's last known location, the city of postmark. It was understood that Reader would set the wheels in motion. Kovacs and the unnamed one would find each other, somehow, through some mix of scattered markers and a little blind faith. Also agreed upon, the letter would not be sent unless Reader found no other recourse except one requiring his own demise.

Kovacs had promised himself it would never come to this. He was warm to the idea that he would live out his days humbly, needing nothing more beyond the boundaries of the Buddhist monastery he calls home sequestered thousands of feet up a steep traverse. He is frightened, but not from the greater danger that resurfacing holds. It is more the re-assimilation into a life of material need and torrential distractions. He has been happy here, sharing every waking moment with his God for three decades. He fears a return to the external world, with all its pitfalls and hollow spectacle, will drive a wedge between himself and the Almighty. He convinces himself, for a moment, that he is unnecessary to the cause. The chosen one belongs to a new generation, one more savvy than when Kovacs was younger. He wonders what he himself could impart to a person so worthily selected that could prepare them for what lies ahead. He decides maybe he should stay.

Again, he spies the letter resting on the table. It represents a greater calling. Reader has certainly sacrificed himself. Kovacs concludes he owes Reader his end of the deal, to complete the task to groom a savior. Perhaps in his return, redemption and atonement will be found for his own regretful acts, sins committed long ago in the throes of arrogance and ignorance. Misdeeds nurtured in the misguided desire of others to reach past the heavens.

Despite being a man of extreme dedication and duty, he must reach deeper within to bolster himself for this challenge. He must leave his home and depart his family of brothers. There is sad news to deliver. He will never see any of them again. He will bid a tearful farewell and journey forth with love as his calling. He knows he is the only one prepared to answer this clarion. A momentary prayer, then he removes his robe. A suit coat pulled from a sealed chest hangs like a drape on his diminished frame. He descends wooden steps from his chamber, somber yet charged by what awaits. Once again, he will lose himself in the confusion of the human masses, with single-minded purpose to find another who must save a broken world.

Seven
Present Day

"Mr. Carpenter, of course the first question is, *how are you doing*?" asks a doe-eyed, foot soldier among an army of press correspondents squeezed into a small auditorium. The question's target, James Carpenter, is seated in a director's chair on the small stage, wearing a comfortably fitted white linen shirt, perfectly tailored blue jeans and leather sandals. A neatly trimmed coffee-brown beard graces his confident jaw.

"I am just fine, thank you. Before I go deeper into this, I want to thank everyone, everyone in the entire *world* it seems for their unflagging support and wishes". He beams with radiant brown eyes, projecting unquestioned confidence. "You just don't know how much that makes a difference until you've been where I have the last few weeks." To a person, the press corps wears a posture of admiration and awe towards their subject. All of their instinctual, confrontational urges have been stowed away. "It goes without saying that the medical team at Mount Sinai was magnificent. I don't think I would be here talking to you if they had not been watching over me night and day. But, to answer your question, I can't recall feeling better, ever."

"Mr. Carpenter, will the medical team be making an appearance today?"

"As I understand it, they are going to be shy. Press conferences aren't their cup of tea, apparently. Unfortunately, you will need to find another time to get the medical details. I might be able to assist, though. I was there, you know." Carpenter smiles short of a chuckle.

Another reporter rises. "Mr. Carpenter, can you put to rest speculation of where the bullet... excuse me, I know this sounds insensitive..."

"Not at all, please," Carpenter implores.

"Well, it was reported the bullet pierced your heart. The bullet being a high-caliber, military-grade custom round. It just seems unlikely that..."

"Those reports are rumor. The bullet grazed the left ventricle and passed harmlessly through my body. I was blessed. The odds, I am told, were well beyond impossible, and I just," Carpenter pauses, emotion catching up with him. "I got lucky, really."

The next reporter stands. "Mr. Carpenter, Jim McKee, World Headline News. Over the past few weeks, there have been a good number of reports detailing your background, your interests and occupations. I was wondering if you saw any of those reports and if you had any comments or corrections. I guess I'm just asking you to describe yourself in your own words. Tell us about yourself."

"My interests are legion. I can't say I have one that I favor or excel in particularly more than another. But, I look at the issues and problems facing our world in this time and just examine if there is some contribution I can make using my skills as a problem solver." He scans the group pensively, seeking a deeper connection. "I've had some good fortune and a whole lot of help from scores of very talented people. I've also had some plain old dumb luck as it turns out."

McKee continues despite another reporter standing for her turn. "But, if I may, Mr. Carpenter. As a follow up on your very humble response, one example, in the field of agriculture. You've developed several strains of drought-resistant grains and high protein legumes designed for the African continent that have, by some estimates, saved hundreds of thousands of lives." The reporter's query is presented without malice, more as an invitation for Carpenter to boast. The reporter raises a hand to ward off interruption. "Although not officially announced, there are insider reports of research guided by you that will soon produce a genetically modified mosquito with an enhanced immune system that actually *combats* malaria. Once released among the general population, it is believed that this elusive and highly destructive disease will be eradicated in under three years simply by these mosquitoes breeding with the current population."

"Well, I..."

"There is the clash in Tanzania, the end of which was brought about by your insertion into the peace negotiations that, by all accounts, were crumbling rapidly. Your contribution brought an end to a bloody civil war in only a couple of days. There is more…"

"Oops, looks like I've been outed," Carpenter jests, punctuated with a laugh; the press corps joins him. "I propose, Mr. McKee, that your account of my achievements is merely one version of the truth. Although the mosquito you mention is only rumored and there are no releases to officially back your claim. Overall, you are essentially correct." Carpenter stands and paces a few steps in front of the gathering. His firm posture carries a lithe but sculpted frame. The quiet force of his presence vibrates the room. Dark, shoulder-length hair sets off his rich complexion; one of ambiguous origin. "I must point out, I was only one of a good number of folks who participated in the lengthy, arduous labor needed to accomplish all of this. For the most part, I was merely directing traffic." Carpenter pauses; his eyes scan his audience, further engaging the crowd. "Because of some early successes in my life, and the financial freedom that success provided, I am fortunate enough to enjoy the luxury of cherry-picking the things I wish to undertake. I am able to focus my attention on the ones that suit my gifts, ones where I can envision a path to a clear resolution based on my unique abilities."

McKee presses on. "But you have yet to fail. You are only in your early thirties with a flawless track record, and until now, you have managed to remain in obscurity for the most part. Within the realms you inhabit, you are quite revered. But to us ordinary folk, you are an unknown."

"Well, until a couple weeks ago," Carpenter inserts. "But seriously, and ironically, it seems my misfortune to step into the path of a bullet has brought my persona into the spotlight more than anything else in my life. I'm not sure how long I wish to stay there, but I will be accessible for as long as it interests the curious, or as long as I feel it isn't interfering with my work."

"Mr. Carpenter, Myrna Rand, BBC London. So, to the raw bit of it. Why would anyone want to shoot you... attempt to kill you, actually? Do you ever recall any association with the shooter?"

"I am unaware of any. My staff has combed our scheduler archives and communication channels. There is no record of any encounter with William Reader. I think it is a mistake to apply some greater purpose or insight into the motives of the shooter." Carpenter gazes thoughtfully around the room. "We can never understand the disconnected chaos that reigns in the thoughts of a madman. I don't know any reason why anyone would want to kill me. I am fairly sure even *he* didn't know."

Eight
Present Day

To Alex Traeger, the project sounded interesting at the outset. One of the first settlement structures built in the New World, and one of the rare few still standing. The plusses were numerous. A chance to connect with centuries-old history and a welcome challenge to depart the open range of whole-cloth invention to the precision landscape of meticulous restoration. Also, the rebirth of a treasured landmark would garner greater notice from a wider audience, attention bringing priceless value to his one-man firm. Maybe more importantly for him, he imagined, it would be soul-nurturing work. Adopting the role of healer for a weary building steeped in rich heritage and sentimental grace felt noble to him. Sub-standard pay was the downside. But as business, it would establish a foothold, open a new marketplace, and launch a profile within a niche realm of architectural design. But greater than all those reasons, it just felt right.

The photos sent by the historical society portrayed a once proud structure now beaten down by the ravages of time and the elements. It may as well be a mirror, he thought. It would be a chance to heal his own worn heart and its craving for renewal. He would bring newfound luster to a past desperate for mending.

To know the building, one must know its era. So, this time "Project Lead Architect" would be synonymous with "Research Historian". The task would require meetings and study, talks with the learned locals, trips to Richmond to comb property records and seventeenth-century shipping manifests. He would receive firsthand demonstrations by colonial craftsmen on the tools and techniques of the day, all the things necessary to flesh out his understanding of the structure's personality. The finished work would need to portray a seamless rebirth of the past into present. Every residual saw mark and chisel strike must be authentic in execution. Replacement nails and mortise joints would have to be hand-crafted and aged to match those still anchored firmly after 470 years.

As the project progressed, he found the most difficult aspect was one he never considered, one not architectural. History is one thing, but one must become absorbed in purpose as well. This being a church unexpectedly brought a struggle as he delved into the religious legacy woven into the building like a dovetail joint. For those who commissioned him, it was all second nature, doctrine assumed, inarguable. But to him, it comes across as glorified mythology, stories meant for others, not for him. Early on, he asked questions of his employers to probe an understanding of the building's deeper purpose, questions all politely answered. But, whatever these doctrines possessed as truth for them in the structuring of their lives, found no resonance where he was concerned.

To avoid undue tension, and the potential tarnishing of the project's air of good will, his questions now go unasked. Specifics regarding the spiritual necessity for objects like baptismal fonts and tabernacles for reserved sacraments remain open ended or are relegated to web searches. No deeper insight is gained on the modern need for props like sacrificial altars, and the most disturbing object of all, a device of Roman torture embraced as the most sacred and core symbol of their deepest beliefs—the cross. Although unimposing in form, its original purpose was as a killing machine of unthinkable horror. Slow patient death, brought on by the gradual, cell-by-cell destruction of the body and exposure to the elements, eventually culminating in languishing suffocation. The end was welcome when it finally came.

It isn't as though he is a complete stranger to these things. For anyone raised in Western culture, basic familiarity with the trappings of Christianity is inevitable. He even attended church as a child with his mother, though only briefly. But his recent immersion into the subject has stirred some unsettled energy. Perhaps for the first time, he is compelled to understand the deeper reasons behind the religious practices. It places him directly in the path of core theology, practices that beg acceptance or rejection and nothing in between. The architectural mission owns his full attention. But to bring justice to the handiwork, he must consider the spirituality involved and deign to understand why others find sacredness here.

His employers are all good people. He considers himself a tolerant man. But for some reason, a surge of callous judgment overtakes him when subjects like the Communion mass are breeched. How can ingesting a stamped wafer of bleached flour and a sip of sugary wine bring any scintilla of salvation to one's soul? He knows the tradition goes back two thousand years, but that's exactly the point—two-thousand years. Shouldn't something have evolved by now beyond this crude, ritual ceremony to bring more depth to one's experience of existence? Maybe more attention should be given to immediate solutions to the problems of our troubled world. Maybe that would bring more personal fulfillment than pleading to a silent god? There is also an additional two-thousand years of accumulated science and philosophy, twenty centuries of the understanding of human behavior and psychology, and the steady progress of human civilizations. He wonders, shouldn't we have a greater grasp of ourselves from all this to not bother any god about it? When do we finally grow up and decide there is everything we know and nothing more matters?

And about this god... If he truly exists, where is he? Prayers are spoken to end suffering, but suffering continues. Petitions offered to feed the starving, but children die every day for want of a bowl of rice. Prayers are solemnly uttered to end the violence of war, but the blood still flows on... and on... and on.

Alex Traeger, a divorced father of two, is a man searching, not knowing where to begin and unable to grasp the sheer magnitude of what he is even asking. He takes a first step venturing from the security of complacent routine to lose himself in a project with nobility of purpose, and a goal of virtue. He will invest his being in something deeper, bringing a grand old church back from the dead to rediscover its vibrant youth. And maybe, in the course of his journey, it will return the favor.

He isn't even sure why he feels compelled to consider these questions now. Maybe because he feels ground down by his divorce, maybe it is middle age or the unexplainable actions of a personal acquaintance named William Reader. As a whole, or in part, these events have him reaching for something to balance the turmoil, to find meaning in it all.

Nine
Present Day

"Hey, Pat, thanks for coming."

"What is it, Ivan?" Patricia Hamer asks, reaffixing her gaze to the fashion magazine she plucked from the park-adjacent magazine kiosk she was summoned to by Ivan Myer. "I don't know what people see in these rags. These women need to eat something," she says shaking her head and replacing the magazine. "So, Myer, what's with all the cloak-and-dagger? This couldn't be managed in an e-mail or a phone call?"

"Look, Pat, in all the years we've known each other, have I ever done this?"

"Exactly," she buzzes back, irritated. "Look, I've got piles of stuff back at the office. Can we get to the point?"

"I just think it's wise to be precautionary, okay? I've been looking further into William Reader."

"You what?" She glares back at Myer, cursing how much time she's already wasted. "Look, this conversation is over." She hikes her purse to her stiffened shoulder.

"Wait. Just hear me out, Pat." Myer's voice fades in volume while scanning to see who might be listening in.

"Look," she sternly says, "I know you are fully aware our involvement is over in that case."

"I don't know, it all just seemed too cut and dried," Myer replies with firm conviction.

"It is cut and dried. Reader did it. *Why* is there still a mystery?" she snaps back. "There were no accomplices, no direct contacts. The weapons were untraceable. He had no deeper agenda than hating James Carpenter. Oh, and we could both get lambasted for having this conversation."

"Hey, I know," he capitulates, hands raised. "Look, I just did some checking in my spare time. I agree, he was a strange bird, but..." A man reaches for a sports magazine just behind the detective. Myer examines the man's face closely. Uncomfortable, the man pulls away.

"What the hell, Myer?" Hamer scolds in whispered embarrassment. "He just wants a magazine. Honestly, no more crime novels for you."

"So, we all know," Myer stands closer to her and whispers back. "We all know the Reader background, tenured college professor, otherwise a loner, but still well connected. You know, not a recluse, just keeps to himself."

"And your point is."

"So, guys who end up with accolades in his line of work have academic legacies and are highly publicized are generally easily traceable. You remember, he was a bona fide genius. He graduated from high school at fourteen and had a PhD by seventeen."

"Yeah, I was the one who told you that."

"He teaches for six years then publishes some masterwork on human social systems. He supposedly developed this theoretical model for cultural evolution… foundational… mutational… whatever… apparently tapping into some breakthrough," he patters on, his face growing more serious. "Some expert described it as developing a process to uncover a sort of *cultural DNA*. He was claiming that there were certain markers, commonalities and patterns. I don't know, *lynchpin variants* in all societies, catalyst individuals that yield breakthroughs and advancements. He claimed he could map them, predict future trends and stuff like that."

"I don't get it." She shakes her head. "I don't think I want to, either."

"No, listen, honestly," he begs. "So, in the physical world, and I'm paraphrasing Reader here, there are vital chemical compounds, proteins and molecules that are the building blocks and mutational triggers for the evolutionary advancement of species and life itself."

"You do recall I have a degree in this kind of thing," she interjects, her tone no less irritated.

Myer forges ahead. "Organisms exist because, at a molecular level, these elemental substances have adapted to the environment that surrounds them. Well, Reader proposed that the same thing happens in the cultural domain. As humans evolved physically, a similar process occurred in tandem for behavioral systems. He viewed cultures as actual organisms."

Hamer finishes his thought to hopefully bring a quicker end to his rant. "So, just as if you have a given peptide or protein chain in the cellular world, there are predictable, provable, observable outcomes brought on by the introduction of other environmental variables."

"Right," Myer resumes. "He theorized the same was true of social structures as well. Certain individuals hold critical mass in the mechanism of society as a whole. And we're not talking Einsteins here. A lot of these people may not even know they *are* one of these people."

"That's a nice lecture, Ivan. And you somehow sound much smarter now. And okay, he's a genius who went a little mad, not really that unusual. Ever heard of Ted Kaczynski? Why do I need to be here?"

"We missed something, something really obvious. His bio says he went on to Princeton circa 1985 to 1988, given special dispensation, despite his relative youth, to be some sort of researcher."

"Yeah, BFD."

"There is no record of him ever being there. There are no traces, academically or professionally that he ever set foot on campus."

"You must be missing something," Hamer replies, her curiosity awakening slightly, melting her edginess.

"He never published anything, there was no office assigned, no pay records, no driving records, no state income tax records, no federal ones either for that matter."

She pauses, squinting, trying to summon common-sense scenarios to talk Myer off the ledge. Nothing emerges. "I still think you missed something... an assumed name, maybe?"

"No, look, the research project title he has listed in his bio never existed. The department was even a mirage. He was never there."

"So, he padded his resume and..." She stops herself. "Wait, how do you know this?"

"I know a guy."

"Jesus, Ivan. I think you just need to back up a bit and chill."

Myer's motivation builds knowing he has her full attention now. "Look, there's no record of him *anywhere*, really, from late 1985 to mid-1988. He fell off the Earth. It's like he took a ride on the mother ship."

"Maybe he was doing something covert. Great minds are often called on for that," Hamer says, taking a stab at a possibility.

"Maybe, but if so, it was *way* off the grid."

"And how would you know this?"

"I know another guy."

"Christ, Myer. You and your *guys*."

"Some of them are girls, actually. Just to be accurate."

"So, why tell me?"

"I had to tell someone. I trust you more than anyone, and I thought your skills might be able to brainstorm this with me," he softly offers as an olive branch.

"Sure, let's walk."

Myer begins down a sidewalk path into a park area, holding a deliberate pace. Hamer humors his desire for stealth and buys a newspaper. She pretends to read while ambling a few feet behind him, then reopens the dialogue. "So, this guy with some brilliant breakthrough publishes the cultural equivalent of relativity theory claiming he has supposedly deciphered the very fabric, the periodic table if you will, of our cultural existence. Is that correct?"

"Sounds pretty spot-on."

Hamer's agitation tapers as common sense begins to provide her with an answer. "He then disappears, leaving no trace on the planet of his whereabouts, at least according to a couple of *guys* you know, correct?"

"Check." Impatient, Myer finishes her thought. "And then he shows up again like he beamed back down and he doesn't miss a beat, just goes right on teaching and researching."

"And... I don't know... I really don't," she wavers, her doubt recharged. "I'd love to find some reason to believe it's all the Bilderberger's fault or the work of the Illuminati, but this is just too..."

Myer stops to face her. "So, speculate then." His expression asks for her gift of reason to make sense of it. "A guy like him, if he really has tapped into the core elements of human societal evolution and structure, what is the value to some group or project? Think for me here, Hamer."

"Again, I don't know exactly. All that comes to mind are these far-fetched Orwellian scenarios. But here we are thirty-plus years later, and if he was involved in something it would have happened by now." She pauses to allow the obvious to snuff the young flame of Myer's conspiracy narrative. "Look, we all know about these very serious black-ops projects that the CIA was conducting decades ago that just come off as ridiculous now—you know, remote viewing and LSD experiments. They were all hush-hush and uber-top secret, but now they're just fodder for Hollywood intrigue." She pauses to see if Myer is content with the explanation. His mouth begins to signal an urge to speak. She quickly intervenes.

"He was probably doing something like that, Ivan. You know, something to stir up the collapse of the Soviet Union, or something. And if that's what he was working on, it looks like he was actually successful. But, based on his last few days here, the ones we *do* know about, he may have been involved in one of those LSD projects."

"Well put," he concedes. And since you bring it up, what about the victim, James Carpenter? Maybe the link is right there in front of us. I think I know where to look now. The answer lies with the target, not the shooter."

"*WE*? Don't count me in on this. *We* were pulled from this case over three months ago. It was open and shut, remember." Her face assumes a more stern posture. "Why you are still investigating is your business. You can choose to bring heat down on yourself if you want but, I need my job. Frankly, I respectfully submit that you are wasting your time. And by the way, Carpenter wasn't even born yet in 1985."

Ten
Present Day

The midday sunlight stretches its full reach into narrow alleys and soot-grimed corners of shop windows and doorways. There is not a cloud anywhere to obstruct the broad reach of the burning ball that simultaneously stirs life and furthers the decay of everything on the Earth. The city drones, the collective resonance of each singular human action melding into a solitary, indiscriminate hum.

A small shadow grows on the street. A faint wail finds its way through the bustle. Terror and exuberance all at once, arriving from an unexpected direction. The wail amplifies, a hysterical human voice from above rapidly draws nearer. Sudden, upward glances find a man tumbling through the air. The wailing arrests with the grisly percussion of body meeting pavement. A car skids and swerves, but not enough. Tires snap legs, already broken from the fall, now shattered and pointing askew in opposite directions.

Screams and groans come from onlookers. Cell phones find index fingers, 9-1-1 times several dozen, though no one believes it will make any difference. There is blood everywhere. Spilled entrails glisten in the day's brilliance. A man arrives to help first, then a woman. Others follow, weaving between the red stains and bits of tissue, strewn human confetti. They stare, some cry, some gape at the horror as they try to piece it back together in their mind.

Lying on his twisted back the jumper twitches, fingers, and then a shoulder. Eyelids flutter, each at a different tempo. The broken mouth opens, a faint intake of air. One eyelid raises, it remains lifted, then the other. He looks upward beyond the gawkers into another space, a childlike gasp of amazement escapes from the broken body. Something seen, but only by the victim, observed in another reality. A semi-toothless smile grows through the blood and violated facial structure. Garbled words follow.

"Yes, oh yes… here once again… Oh, the glory… such beauty… I want to stay forever… no… NO! Let me stay!" The face screws in agony and horror. The eyes return to the physical reality. Pain controls his shattered face now. A cry of anguish is interrupted by a cough and spewing of blood, even more trickles from his nose, ears and eyes. A chunk of skull dislodges onto the pavement, exposing brains. The crowd shivers and cringes but can't look away.

Sirens rise above horrid howls. His eyes roll back showing only white, then gradually return. He is trying to die, but cannot. Bystanders privately wish they could engineer a merciful demise, but there are too many witnesses. It would be murder. They must mutually suffer, praying he finds his end soon.

EMTs wind through the chaos, giving the crowd an excuse to shy away. The man conjures a joyful strength through his languishing, "I was there… Oh, god, I was there." The medical team collects him one part at a time. Bowels are gathered and randomly returned to the burst abdomen. Blue latex covered hands reassemble the skull in whatever way it seems to fit. A cautious, but swift journey to the ambulance and then they speed off to find the nearest ER. The crowd remains, mulling. Horror stricken zombies ambling, confused and disoriented.

Inside the ambulance, commotion reigns. "Get the bleeding under control. Bind the head wound. Get some tourniquets on the legs. Cut his shirt off." The lead tech barks over blaring sirens and the racing engine noise to three others glaring at him in disbelief. The lead EMT looks for where to begin, but this is not a stabbing, or even comparable to a serious auto accident. This man is literally in pieces.

"C'mon, Dan," one tech mutters in return to the team lead gesturing to the ambulance floor half covered in blood. "Let's just sedate him, relieve his pain, and let the ER make the call."

"Agreed, but we need to at least try and stabilize him," Dan replies calmly.

"Why isn't this guy dead?" a female tech, Alison, whispers to no one in particular.

"I think it stopped," the first tech announces, amazed.

"What?"

"The bleeding."

"But we haven't even finished treating it. There's no way he's clotting yet, and there's too much damage," Alison bursts out, perplexed. "He really should have bled out by now."

"I'm going to eighty-six the tourniquets. Honestly, there's no more bleeding."

A third tech gasps.

"What is it, Sonja?"

"His fingernail... it... it's growing back."

"What do you mean?"

"I had to peel off the old one when I clipped the pulse monitor to him. Look at it now."

"Maybe it was damaged before. It came off because it was ready to," Dan suggests

"Here's the old one." Sonja produces a biohazard bag containing a fingernail and two teeth. "Does that look previously damaged?"

"Not really."

"It was hanging off his finger, but otherwise it's in good shape."

"Came off from the impact, no doubt," Dan reasons, meaning to keep the conclusions grounded in the obvious.

"Right, but look at the finger now," Alison joins in.

A healthy, brand-new fingernail has grown an eighth of an inch where the old one was ten minutes before.

"Have you ever seen that?" she asks with mild defiance.

"Hell, no."

The ambulance climbs a small hill to the ER entrance. An admitting nurse races to the gurney already rolling to the hospital entrance.

"What have we here?"

"He's a jumper, probably over twelve stories. Severe head trauma, burst abdomen, major facial lacerations, shattered legs, that's all we could get to.

He's all messed up, basically," Dan answers coldly, considering the apparent futility

"Yeah, twelve stories, onto pavement? He should be dead. Good work," the nurse replies as a compliment.

"We didn't do anything, honestly. He's a gifted healer, I guess," Dan returns while turning to rejoin his EMT crew.

The nurse rolls the gurney into the ER entrance. The wrecked man looks up to the nurse finding her eyes.

"I was there. It was so peaceful, so wonderful."

"My god, and you're talking, too."

"Nurse," she calls to another "Get this man prepped for surgery, and we need to sedate him right away. I don't want him freaking out on us. If he tries to move he might just fall apart."

"I'm gonna be all right, you'll see, miss. I can't die," the man mumbles in his oxygen mask.

"Not if I can help it, mister."

"No, you don't understand, ma'am. I can't die."

Eleven
Present Day

"And you can't adjust your Pilates schedule to accommodate my commitment to this restoration project? This is a big deal for me," Alex Traeger implores via Bluetooth of his former wife, Valerie.

"It's pre-paid, Alex. I'm committed to the timeslot," her frigid, rigid voice replies.

"And they won't let you switch from Friday to Tuesday?"

"It isn't so much that. Tuesday nights I go to my divorce survivors group, and besides, if I switched, that would be two days in a row. I'm Monday, Wednesday, and Friday. You can't do the same workout two days in a row, and that would be three, really. The body needs to rest," she tersely informs, irritated at having to explain.

Traeger's hands strangle the steering wheel. "You know, this is the kind of thing…" He pauses to harness calm. "I was always the one that had to work around your schedule. I guess even divorce and distance can't change that."

"Really, Alex. You want to take it there?"

He looks ahead to an oozing river of red taillights ahead of him, nothing to indicate the cause of the traffic jam. There is no exit ramp to provide an escape for miles, only endless dots of red, winding into the dark night. He sighs into a response. "Sorry, I'm frustrated. I am trying to expand my professional scope here and I'm still hitting roadblocks. Why do the kids need to be picked up, anyway? They are in middle school now. Is there a carpool? Hey, I'll pay for an Uber. Can we at least look at a bus schedule?"

"No, to all of the above."

"No, and no further discussion, just *no*?" Traeger rolls his eyes, his teeth clenching hard.

"There is nothing to discuss; the kids need to know we are there for them. Strangers don't need to be chauffeuring our kids."

"*We* are there meaning me *and* you?" Traeger carefully tries to navigate the ensuing minefield that the conversation is heading toward. "What about your mom? What's she doing that time of day?"

"You really want to bring her into this, get her running commentary? Have her spew her callousness about their flawed parents to our children on a weekly basis?" she reminds.

"Yeah." Traeger exhales forcefully, no retort available. "I see your point, but, can you grasp my situation? I'm going to lose a whole day out here every week to commute the late train back to Maryland on Thursday night and then try to manage this project remotely on Fridays all because of a twenty-minute trip to pick the kids up from school."

"That's how it works sometimes, Alex."

As a distraction to steady surging frustration, he raises a coffee tumbler to his lips and gulps, filling his mouth with cold bitterness. With nowhere to spit it out, he swallows stagnant remnants from his morning brew. He winces and answers with a little frustration leaking out. "Except for you. Your schedule is unaffected. And, oh by the way, what was your motive when you set up the Friday class, anyway? You conveniently made yourself unavailable because you knew I'd, once again, adjust my life. You knew this was looming once the school year began, but you did it anyway."

"I'm hanging up, now, Alex. I'll see if I can arrange my week differently, how's that?"

"Sure, let me know."

The conversation over, the communication ended, Traeger knows the last offering was a hollow dismissal, a patronizing *run-along-now* pat on the head. Again, it is he who must compromise. When accepting the church restoration, he'd understood the distance might be an issue. He would be committing to weeklong stays away from home for a while. Now, Thursdays will be marathons. He'll have to plan his design meetings and construction decisions to avoid critical operations on Fridays. It might even jeopardize the commitment date. His life has just become rapidly inflexible. He scolds himself for expecting change in his former wife's behavior pattern. He should know after living with it for sixteen years. It was the wedge between them—self first, then the other. He knows his own inflexibilities and self-attentions put him at fault, too. But, she always had a knack for choosing vital moments for her version of suburban diva, and usually over items of low consequence like Pilates classes. He catches himself mid-thought to erect a mental barrier. He is peering into the past again, anathema to his new credo to "strive ahead." He will adjust his life again. But it will test him that much more.

Twelve
Present Day

"These arrangements are only temporary. Soon, we will be formally announcing a move to more suitable accommodations. We need more space and more sophisticated site infrastructure to accomplish our objectives. We hope to be sharing some exciting breakthroughs with the good people of this humble planet," James Carpenter reveals to veteran television reporter Christy Raines.

"Can you give us a hint, a tease as to what this might mean for the average person? How will our lives be affected by these *breakthroughs*, and what will they cost?" she politely probes as she strolls aside Carpenter on a stone path weaving through a lush botanical garden. A few steps ahead, a camera crew captures the conversation. Her seasoned, professional manner is now fully engaged with Carpenter, but her private thoughts include a concern for how the camera will treat her today. The setting is emotionally uncomfortable. Natural light is unforgiving. It overpowers the fine art of hair and makeup and may possibly expose her true age. She knows Carpenter's youthful, mid-thirties presence beside her will serve to age her even further. Discomfort also arrives with the thought that the production roster includes head-to-toe shots. Even near starvation can't remove the thickening of middle-age, pounds amplified even more by the effect of television.

"The breakthroughs will cost nothing, Christy. That's always been our position here. We feel profiting from or pricing out a portion of the population from something that would so clearly be a benefit would be unfair and immoral. Everyone deserves the opportunity to be a better person," Carpenter dispenses with calm rectitude.

"That's very generous, but how will you cover your costs and continue to operate if there is no revenue flowing to offset the expenditures?"

"All of our funding is brought in through donations and private grants from anonymous angels. They understand the importance of our work to empower an evolution of mankind. We are paying our own exceptionality forward in hopes of fostering opportunity for those who have not been so blessed."

Raines' self-concerned thoughts are melting away. Carpenter's calm air and gentle confidence are putting her at ease. "Noble indeed. Your approach and unshakable conviction project a genuine sense that you can actually accomplish anything you put your mind to. I can't quite put a finger on it, Mr. Carpenter, but there is something you possess... a presence about you... something ageless, really."

Her calm comfort summons an inner discord. Her professional self is gnawing at her to maintain staunch objectivity. She has always been renowned for her consummate professionalism, a proclaimer of the journalistic ethic founded in cold impartiality. She considers maybe Carpenter has her too easily undone, even intoxicated with the authenticity of his open-hearted concern and genuine, self-effacing charm. In all her career, she has never once lowered her standard to champion a cause. She argues back to herself, *if the world is served rightly, there is no harm, in fact harm could be done by the not doing of it.* Maybe here, she wonders, is an exception where support is in order rather than contentiousness.

In all her years, in thousands of interviews, Carpenter is a subject like no other. His appearance speaks of poise lending to an air of composed purpose. His physique bears a relaxed vitality, powerful, but not at all intimidating, leaving her at ease and drawn in.

"I must apologize, Christy. I need to hold you to the time allotted, today. My schedule is unalterable... " Carpenter's attention is drawn away. He looks past her and nods, then motions another woman over. Raines turns to see a woman approaching.

"Christy, I'd like you to meet Marianne. She is my partner in crime, so to speak. She keeps me put together." He smiles and she floats in. Raines' heart sinks unexpectedly to sadness at Marianne's flawless beauty. Long black hair sets off her perfect form and confident bearing, a woman indelibly comfortable in her perfect skin. "We are set to continue in three days again, are we not?" Carpenter asks.

"Correct. Three days is perfect. It will give Tommy and me a chance to get a head start on the editing and post work. Thank you so much, Mr. Carpenter. Nice to meet you, Marianne."

* * * *

Inside the remote truck, a high-tech RV, Tommy, the chief cameraman and editor, mans joystick controls and multiple wireless mouses to review smooth edit points in the raw footage. Raines stands over his shoulder, chin resting on her fist, taking the viewer's perspective as the pieces are adroitly forged together.

"Christy, I know you're not a big fan of this, but I think it has much more impact if I pull out and keep both of you in the shot," Tommy proposes.

"Why? You can't see his face as clearly then. This interview is about him."

"Right. I'm not going to leave it there, just more than we usually do. There's something about the two of you moving together... I don't know... it's hard to describe. There's this symbiosis thing going on. Oh, and I'm going to leave in more of the close-in work Jimmy shot from the stationary angle."

"Close-ups of me in outdoor light? Whatever, Tommy. You're the visual guy. You've been my eyes for twelve years, so I trust you."

"Cool."

Tommy spins the editing wheel zipping through footage, deleting, reserving, and trashing, while jotting notes on voiceover cues to tie it all together. He spots a reaction moment from Christy and pauses the feed. "See, this is money, Chris. I've never seen this expression from you. If I didn't know any better, I'd say this guy is under your skin."

"Right," she interrupts, "that's exactly why we should shit-can it."

"Christy... babe... this is broadcast gold. I've never seen you so genuinely human in... ever. That look on your face is tweet-city, social media pay dirt."

"But," she hesitates.

"What?"

"Look at my wrinkled neck." She grimaces. "And the bags under my eyes. I... I look so old."

Tommy spins in his chair and meets her defeated stare. "Christy, I hate to be the one to break it to you."

"Yeah, right, I *am* old."

"Look Chris, maybe for a politician or a young grandma you're a spring chicken, but for a TV personality..."

She stares back icily. "Yeah, I see. No need to embellish... *babe*."

Thirteen
Present Day

Negotiating thousands of worn, weathered stone steps descending from the Himalayan peaks is a test for a seasoned climber, but for a man over seventy years of age it presents a formidable obstacle, even with help of a local Sherpa. The treacherous staircase was merely a starting point for an arduous journey ending halfway around the globe in Baltimore, Maryland, the city of postmark inked on William Reader's empty envelope. Leaving the security of the Tibetan monastery is tempting fate, but it has been thirty-one years since he last stepped beyond the temple grounds where he secreted himself high above the rest of the world. The dangers that sent Jonas Kovacs into hiding are still very real, but the chances are slim they would have learned he was in circulation again this soon.

To pass the greater distances safely and undetected, help was needed. The monks, although men of peace, have their own reciprocal acquaintance with marginal entities, necessary insurance as guard against unwanted incursions and meddling in their vulnerable existence from others of truly wicked intent. Their underground connections produced guides, papers and a loosely affiliated network of individuals of trust to anonymously usher him through Nepal then India, on to the Arabian Sea, north through the Suez by tanker to Israel, and lastly a tag-along seat on a charter flight to the U.S. out of Tel Aviv.

Venturing through the Middle East, a geography thick with spiritual gravity, was a worrisome, but unavoidable turn. No one knows stealth like the Israelis. But long ago, not only had he run from his enemies but also from a past that might now take interest in his return through such hallowed ground. In the tempestuous crucible of the Holy Land where time is measured in millennia, thirty years is but the blink of an eye; Kovacs' transgressions, for him long ago, are only as yesterday's here. It is a place where forces of consequence, some not of this earth, wisp unencumbered like scalding desert winds in search of retribution. This is his worry; mortal sin has a way of finding you out, and exacting its due. He hopes the worthiness of his current quest will expunge the burden of his spiritual debt accumulated by acts of more than three decades before.

Touchdown at a small airfield aside the Potomac River and a cab ride into the heart of Baltimore has Kovacs once again surrounded by mountains, this time the man-made variety. Not even close to the density of a city the scale of New York or Chicago, Baltimore's structures are lesser in stature and more scattered, but his time so long removed from modern civilization makes the high-rises seem to reach into the heavens. All about, people, charging and bustling, staring into their palms at rectangular devices, talking at them, presumably devices of communication, or information, but with no cords. Automobiles whisk by, some silent as if no motor exists at all. Tattoos are everywhere.

He had hoped he would be afforded time to gently reacquaint himself with the rhythm of the world before it shrouded over him again. But in a few short hours he has found his being left bare and exposed. The first intruder is the unrelenting cacophony. In Tibet, whole days would pass where the only sound might be the whistles of wind. But now, inescapable clamor reigns. An assault of traffic—trucks grinding gears, tires clicking over manhole covers, horns and sirens. Thundering rumbles of bass come from cars that look more like full-scale toys, a sonic quake of music sounding incomplete. Beats and shouting with melodic tones left abandoned. Blaring voices thump curse-laden braggadocio, the crudities employed more as punctuation than as meaningful expression.

The delicate cocoon woven around his inner being by well over a quarter century in virtual isolation is succumbing, rapidly tearing open, giving way to the serrated existence surrounding him. The journey here, one plentiful in its own jagged edges of randomness, had less of an effect. The stops were temporary and he was always under the care of others possessing keen familiarity with the terrain, providing security and allowing him to remain removed from the details. But knowing he must remain here to fend for himself requires interaction and upright awareness. He alone must conjure a method of survival.

This raw, unfiltered place is now the battlefield, he thinks. He is boldly aware of the onus now resting upon his shoulders not unlike the dense wood of the cross. The thought of it oddly comforts him; it is a kinship with his beloved Savior. It swells his heart with purpose and selfless devotion. Divine grace has delivered him temporary strength.

His destination achieved, Kovacs aims to steer his thoughts away from the overload of stimuli to consider how he is to find William Reader's *chosen one*. Looking around the city it seems an impossible task. Reader left no clues, at least none apparent. Kovacs is relegated to his own instinct and omnipresent faith. A slight sense of panic builds, quickly soothed by something familiar in the distance. Among the collage of concrete and steel, he spots a simple, comforting thing. Atop a smaller building three blocks away—a cross. It is a church, a structure dwarfed by its neighboring giants housing the businesses of worldly pursuits, like a cottage hidden in a forest. He will start there, in a place of peace.

Long shadows from high above contrast a thin stripe of light angling across the church's face. The church's name, *Mount Calvary*, seems apropos. Both timid and eager, Kovacs enters through the large wooden double doors. A service is in progress, the celebration of daily Low Mass. Familiarity rises, a ritual instilled within him so long ago. He finds a pew in the back.

The mass progresses, sermon, intercession, confession, and consecration bringing a rapid sense of the cleansing of thirty years of self-imposed exile. The Communion awaits—he approaches the altar rail and kneels with a contrite but wounded heart. He extends his palms upward, one laid upon the other to receive for the first time in a very long time. Vestments sway before him, wafting a faint perfume of frankincense released from the silken fabric, landed there from a recent Holy Day celebration. It recalls in him the meaning of it, a gift of the Magi to the infant Christ, a symbol of the child's spiritual divinity. A disc is placed in Kovacs' open hand. "The Body of Christ," he hears from above. A silent prayer of humility, then consumption, to eat of his flesh. The wine follows. "The blood of our Lord that was shed for thee." He drinks. The fog begins to lift. Light and unrestrained, he looks skyward in thanks. The prodigal one has returned and received his absolution.

Again in his pew, Kovacs feels renewed and bolstered for his task. Although salvation and redemption have found him temporarily, revelation is tardy. Impulsively, he bends to find the kneeler again. He bows his head, prays, and clears his mind to allow for the spirit to answer. William Reader returns to his thoughts. He was a man of rare brilliance. Kovacs hopes Reader had found some measure of understanding in his final days. He regrets not being there for him. Instead, he ran. But he had to. No good could have come of his own murder. He is here today to act as the catalyst for future change, to undo the past.

The first time they met, he knew Reader was an exceptional being, blessed and possessed by God, but unaware of it himself. Kovacs tried to make that apparent to him, but Reader's own brilliance was also his obstacle. There was no room for *unanswerables* in his realm. There was no tolerance for a blind assumption of an invisible dominion belonging to a superior being. There was only here and now and what had been before. This, despite the irony that Reader's own chosen field of study, human behavior, is rife with subjectivity and perpetual mystery of its own, requiring its own measure of blind faith. The first thing Reader ever said to Kovacs was, "You can save your breath, Padre if you're thinking about having a go at converting this man of science," which of course told Kovacs there was imminent hope. Vehement rejection is the other side of the rigid coin of faith. Kovacs prayed for Reader's epiphany, but if it happened, he was not there to see it.

It was a coffee shop, one not far from where Kovacs is this very moment. He remembers, it was 1985, the venue of their first real meeting. Kovacs decides that is where to start, at the beginning. Of course, the answer will lie in some form of Reader's penchant for rebellious irony. Wickedly clever, he possessed a dry, acerbic wit with the ability to insult someone right to their face without them even knowing they had been humiliated. They might even laugh at it themselves. That's how Kovacs will know; there will be something right out in the open, hidden in plain sight, but only discernable to those with inside knowledge. Kovacs thanks God for the answer to his prayer, and departs recharged for the journey.

Fourteen
Present Day

"Ivan, really, this is even more cliché than the magazine stand. Christ, you're even wearing the obligatory rumpled trench coat," Patricia Hamer muses sardonically at her inquisitive colleague Ivan Myer.

"There's a reason things are cliché; it's because they work, and the trench coat was a gift," bristles Myer with a friendly half-grin.

"So, why have you dragged me to this secluded pier, pray tell? And I'm disappointed. You didn't even require a pass phrase... you know... *the tuna are swimming closer to shore this time of year...* and I'd have to reply *because the mackerel become precocious as the summer wanes.*"

"Very funny," Myer dribbles out with a smirk. "With the mocking portion of our meeting behind us, can we proceed to the serious business?"

"Yes, please, although your last screed on Reader at the kiosk was teetering dangerously on the boundary edge of marginal and wacko."

"Think what you will, my payoff will be your jaw dropping after I have presented this gem."

Hamer shakes her head dismissively and looks up into the moonlit autumn night. A marine layer is trying to decide if it should roll in from the dark ocean off shore. Fog *and* trench coats would be too much to bear, she thinks. "Very well, let's get on with this."

"So, there's this guy I know—"

"A *guy you know*? Well, imagine my surprise."

"C'mon Pat, let me just..."

"Right, sorry."

"This guy works in Homeland Security. He's tasked with what he calls—" Myer flips some pages in a tattered spiral notepad. "Ah, here it is. It's called *atypical phenomenological incident analysis*."

"Only in government does that phrase exist—translation?"

"Weird stuff, the unexplained."

"Oh, goody, X-files. Please go on." She punctuates her incredulity by lowering her head and shaking it.

"Pat?" Myer raises an eyebrow.

"Alright, continue. I'll shut up."

"So, he and his team track events across time, coordinating video files and stills from public security cameras, satellite scans, social media, drones, you name it. He looks for anything that might be considered out of the norm. Most of what they find is ultimately explainable, but every once in a while they come up with something that stretches the envelope." Myer produces a tablet device from inside his overcoat, taps it a few times, and continues. "He gave me a link to this video composite, a chronological patchwork that speaks for itself. However, I may provide some play-by-play."

Myer taps the screen twice and a video queues up, presenting in a grainy black and white and time-stamped. The camera is angled from just above a city street. Normal foot and car traffic passes and then is rapidly interrupted by a body speeding into the street pavement. Hamer snaps her head away in shock and mutters, "Good god, Ivan." Myer pauses the video.

"Sorry, I should have warned you, it's a bit graphic. Anyway, that was a jumper, see there, and there, he's pretty jacked up. Probably should be dead."

"You mean he's not?"

"No, watch."

The video montage continues, showing an ambulance arriving, gathering the jumper, and transporting him to the hospital.

"So, here's the art in what my friend does. He pieces together the ambulance's course on the way to the hospital via intersection cams... there... and there... notice the chronological time code... and now we're at the hospital." Hamer's brow crunches up. Her keen investigative mind working overtime to find any weak link in Myer's case. He continues. "Zooming in so you can see that the jumper is actually speaking to the nurse." Hamer's eyes reflect surprise, but her skepticism remains perked up. "Now, fast forward, one day later, a hallway cam outside his room. We can see him there, tubes and respirator. Now, a day later he's propped up reading a magazine. Day three, now. Again, the cam outside the Emergency Room entrance."

She taps the pause button. "I don't get it, what am I looking at?"

He resumes play. "That's him walking out on his own two feet."

Hamer raises her head and looks at him in chilled disbelief. "I don't believe it," she voices with firm conviction, maybe more to convince herself. Myer drags his finger across the tablet twice and taps again. "Here's a different rendition... sooo, again the cam outside his room just before the emergency room exit shot... and tracking him through the hallway... aaannnd out a side door. No limp, no bandages, he's even got all his teeth."

Her armor of skepticism is succumbing. She is no longer able to disguise her thoughts with a false expression of doubt. "It's him? Oh my god, that's impossible. I can't believe they discharged him. They should at least have him under observation. The lawyers alone would—"

"They didn't discharge him. He just strolled out on his own."

"Did your guy follow up, locate him? What's the jumper's name?"

"He had no ID. He was a John Doe admittance. And get this, all they did was sew him up and hook him to life support. He was scheduled for a dozen more surgeries, but they got put off because he was healing on his own."

"How do you know that?"

"As you brought up, Homeland did do follow-up with the hospital."

"C'mon Ivan, this is just video trickery, mind freak stuff."

Weary with her persistence of contrarian argument, Myer leans in with evangelical conviction. "Pat, this is real. Trust me."

"Why did your guy share it with you? Why did he think *you* would need to see this?"

"Well, it wasn't so much just me. There's this kind of semi-private, insider-only, web-based video farm for cases deemed unclassified." He stifles the beginning of an eye roll on her part and presses his case further. "Honestly, it's partially for amusement purposes. Anything not considered a security situation is just dropped there for privileged collective consumption with the hope someone in the universe of learned users might notice something the experts missed. My guy just sent me the link and a password."

"That's kind of creepy, Ivan. It's just snuff voyeurism." Hamer gathers her wrap tighter around her shoulders fending off the brisk churning air.

"Sure, but I can't help but think there's something to this one case."

"Why?"

"Well, it kind of reminded me of someone else who should be dead."

"Who?"

"Carpenter."

Hamer turns and walks from the cone of brightness provided by a light pole, then proclaims into the night, "That's a quantum leap, Ivan."

"I don't think so. He went down with a massive shot to the chest and was better than good in a week."

"You don't know that. He didn't surface for nearly a month after that."

"Yeah, but the chatter in the system is, his case was pretty much like the jumper here."

Hamer slowly turns, greeting him with the expression of a scolding mother. "Chatter in the system?"

"Yeah, nothing is ever really secret," he tries desperately to explain. "Ask yourself this, Pat. How come no one has ever heard from the medical team that worked on Carpenter? Also, after two days he was moved from the hospital and managed by his own people. That is undeniable fact."

"It still doesn't mean anything."

"Not in a court of law, but you have to admit this just tickles the nerve endings of your investigative instincts. There is something going on here."

Her patience exhausted, she sternly asks. "So, here's where I ask, *a-gain...* why the hell are you dragging me into this?"

"For the same reasons I always do, to get your opinion, your perspective. I know you are a skeptic, so help me assemble the missing pieces. Ground my theory with some Hamer brilliance. Tell me where it falls apart."

She ambles a few steps back into the light, her low heels tapping the pier's thick wooden boards. Waves crash in the darkness beneath their perch. Her breathing finds a rhythm with the regular tide. She rotates her head back to look at Myer.

"So, let's say you're right. I'm stuck on the jumper, Ivan. I can't get past that. Sure, one in a million survive, but three days and he's good as new? My forensic self just screams out: *Impossible*. An impact that traumatic... it... there's no way in just three days he is ambulatory."

"Right. There should be brain damage, spinal injuries. He should be a paraplegic at best."

"Absolutely. But seriously, Myer. The Carpenter tie-in, I'm just not seeing it. There, you wanted skepticism."

"Okay, point taken. Ready for the coup de grace?"

"What, more?" Hamer shakes her head.

"I asked my guy about it. He says there are others. People walking in front of buses and commuter trains."

"That doesn't impress me, Ivan."

"No, I mean the same result. They miraculously heal in short order and just walk away, some right at the scene. There are too many to have all of them be fakes. We're just learning about it because technology gives us the ability to piece the puzzles together."

"How commonplace?"

"Two— three times a month."

Doubt, or perhaps a growing dread at the nagging irritation of something unexplainable, overwhelms her once again. The cold air and her discontent answer for her. "I... Ivan? It's gotta be a hoax. It's crop circles all over again."

Fifteen
October 11, 1988

Morning rays, glowing brighter than usual, politely invite themselves through the double-hung window of the third-story walkup belonging to Jonas Kovacs. The celestial spotlight shines down over a scattering of Spartan furnishings, the humble trappings of his existence, a monastic cell burrowed into the cityscape. The screaming of a tea kettle shatters the silence. Sweet, peppery notes of bergamot announce Earl Grey as his chosen companion for morning devotionals. After a precise two minutes in the pot, he tilts a generous pour into a handmade pottery mug, a cherished gift from a friend. The bloom of the day has begun.

Always too hot at first, a few minutes of rest will leave a perfect sip. Morning prayers ensue, soon interrupted by a flittering companion. A monarch butterfly lights delicately upon the page. Kovacs sits motionless to savor the gentle moment and ponder its grace. It is curiously late in the season for a monarch, and even more curious that somehow it entered a sealed room.

Anxious, the black-and-yellow winged angel flutters away towards the pure rays of the sun. Kovacs rises to open the window and hasten its freedom. Raising the creaky window frame, the crisp autumn air fills his nose. The remains of summer are stirred with a looming chill of winter's inevitability. Briefly immersed in his senses, he has lost track of his airborne friend. A quick scan of the surroundings yields no trace. Swiveling his head outside the window brings the same result. He leaves it open, hoping the butterfly will find its way if it hasn't already.

He returns to his meditation reciting prayers that inspire, then prayers of need. He raises the mug to his lips. There is an odor, one not so sweet as bergamot. From the mug he sees vapor, but not steam, more like smoke. Inside the cup, the monarch is floundering and failing, but more than that, it is dissolving, consumed by the liquid, then vanished altogether.

Kovacs rigidly stands, horrified. Bewildered, he steps away. Inside the teapot only threads remain: the bags are extinguished, eaten away the same as the butterfly. New prayers come to mind, ones scrambling for guidance and enlightenment. What if he had sipped from the mug? Images of his body writhing on the floor, suffering in agony, overwhelm him. He could easily be a corpse; instead, saved by a butterfly. A lowly insect, but one bearing a moniker of royalty. An unlikely visitor, an impossible one has been sent to save his life—an angel indeed.

Questions auger rudely, now. Who and why? They rip the remaining tranquility from his being. This was no natural event, no accident of flawed manufacturing. This was deliberate. A prepared act to bring about his termination. No explanation of malice makes sense save the project that brought him here in the first place.

Outside, a sturdy vehicle races to an abrupt stop. Kovacs angles to gain a view, one inconspicuous from the street. Determined footfalls march to the building entrance and then set upon the stairwell trembling the apartment walls. He suspects their task is to remove a body—his. They won't expect it to be still standing, still breathing. The marching halts just outside, followed by a polite tap on the door. Kovacs is frozen; he dares not make a sound. From outside, a mechanical whirr decimates the deadbolt. When they enter, they will find him alive and then remedy the glitch in their plan. He grabs his wool coat from the sofa and rushes to the open window. The escape meant for a butterfly is now his own. A moment later, he is tiptoeing down three flights of black steel fire escape, dashing furiously to freedom. The apartment door swings wide. Two grizzled men spill into the room dressed uncomfortably in business casual attire. There is no body, dead or alive. They must report a failed assignment.

Kovacs runs until his legs and lungs scream to stop. He is safe now, for the time being, but everything has changed.

Sixteen
Present Day

"Do you know how this thing is attached?" Alex Traeger asks of anyone within earshot. The architect, perched precariously on the twelfth step of a sixteen-step extension ladder, is attempting to remove the large cross from the wall a dozen feet above the church altar. The ladder leans, angled against the back wall of the sanctuary to the right side of the cross. The means of attachment is undetectable but stubbornly effective. Adroitly, he retrieves a small flashlight from his rear pocket and shines it into the thin gap between the wood of the crucifix and the plaster wall. No enlightenment is gained.

"I think it's definitely some form of hardware, but not screws or nails," replies a voice from behind belonging to parish priest Stephen Archer. Traeger dares not turn to look back, his balance too much in jeopardy. "So, maybe a cradle device, something held in place by gravity, not part of original design?" Traeger pants between awkward poses.

"Correct, Alex, it was resituated in the 1950's for safety reasons. Whatever is up there is much more reliable than before," Archer returns.

"I'm guessing a good upward thrust on the bottom piece will..." Traeger interlaces his fingers beneath the bottom of the cross and begins pulling upward. Nothing. He tries again with more force. He hears a creak, but no movement results.

From ground level, he hears, "Alex, wait let's get some more help." Ignoring reason, and with defiant determination, Traeger lifts with more force and a grunt. The cross disengages from its cradle throwing its top-heavy weight slightly away from the architect. Traeger grimaces as he wrestles the awkward heaviness of the wood. He releases his grip from the bottom so it can slide into his arms. The crossbeam lands on his inner arms at the elbows, the force enough to give question to his stability. One foot suddenly slips off the rung. Desperately, he hugs the cross against the ladder and finds purchase again. Adrenaline thumps electric bolts through him. The aluminum frame quakes, Traeger's legs are vibrating with fatigue and fear, slowly losing the battle with the eight-foot-high cross.

Hands belonging to several panicked onlookers extend from below. Traeger cannot release the crucifix, worried he may send its gravity downward. He steadies himself, carefully resting one hand against the wall, retreating down the ladder one laborious rung. He repositions his hand, but it slips slightly, the result of a wet palm. Sweat maybe? He spots a full hand-print on the wall the color of deep red. His shirt sleeves glisten scarlet. "Oh shit, I've cut myself," he yells. One foot slips again to the rung below. He traps the cross against the ladder, his body now vibrating at full tremble. The ladder wears slippery red drops, with more falling to the floor.

"Hang on, Alex. I'm coming up to help. Everyone! We need you over here now," Father Archer barks.

There is no pain, no apparent source of bleeding. He is frozen and puzzled. Descending is his wish, but he is paralyzed, his arms nailed to the cross, hands glued to the ladder. He thinks it, but cannot move to climb down further. Suspended, he alone bears all the weight.

"Alex, down here. I have it now, just a couple steps down and we can get some more hands on it. Breathe and step, you can handle the weight. It's going to be alright," Archer calmly instructs. "That's it... Let go... now another step... okay... we got it now."

Back on solid ground, Traeger examines his red-soaked shirt and hands. His jeans and shoes are also spotted red.

"I'm bleeding. Where is it coming from?"

"Alex, I don't think it's blood." Archer replies.

"But I'm covered," Traeger returns in disbelief.

"Trust me, it isn't blood, Alex. And what the hell were you thinking doing that on your own?" the priest blares, scolding Traeger.

After a few deep breaths, the excitement over, Traeger is satisfied he is unharmed. He examines the backside of the cross. Archer pitches an impromptu forensic opinion. "Look... here, see the channels cut into the wood. It seems insects have burrowed in. When you dislodged the cross it disrupted a fluid of some type."

"Father, that's the substance left behind by the insects we found in the bell tower," one of the onlookers contributes.

"There is insect infestation here?" Traeger blasts both as indignity and as release. "I think I should know this. Why wasn't I informed?"

"It was over five years ago and isolated to the one area. It was managed. I guess they found a home down the inside of the wall here and into the cross. We simply forgot about it, Alex," Archer calmly submits.

"Why is there blood... or... whatever this red liquid is?" Traeger asks, calm setting in.

"It's some secretion, at least that's what the exterminator said," the first onlooker returns.

"What bug is it?" Traeger posits.

"I honestly don't recall," Archer answers. "Some sort of beetle, I think. Is it important?"

"Not really. I'm going to clean up. If you see the plaster guys while I'm away, tell them they can get to work on the back wall now, but we need to have the exterminator in again to check where they came from, so leave the area around the mounting untouched, please."

Exhausted, Traeger finds a careful resting place in the front pew. Clean up will have to wait for a second wind. High above, he sees his red hand print and next to it the silhouetted shadow of the cross, a ghost left behind. He stares into it. The cross, gone, still lives on.

Seventeen
October 13, 1988

"It was an attempt on my life, William. I am very fortunate to be here talking with you," Jonas Kovacs rattles off nervously through the restless, random surge of an unsettled autumn breeze to his colleague William Reader. The professor listens skeptically, sitting atop a weathered picnic table. The location, rest stop roughly thirty miles due west of Baltimore, was one chosen for its seclusion and anonymity.

"Well, it could have simply been some chemical reaction to—"

"William, dammit, they sent men to make sure I was dead and now they are searching for me," Kovacs fires back, pacing in front of Reader, fear permeating his words. "I have been hiding in churches the last two days. It was very risky for me to contact you, and I made absolutely sure I wasn't followed here."

Reader's innate lack of natural empathy has him struggling to process his good friend's emotion. He answers the only way he knows how, with awkward logic. "Look, Jonas, I'm sure there is an explanation that makes rational sense."

"This has gotten way out of control, William. Forget that I was almost murdered, look at the project. What was agreed upon at the start seems to have been completely abandoned, and any hope of regaining the proper course is growing ever smaller."

"Plans always change, especially in this case. You must understand we are pathfinders, pioneers. You knew that going in. This is uncharted territory."

Kovacs' conviction burns stronger. He looks at Reader with determined eyes. "We're being pushed aside. We were told, as the project moved ahead, you and I would be the most important ones. I fear the opposite is true."

"It concerns me too." Reader sighs, his own conviction now sounding hollow to his own ears. The moment brings a pause surrendering the air to the distant hum of highway traffic.

"We have been misled, William." Kovacs utters with despair. His inherent trust in others melts away like the butterfly in his tea cup from two days before. He sneers. "She has another purpose in mind than the one that brought us all together."

"That is one possibility," Reader admits while rising from his perch and angling away. The spectral autumn colors of the distant forest fill his gaze, its beauty a welcome counterpoint to the disnature of the subject matter occupying his thoughts. He answers, seeming more to address his own thoughts than the cardinal's. "It would appear she has found something of great importance to her, something where your continued presence would present a threat," he reluctantly submits, resigning himself to Kovacs' version.

A gust of chill wind from a looming storm cuts through, ripping dried leaves from their arboreal anchors and tumbling them to chaos. "But what?" Kovacs replies.

"Something in the artifacts," Reader spills out. "Something unlike anything to be found anywhere else."

"I was only told of the original purpose. If there was a hidden plan, I was unaware," Kovacs laments. "I think now maybe, I was told a tale. I am a pawn, a delivery boy. And now the package delivered, I am expendable." Kovacs' lips curl in bitterness and disdain.

"Perhaps it is something not of treachery but simply actions based in greed," Reader submits. "Maybe she is merely protecting her self-interest."

Kovacs churns urgently with greater impetus. "That is possible. But she knows me well enough to know I have no interest in any financial gain. She knows I would simply walk away if that were the case." Kovacs runs the tips of his fingers across his crimped forehead. "It is something more. She knows where my allegiances lie. Perhaps I am an obstacle to her greater purposes. She has found something of greater worth than monetary reward. Trust me, William. I feel it in my soul."

"You know such feelings have no bearing in my paradigm," Reader blurts.

"I do. But I know you value my instincts, if for no other reason than for amusement and curiosity." Kovacs smiles a little at the characterization, but grim thoughts creep in. "Take heed. It is me they want today. You may be next, my friend."

Reader replies, still struggling with one last shred of hopeful repudiation. "If they have another purpose, it may be prudent for them to dispense with loose ends, but I am not a loose end. I am sad to admit you are correct, though. To them, *your* usefulness is ended."

"Why do you think you are safe?" Kovacs pleads.

"This project, no matter what it is, will take years to come to fruition. My role, my skills, are needed on an ongoing basis. I too sense her motives are grand, something of global proportion. I can maintain objectivity and convince them I am a friend of the project. I can persuade them I am committed as long as they need me and continue to be a powerful voice for the finished product. I can sell them on the idea that without me, all their hard work will be squandered further down the road. I alone know how to read the future landscape at the scale she is attempting to reach. I think, for now, I am safe."

A cautious grin paints Kovacs' face. "William, you are many things, but a salesman you are not."

"I really don't need to sell them. I actually do have some curiosity about where this all leads. I am a man of science and relish the fascination of it. In you, they see the scrutiny of ethics. They can't have that around. They know you will tell the world, possibly derailing their final goals."

"My friend," Kovacs pleads further to the purer humanity Reader buries beneath his genius. "You are also a man of morals. You just don't allow them to occupy your consciousness."

Reader takes a moment to digest his friend's observation. "Jonas, do you have somewhere you can go? And, I mean far away." A feeling foreign to the professor washes through him. He realizes he will miss his counterpoint, Kovacs.

"I... I don't... well..." A possible refuge occurs to him. "Maybe, some trusted friends from years past."

"That sounds like the right place. Don't tell me where. It is best I don't know. We can sort out the details at another time before you leave. See if that destination is one available to you, then we will talk further. Reader now fully present, his clouded perception of ulterior motives burned away, he asks, "So, good Cardinal. What is the grand plan, their plan, really?"

"Only one person of the group *really* knows."

"Yes, Brandt is the epicenter. It was all initiated by her," Reader concurs.

"She got the government channel involved. It's all off books, so no chance of tracing it. The money is already in the bank, and government money never goes away once it starts in this kind of thing." Reader moves in to address Kovacs more intensely, his genius now gaining clear focus.

"Kipner and Chandler are only pawns—worker bees. Brilliant, but worker bees nonetheless. And when their job is complete, they'll be the first to be eliminated. Especially Kipner; he'll never be able to keep any secret for very long." Reader's cadence quickens, the vision clear to him. "The government men, Smith and Jones, who knows what their future is? But Brandt is the queen bee. The science belongs to her and we both know she is capable enough to know what to do with it."

"Yes, she is driven beyond any passion I have ever witnessed," Kovacs agrees. "We should warn the others," he pushes out in one last bit of hope.

Reader reaches out, laying his hands on Kovacs' shoulders. His humanity gazes out from beneath his callous shell. "We can't. I'm sorry, Jonas. We aren't sure who else may be involved behind the scenes or where this is all going. We are making assumptions, here. Even though they did try to kill you."

It is Kovacs' turn to rise and look into the trees, resolved that Reader's analysis is flawless. The vision of his own life, once so dazzlingly laid out for him, must now instantly disappear into another uncharted universe. He will go where he will not be found, leaving all ties. He slumps and sits on the picnic table bench, staring at the ground. He makes one last plea in despair. "There must be another way."

"I am afraid there is none."

"But what becomes of me, William?"

Reader takes one knee before Kovacs' deflated form. He captures his friend's eyes and looks sternly into the man of faith and offers some of his own. "Jonas, friend, your importance is not over. To them, maybe, but should their intent be truly malicious, you will be the only one remaining who knows there may be devastation ahead." Reader smiles to bring hope. "The rest of us are earth dwellers. You know I do not believe the things you do. But, given the possibility I am wrong, you are the only soul who can carry the cause forward."

Kovacs returns a thankful smile. "When will that be?"

"It could be months or years; it's hard to know."

"How will I know?"

Reader takes to his feet. He paces furiously for a moment. "I... I will take it upon myself." Reader relays with fervor. "If you hear from me, you will know. I will not know where you are, at least at first, but I am clever and smart. I will learn of it and contact you."

Kovacs stands and rests a hand on the professor's shoulder. "William, I am afraid something has been set in motion we may not be able to stop."

Pondering the evidence, Reader scans his accumulation of human understanding. His unique intuition flutters through possibilities. Leaves scurry and rustle about his feet, all orange and brown, amber and red, except one, an unusual royal purple. He picks it up between his thumb and forefinger and presents it to Kovacs.

"There is always one, an opposite, an outlier. It is the collective law of human existence. The universe is consistent—black and white, yin and yang, light and darkness, zero and one. What is in motion will also generate another we do not know of, an opposite, a canceling presence. I will dedicate myself to finding that person."

"Who, then?"

Reader rolls on, his intellect extruding solutions faster than he can express them. "The one," Reader utters almost trancelike. "In every generation there are evolutionary individuals, catalysts, unwitting players of exceptional circumstance, persons possessing an inherent balancing force." Reader turns, his face stony with pure understanding, all possibilities reduced to one. "This event, being as big as you believe it to be, will surely have a neutralizing counterpart—a spawn of synchronicity. I will find that one and let you know by some arbitrary, but obvious means."

"By some *means*? That sounds precarious, my friend."

"You are a man of faith, Jonas. Have faith."

Eighteen
Present Day

"Did you have a chance to look over the interview outline I e-mailed?" Christy Raines inquires as prelude to her follow-up interview with James Carpenter.

"I did, but maybe we should go over it again." He smiles with welcoming eyes. "You know, more personally, face-to-face, in your words?"

"Sure." She smiles back. "Today we would like to drill deeper into your work, explore what you might have in store, breakthroughs and the like. Just to give you a head's up, you'll get some devil's advocate questions and a modicum of adversarial posture," she warns with professional resolve.

"I insist on it, actually," Carpenter responds with unflappable calm.

"Thank you. Now, I wanted to begin on the path over there where we left off, keep the continuity in flow with our last conversation."

Carpenter nods. He stands before her, his posture shamanic and regal. "Can I take a moment to just say, even with your notable accomplishments," Carpenter pauses, his demeanor intensifying as if looking from another place past this moment. His unblinking eyes peer into her soul. "I see within you so much more."

"Thank you, Jaaa—Mr. Carpenter. That's very kind," she responds in kind, calm and receptive.

"*James*, please, Christy."

"Sure, *James* it is, then," she reluctantly yields. The struggle within stirs once more. He has once again drawn her out from her professional veil. The ease with which he does so, moderately upsets her. But his pure, genuine nature has captivated her as well.

"May I be frank, Christy?" Carpenter's eyes pour out a depth and assurance, undoing her composure to a degree. "The promise you hold for the world is your unique gift, the gift of communication. But ours is a superficial world. I'm sure it has crossed your mind, the fleeting impermanence of your future."

She nervously tosses some strands of hair into place and straightens her posture. Her hands find sanctuary behind her, safely out of sight. Manicured nails offer limited distraction from the seasoned appearance of the rest of her hands. She is dreading his next words.

"I see who you are and what you do, and all of it exists at the mercy of a fickle public, one that worships youth and beauty over all else. Your time in the spotlight is rapidly setting. Yet, your skill and talent could endure several lifetimes." She feels her staunch resolve crumbling away as he reads back to her every intimate concern and emotion she harbors. "Soon, your audience will heartlessly choose to look elsewhere, coldly casting you aside, wasting your talent," Carpenter serves up with frigid certainty cushioned in keen awareness.

"I... I suppose, James... I try not to think about that," she fumbles back sheepishly. "I cherish my gift, and I guess I always believed it would buy me more time than most. I guess I'm in denial about it, though." She clumsily punctuates her confession with nervous laughter past the growing lump in her throat.

"What if that never needed to happen? What if I could assure you that your talent would not be squandered?"

"Assure me?" Her heart leaps at the possibility "How?"

"We are organizing a new test group for an innovation of unique precedent. I think you would be a stellar candidate. At this stage, it must remain confidential, but you would chronicle your experience with us, personalize the process from the inside. When the time is right, you will be the one telling the world how it all works, step-by-step, in your own words."

"*Innovation*?" she questions. Her curiosity is piqued, with a blossom of hope right behind.

"It's sort of our own version of a *makeover*, but it's so much more," he reveals in measured words. "I think you would uniquely understand what we are trying to accomplish and be able to communicate to your following just how positive our work is."

A whirl of emotion has Raines swept away. Her objectivity is now cast far from sight. All at once, she is overcome with the promise of Carpenter's words. But it is more than his words. His countenance, so calm and reassuring, stirs an allegiance within her. He speaks in global scale but with an attention given directly to her. Her vulnerability exposed, she is lost in a sense that she is all that matters to him and wants nothing else than to be near him and participate in his vision.

"Sure, James. What do you need me to do?"

Nineteen
Present Day

The building remains, but the face is changed. Coffee is no longer the drink of commerce, now vintages and varietals, the grape not the bean. Jonas Kovacs steps into a swirl of human activity where once stood the "Java Hut," the homey establishment where he and William Reader first became acquainted. His dated, rumpled appearance draws awkward glances from the cosmopolitan clientele.

Sand-blasted brick and mortar encases accents of brushed steel and reclaimed barn lumber, fused beneath narrow halogen beams from above and cool spot washes from the floor. Toned, postured pencil skirts float in Versace heels exchanging skillful dialogue with fit Hilfiger blazers atop Ralph Lauren denim. Surging pulses of music fill the ear. Muted video monitors act as windows looking out beyond the distance of plain sight, framing dissonant images laid side by side. Hip-hop fly-girls bounce next to pans of typhoon devastation, alongside Brahma bull rodeo riders, adjacent to sharks ripping a seal to pieces. Visual charcuterie for pairings of Pinot Noir, Merlot, and Malbec Reserve.

Outside, the late-fall sky submits to growing darkness, leaving the interior space in command. The strict columned pattern of downward light means each step Kovacs takes finds him in full brightness or darkness. He ambles and twists randomly through a forest of fit bodies as he seeks a starting point to digest the alien landscape. It resembles a discotheque from his era, but without the dance. Here, the years of peaceful expanse in the Tibetan ranges seem as a distant dream, so far removed as to seem alien.

The stale stench of purposeful shallowness stains the atmosphere. The mind is numbed by sensory overload, a narcissistic mosh pit of escapism practiced at a synaptic level. He braces himself with the realization that what called him here must not be overshadowed by the atmosphere of self-consumed superficiality.

His thoughts turn to Reader, the scholar of the human social soup. Not long before, he senses, Reader himself walked here, immersing himself in the crude simmer. Kovacs considers that, if Reader felt the world was lost, he would have quickly turned from here and brushed his hands of it all. Instead, he chose, after thirty years, to summon his friend from halfway around the world. Kovacs owes it to Reader if no one else. He must follow through to the bitter end. But, it briefly crosses his mind in this glamorous bog of human existence, whether the journey will be worth it.

He tries to think as his friend would. Where would a clue reside in this place? What would draw his attention? To oblige the house, he orders a "red wine." Glass in hand, he wanders, trying to slough off the sensory assault and become part of it. Despite Reader's deep interest in human activity, Kovacs decides the professor would not have lasted long in this place. He examines the detail, but from a distance. Another sip of wine, a superb aside—it has been three decades, after all, since he has tasted it. It is pleasant, but a vintage incomparable to the wine he sipped earlier in the day while on his knees. He finds a lone stool and sits, seeking repose. The weight of the journey presses upon him. He will be too exhausted soon, and still needs a room for the night. A YMCA stood just a few blocks from here in 1981. Hopefully it is still in existence. He decides he will finish his wine and return to this den tomorrow at a quieter time.

He snaps back to the present moment and the room surging before him. His eye is drawn to an expansive crimson wall at the other side. It wears a mesmerizing pattern woven behind a scattering of patrons. He approaches to discover the pattern is simply writing—random scribbles—the collective scratchings of tipsy patrons and giddy out-of-towners, poetry and proverbs, silliness and sleaze. He reads on, sipping again, taking them one at a time. He spots a crooked column of light from above. The others shine perfectly vertical. One of the halogen cans is tilted out of place. The angled beam reminds him of the stripe of light painting the front door of the Mount Calvary church, this beam like its twin. He steps through, weaving oblivious patrons, to the wall of writings. Looking straight ahead, a cryptic etching is illuminated by an LED candle resting just beneath it on a bistro table against the wall. A lone remark is revealed.

Extra Regale
    W.R.

Twenty
May 24, 1986

One pair at a time footsteps reverberate from cavernous warehouse walls, echoes that relay magnitude and consequence. Six steel fold-out chairs placed in a half-circle face a wood-framed easel-style blackboard. This is the final destination for each as they arrive. A haze of guardedness taints the atmosphere. Reticent to exchange formal greetings, the six individuals occupying the cold metal seats muster only nods and muted grunts to the others. There is no need to uncloak from presumed anonymity when fifteen minutes later a departure may seem the more prudent option. All arrived ignorant of the purpose except for being told they have been chosen as a *select member* to participate in a *once-in-a-career opportunity*, a *seminal experiment with global implications*. It was a sales pitch taken much more seriously than any other given the name making the request.

A worn wooden door bursts open from a far wall. The big bang produces a seventh member pushing an office desk chair, the *name* arriving in the flesh. Casters squeak like weary mice riding rough over small bits of debris left strewn from years of neglect. The six wheels screech in anguish to keep up to the determination of the driver. The journey ends beside a blackboard. A beefy hand envelops a piece of chalk from the easel tray and, like a grammar school teacher, begins writing a name in the upper left corner.

"Everyone, as if you didn't know, my name is Adeline Brandt," she proclaims as she crosses the "t," underlining the full name with a swipe. Facing her guests, she breathes a purposeful breath and assumes the determined posture of an evangelist. "Fortunate people, such as ourselves, the rare breed of individuals possessing uncommon talent, skill, and the benefit of good fortune, may, only once in our lifetime, be presented with an opportunity to alter the course of the human condition—Jonas Salk, Albert Einstein, Genghis Khan, Robert Oppenheimer. When fate fuses together the golden combination of right place–right time, with capable knowledge and technology at the ready, and then presents it on a silver platter, it is not just one's privilege, but one's *duty* to act. To turn away and ignore it is to commit mortal sin against the cause of mankind. This is not a *calling* I am about to offer you; it is a *telling*. You must accept it or live the remainder of your life knowing you interfered with the very evolution of humanity."

Brandt, a square-framed woman with sturdy shoulders and blocky features, strides before the grouping. At row's end, she pivots on a thick leg and returns to the other side, a bulky human pendulum pacing the full row of chairs and back again. She wears matronly gray, looking almost like a prison warden in her frock and flats. Her hair is mud brown and whipped into a tight bun, awkwardly pinned by several daisy barrettes. Her puffy face hides behind brown-rimmed discount-store, half glasses. "I have gone to great lengths to research the backgrounds of everyone in this room. It is my firm belief that the assembled can cultivate extraordinary breakthroughs, but it is imperative that all participate." She pauses to face them and glare past their defenses. "That said, and before you start raising your hands like inquisitive preschoolers, I want to point out that everything discussed here is confidential. If you came here with ulterior motives, you will leave possessing nothing of substance to thwart our efforts."

"I am quite certain there is no other group of individuals even capable of comprehending what we plan to accomplish. But, just the same, knowing the players involved may be enough to prick up meddlesome ears in the outside world. Ears that belong to stilted imaginations unable to grasp the importance of what we seek. So, I ask that you respect our anonymity should you decide to bow out." Six heads nod affirmatively. "Of course, I am familiar with each of you and your various talents and achievements. As far as my contribution, well I'm sure—"

"If I may, Miss Brandt," a younger man with an Austrian accent brashly interrupts. "I think you could dispense with the formality of telling us who you are and what you do. I'm sure we all know very well that you—"

"Ah, yes, Mr. Kipner, wunderkind extraordinaire, and it's *Doctor* Brandt, actually," Brandt retorts acerbically.

"*Doctor* Kipner, *actually*," he parries. "I have a PhD as well, Miss Doctor; several really."

A dashing fellow interjects, "Look, before we all start off on the wrong leg here, maybe we should introduce ourselves, *Doctors*, to each other. You know, just to break the ice a bit, get to know each other before we build an ego-fueled bonfire. Doctor Brandt has the advantage of knowing who we are, but the rest of us do not."

"You would be the one sent by the Vatican," Brandt interrupts.

"Yes, Cardinal Jonas Kovacs," he replies cordially.

"Ah, yes, one of the non-scientists," she colors with a mild tone of superiority. "Welcome, Cardinal Kovacs. It is clear where your background lies. Kipner, please share with everyone your unrivaled expertise?" she capitulates edgily to Kovacs' request.

Kipner volleys his response smugly as if rehearsed just for the occasion. "Biogenetics, gene mapping, hybridization. I obtained three doctorates before the age of twenty-four and would share with you what projects I have worked on but they are highly classified, and some still in operation. I have weapons work, disease management, disease *promotion*, etcetera." Kipner turns his head, a passing of the baton to the man seated at his right.

"My name is Doctor William Reader," the somewhat more seasoned and casually unkempt fellow begins, "I only have two doctorates, but obtained each before I was *twenty-two*," he boasts with feigned pretention aimed as a gentle poke to his predecessor's over-seriousness. "My field of study is anthropology and sociology, but my realm is much more than that and, as of yet, goes unlabeled. Let's call it the study of mass behavior and population dynamics, a field of study of my own design that I call *cultural genetics*. I will not regale you with the details here, however; I'd prefer to explain that at another time." Reader relaxes back into his chair as a cue for the next in line.

"Marcus Chandler, everyone," recites a gregarious man in his mid-forties. His demeanor and tone speak of a no-nonsense frankness, but an impish gleam sneaks from his eyes. "I hold degrees in aerospace engineering and biological design. I specialize in structural configuration of unique laboratory environments. I cut my teeth with NASA on space shuttle technology, engineering containment, and isolation units for extreme environments. I am more often than not inventing new technology on the fly to accommodate innovative experimental techniques, supercolliders, hyper-sterile and zero-gravity horticultural facilities, that sort of thing."

The two who remain unintroduced carry themselves differently than the rest. They are both bald and wear black suits. A pause grows pregnant. They wear a posture reluctant to contribute. One finally speaks drolly as the stares from the others prod an utterance given solely out of obligation. "My... my name is Mr. Smith, and this is Mr. Jones," he spills out with a crooked smile. "We are the *executive producers* here, specialists in mitigating red tape. We have no doctorates, not a single one. We didn't even finish grad school."

Their lack of credentials raises a subdued, collective brow. They smell of government types to the others, and not the good kind hailing from a sympathetic branch like CDC or NIH. These two wear a facade concealing misdirection. The ilk who make their nests in the gray areas of forgotten budgets, parasites attaching themselves to open-ended project money.

Kipner can't resist. "So, if I may, Miss... uh... *Doctor* Brandt, it appears, despite all our celebrated accomplishment, this is going to boil down to just another black-ops, below-the-radar endeavor where these two end up stealing the glory and we end up getting audited by the IRS to shut us up. No offense Messieurs *Jones* and *Smith*."

"I find myself reluctantly agreeing with the boy," Reader seconds. "I know how these things play out. This just reeks of bureaucratic bondage."

"Look," Chandler jumps in. "I have worked on a lot of government-funded operations. It can work, and really quite successfully if the G-folks just stay on the sidelines. If you two can do that, then I am in. I need assurances, though; it seems like we all do."

"Look, we are all here for one thing," the other bald man offers.

"Which one are you?" Reader needles.

"I am Jones. As I was saying, we are all here for one thing. To break through barriers, to push the envelope. If that weren't true you wouldn't be here. *We*, me and Mr. Smith, only want one thing, to watch you all thrive unrestrained."

A lengthy pause settles in. Brandt breaks the silence. "Very well, I'm sure all of you can distill the nature of this project, based on the skills of those assembled. As you well know, I have been hailed as possibly the most brilliant mind of our age—at least that's what the *New York Times* declares." She lingers to share a laugh with herself. "They really don't know the half of it. I will tell you now with absolute certainty. When finished with our work, we will be able to alter lives for the better and provide unlimited purpose to each individual. We shall transform the human experience in ways never imagined, evolution on an exponential scale, ending hunger and curing disease. Look around you, the skeletal space we occupy here today will pulse as a vibrant crucible of scientific breakthrough with you thriving boldly in the belly of the beast."

Kipner clears his throat with a question meant to provoke. "Ok, I'll bite; which diseases?"

Brandt turns to Kipner. With unblinking, steely eyes and a one-sided smile she responds,

"All of them."

Twenty One
Present Day

In his time here long ago, the Central Branch of the Enoch Pratt Free Library in downtown Baltimore was a home away from home, a quiet environment for a quiet man. Located less than a mile walk from his present-day homeless shelter, Jonas Kovacs guides his way via memory, still as keen as if it were yesterday. The library seems the best start to gaining more knowledge in deciphering William Reader's cryptic wall scribbling of *Extra Regale*.

To Kovacs it reads as some fashioning of Latin, but one not common, or even proper. *Extra* means "out," or "outside of," *Regale* translates to "the royal." Separately they mean nothing to him or the context of finding the chosen one. Together they make absolutely no sense. It would seem Reader's intent was to leave a clue with some relevance to something Kovacs would have familiarity with, but others would not. Perhaps, Latin seemed a good choice, one of several languages Kovacs has mastered but one obscure to the layman. Beyond that, the words have no substance to his understanding. He is certain there will be a dusty volume of Catholic history on a shelf somewhere that will render an answer.

Passing through the main arched entrance, Kovacs is struck by the library's immensity. An enormous building occupying an entire city block, it seems so much larger now than years ago when he was more a denizen of city life. Row upon row of bookshelves stand proud and timeless, but an unexpected addition to the vast space are the dozens of flat television screens attached to typewriter keyboards. But maybe not typewriters and maybe not televisions, he considers. Peering over a stranger's shoulder, he tries to glean a functional purpose to these devices so out of place in a temple dedicated to the worship of print.

"Can I help you, sir?" a female voice wafts in gently from behind Kovacs.

"Oh, um, yes, I was wondering if you could show me to the reference materials?" he timidly responds turning to greet the voice, which belongs to a slender, young Indian lady with a nametag reading *Suri*.

"We have thousands of reference materials," she says through a smile. "What specifically are you looking for?"

"The origins of a phrase... maybe if I start in the card catalog, I can find something to..."

She stifles a reflex to laugh. His sincerity gives her pause to realize it is a serious question. "Card catalog, sir? We haven't had one of those for nearly fifteen years."

"Well, then how will I be able to find anything?"

"If I could suggest a web search. That might go much quicker for you."

"Web? Search?" Kovacs' face goes blank as his brain tries to put meaning to the words.

Suri and several nearby library patrons pause to gape incredulously at the improbability standing among them.

"Bro, planet Earth calling. Hello?... Internet... World Wide Web," interjects the young man whose shoulder Kovacs was peering over before. Kovacs' confusion grows at words spoken to him in English but making no sense at all.

"I got this, lady. Sit here, man." The young man offers a stool next to his. "My name is Drake, and you are?

"Jonas."

"So, seriously, straight up, you have never heard of the Internet?"

Kovacs has a question of his own about why the man is wearing a winter ski cap and summer shorts at the same time. "No," Kovacs responds, leaving his query unasked.

"Have you been living under a rock, or something? No offense," Kovacs newfound tutor asks through his lumberjack beard.

"More like on top of a rock, a very large one," Kovacs clarifies.

"Whatever, bro."

Drake patiently tutors Kovacs on browsers, keywords, and mouse techniques. Twenty minutes later, confident Kovacs is comfortable, Drake bids adieu, seizing a worn backpack and leaving his elder student to his own devices. Kovacs gleans browsing skills quickly. He searches for tie-ins to Baltimore and Reader's name with the Latin phrase, crafting possibilities that there may be some magical combination. The result is nothing that could even remotely be considered a starting point. The phrase, even by itself, yields nothing. It doesn't mean anything to the *World Wide Web.*

A roiling tsunami of hopelessness washes over him. He thinks now he must rely on luck and his good friend Reader's blind faith. Among the searches for the phrase coupled with Reader's name arrive companion results of the day of his death. When the letter arrived at the monastery, Kovacs knew his friend was gone, but until now, he has not known the circumstances. Reluctantly, but with reverent curiosity, he summons the news reports to his monitor, hoping they will shed clarity on his friend's uncharacteristic act of desperation.

He reads of an apparent madman bent on the destruction of a rising earthly saint named James Carpenter. Overlooked go Reader's academic contributions, eclipsed by his single, violent act. Inarguably, the press narrative plays as insanity. Reports of custom-crafted firearms and ammunition slice crossways through Kovacs' memory of the man he knew, one dedicated to discovery and the pursuit of truth. It chills his soul to think the gentleman with whom he shared late hours discoursing on the origins and righteous reasons for mankind's existence somehow arrived at a place where his last act was an assassination attempt. More than thirty years have passed. Could the man he knew be capable of such a monstrous act? Could reasons exist that would justify attempted murder? His friend always had deeper motives in mind for anything he undertook, at least back then. But what chain of events could have led the Professor to such a twisted conclusion? It seems implausible in much the same way as assigning grandiose meaning to a scribbling on a barroom wall.

Kovacs' attention moves to the victim of Reader's crime. A man so young wielding such dramatic impact, and already on a global scale. He reads, in article after article, that Carpenter is surrounded with bold successes. He and his Institute bring improbable stabilization to troubled nations, forming innovative solutions to the ageless problems of hunger, disease and despotism. This one man harvests peace from hopeless circumstances involving factions engaged in centuries-old, bloody conflicts. Within Kovacs wells a dissonant respect, as if he has known this man before. All at the same time, Kovacs loves him and fears him in equal measure. And yet, he does not know him at all.

The importance of his mission, the meaning of the phrase, falls temporarily to inferior status. He hoped it would be easy, but instead, it requires some divined intuition on his part, and maybe some divine intervention. As impossible as it seems now, when it is revealed, he is sure it will be something obvious, given Reader's penchant for hiding things in plain sight. But at the moment, Kovacs remains ignorant of a solution to Reader's puzzle. What it all means, he concludes, will be revealed when the time is right.

Twenty Two
Present Day

"Is that the cross, Daddy?" asks Jason Traeger of his father. "The one that almost killed you?"

"It did not almost kill me, but I could have been seriously hurt," the architect corrects his son with a tempered, fatherly tone and cautious reserve to douse any thoughts of dread. Although the child was more accurate than Traeger would readily admit aloud. His seven-year-old daughter, Melissa, remained with her mother today. Traeger strongly suggested she attend, but an equestrian outing labelled "important" by her mother took precedence. Traeger bristled at the excuse that a weekly horse ride was more important than attending a seminal moment in her father's life, but he conceded rather than fomenting another cell phone confrontation he was sure to lose with his ex. At least his son can share the day.

"It looks very heavy. I think it would have crushed you if you fell," the nine-year-old dictates with coarse, forensic certainty, a trait passed from the child's mother—raw judgment not meant to inflict a wound, but still leaving a mark.

"I am certain I would not have been crushed, Jason."

"Why did they make the cross so heavy?"

"It isn't heavy on purpose, it just is. It is made of very dense wood."

"Okay, everyone, let's gather outside at the front steps. It is time for the dedication ceremony," announces Father Archer to the scattered congregation and guests.

Outside, they find a different gathering with media. Cameras and microphones are unexpected pageantry to Traeger but he welcomes the publicity. Father Archer addresses the assembled.

"Faithful parishioners and appreciators of history, welcome to our new *old* house of worship," begins the priest from a temporary pulpit situated on the highest stone riser of the church entrance. "Nearly five centuries ago this structure was erected to the glory of God by a handful pioneers brought here for one sole purpose—to enjoy the freedom to practice their beliefs without the interference and persecution of others. They braved the turbulent Atlantic Ocean, a hostile landscape, starvation, disease and the occasional attack from unfriendlies. This building has housed many a denomination—Puritans, Anglicans, Baptists, Adventists, and is currently the grateful home to the Roman Catholic faith. It remains a stalwart monument to the glory of God. And now, thanks to the fine efforts of several dozen craftsmen and one visionary architect named Alex Traeger, we will more gratefully enjoy the worship of the one true God from inside these four spectacular, renovated walls. We dedicate this building and its rebirth, dare I say *resurrection,* to the grace of our Lord, Jesus Christ. Now if you will all join me in solemn prayer."

Archer leads the gathering through prayers of thanksgiving and blessings, then a generous sprinkling of holy water. Alex Traeger tries to lose himself in the depth of the moment; he has worked hard and with purposeful commitment to his client's wishes, but he cannot muster any spiritual inspiration from the ceremony. He wishes he could, but even after months of immersing himself in the practices and architectural importance of the building's features, he remains unmoved. The prayers ended, Archer invites the gathering to a reception and casual "Q and A" walkthrough of the building.

"Daddy, was he really talking to God?" Jason asks of his father.

"I... I think he believes he is."

"Does God talk back?"

"I..." Traeger thinks about it. His answer to himself is "no," but unexplainably he cannot bear to assign such finality to the boy's desire to know. He himself does not believe, but he does not feel he has the right to decide that for his son. It is tantamount to revealing the truth about Santa Claus, but not even that. He has discovered he has an unexpected reverence for the idea of God, even though he defaults his spirituality to one of agnosticism. "Let's get some cake, son," Traeger responds, knowing it will deflect, even if only temporarily the question for another time when maybe he has a better understanding.

Twenty Three
May 24, 1986 – Later in the evening

"Cardinal Kovacs, right?" echoes through the dim illumination of an underground parking garage located two blocks from the initial group meeting with Adeline Brandt.

"Yes." Kovacs turns to the voice. "Professor Reader, hello."

Reader treads gritty concrete to extend a hand, met firmly by the cardinal. "In the flesh, Padre. Look, I don't know about you, but that was the strangest gathering I have ever been party to"—Reader smiles as prelude to a jest—"and I'm in academia." Kovacs chuckles at Reader's humor.

"I'm making an exception in your case from that comment, of course," Reader resumes. "Would you care to join me in a cup of coffee? I need to commiserate with someone who apparently has his feet on the ground, someone who can help me collect my thoughts about all this. Can I buy you a cup?"

The two surface onto churning, nighttime streets in central downtown Baltimore. Not far away, they find comfortable digs in the form of a brash new-concept coffee house called the Java Hut. They land in a diner-style booth featuring brass nails hammered into crimson leather. The random noise of fluttering conversation fills the air, sprinkled with clinking dishes and steamy blasts of frothing milk. Their mugs arrive. Coffee, black, unadorned by barista artistry.

"Thanks for joining me, Jonas. It's pronounced *Yo-nas*, correct?" begins Reader. He pauses for a sip to find his opening words. "Needless to say, I'm still trying to sort out the meaning of all that business. The abandoned warehouse, the savant geniuses and *G-men*, the impossible claims of universal cures and ending world hunger." Reader sips again. "I sense I can trust you, Jonas. You were the only one there concerned with everything else and not with how it will benefit you. I hope the feeling is mutual." Reader pauses, then smiles a bit. "Now, before we go on. Let me spare you some time. If you're thinking about giving a go at converting this man of science, you can save your breath."

Kovacs grins with a sparkle in his eye. Any further tension between them dissolves. "I have no intention of converting you to anything. It may surprise you that I am a man of science, too. My initial studies were in physics in Budapest before I decided to join the priesthood. Now, I am a man of God first, who is also a man of science. There is no conflict, as I see it. They are really one and the same. God invented science, you know, William," Kovacs posits with another smile.

"If only he had included proof of his own existence in that science. It would all be so much easier," Reader answers in his own lightened tone.

"Well said, my friend. I'll have a talk with him about that." Kovacs winks, then sips from his coffee.

"I would appreciate it, Father." Reader adds more sugar to his cup to punctuate his thought. "I guess the first thing I want to ask you is, what brought you here?"

"A request from Brandt. She approached the Vatican and they assigned me to the task."

"She approached? The Vatican? Do you know how incongruous that is?"

"It's true, Professor. I was told to cooperate in every way."

"In regards to what?"

"Religious relics and artifacts."

Reader's brow furls at even more mystery. His eyes squint as if they are looking further into himself for an answer to his conundrum. "The plot thickens. Again, this is not something Adeline Brandt is interested in... would ever be interested in."

Reader adjusts a spoon and squares a napkin to reside parallel to the edge of the table, a subliminal ordering of things as a balance against his thoughts swelling with uncertainty.

"I know nothing of Adeline Brandt. You seem uncomfortably... *impressed*... by her," Kovacs probes.

"Well, yes. She is the foremost pioneer in several novel disciplines, most notably genetics and DNA mapping. She is a walking phenomenon of genius, and the only reason I showed up, or assign any value to this meeting," Reader professes.

"You mean her talents are legitimate."

"Legitimate? There is no word to describe the level of cachet she brings to whatever it is she is involved in. Anyone situated in deep academia would pay close attention." Reader hears himself and realizes there are no real words to describe what he is trying to impart. "Look, if she held a bingo game, I would be there."

"I have never heard of her," Kovacs confesses.

"You wouldn't. Her circles of influence are rare and stratospheric." Reader squirms again to make sense of his dilemma. "Relics and artifacts? Seriously?"

"Yes, I was given a listing of all artifacts known to exist in shrines and churches, many only known to a very few. You know, things like Saint John the Baptist's tunic, a ring thought to have belonged to Saint Peter. The actual wood of the cross, things like that."

"The end game being?"

"Authentication. Doctor Brandt approached the Vatican with a bold idea to validate the claims surrounding controversial religious relics through her advanced science, to determine if they are genuine or not. She offered to do so with no compensation and signed a binding confidentiality agreement regarding any findings. I have no knowledge of how she will do this. I wasn't there, but apparently her presentation was persuasive to the Vatican."

"So, Jonas, how does all that fit in to you being here?"

Reader's skepticism is chipping away at Kovacs' confidence in his assignment. He continues but with new thoughts swirling. "I am here to contribute needed historical context and to supervise the Vatican's interest in the project. I am the middleman between Brandt and the Vatican."

Reader senses Kovacs' concern. He offers a more stable outlook. "Look, I believe you, Jonas, but it doesn't add up. She has absolutely no interest in anything religious. I don't know," Reader interrupts himself to stir a thought. "Maybe she is just using your artifacts as a beta test for her science. I guess that is possible."

Kovacs leans in, finding full allegiance in his new friend across the table. "Do you trust her, William?"

Reader aligns all the packets in the sweetener caddy into perfect symmetry, fronts and backs facing the same direction, colors grouped with like colors.

"I'm not sure. She doesn't evoke an air of selflessness. She is inarguably out for her and her alone, always has been. If there were some monetary gain or personal glorification to be had, it would make more sense to me. But, she isn't a bullshitter either. Her arrogance won't allow her to stoop to petty deception. If she means to authenticate, then I think you will get accurate results. She is proud of her science and wouldn't compromise its purity. That is *her* religion. If there is more to it than that, then I can't imagine what she might be considering."

"So then, Professor, do you plan on following through with this?"

"I must. I am a slave to the curiosity of it. I need to know. She is right when she says this is a once-in-a-lifetime opportunity. I also just happen to fit in well with strange gatherings." Reader grins at his last words. "What about you, Father?"

"I am bound by duty. The Vatican has sent me here. I must continue."

"Very well, then we must remain thick as thieves, share our thoughts and knowledge in confidence. Do you agree?"

"I do, William. I believe God has brought the two of us together."

Twenty Four
Present Day

Not far from the old Java Hut site rests a new coffee house. A block here and a block there away. Jonas Kovacs sips his morning tea at a window counter seat framing a panoramic display of the ebb and flow of the street beyond. An aquarium of humanity swims before him. Morning devotionals behind him, he requires more than his usual routine to consider where his quest for Reader's chosen one will continue. Words from over thirty years ago echo in his thoughts, his own proclamation that God brought the two of them together. So long ago, and so naïve he was, when there was nothing but the future ahead for both of them.

He still believes it was an act of God's hand, but if there were supernatural forces influencing fate, they seem more distant than ever now. The events that have taken place since that day long ago would argue against divine handiwork. Reader is gone and Kovacs is charged only by a desperate shred of hope. He reminds himself that God has his own timetable, one not dictated by days or months or even millennia, or nagged at by the burden of desperate impatience. God knows nothing of waiting. It is an experience known only to those subject to time's incessant winding. God's realm has no clock. Whether alpha or omega, it is all in the present.

Extra Regale—he has replayed the phrase several hundred times, subconsciously, out loud, even with greater emphasis on different syllables. It is rapidly morphing from a phrase of hope to a taunt of despair. He sends a thought, a cursed sneer Reader's way wherever he now resides, chastising his friend for non-specifics. Kovacs shuts his eyes to bring calm. A prayer rises up within him. He breathes deeply, awaiting an answer. Silence is returned.

Whatever became of Brandt, he wonders. She disappeared, or so his deeper Internet searching at the library indicated. There was no obituary, so she must still be alive. But there were no indications of further work. She disappeared at almost the same time he himself fled to the other side of the world. And yet he finds it impossible that someone possessing her abilities could simply disappear into obscurity.

Sunlight peeks through the thin space between two distant high-rise towers, casting a narrow beam of light through the window and across the countertop holding Kovacs' teacup. The stripe of daylight streaks across the leavings of a departed patron, a spent coffee cup, crumb cake crumbs on a plate, and a newspaper. Kovacs leans to one side of his stool, extending his reach and clutching the tabloid. It reads of social injustice, landlord squabbles and price gouging conspiracies at in-town convenience markets. Deeper into the pages, he finds a notice for Sunday service times in the downtown area, a notice unchanged from his time here long ago. It settles him to know there are still constants in this world.

On the opposite page lies a short article about a restoration project of an historical landmark, a house of worship in Virginia, orchestrated by a budding architect named Alex Traeger. It warms Kovacs' heart to read of tradition and longevity restored, to learn of a humble, broken structure given new life. He reads on to become captivated by the renewal of a dying building and the man who cared enough to remake its existence. Something else is wriggling and poking at Kovacs. Something else about the article is drawing his attention. It is the architect. It is his name, specifically the letters, ones he has recently spent a great deal of time with, but arranged differently. One letter at a time he crosses them out—"E", then "X", then "T". When finished, Kovacs is torn in two, one half in glorious relief, the other filled with disbelieving incertitude at the seeming randomness of Reader's choice.

For now, he opts for glorious relief recharging his spirit and Reader's playful way of hiding things in plain sight. The puzzle is a marker for Reader's own impudent arrogance. It is insulting in its own way, a wink and a nod now obvious to Kovacs. The puzzle is a simple one, really. *Extra Regale* is not a phrase or a grand reference, it is a childish anagram. Hidden inside the puzzle is a poke to Kovacs from Reader to say, "I'm going to give you a *real* clue, but because it's you, I'd better make it an easy one." *Extra Regale* equals Alex Traeger.

To know for sure, Kovacs must find him.

Twenty Five
Present Day

He wears fine creased slacks, a high-thread-count linen shirt with the collar strategically opened just so. A slate-gray Armani blazer rides over one shoulder. From a distance, via remote, he unlocks the door to a convertible Jaguar coupe. The underground lot is isolated, but well lit. He feels safe, comfortable in his stride, savoring the victorious dealings of the day now gently fading behind him. It is the last pleasant thought he will ever have, one violently interrupted by rupturing voltage. The chilled control of life succumbs to the lightning-bolt force of a Taser that induces involuntarily evacuation of bowels and bladder. His limp form thumps rudely to the concrete and is callously deposited into the trunk of his car and quickly chauffeured home.

By sheer acreage, it is an impressive spread but incongruous to a man of his outward elegance. It looks more the turf of alligator hunters, or moonshiners—crude, rustic, and unrefined, more a compound than a sanctuary.

He wakes, strapped to a chair made of wood, but one of sturdy make. He will not be able to free himself no matter how urgently he struggles. He built it to be strong for that very reason. A female approaches from a dozen feet in front of him. A small red light behind her beams; video rolls to capture the moment. For him, the tables have surely turned.

"Hello, Stanton, remember me?" the young woman barks as she steps into the harsh light hanging from above. A chill of horror rips through him, greater still than the fear of waking to his predicament. His eyes are playing tricks, he thinks. The woman standing over him cannot be real.

"Yep, it's me, mother-fucker. Karma is a bitch."

"Who are you?" he mumbles through his recovering haze. She brings her face in closer.

"I think you know... Surprised?"

"It's impossible... There is no way. I'm hallucinating... You... you are dead," he slurs in horrified tones.

The woman pinches her arm. "Ouch!" she screams, feigning pain. "That actually hurt. Do you think a dead person feels pain?"

"Oh God, this can't be real," he weeps.

"GOD! GOD?! You of all people, talking of God!"

He blinks furiously, apparently trying to erase the image from his eyes. This must be a mirage, surely a trick of the brain.

"I tried to tell you. Do you remember what I said to you, then? I told you I would come back," she scolds, poking his forehead with her index finger. "I told you that you would regret what you were doing, but you didn't listen. You cut me into pieces and dumped my body, what you left of it, in a swamp, yet here I am. It's *a* meer-aaaa-cle," she blares, waving her arms as a would-be revival preacher.

"What..." his dry, trembling throat chokes trying to produce the next phrase—"what are you going to do to me?"

"I'm kind of a show-me-don't-tell-me girl. So, I'll spare you the dry details and just... well... let you *experience*... Isn't that what you said to me?"

She clutches a roll of duct tape and crudely wraps it around his head and across his mouth several times, strapping his skull to the chair-back, ensuring he will never speak a coherent word ever again. She wanders the room, a well-equipped workshop in an over-sized garage. A treasure trove of commercial grade construction tools, but these more frequently used for purposes not imagined in their original design. She finds an air compressor and some pneumatic tools. They will do. Fearful tears well and fall from the man's eyes at the noxious grind of the compressor building pressure. Snot oozes from his panting nostrils. Involuntarily, he feebly lurches to free himself again. She discovers a razor knife and approaches, nuzzling her mouth to his quivering ear.

"I have a brilliant idea," she whispers.

She takes a peek at the gauge: optimum pressure. She brings the razor knife to his crotch and slices through the fancy fabric of his trousers, spilling his genitals onto the wood of the chair. "Going commando, I see? Good lord, did you shit yourself? I'm sorry. This must be humiliating," she sneers with a vengeful laugh.

A nail gun is secured to the compressor hose. The cartridge houses framing nails measuring three-and-a-half inches and coated with resin to insure they never unstick: nails made for securing two-by-four lumber. The trigger is gently pressed down. A percussive puff of air releases, followed by a wretched wail forced past silver duct tape.

"The bleeding will stop soon, I promise. I'm pretty sure the pain won't. Sorry about that, Mr. Stanton." She role-plays polite concern.

The woman slides a second chair over from the far corner and seats herself down, backwards, arms resting on the chair back. She leans in, inches from his pained face. "Poor Mr. Stanton, did you ever think you would see me again? I pity you because you had no way of knowing. I will tell you so you do not die in ignorance. We are sworn to secrecy. But, since you will be dead soon and I know you are not one of us, I will let you know the mistake you made. You picked the wrong girl to rape and murder. I have connections. I am part of an inner circle. You cut me into pieces, but it doesn't matter. I am an Eternal. I cannot die. You, on the other hand, will. You will suffer a brutal death and then be exposed to the world as the perversion you are. Are you ready for that now? Shall I finish you so you never do your evil again?"

His tortured eyes and distorted face concede "yes." She nods with a teasing, pleased smile and says. "Very well, let's get on with your wretched penance."

Patiently and playfully, she empties nails into his body, one by one. Twenty shots find joints, bones and viscera—a modern-day crucifixion by power tool, executed in sitting position. She avoids vital arteries and organs to prolong his suffering. He tries to pass out but she won't allow it, administering a different pain with the razor. She stands back like an artist from her masterpiece to watch his eyes reflect a trip to hell. With her last shred of mercy, she decides it is complete and presses the business end of the nailer to his panicked left eye. The trigger pulled, his skull fuses to the chair-back. It is over.

Twenty Six
Present Day

"Hey, Myer. Thanks for meeting with me." The formerly athletic build of Detective Anthony Petrangelo slides into a barroom booth opposite Ivan Myer.

"No worries, Tony. What's up?"

They shake hands.

"I suppose you heard they caught the Durham Devil," Petrangelo imparts with a smile that telegraphs the dropping of another shoe is coming.

"I did. That's really good news. How did that case break?"

"He was murdered and the local blue got an anonymous tip where to find him." Petrangelo dishes up matter-of-factly, then leans back and signals the bartender.

"Okay, so why did you need to talk to me? Sounds like the case is closed."

Petrangelo slaps a large manila envelope on the table between them. "I called in a favor and got the case file. Check it out."

Myer digs into the folder and pulls out copies of pictures and text. A glass of beer lands in front of Petrangelo. "His name was Harris Stanton, age forty-three, an antiquities dealer who operates... *operated* up and down the east coast."

"And you want me to see if I have any insight on the killer?"

"We know who killed him."

"So, why am I here?"

"You said you were interested in *bizarre*. Just take a look."

Myer examines the documents now spread across the table. His eyes strain back and forth examining the macabre corpse of a mass killer, cringing at a framing nail planted in the victim's eye socket. "Wow, he's a mess."

Petrangelo nods affirmatively while sipping his beer. Myer continues, "I still don't see it. I'm at a loss. Give me a hint. What's the backstory?"

Petrangelo's left index finger singles out a page from the scattered pile and carefully pushes it in the direction of Myer, who snatches it up.

"He kept trophies, Myer, freezers full of them. Look at the document. Look at the perp profile, then the victim roster, the ones identified by remains at the scene," Petrangelo guides.

Myer goes back and forth trying to find Petrangelo's mystery. He finally sees it. "Oh, really? That? It's a typo, a clerical error, pasted into the wrong column on the spreadsheet. I've seen this before."

"Not so fast, Myer. This was three weeks ago and the science is indisputable—two independent labs. They found him a month ago nailed to a chair in Durham. On his own property, no less. Turns out he's a classic ghoul with rows of appliances full of specific body parts in his garage: feet, hands, and heads only. The rest of the remains he dumped at random locations. We don't know how, but this young woman managed to get him duct taped to a chair on his own property, most likely by tasing him. Crime scene photos show burn marks on the back of his neck."

"How do we know about this woman? How do we know it *is* a woman?" Myer questions.

"She left a video at the scene, along with plenty of DNA."

"Such as?"

"Strands of hair, epithelials, fingerprints on the murder weapon. She spit on him. It's a slam dunk, really, like she wanted to be found out."

"So, Captain Obvious here, why don't they go arrest her?"

"Right. I never thought you'd ask. There's the *typo* problem... that... well, it isn't a typo. You see, not only did she—Amanda Tisdale—dial up as the killer, she's also one of the victims."

Myer slumps back in the booth and wriggles a bit. "What?"

"That's right, she's in both columns on the spreadsheet because the science verified it. In the third freezer from the left they found her hands, feet, and head, DNA confirmed... twice."

"There must be some mistake," Myer refutes, adding emphasis by shaking his head. "Okay, try this on," he theorizes. "She killed Stanton and then a short time later... " Myer's brain grinds away at possible theories. "Maybe Stanton's accomplice finds her at the scene and offs her using the same M.O."

"Nope, no accomplice, and comparing the time of death, her parts in the freezer come in around seven months ago, which is just about the time she was reported missing."

"A twin, maybe?" Myer grasps desperately for some logical explanation.

"Nope, her family reports no twin. They haven't seen her since she disappeared. Can you imagine how they are taking this?"

Myer feverishly shuffles through the case documents one more time looking for something he might have missed, something the investigation may have overlooked. He falls back in his chair, exasperated. "I don't know. There is no explanation. How can they file a report like this? It's irresponsible. The killer is also a victim? We all know that is impossible. It just plays more like shoddy work than anything."

"What can I say, bro? Science is science. What are they supposed to do?" Myer's colleague tries to sympathize. "There's no way they could ever prosecute her even if they catch her. Can you imagine a jury hearing that?"

"You know," Myer half-whispers to himself, perhaps in confirmation of an earlier realization. "This kind of thing just keeps showing up; unexplainables, the impossible becoming possible."

Petrangelo leans in and collects the file documents, sliding them into the envelope. "It's some crazy shit, Myer."

"I need to think about this Tony." Myer pops to his feet, tosses some bills on the table and exits. "Thanks, I owe you."

Twenty Seven
Present Day

"Thanks for coming in on short notice, Christy. I know you need to run to catch a flight but, I didn't want to give you fantastic news without being face-to-face."

"About?" Christy Raines replies, immediate suspicion nudging at her instincts.

"A promotion. We want to bring you on to the decision-making side. You have more than earned this. Let's celebrate," her managing editor, Pete Kilgore, gleefully answers as he reaches into a desk drawer to retrieve a bottle and two glasses.

"Decision-making side being?"

Kilgore pushes a glass Raines' way. She ignores it. Kilgore raises his glass and toasts alone, then spills a mouthful down his throat. Fidgeting in his chair, he clutches a foam stress ball from a nearby desk caddy. "We're moving you to the production side. We need your polished skills to navigate the intricate landscape of twenty-first-century journalism. We've decided your accrued talents are being squandered in your on-camera role. It's time for you to move on to bigger things. You are worth so much more if we—"

"I don't want it. I'm happy where I am, Pete. Look, I gotta run." Raines rises from her chair as if electrified, her intuition wildly waving red flags. Kilgore's transparent, over-glossy sales pitch and faux exuberance smell to her of a Faustian bargain in the works.

Kilgore pushes harder. "Christy, this is once in a lifetime. You need to say yes. I've called in some huge favors on this."

"Bullshit, Pete," she fumes.

"Christy, really?"

"Yeah, really," she snaps back.

Kilgore spins his chair ninety degrees to enjoy the cityscape from his thirty-second-story picture window, or maybe to avoid the blazing eyes of Christy Raines.

"Pete, you insult me. You forget what I do for a living. You, of all people. I am a walking, talking bullshit detector, best ever. I know what you are up to. You were never able to lie to me with a straight face. What's up, Judas?"

Kilgore turns back to face her, but his eyes retreat down upon meeting hers. She leans above him, glaring downwards with both arms staked to his desktop. "Look, Chris," he reloads for another attempt. "We go back a long way. We've scratched each other's back countless times. I hate to be the bearer of bad news, but the board has no spine, so they make me do this unsavory business." His hand finds the second glass. He downs the contents.

"The truth is they have this crazy idea that the viewers want softer news and less complicated subject matter," Kilgore confesses. He limply clears his throat and swivels his chair back to enjoy the skyline view. "You know the game, Chris, it's all about demographics. It's always demographics."

"You sack-less wonder," she scolds Kilgore, wagging her head. "So, they want to go Hollywood and you're all in. Are they going to write the copy too? You are totally their bitch, Pete."

"It's a goldmine. Look, Chris, you are a legend. You are an icon, but there comes a time to bow out gracefully and you, my dear, will do so with your dignity intact. You're one of a lucky few. You'll get the lifetime achievement awards, the speaking tour, an occasional primetime interview special. You are still gold, baby."

"You mean golden, like golden years gold. I'm nowhere near ready to fade away, so tell the board to jam it up their clenched, caviar-fed asses." Raines' ire melts to melancholy. She harbors regret at releasing her venom at her long-time colleague. She knows the true caldron of anger simmers from the inevitable oozing forth. Her time has come. Her truest love and passion, her career, is being ripped away from her.

Kilgore rises and tilts his head slightly, palms open towards her. "Christy, this is exactly the wrong way to go about this. Look, take a few days to mull it over. We can talk then. You will still be a news contributor but also a valuable asset to the production team. I'm just trying to extend your career. There was considerable thought given to dismiss you, buy you out, and forfeit your option years."

Raines retracts, slumped. Resignation envelops her. She takes three steps to exit, then pauses and pivots back on a Louis Vuitton heel, her ire stoked once more at a eureka realization. "Oh my god, Pete. I get it now… *Zarabeth!*"

"Now, Christy, look." Kilgore tries to calm the brewing storm.

"No, it makes total sense now."

"I would be lying if I said that weren't true, but..."

"Pete, you know she's slept with half the board, even some of the women," Raines fires out, her scorn redoubled at realizing her replacement.

Kilgore smiles slyly, chumming up to his long-time friend, trying to quell her agitated state. "The sad thing is they would have given her the gig anyway. She didn't have to shag the gray prunes on the board. She spread her legs and got nothing else for it."

"Zarabeth? She's got to change her name to be a serious journalist," Raines' anger now morphs to spite and contempt. "It's a name that belongs to a Wiccan priestess, not a serious news person. For Christ's sake, her degree isn't even journalism, it's *communications*."

"Actually, they kind of like her name. It did really well in the forum testing. She's perfectly ethnically ambiguous and she's smoking hot. She kills in the eighteen-to-thirty-four males. We're going to compete with SportsCenter. Can you believe that? News head-to-head with sports."

Raines resumes her journey, reaching the office door, her salvo spent. "Pete, I don't know what to say. I know you probably gave it a half-assed try and your hands are tied. But, one thing is for sure, I'm seeing out the Carpenter makeover story. I'm committed contractually."

"That's exactly what they expected. Do your best work. Go out big, dear."

"Whatever, you son-of-a-bitch."

Twenty Eight
Present Day

Working on Saturday, Alex Traeger catches up on paperwork loose ends. Adjusting his schedule to accommodate his ex-wife's yoga routine resulted in time lost and backlog. He hopes today and another weekend day will bring him up to date. The silver lining is the fact that, the labor is in solitude, leaving him peacefully alone in his office.

His attention is nudged by a sense of another in his presence. The shape of a man just feet away startles him. An elderly gentleman stands in the office doorway. Traeger heard nothing, as if the man is an apparition.

"Can I help you?"

"Possibly," answers the man. "Would you be Alex Traeger?"

"I am. What can I do for you?"

"I hope you don't mind my intrusion; the front door was unlocked."

"I must have forgotten to check it. No worries. Please come in."

Daylight angles in through a narrow side window, leaving a thin stripe of light across the floor in front of the elderly man's shoes.

"My name is Kovacs, Jonas Kovacs. I need to...," he pauses realizing the gravity of the conversation ahead. "I am here to ask you a question."

Traeger's curiosity stirs. He looks at the man, well into his eighties, and decides he is not client material. Perhaps he is homeless, he thinks. "Sure, please take a seat."

Kovacs ambles over, lowering himself into an upholstered leather chair, one of two placed opposite the architect's desk. "Mr. Traeger, I was referred to you by a friend. He *suggested* I contact you."

"Do I know him? What is his name?"

"I believe you may. Your paths may have crossed. If not, I will leave you in peace. His name is… was… William Reader."

Traeger squares to his desk and eases his wheeled office chair back a few more inches away from the name, one he did not expect to ever hear again, one he hoped to forget. Traeger's calm has been pierced at the mention of Reader, an unwelcome provocation coming from a stranger.

"I am not sure I would call him a friend, Mr. Kovacs; acquaintance is more like it."

"But you knew each other, correct?"

"Yes, and you aren't here on business then, Mr. Kovacs."

"I told you, I think he decided. He wanted us to meet."

"For what, exactly? Why would he tell you that? When did he tell you that?"

"He seemed to think I needed to reach you and talk to you."

Traeger's tone has firmed up, the guest now becoming more discomfort than mystery. An odd man he knew so little about, from his past, continues to bring him unwelcome strain. "I can think of nothing to enlighten you any further about Reader. What is so important that you think you need to talk to me about?"

"Changing the course of mankind."

Traeger's eyes widen. His fingernails dig into the arms of his chair. The withered old man has unexpectedly caused him to feel threatened. The proper response, he thinks, should be laughter. But the visitor's words come packed with a magnitude of deeper importance. The architect breathes deeply and sinks in his chair. "Look, Mr. Kovacs, I…"

"I apologize, Alex. I am an unassuming man, but I feel nothing is gained from tiptoeing around God's truth."

"God's truth?" Traeger tosses back incredulously, wondering how God has now become part of the conversation. "What does *that* mean?" He breathes deeply and decides the best course is to shut down the conversation. "Now, if you will, I really have work to do."

Kovacs remains motionless. Traeger squirms at the lack of response. He impulsively clutches a snow globe paper-weight, the world inside now in sudden storm, a flick of the wrist unleashing a blizzard of unrest. "Honestly, I never really knew him, sir. I may have talked to him ten or twelve times, *ever*, and mostly small talk."

"I have no reason to doubt you, Mr. Traeger. William was unique. But he was never shy about the deeper things. He cannot tell us the meaning of his actions, for he is gone. But I do know this, one of his final acts was because of you. I have no knowledge as to why, but he chose you."

Traeger is numbed and shaken. Seeking space, he drifts over to a narrow window to look outside. Maybe a reminder of greater, more peaceful space will quell a surging sense of torment. Once again, he has been yanked back into the actions of William Reader and the cloying intensity that comes with it.

"Chose me?"

"I really don't know why, Alex."

"You are confusing me, Mr. Kovacs."

"Are you a Christian, Alex?"

An odd question for the moment, Traeger thinks. "No, sir."

"Do you believe in God?"

"I wish I did. I could use one right about now. Why do you ask?"

Kovacs rises, eases closer to Traeger at the window, and gently offers, "I am at a loss, as you are. His choice is as much an enigma to me as to you. But, he would not take this sort of thing lightly, and therefore it is important to me. You see, I am a man of God, and God has a hand in all things that matter to him."

"Define *man of God*."

"A great while ago—and telling you this carries with it some chance of danger for me—I was once a resident of the Vatican, a cardinal, actually. My path was set; I was on a course to one day even be considered a candidate for the Holy Father. Perhaps right about now, had I remained."

"What happened, Mr.—Cardinal?" Traeger is dumbfounded, still unsure about this man's level of coherence. Everything he says is uttered in grave concern and conviction, no inkling of ranting tone or disturbed expression. But the content is outlandish and otherworldly for conversation with a stranger.

"I was unknowingly assigned to a matter destined for disgrace," Kovacs continues. "I was misled and had to go into hiding for a very long time, emerging only a short time ago. This sordid business I speak of was where William and I met. In over thirty years, William and I had no communication. A few months ago, I received a letter from him. It was a summons to return and seek you out."

"Me? For what?" Traeger pushes out with timid disbelief.

"I cannot reveal that, at least not until I am certain you will understand the full depth of what you have been brought into. I am afraid if I told you now, you would resist me."

"You're right, I probably would," Traeger says, thinking it the most sensible thing Kovacs has said thus far. "Maybe it would even put *me* in danger?"

"I assure you, no."

Traeger returns from the window to face Kovacs. He gazes deeply into his eyes, trying to reach any rational bit that may remain inside the old man. "Look... Cardinal... I am a very busy man. This is all very compelling, but I am just trying to put a wrap on this day and get home to a steak and a few beers. If William Reader actually made some mention of me somewhere that made you believe you needed to talk to me, I am sure it was delusional. In case you are unaware, he did try to assassinate a guy, then committed suicide."

Kovacs stirs, ready to respond. Traeger tersely interrupts. "Look, I don't doubt you, and you seem to have some sense of urgency, but the man you knew long ago turned into someone very different. I seriously question that I am some *key* to anything."

Traeger's summation of Reader is indisputable. Kovacs decides another opportunity will be provided if Traeger is indeed Reader's true choice.

"Mr. Traeger, I believe I am needlessly complicating your life. Please accept my apologies. I promise, I will only contact you if something meaningful arises. Until then, I will commit myself to finding answers to your questions. I at least owe you that."

Twenty Nine
Present Day

"This is impossible, Ivan. Look, I called in some favors, got access to the evidence lab and looked it over myself. There is no explanation to be had by science as I understand it," concedes Patricia Hamer across an open-air bistro table in downtown Baltimore. Cumulus clouds float above, debating whether to gather and storm or not, making their presence known, alternately blotting the sun and allowing it to shine.

"You have me worried, Pat. It's usually the other way around: *I'm* the one that's supposed to do that to *you*," Myer says with mock concern as self-amusement. He leans contently back in his chair, hands laid across his filled belly.

"The facts are inarguable. This Tisdale girl, she is indisputably both victim and perpetrator."

"Again, this is not like you. Crazy-ass theories are my department, not the other way around."

Hamer stiffens her posture to signal her seriousness. "I am not *concerned* with that," she voices like an irritated school teacher. "You are describing an emotional condition. Any disturbance you sense is because I cannot discern the whole, factual truth, which I will do, sooner or later. That is inevitable. My agitation stems from the unresolved calculus here. The Tisdale girl cannot be in two different states of being at one time. She is either dead or alive, not both. This whole thing means I have to expand my paradigm, and that includes considering the impossible."

"Go on; I'm enjoying this." Myer crosses his legs at the ankles and laces his fingers, settling in to enjoy her dilemma.

Hamer pushes her sandwich wrapper aside with a few bits of chicken salad and a half pickle spear as passengers. Reaching into her satchel, she pulls out her phone. "This whole bit she does right before executing Stanton. She says... hang on, give me a sec." Hamer taps her phone twice. "Okay, here it is." She recites Stanton's words from her notes.

'I tried to tell you. Do you remember what I said to you, then? I told you I would come back. Then later, she goes on... *We are sworn to secrecy and I know you are not one of us... I have connections... I am part of an inner circle... You cut me into pieces, but it doesn't matter. I am an Eternal. I cannot die.'* Hamer stops and looks up from her phone, her face bewildered but focused. "I think she lost herself there, Ivan. She got out of character. She forgot, or didn't care, that she was recording, wanted to rub it in to Stanton, let him know he was done in by his own greedy lust. But she inadvertently revealed something in that moment when she was riveted between herself and Stanton, temporarily oblivious to the camcorder."

Myer bites down on the partial pickle spear he liberated from Hamer's leavings. "Do you really think there is some *inner circle* of people who have figured out how to cheat death?" He pauses, eyes frozen at her admission. He shifts closer in. "Let me be you here, Pat. So, maybe she was lying to Stanton, messing with him."

"Unlikely," she parries back. "He's literally a captive audience, condemned to death. She has no reason to lie. The truth hurts him more. C'mon Ivan, after all those years of conspiracy crap you dished out in my direction, you are now going to back away from the real McCoy?"

"Touché." Myer drifts deeper in thought. An image floats from the depths. "I'm remembering the jumper, the guy I showed you at the pier?"

"Right, he's got to be one of these *Eternals*."

"There must be some cadre, or secret society of individuals out there who have somehow tapped into some fountain of youth or life-extension project," he proclaims, bouncing his hands off the table.

"More like death avoidance, perpetual existence. But how do they do it, Ivan?"

Myer reflects incredulity, something not common to a man who deals in the unusual on a daily basis. He whispers, "You're talking about resurrection, really. Is that what we are saying?"

"And who? Who gets to be part of this and why? The rich and powerful, the connected?" Hamer rattles off with a measure of sanctimony.

A curious cloud comes between the sun and their table, casting a shadow.

"I almost forgot," Hamer returns to her phone. "I have some background here on Amanda Tisdale, some casework from the time around her disappearance. It didn't seem like much then, but among those interviewed as persons of interest is a congressman—a committee chair, no less, appropriations committee chair. Let's see, yes—Jeb Hill from Louisiana's fourth district."

"And they didn't think that was relevant?"

"Yes, they did, actually. The investigation questioned him twice and he was cleared. But in the press there were allegations of a relationship. She was an intern for a representative from North Carolina. They clearly knew each other and spent time together. He even pressured FBI brass into driving the investigation further. For my two cents, he was acting out of concern, not pretense. He cared about her."

The cloud above moves on.

"Okay, Pat, see how this registers. Congressman Hill, a very powerful man, gets invited to be one of the inner circle of these *Eternals*. Wanting to impress his young trophy, he spills the news to her during pillow talk that he has influence and can offer her a chance at immortality. Of course she buys in and goes through with it. Then some random serial killer offs her, not knowing she will reconstitute and come back to nail gun his junk to the seat of an oak, Shaker-style chair."

"Well stated, if overly graphic, but essentially correct."

Myer shakes his head in wonder with an angled smile "So, here we are just having a casual conversation about the reality of eternal life. Is that what we're doing?" Myer nods for emphasis, his eyebrows stretched up.

"Yes," Hamer replies, now returned to her usual unflappable self. "We are accepting that there is some group out there that may have figured out how to live forever. Not only that, they might just be able to come back even after they are dead."

"Does that stir you at all, Pat?"

"I still think there are other possibilities we have not considered, ones not occurring to us here and now. But if this is true, it scares me, Ivan. It scares the hell out of me."

Thirty
June 13, 1986

"Phase one will necessitate high-precision incubation environments capable of micro-temperature adjustments in increments of hundredths of a degree. We must be able to isolate several dozen alternate environments within the array, with capability to read and record real-time fluctuations within each chamber independently. We will be capturing the temperature of origination, and the resulting thermal variance throughout the process," rattles off Adeline Brandt to her team's engineer, Marcus Chandler. He furiously scribbles notes in a graph-lined lab notebook.

"That should be attainable, Doctor Brandt. I need to ask—"

"There's more," she bulldozes on. "We need on-demand spectrographic analysis at a micron level and the capability to measure emission data throughout the incubation period."

"Very well, but I must point out, Doctor, that given the level of *confidentiality* you have proscribed, there are only three manufacturing facilities on the planet capable of delivering such—"

"You needn't trouble yourself with that," she replies with dismissal. "Smith and Jones handle all delicate logistical matters. At this time, I only need schematics from you. Eventually, you will interact with the contractors, but you are premature in assuming we have not established discreet channels," Brandt instructs.

"Of course. It would be immensely helpful if you could clue me in regarding what we are incubating, Doctor Brandt."

"We will be culturing genetic material. We seek to activate dormant DNA."

"Dormant? I don't understand."

Brandt rises her chunky frame from her seasoned oak swivel chair. She lists to one wall of her temporary office, a partition housing a picture window overlooking worker bees in hardhats erecting her future domain. Like a pharaoh monitoring the gradual rise of his pyramid, a monument to a timeless legacy and gateway to the eternal afterlife, so she admires the fleshing out of her future hive. Welders spark torches, forklifts caravan raw materials, and the nameless drones piece it all together. The confluence of a dream still being dreamed. She returns from her moment to answer Chandler.

"Mr. Chandler, of course, forgive me. Your expertise does not encompass the biological realm. As we speak, other members of our team are analyzing and cataloging a large sample of ancient DNA recovered from sources of distant origin. It is my belief..." She pauses to find the most delicate phrasing available. "I have reason to believe..." She contemplates how to inform him while not informing too much. "There are legacy DNA chains that contain properties that may lead to tremendous advancements in the quality of human existence. My efforts are dedicated to perfecting techniques to ... how shall I put it...? *Reconstitute* lost DNA. As far as your contribution, and based on your need to know, the environments you will be designing will comprise a surrogate womb for this rebirthing."

"Rebirthing? That has complicated implications," Chandler returns nonplussed, trying to comprehend the scope of her ambition.

"I have had tremendous isolated successes in culturing aspects of DNA in my crude lab environments. In order to reanimate the fullness of the genetic spectrum, I need much more sophisticated means. You will provide that through your own unique genius," she conveys, laying her hand gently upon his shoulder.

Chandler smiles at the compliment, something not common in the rarified elitist circles of uber-science where intellectual macho is currency. For the most part, Chandler isn't even acknowledged as a person of science where Brandt and Kipner are concerned. Despite the innovations and breakthroughs engineers provide to the brilliant class, their vehicles to facilitate the birthing of the theoretical and nurture their own vainglory, engineers are seen as subspecies in the hierarchy. Brandt continues her laundry list.

"I estimate we will possess viable samples within eight weeks. Can you deliver?"

"Well, I can. It all comes down to resources. With enough money, I—"

"Money is not an issue; Misters—"

"Right, Jones and Smith, say no more," Chandler finishes her sentence, now emboldened with the keen awareness of the project's gravity and Brandt's unchained momentum. "I can have the schematics completed in eight weeks. Tell them I need a manufacturing entity ready to tool up in that time. I assume this structure is the venue we are discussing."

"No, we have another location, one not on any regular map, a leftover bunker from the Cold War. It's private and safely removed from meddlers.

Smith and Jones will drive you there when we are done here. Do you have any other questions?"

"Yes, a burning one. From what ancient source are we drawing this DNA?"

Brandt marches uninvited into Chandler's space, darkly towering over him. "I believe I made it clear that this is of no concern of yours. Are we in agreement on that, Mr. Chandler?"

He cowers, sensing a deeper darkness. "Absolutely, Doctor Brandt."

Thirty One
Present Day

"Aging is not a function of time. It is an error of replication. Why does your dog show gray after only ten years, but it takes you fifty? Well, if you're lucky."

A gleeful chatter rises from a grouping of several hundred select individuals attending a pre-admission orientation seminar hosted by James Carpenter. Collectively, they are a who's who of industry, politics and celebrity. Waltzing the platform, Carpenter engages his audience with skillful aplomb. His countenance possesses the rare quality to engage each listener as if he is speaking directly to him or her. At each side of the stage, large video screens project the logo of The Carpenter Institute upon a field of cerulean blue.

"The process of aging is determined by the body's ability to regenerate cells. Each time the body reproduces cells, there is a slight degradation. Each generation of new cells brings more errors and further deterioration. An example," Carpenter pauses as if he is searching for his example, while his next words wait patiently on the teleprompter. "If you take a picture of yourself and run it through a photocopier, then copy the copy, then copy THAT copy over and over, after a while, the image becomes grainy. After thousands of copies, it may even become unrecognizable. Even at the smallest margin of error, defects eventually emerge. The same happens in the human body except these replication errors lead to devastating life events like bone loss, strokes and cancers and, of course, irreversible aging. He pauses again for effect, and then whispers, "We all know death is inevitable."

He slowly pans across the crowd. "We all die of something, but if the cause isn't an unfortunate accident, it will be the fault of the body's imperfection." He waits again, his face assuming calm confidence. With robust tone he launches a revelation: "That is, until now."

Murmurs bounce through the audience. An energy of hope and curiosity rises as they wonder if they truly heard what their ears told them.

"As you know, The Carpenter Institute has a dedicated mission to improve the lives of all of the citizens of planet earth. When we started, our primary initiative was to eradicate devastating illness." His form tightens in evangelistic vibrancy. "In the past decade, our geneticists have made breakthrough discoveries in the areas of aging and cell regeneration. Now, we are forging breakthroughs that will reinvent life as we know it."

The murmur has grown to a buzz of hopeful astonishment. Carpenter's tease tempts images and fantasies of longer life among the assembled. Hope is fueled by the postponement of the fear of death to some period in the distant future.

"Truly, I tell you, the door has been unlocked. You can live far beyond the limits of today, and not just *live*, but continue on as your most perfect self. Our gene therapy not only insures extended life, but optimizes your entire physical being." His voice swells again. "You will live on at your physical and mental peak, aging will reverse, and all for a time well beyond your wildest dreams," Carpenter champions.

He glides downward. At the edge of the stage, he takes one knee, positioning himself closer to the eye of his audience. He whispers into his headphone mic, "All *you* need to do is say, *yesss*." He rises again with voice swelling in glorious proclamation, "You need not say goodbye to your loved ones so soon. There will be no regrets, ever, no mistake that cannot be undone. Time will virtually stand still and you will enjoy the fullness of who you are without being cut short in your prime."

The crowd is stirring and electric. Carpenter seizes the energy. "For the whole of mankind, my voice speaks to you, you are important to us—the inhabitants of planet Earth. We need you here. We need your unique gifts to right the wrongs, to build the future, to *be* the future," he emphasizes, pumping his fist to the heavens.

Applause and cheers beckon to Carpenter's ears and deep into his heart. The furor wanes, the crowd waits, hungry for more. With unrelenting conviction, he resumes. "So, dear guests, the moment has arrived, renewal awaits. Of course, you are free to leave, and there will be no judgment cast upon you, but remember you are beholden to the pledge of confidentiality. You must remain silent. I do encourage you to stay, partake—indulge yourself in forever. I will see you on the other side."

Carpenter exits the stage. Double doors open at one side of the auditorium, the gateway to a promise of paradise. Most of the attendees eagerly follow. Some hesitate, opting to observe if others decide before proceeding, seeking assurance they are not alone. Two remain anchored in their seats, on chair's edge, uncertain, afraid, tearing up at their decision to remain as they are, temporary beings subject to the callous whims of nature.

Thirty Two
May 14, 1985

"Cash is always available. We're talking about the United States of America, here. If there isn't a budget we'll make one. If the currency is short, we'll print more," boasts the man who calls himself Jones above the white noise of Learjet engines.

"But it must be covert, under the radar," cautions Adeline Brandt.

"As you are to science, we are to bureaucratic cash flow. You shall have what you need," confirms Jones's counterpart, Smith.

"Why are you so eager to help?"

"Because we believe you can give us what we can't get any other way," Smith admits lustfully.

"Which is?"

"What money can't buy. We have researched you, reviewed your body of work. We know you are pioneering breakthroughs in life extension. Money is easy, but you can't take it with you, so we think we'd rather stay as long as possible," Jones proffers with a one-sided smile.

"How do you know I am doing that?" Brandt asks, swiveling nervously in her passenger seat.

"Because we are very good at what we do," Smith responds.

Brandt screws in further discomfort at his reply and the unfamiliarity of being at a disadvantage. "Very well, yes, this project encompasses that realm, but I am not sure if I trust you with more."

"We have no way of providing guarantees," Jones concedes. "You just need to trust us and it will all be fine. If you can deliver what you promise, you will hold all the cards. There are many powerful people who would prefer to remain in their current positions. And we would enjoy being the arbiters in those negotiations. I see no reason some multi-national or government entity should control something so important. So, in that, you have your reassurances. We have every reason to want you to be as successful as possible."

Brandt considers the alternatives. His case is iron-clad. She needs these two men to fulfill their promises in the same manner she must achieve hers— grand in scale, but quietly so. Brandt makes her offer. "Okay, what I need from you is a resource conduit. I also need a sequestered venue, maybe more than one. Money always comes with strings attached, and government money comes with steel cables. I don't need meddling and oversight. This endeavor, if successful, will alter how planet Earth understands human life. Interference from bureaucrats or politicians will be unwelcome and will strangle the outcome in its crib. Compromise will mean failure. If you two want to be part of the final solution, you will have to deflect all undue curiosity," she cautions intently.

Smith rises from his sofa-style chair to refill a Bordeaux glass. He turns and pours the same for Brandt, while beginning again. "Look, Doctor, we understand the gravity of all this. By way of offering perspective, and for the sake of easing your concerns, Mr. Jones and I have established foreign aid for countries that don't even exist, increased budgets for weapons programs literally unable to leave the launching pad, and even created entire phantom federal agencies out of whole cloth that will never be expunged by any act of Congress. You needn't worry."

Jones completes Smith's thought. "We should assign an ironic acronymic title... something like 'HELP': the Health, Education, and Labor Project. It will go a long way to deflecting snoopers."

"Did you just pull that right out of your ass?" Smith questions his cohort with gleeful admiration.

"Yep."

"You are an uber-crat, sir, ridiculously impressive," Smith concedes raising his glass.

"Look, gentlemen, I hate to interrupt your intellectual coitus, but are you certain we can do this without triggering red flags? Is that possible?"
"Damn straight, consider it done," Jones boasts punctuating his bravado with a robust swallow of his own libation, twenty-one-year-old single malt scotch.

"I mean this. Our necks are riding on this. Your cavalier tone concerns me," Brandt delivers with stern rebuke.

"Well... now I am not so sure. Do you mean *our* necks? Smith's face transforms to one of grave seriousness for a brief moment then sliding into a grin and finally a belly laugh, "Oh, goddamn, I can't keep a straight face, and I really tried."

"I am deathly serious," Brandt admonishes coarsely to dispel their frivolity.

"Look, Doctor," Jones renders with a renewed sense of command. "Everything is quite alright. We are enjoying a joke with you. But, know this, when it comes to the work, we *are* deathly serious. You will have your money and be able to do what needs to be done. Let me reiterate—foreign aid budgets; non-existent countries."

"Very well, so with the resource matter is settled; what about the venue?" Brandt presses.

"In the backwoods of Maryland, West Virginia, and parts of Pennsylvania lie a treasure trove of decommissioned sites that have loads of potential. This is where you will set up shop."

"Decommissioned sites?"

"Yes, at one time these were highly guarded, secure locations, havens of survival built for chosen survivors for a day that never came."

"Because?"

"They are bomb shelters, okay? I know that sounds unglamorous, but they are vaults, vaults unremembered on any map except where classified in files over fifty years old, now warehoused in oblivion. This is what you need," Smith assures. "We can get you as many as you need with uninterrupted electricity. No one will bother you there."

"Very good," Brandt acknowledges with satisfaction. Sipping her wine, she looks out her porthole window. "Where are we going, anyway?"
"Nowhere; we just like to conduct business where there is no possibility of surveillance," Smith answers.

"Whose plane is this, then?"

"It's ours. Again, foreign aid, non-existent countries."

Thirty Three
May 9, 1986

A scent wisps as ghosts stirring the important air of a sanctuary unlike any other on the earth—the Vatican. Like a perfume past its prime, the aroma hangs; the unique blend of centuries-old plaster, medieval tapestries and Renaissance oil portraits. This hallowed ground now serves as the uneasy home of a newly appointed cardinal named Jonas Kovacs, one of the youngest ever in this modern age. Plucked from Hungary, he garnered attention for his shrewd ability to attract new followers in a region where the faith had languished for as long as anyone could remember. His unique gift is to reach souls thought unreachable. This, coupled with brashly handsome charisma, is rare, and welcome. He brings fresh thoughts to an aging stagnancy of doctrine. Characterized by an unabashed, unconventional voice, he expresses the true nature of Christ in a unique way, a quality not always eagerly embraced by an institution of deep tradition and uneasy with innovation. Despite this, his value was apparent and he was quickly afforded a fast track up the Catholic hierarchy.

Brought from the vibrant but unsettled atmosphere of Eastern Europe, he is still trying to assimilate himself within the structured politic of bureaucratic Christianity. He sometimes considers that maybe his gifts are wasted here. Not very long ago, on his turf, he could spontaneously reach out to anyone seeking answers and guidance and maybe spark a rare opportunity to influence grace. Now, he is relegated to serve as a glorified minion in a gilded cage, his talents rendered impotent. He cancels his growing angst by embracing pure faith, remembering that the hand of God placed him here. The purpose will be revealed when it is his to know. One day, he imagines, he will possess the maturity and influence to administer his own vision, one guided by the very hand of the Lord, one delivered to even larger populations, perhaps even as the Holy Father himself.

Striding uncertain steps down a marble hallway, each tap of his anxious heels booms louder, reverberating and amplifying each rigid scratch of friction rendered from his cloying vestments. He marches closer to a task of raised significance. At least, that was the message relayed to him. A clutch of senior cardinals issued the summons under the auspices of a "calling bearing critical nature." He, being the junior, is compelled to comply.

Massive, ornately carved mahogany doors part wide upon his approach, opening to a Renaissance styled room, an ornamentation weary with time. Majestic frescoed ceilings and sculpted plaster apply vintage character to a tired space where greater glory has come and gone. Four fellow cardinals, ones in residence here since before Kovacs was a teenager, embrace his arrival. "Cardinal Jonas, such an honor to be in your presence," comes a greeting from a gray-haired man with rosy, spider-veined cheeks, a hue complementing his rouge vestments. "These are Cardinals Vincenti and Monihan, over there is Cardinal Rodriguez. I am Cardinal Grant."

"Mine is the honor, brethren," Kovacs replies, involuntarily bowing despite there being no protocol requiring it.

"It is we who are honored, Kovacs," Vincenti trills.

"Very well, we are all honored, then," Kovacs replies. A shared grin breaks the tension ever so slightly.

"Would you like an espresso? Tea? Perhaps a libation? It is the late afternoon, after all," Monihan suggests, a subtle hinting at his own beverage preference.

"Some tea might be exactly what I need," Kovacs requests. "Earl Gray? Do you have any?"

"I am sure of it," Monihan answers, passing the order with a nod to an attendant. Implicit is his own choice to the attendant, the usual, one more robust.

"How may I be of help, Cardinal Grant?"

"In due time, but I must express that we have heard such marvelous things about you, young Cardinal Jonas. I am personally embarrassed that I have not found time to meet with you before now. As far as our duties here, the four of us are purposefully removed from the general population of the holy city. Our work is the kind that does not benefit from greater exposure. You see, we are guardians of a sort. We oversee antiquities, protect information dating back to the origins of the faith. Despite the sworn commitment to Christ made by all who reside in this city, it is in the best interest of those with greater experience and knowledge to decide what needs to be known and what doesn't. Some of what we do is considered, well... how would one say that?" Grant questions his colleagues.

"Delicate, potentially volatile," Monihan steps in.

"What do you mean by that? How can truth be controversial?" the youthful Kovacs innocently implores.

Grant gestures to a finely embroidered armchair, inviting Kovacs to take a seat. Three steps places him in upholstery weaved during a century long before this one. The others follow in respective chairs all facing each other.

"As you know, ours is a religion of faith, subjective in nature," Grant continues as they settle in. "We find our fullness in the mystic realm, reaching beyond the three dimensions that tether our physical selves to this crude, earthly existence. But as much as we may desire it to be, we cannot remove ourselves. We are all creatures woven into the fabric of the physical realm, we seek..." Grant rubs his chin trying to conjure the correct words, "*confirmation* that all we hold spiritually dear can be verified by physical markers, by a concrete trail of evidence."

Rodriguez breaks in to finish the thought. "It shouldn't be of concern, but it does matter. We all need touchstones, as it were. So, we seek more, something visceral; we gain comfort in *proving* our faith, in knowing there is a corresponding trail of history. Do you understand the inconsistency there, Jonas?"

"Yes, I do; *faith* is not tied to *physical proof*."

"Bravo, Kovacs!" Vincenti blurts out.

Grant resumes. "So, we are the fortunate ones assigned to mediate the struggle between spirit and flesh that makes up the Catholic Church. The four of us have been allotted a thankless task, until recently, that is."

Monihan forcefully takes the floor after a generous sip from his glass. "You see, what my brother is trying to prepare you for, but is unable to do so without his signature flourish, is that we are the ones trapped in the middle when there is dispute or uncertainty about a given artifact," he spills forth with a gravelly brogue. "Inevitably, we will unfavorably stir some faction or offshoot, should our investigation find something contradictory to what they imagine it should be. For example, if we took all the claims of this *splinter* and that *chunk* as being the actual wood of the cross, we would be able to construct a half dozen crucifixes."

Kovacs interrupts. "This is all very compelling, my brothers, but I am still not certain why you have summoned me."

Rodriguez answers, his English spiced with Latin flair. "Jonas, we have been approached by an American scientist who offers a method that may settle, once and for all, the doubts that cloud the ancient physical history of the church. We might finally put to rest the uncertainty that casts doubt on our mystical relics. We have been plagued by disputes surrounding unverifiable claims of dubious authenticity tainting the entire catalog of artifacts we hold dear throughout the Catholic world."

"A scientist?" Kovacs asks with a raised eyebrow.

Monihan bursts in again. "Yes, she is brilliant and highly regarded. She unravels what is referred to as DNA, apparently the key building block of all life."

"Yes, I am familiar with that. Where does this all lead, if I may ask?"

"Don't you see, Cardinal Jonas, we can finally authenticate Christian history. Even if only half of the relics are identified as belonging to the age or the region they are claimed to originate from, it will give powerful meaning to the church as a whole. If only the relics claimed to be the actual wood of the cross were confirmed, we will establish a sturdy scientific foundation to attract more skeptical converts," Cardinal Grant concludes.

"But why should proof matter?" Kovacs asks.

"It is a gateway," Rodriguez responds.

Monihan finishes Rodriguez's point. "Yes, the lost souls who find faith to not be enough will now be within our reach. When they see there is physical evidence to back up the history we profess, they will be more approachable, they will be more accepting of the mystical aspects of our beliefs."

"I thought it was about faith." Kovacs blithely submits.

"Cardinal Jonas, you have a background in science yourself," Grant administers, gently wielding his seniority. "You must trust us. Your unique abilities will bring understanding to this. You must go with the power of Christ, meet with this scientist, do what she asks knowing you are doing God's work," he commands. "It is by our authority."

Rodriguez joins in again. "Cardinal Jonas, we have been asked to provide a representative to guard the church's interests and oversee the process of verification. We have been bestowed great liberties where this is concerned."

"Why? What is hoped to be gained? Have you any insights about the motivations of the scientist?" Kovacs asks, his instincts overruling his naiveté.

"We presume she seeks public recognition, verification of her scientific method. She wishes to boost standing in the circles she and her operation occupy," Grant replies. "Our large pool of artifacts is perfect for this initial test."

"Very well. I suppose I ask too many questions. It is not my place to question your collective years of experience. I will do as you need done. When do I leave?" Kovacs asks, being a good soldier.

"I am afraid we haven't given you much notice. You leave Thursday to Baltimore, Maryland, in the United States. We have arranged a flight for you. You will communicate back to us the progress of the initial meeting. There are six other participants who will join you there including the scientist, Doctor Adeline Brandt. Your specific task is to coordinate the retrieval and delivery of the relics, working with us to gain access to them and to then guard their whereabouts. We are counting on you, Jonas."

"I fully understand. I embrace the challenge knowing it is for the good of the church and to seek favor in the eyes of God."

Thirty Four
Present Day

Alex Traeger pauses, straining to recall what exactly he was searching for in a cardboard moving box. He shakes his head as dismissal of any urgent concern to remember. Whatever it was, he is more content unearthing treasures and keepsakes that usher greater validation of the most important thing in his life—his children. Scattered about his condo office floor are field day ribbons, report cards, and other keepsakes of their younger days. They summon a smile and a sad reminder of the reality that they are growing up, and apart from him, still hoarded by their mother. Photo prints and crayon drawings signifying years of their lives comprise a portfolio of, sadly, less volume than he expected.

At the bottom of the box lie several CD-ROM discs and the recollection of the reason he began digging in the first place. His ex had their entire family photo catalog saved to CD just prior to their divorce. She offered to do it out of her sense of goodwill. There was no legal requirement. But, knowing her way, he suspects she was sending a discreet message that he should be happy with pictures, since she would exact her spite with demands of unequal custody in her favor.

A few days ago he received a text from her requesting copies. Discs had been compiled for each of them, but she too busy, or unwilling to be bothered with the effort to locate the ones she was given, took the easy out and asked for duplicates. Weary of verbal battle, he decided to keep the peace and submit to her request. For Traeger, it was nothing too difficult. His copies were at the ready, easily found inside the cardboard cube, still resting where he left it the day he moved in months ago. He was too emotionally exhausted to do more, the wounds of divorce still fresh.

Five CD-s in all, four in plastic cases and one in a red paper sleeve. Valerie would never use a sleeve, he decides, so a mystery begins. Traeger examines the different disc to determine its origin. There is nothing written on it. It is familiar to him, though. Scouring his memory, he cannot place where it came from. It was given to him, somewhere on the school campus, maybe? The campus, he remembers now. The CD falls from his paralyzed hand, a chill snaking his spine. It was the strangest thing. A man he hardly knew had handed him the disc. "Vacation pictures," he called them. The man was William Reader.

Why he kept the professor's disc at all baffles him. Perhaps he suspected someday Reader might ask a "What did you think of my vacation?" question. So he'd kept it shoved in a desk drawer to have some readily apparent knowledge should it be needed. The two had only talked a couple of times before that, both initiated by Reader with an uncomfortably eager approach. It played off as Reader hoping to befriend the architect, an awkward acquaintance at best. Traeger slumps in disbelief that he neglected to mention the encounter to the investigator during questioning about the shooting. He merely forgot it ever took place.

His tentative hand finds the CD again. He rises, humbly slipping into his office chair. Rummaging some loose papers on his desk, he locates the business card of the investigator, Patricia Hamer. Seeking penance, he dials four numbers, but then pauses. Curiosity is winning. Traeger sets the phone down and warily places the CD in his DVD drive. Nothing happens. He searches the drive's contents and finds that the CD has folders, a dozen maybe, each named after different locations in the Caribbean—Tortola, Jamaica, St. Bart's and so on, all dated roughly nine months before the shooting. He opens the Jamaican folder. Twenty-two image files of beaches and pool bars and fishing boats, drab, boring, unimaginative, obligatory, and random. The pictures seem to be taken without purpose, even as a record of a routine vacation.

Another folder and then another, photo after innocuous photo. If it were anyone else but Reader, Traeger would have given up browsing by now, the disc's next destination the trash. The third folder from the last is titled "St. John's." A blurred memory surfaces; something about that name resonates. He looks at the photos, sixteen of them, one by one. Fifteen of them are identical and one is different. The identical ones show Reader from the chest up in a white linen shirt, half unbuttoned, wearing sunglasses and a relaxed smile. Untamed, breeze-blown hair attaches an appearance of blissful abandon. There is a simple church on a hill above the beach in the background. The final picture shows Reader with his right hand raised, pointing to the cross at the top of the church. There is no rational explanation for having this collection of images. But it occurs to Traeger that Reader may have actually been irrational at the time he compiled them.

Traeger's instincts are sparking unease. His breathing quickens. He feels his shoulders clench. A dark sense tumbles inside that his next action will bring about some measure of profound consequence beyond his control. He can't discern how he knows, but despite the pounding impulse to walk away, he is compelled. He wanders the arrow to Reader's face, gradually circling it, muttering out loud, "What are you up to, Professor? Why would you give me this?" Next, he journeys the pointer up the outline of Readers arm, toward the cross. On its way, the arrow quickly changes to a cursor. He almost missed it. He repeats the movement with deliberation to find the spot where it changed, the very tip of Reader's finger aimed at the cross. The mouse pointer rapidly shakes on the screen, the result of Traeger's hand trembling. He presses through doubt and clicks the mouse.

A text box opens.

Lightning bolts shoot up his neck. Hairs stand on end. His memory pokes through the fury to remind him of the St. John's connection. It was the last thing Reader said before walking into a hail of gunfire minutes after he shot Carpenter.

"St. John, *Beloved.*"

The cursor blinks in the box, seeking a password, he thinks. Through the blur of adrenaline, his trembling fingers type b-e-l-o-v-e-d and strike the return key. Another text box opens bearing the words "type your name." He reluctantly obliges, but does so out of some peculiar sense of duty. The screen dissolves. The disc drive spins in a frenzy, refreshing the screen with an image of William Reader seated in a muscular, worn leather armchair, puffing a thick cigar. Behind him a stuffed, well-titled bookcase fills the remainder of the image. A puff of smoke clouds Reader's face. It occurs to Traeger, this is no photo. It is Reader returning from death via video.

"Good Day, Alex. If you are indeed the one watching this then all my hard work has a much better chance of mattering than ever before. Unfortunately, it also means I am very dead now and you are unwittingly drawn into something you will probably wish had never been brought your way. If I calculated correctly, my ruse regarding the nature of this disc has you viewing it at the proper time. I suppose I should first explain my actions in relation to James Carpenter. By now, the world has decided I am a madman and all that ever mattered to me has been discredited by the final minutes of my life. I regret that it had to end this way and no explanation from me will suffice to fully convince you otherwise. You will discover how necessary it was the more you learn. I will tell you this, though. My time is near, my enemies have no further value for my continued existence. Soon they will finish me." Reader pauses and slowly pulls the cigar to his lips. His last words heard aloud by his own ears sinks in with finality.

Traeger's heart is thumping viciously. The thought of James Carpenter's would-be assassin speaking his last, chosen words specifically for him grinds his insides, scraping him out and filling the space with spiky barbs.

Reader's face emerges from another shroud of smoke. He leans in. His anguished face wears the blended countenance of determined will uncomfortably shared with assured dread. "An apparent accident it would be, no doubt of it. It is only a matter of time. But I would rather not give them the satisfaction of departing politely. I prefer to go out on my own terms and I refuse to bow out gracefully. Mine will be a bold statement worthy of my station. I will snap the world's attention to something gravely critical."

A momentary gleam of hopefulness rises in Reader's eyes. His mouth turns upward, perhaps even to smile at his next thought. "Soon, or perhaps already, an unnecessarily and overly serious elderly man will approach you. He won't know why you are the one he is to meet, but give him the benefit of the doubt and listen to him. He is the most honorable man I have ever known and you should trust him with everything you have. He is wise and deeply knowledgeable on the course your journey must now take. I will leave it to him to tell you what you need to know when you need to know it. We met years ago, participants in a project destined for infamy. For my part, my pride, arrogance, and ignorance eagerly lent my unique skills to setting in motion a power that will change the world for the worse—the entire world. You must heed this."

Traeger grows numb with fear. *The entire world?* He briefly quells his anxiety concluding that Reader is crazy and delusional. But there is no similar rationale to dismiss Kovacs. It is undeniable. Why would Kovacs participate in a madman's scheme?

Reader leans further forward, staring through the monitor screen. "You are, no doubt, asking why you are part of this. The reason is, my unique genius and understanding of human systems has determined that you hold a key. My algorithm indicates you to be an extremely rare individual, a once-every-hundred-years vehicle for change. But, I must advise, the forces in opposition are *once-ever-in-time*," Reader brashly proclaims, eyes piercing forth, his tone now grave and commanding. "You are safe for now; they have no idea you are involved. Do not reveal to anyone that you ever received this message, save this one man. He will be grateful to know. Destroy this disc when you are done. Cast it into flames. I wish I could express more, but you would find it unbelievable. I bid you Godspeed." Reader leans back again, drawing deeply from the cigar and exhaling a billowing cloud. From behind the clearing smoke, he restarts.

"Alex, I am not a man of faith. I have no greater belief than my accumulated knowledge, keen intuition, and what I have learned from my work. My friend, the old man, he is the man of faith. He will inspire you. Now, go, seek him out and make right what I have set in motion. The sake of all mankind now rests in your hands."

The screen dissolves again and, the computer restores to Traeger's desktop image, a photo of his children from a Christmas several years prior. A time holding more promise. Panting and hyperventilating, Traeger struggles to recover. His hands are welded to the arms of his chair with knuckles pale white. Through the turmoil, he has one clarifying thought, to find Kovacs. But it is a difficult task now having no clue where to begin.

Thirty Five
Present Day

Alex Traeger sits numb, his life impossibly, irreversibly altered. There will be no sleeping tonight. Through the earliest stirrings of dawn, in discordant stillness, he will remain riveted to his seat. Staring at his flat screen monitor, his fingers frantically strike the keyboard, grasping for any germ of insight into his dilemma and the players who presumed to write him in without asking permission.

William Reader's message from the grave casts new light and more shadows on one of the most notorious and inexplicable crimes in years—the assassination attempt on James Carpenter. He patches together keywords— "William Reader," "James Carpenter," "William Reader James Carpenter," "William Reader Project," "William Reader Cultural Theories," and on and on. Reader's links lead mostly to published academia and commentary on his radical breakthroughs and, of course, volumes on Reader's presumed insanity.

His Wikipedia page lists an accumulation of accolades comparable to entire departments housed in Ivy League institutions. It speaks to his pioneering methods in cultural study and the leapfrogging ahead of his newborn science a century beyond the current understanding in a matter of decades. But now, the resume is re-written as a backdrop, and cautionary tale, for his tragic fall from grace, and useless to explain the ominous message Reader delivered to him personally via CD-ROM.

Carpenter's story unfolds as a saga, a hero who arose seemingly out of thin air to blaze trails in diverse, unrelated fields. Traeger reads a tale of a

Renaissance man, and emerging legend, with no apparent concern other than to bring harmony to the planet, articles adorned with sympathy at the heinous act visited upon him. The reports lack details, though. What happens behind closed doors apparently stays there where James Carpenter is concerned. There are no transcripts or eyewitness accounts to explain the breakthroughs. Perhaps his successes are due merely to his charismatic leadership ability, Traeger thinks. But the results are inarguable. In time, Traeger thinks Carpenter may even bring peace to this turbulent planet.

Hours later and Traeger has gained no deeper knowledge as to why he himself was *chosen* by Reader. Except for the shooting, how James Carpenter connects to William Reader means nothing to the World Wide Web.

The answer Traeger needs most is how he himself now resides at the center of the same universe as the genius-madman and the reluctant saint. No web search, no combination of keywords will ever provide the slightest clue. Where is the conflict between Reader and Carpenter, he wonders? What purpose does it serve for Reader to try to assassinate Carpenter? Is Carpenter somehow involved in the "project" Reader mentioned in his video? It seems to Traeger that the two would, more likely be brothers in arms than find enmity leading to one taking aim at the other.

Traeger's churning thoughts brew angry at Reader hijacking him and depositing him in a foreign landscape, one apparently populated with persons willing to murder to achieve an end. Reader feared for his own life, leading him to his own desperate act. He knew the fullness of the facts. Ones he chose not to divulge to Traeger when involving him in... what? Kovacs holds the key, but how will he find him? Traeger opens a fresh browser to try more keywords— "Jonas Kovacs Cardinal," "Jonas Kovacs William Reader," "Jonas Kovacs James Carpenter," and finally all three names together. A few responses come back, but nothing of use. Several hundred returns on Kovacs' name, one apparently popular in Hungary and Eastern Europe, but one not associated with former Catholic cardinals. Traeger falls back in his chair, despondent at the utter futility.

***

"Mr. Smith, I think we finally have an incident meeting the criteria set forth in the Omega algorithm," a spindly, young, mop-haired emo male sheepishly relays to a slender, bald-headed man in a black suit and tie.

"Okay, dazzle me. I really hope this isn't a false alarm,"

"Well... it..." The male brushes his mop to one side and bravely continues. "Well, there are searches for Reader, Carpenter and—this is a first—Kovacs... all from the same IP address, and all within two hours of each other,"

"Are you sure it—"

"It's a residence, sir, not a shared access, so no chance of a false positive caused by multiple users. It's coming from one person and it's just outside Baltimore."

"That is *very* coincidental indeed. You have earned your gold star today, Ernstein."

"Enersteen, sir," he cautiously corrects.

"Whatever," Smith drones back. "Determine the exact location and then notify me. Good work, son. You may have just saved the world."

"What, sir?"

"Nothing, just an expression."

Enersteen returns to where he came from. The bald man grips a cell phone and calls. "Yeah, it's Smith... I think we've got something promising this time."

Thirty Six
June 30, 1979

Shards of glass and splintered wood crumble beneath the heels of a lone pair of military boots treading the remains of a formerly proud, pulsing village near central Nicaragua. The once vibrant main street is now remanded to a gouged shell. Debris lies strewn as fallen confetti from a parade, though a macabre one featuring live ammunition and leaving behind twisted corpses.

Two cars issue wispy streams of pungent black smoke from their smoldering guts into the thick tropical air. The stench of death hangs heavy and stubborn. Stray dogs rip at idle flesh. Flies are everywhere, looking for a fertile rot in which to lay their eggs. Store fronts and cantinas stand blown out and looted, cinderblock shells are all that remain. The outsides are pocked with bullet holes and blood spatter, scars of battle and impromptu executions.

More boot steps, careful and cautious. He scans the wreckage for lingering hostiles. It was over a day ago, but there may be sentries left behind waiting to ambush—coked-up teenagers with twitchy trigger fingers. Across the street, he finds temporary refuge in a hotel of sorts, rooms once for rent, sometimes on an hourly basis. He finds a stool in a shady corner to rest his exhausted frame, then removes a .45 from its holster, one given to him as a *just-in-case* measure by the Grandfather he was named after, Theodore. Before yesterday, he had never fired a weapon, and he still hasn't fired at a person, only in a general direction to desperately orchestrate a narrow escape when the death squads reached the Red Cross camp. He reloads shells from his jeans pocket, ones gathered along the way, tossing aside the ones that don't fit. He exhales a long-sought sigh of relief. Rest is the goal now. Sleep is inadvisable. He will search for cans of food and potable water when he feels secure and rested. They may be needed should the ensuing rescue be thwarted.

It was an aid effort, basic needs and medicine for those trapped between the rebels and the government. Until now, they had been left to their own devices, but the death squads of late resemble blood-thirsty marauders rather than loosely trained military. Anyone is a target now. Suspicion has gone frantic.

His boots, ironic as military issue, are the unintentional gift of a dead soldier, one stumbled upon in the jungle, boots no longer needed to traverse the treacherous undergrowth. It was all he could salvage from the soldier's body, the remainder being encased in the front end of an anaconda who made a bad dining choice, literally biting more than he could chew. The two lay stiff and fused, deaths of utter futility no different than any other in this place.

Who knew helping others could be so dangerous? Landing in this literal ghost town with no thought of where to proceed is a far cry from where he imagined he would be when he volunteered for a semester-long assignment to assist in a humanitarian mission, setting his Dartmouth undergrad work on hold. Even more distant from his schooling is his annual summer haunt in the Hamptons just two and a half weeks ago. He'd kill for a gin and tonic right now. Maybe *kill* is the wrong word, he thinks. He even considers that he'd be safer had he enlisted in the military, rather than enrolling in a peace effort. But that is folly; enlistment would never suffice a man of his breeding.

From the north, muscular rotor blades chop the humid shroud, the approaching sound of imminent rescue. Within the hour he will bunk in a state room near the captain's quarters. The commander will address him as *Mr.* Carlisle and the ship will be at his disposal, in his rightful place, no longer a fish out of water.

The wretched ruin before him assists decisions on his future. They formulate uncluttered. Any further thoughts of altruistic endeavors was shot down in the jungles behind him. He tried a purer path and it failed. The surrounding wreckage reinforces his understanding of the way of things since the dawn of man. Compassion is a fool's hope. Progress is best achieved where personal incentives remain. He resolves he will change the world for the better using more practical means, ones unapparent to the commoners, ones surging in his own DNA. He will lead, but not as a leader, instead as puppet master, a conductor of a vision more easily spawned anonymously and certainly more suited to a man of his lineage.

As he knows the way of things, from first-hand observation, leaders are merely followers of a different sort, men beholden to the whims of a fawning populous that craves only bread and circuses. It has been the way of every civilization of consequence since Roman rule, where *leader* mostly means *figurehead*, front-men molded much in the way of Washington, D.C., and suffering fleeting lifespans. He will be one of the greater others, the playwright crafting the narrative, enjoying the applause backstage while the egos take their brief bows in the spotlight. It is the role he was destined to fulfill and apparent to him now. At least, so it occurs to him in the bleak leavings of man's inhumane treatment of his fellow man. His existence, he concludes, will be of an importance to surpass that of many a ruler.

Thirty Seven
February 12, 1980

Coiled tight against one arm of a saddle-brown studded leather couch, a pedigreed protégé waits in gripped silence. He spies occasional glimpses of his surroundings. The office is small but large in import, the place of business for his father, Senator Bradley Markham.

"Good Christ, Brody, you're a sack-less pissant. You spend too much time around your mother and her doting nannies. What are you so goddamned nervous about?" Before a reply can be uttered, Markham thinks again "Wait, I don't want to hear the excuses, forget it. Clear your head and focus; you're about to witness the making of Capital Hill's finest pork sausage. Listen, watch, but don't even think about opening your cake hole when my guest enters except to exchange greetings. You and I both know you are not cut out for this league of cock swinging. So let's just get through this and then you can get back to your life of... of... whatever your mother has planned for the rest of your life. We both know this is merely an exercise in pretense. Do you understand?"

The gangly twenty-year-old nods his head in reply, sliding slender fingers between his knock-knees, casting his defeated gaze downward to the dense weave of an elegant Persian area rug beneath his feet.

"Son, look I'm not trying to be cruel, but there is no use perpetuating a lie. You are not senator material. I would know. Let's carry out this masquerade and then—""

"Senator Markham, I have Mr. Cranston here to see you," a female voice pierces from a desk phone speaker.

"Send him in, Gloria."

An eight-foot-high oak door swings into the small chamber.

"Good morning, Senator."

A practiced hand reaches out to Markham. "How the hell are you, Brad? Damn, it's been... Jesus, was it the satellite summit... that long ago? Yeah, and that waitress, lordy," Cranston chuckles, a jolly Santa Claus without the red suit and beard.

Markham, fearing an awkward progression of the waitress story, rapidly hijacks the conversation. "Dick, this is my son, Brody. He's staffing for me today."

"Nice to meet you, son," Cranston shoots his right hand out. Brody returns a dead-fish handshake. "Great to finally see you in person. Your father speaks highly of you. How is Princeton treating you?" Cranston questions with a calloused grin pasted beneath his sharp-angled, ever-browning nose.

"I'd like to say I was enjoyi—"

The senator swoops in to steal the floor and avoid a moment growing more uncomfortable. "Dick, glad you could make it. My schedule is tight, so we should get down to business." The senator gestures to a seat opposite his disheveled, paper-stacked desk. Cranston sits, but further down than he expected. His shoulders are almost even with the walnut desktop. His chair is sparsely cushioned with disproportionately stubby legs, a full foot below the senator's line of sight. A closer look might reveal the legs had actually been sawn off a few inches.

"Okay, Brad. Let me get right to it. We've talked before about the importance of opening the long distance markets and the telecommunications infrastructure as a whole. As long as there is a monopoly in the industry, there will never be an expansion of the technology poised to explode into the sector."

"I know that, Dick. I think I'm the one that brought that up last time we talked. It's just... well, it's complicated. There are a lot of union jobs involved and allowing startups to get a foothold may potentially put those jobs in jeopardy. Startups aren't unionized; the phone company is."

"Senator, I circulate among those in the inner circles and I'm telling you. Someday soon, this system you are defending will go away." Cranston slides his corpulent body further up in his seat to improve his diminished vantage point.

"So, what are you proposing?"

"Break it up. Draw something up in committee, bring it to the floor for a vote, and allow the market to do what it does."

"Dick, that's a tall order. You're talking about fucking with one of the largest corporations in the world."

"I'm not talking about dismantling it, just allowing equal access. The rest will take care of itself. It's just good old American competition."

The senator leans back to contemplate, the tired springs in his worn desk chair creaking beneath him. "So, these startups, they'll need venture capital and growth consultants. I may be able to introduce them to someone."

"Brad, most of these enterprises have money in place, scads of it. They just need the right of way."

"You remember this dance, don't you?" Markham counters in a tone designed to inflect a second meaning. "If they want to be successful they will need the guidance of *true professionals*, and I know just the people who can help them."

"Alright, so I need to advise them that it can happen in time, but they will need to plan for... *additional investors*... correct?" Cranston responds as a verbal wink and a nod.

"Yes, investors who expect low risk... no risk, actually."

"This is a little more than we usually discuss, Senator."

Markham drops the pretense. "Let's just say I've done my own research. If these guys want to be stinking rich, they will have to include some of my friends, who in turn support me. Call it a monetary vote for market-based democracy," he says half-smiling at his own ingenuity.

Cranston pauses, working the logistics out in his head. "Alright," he sighs. "I'll get back to you." He stands, opens his briefcase and deposits a bottle of twenty-one-year-old scotch on the desk-top. With a wink he says, "See you, Brad." He turns and leaves, the door closing behind him.

The senator tilts his head, puffs out his chest, and turns his chair on its swivel to face the boy. Where once sat a meek youth now sits a bold fellow assuming a cocksure pose. His arm rests atop the couch, the ankle of one leg atop the other's knee, his chin jutting out like it belongs on Mount Rushmore.

The senator shifts back in his chair. "What's got into you?"

"So, you're going to go through the whole legislative process on this, Dad?" Brody Markham oozes out with a measure of condescension.

"We have to. That's how this works. It's how we feed the campaign machine. Re-election is the first priority."

"Dad, you are sixty-three years old. How long will it take to get this thing written, debated, and passed— assuming it even gets that far?"

"Probably four years?"

"And then the legal challenges once the law is passed. It will probably go all the way to the Supreme Court. How long?

"Probably another three years."

"And when will you see dollar-one of your kickback?

"Son, I don't get a kick—"

"Dad, I may be young, but I am your son," Brody interrupts to shut down the ensuing moral posturing. "I share your blood. I can smell a kickback... How long?"

The senator huffs and rolls his eyes. "Another three or four years."

"So, you'll be well into your seventies, if you are still alive."

"Son, I...," The senator's speech stumbles sensing he is about to be schooled on politics by his own offspring. "Where are you going with this?"

"If you legislate all this you'll be too old to enjoy the benefits before it happens and the Japanese will end up outracing us and own our telecommunications anyway."
"Look, the Constitution says we have—"

"Screw the Constitution, screw the legislative process. Look, this divestiture of the phone company you are planning is important, right?" the boy barks while seeming to levitate from the couch to tower over his father.

"Yeah," the senator puffs with swelling pride at his son.

"It's good, not just for you and your allies, but for the country as a whole, right?"

"Yeah."

"And, of course, the ignorant masses of voters will never understand how important it is?"

"No, I doubt it."

"So, it demands a fast track, a way to put it in play without meddlers interfering and adding needless riders and earmarks cluttering the bill and making it impossible to implement."

"And how do you propose we do that, son?"

"Find a judge somewhere to *discover* a law or a right that never existed before. Tell him to find some fundamental violation of the commerce clause, to pronounce the need for a single carrier has been usurped by technology and the public interest. Ultimately, the public will accept the change because you are toppling an *evil* monopoly. They'll understand that and you end up a hero helping all the Davids fight Goliath. Even better, the process will take a third of the time, and most importantly you and your cronies will reap all the benefits because you are ahead of the pack, you have all the inside information."

"Son, I can't count how many ethics violations your proposal might trigger, but—" Senator Markham's wheels spin, trying to keep up with his son's shrewd suggestion. "Done the right way, with enough massaging and TLC, I think it could work—and we could even maintain adequate distance to disperse curious oversight interests."

"It's the forest for the trees, Dad. Give them what they want and the general public doesn't give a shit if you wipe your ass all over the Constitution."

The senator stands to face his son eye-to-eye. He smiles, shakes his son's hand and says with a tremble, "Brody, what has got into you?" He tilts his head and stares as if looking deeper into his son's soul. "Maybe it's always been there and just hasn't had the opportunity to flower. I am still right about one thing, though. You aren't senator material." he pronounces, his pride now fully engaged. "You can go much farther than that. I can see it in your eyes. You have a gift for this."

"Politics?"

"No, government."

Thirty Eight
Present Day

"ENERSTEEN, get in here, and you'd better have some progress to report," bellows Smith as he leans into a speaker phone.

Basking in the glow of his own importance, Smith glances through his office window to drink in the D.C. skyline. Nowhere on Earth resides such concentrated power and no one on the planet has had more influence on the currents of that power than he and his associate Mr. Jones. Once lowly servants, the two cousins now rule over their masters, the pathetic addicts to ravenous vanity and unquenchable delusions of throbbing egoistical grandeur. Smith and Jones live a cherished existence, one harnessing unequalled power and influence coupled with full anonymity except to the powerful few. The two possess the ultimate leverage. Eternals themselves, they hold sway over deciding who will join them and when. They will all beg for it, of this they are both certain. The privileged class are unmistakably all-in as their lustful appetites and advancing mortality make the decision for them.

"S... S... Sir? You called for me?" stutters Enersteen who managed to stumble his gangly, androgynous form into the office undetected by the daydreaming Smith.

Still staring out the window, he chides, "Did you already forget why I called you in here?"

"N... n... no, sir."

A pause lingers. Smith peeks around his shoulder. "Well?"

"Uh... yeah... Umm."

"Chill, Enersteen. Breathe deep. Grab a seat." The boy meekly finds the front edge of a chair cushion across from Smith's desk. Smith turns his own irritated face to him. "Well? Do you recall my request, son?"

"Yes."

"And?"

"The IP address ends at a condominium complex," Enersteen wisps out, breathless and timid. "It's a service provider LAN and it connects to over seventy-five different units. That's why it has taken so long."

"Have you narrowed it down?"

"We're pretty sure the search in question came from a man named Alex Traeger, or at least from his computer. He lives alone."
"Just to confirm, this is the search that included Carpenter, Reader, and Kovacs in one keyword combination, correct?"

"Yes, sir."

Smith pauses to search his memory. The name is unfamiliar. It nags at him. "Who is Alex Traeger?"

"He's a divorced architect, in his early forties. He has two children, one of each, one boy and—"

"Yes, one girl. Does he know any of the three?"

"There is nothing linking them. Well, maybe one thing." Enersteen's confidence is returning as he recalls something of significance. "Traeger served as guest faculty for a time at the same university where Reader was a professor. But they taught on different sides of the campus and different subject matter."

"So, they could have known each other. What about Kovacs? Where does he fit in?"

"It seems he doesn't, sir."

Smith stands to walk the room, the nagging uncertainty bringing an uncomfortable edge. "There is no way I'm going to accept that answer, Enderton. The name Jonas Kovacs is a needle in a field of haystacks. No one accidentally types that in and searches that name with the other two. It means he knows him."

"Knows him? How could you know... and it's Enersteen, sir."

"Trust me. They have met. It means Kovacs is back, he's alive. It's the only way Traeger could ever know about him." Smith tapers the last bit off realizing it is a comment meant solely for himself.

"Look," he leans in over Enersteen. "This isn't good. Assign a field trace. Put Simpson on it. He's our best. Have him follow Traeger. Tag his car, bug his house, you know all the toppings on the pizza. Got it?"

"Yes, Mr. Smith."

"Ok, now go and have Simpson contact me when the operation is live." Before Enersteen exits, he has his own nagging question. "Can I ask you something, sir?"

Smith nods.

"Why do you call me kid? You're only like five years older than I am."

"It's because I have eternal youth." Smith smiles at the secret only he knows. "But seriously, it's just an expression. It's more because I'm the boss not because I'm really *thirty-five* years older than you."

Thirty Nine
Present Day

"Greetings, everyone. Seeing you all here fills me with such hope, all of you glowing brightly," a beaming James Carpenter says to a loose gathering casually seated about him. The room is grand but not imposing, soothing even, a spiritual retreat lobby adorned in spa-contemporary. The lone exterior surface is a seamless, towering pane of glass. It pulls in the hues of the rolling hills of north-western Maryland, the view invited in to be one with the gathered. The opposite wall features a gentle cascade down its length—a perpetual flow of spring water, resolving in a tranquil pool where koi swim freely. Above, muscular timber beams brace firm in unfailing support. The floor is quarried black slate, laid evenly in altar-sized slabs. The rocky darkness is broken with a scattering of eclectic rugs and animal skins. A third wall houses a hearth with a fireplace large enough to torch full-sized pine tree trunks. Where the fourth wall would be lies a passage that disappears far off into the remaining structure: the place where the science happens.

"You have all made a very important decision to be here, one not wagered lightly. If you harbor any remaining doubts, you should know, once we have begun there is no return." Carpenter pauses to allow the room to contemplate the finality. Satisfied, he continues. "Change is frightening to us all, but this change is the best and last. So, if you have arrived at a different conclusion, please feel free to return to your lives as they were with no judgment laid upon you." Carpenter spreads his arms with palms skyward and angles his head patiently side to side to view the full complement, awaiting responses. The gathering remains seated, content and silent.

Carpenter assumes a comfortable pose aside the hearth. "Perhaps you already know, but all of you are here because you possess unique gifts. Look around you. The collection of individuals here, such brilliant minds and storied achievers. And, not only that, you are now pioneers. The first to usher in a new way of life on this planet. You will be disciples of a sort. Your mere presence among the rest of humanity will be a testament. Your transformation will bring others to join us and share in a life uninterrupted, a life of endless growth and higher awareness."

Carpenter steps from the hearth to a seat cushion near the center of the group to address them at their level. "You see... here in this place, we have conquered death. Now it can be told, now that you have committed to see it through. What we will do here, all of us together, is to transform your being. To tap your physical body's own regenerative gift and render it flawless. You will become what we refer to as... Eternals."

Seated ten feet away, riveted to Carpenter's confident manner, is Christy Raines. In her heart, she is losing the battle to maintain a reporter's distance. She has interviewed presidents and dictators, Hollywood elite, Nobel laureates and serial killers, but Carpenter is like no other. She is struggling to categorize him, even just to find a starting point to define the man. Not at any one time is he only spiritualist, or scientist, neither a healer nor political animal. He seeks no apparent power or control, only to share a discovery with the fellow citizens of this planet, and at no expense or committed allegiance on their part. He is pure enigma, simultaneously captivating and disquieting.

She scans the room for expressions or body language to betray similar feelings among the gathered. To a person, they are mesmerized, enchanted in the moment, drawn to his words of hope and positive change. She scans further back into the shadows further against the far wall. Standing at attention, the stewards, the caretakers, and hired hands. They are also enrapt—save for one.

So as not to draw attention to herself, she watches him glance by glance. The observable difference is that this man is studying Carpenter rather than admiring him. He examines the gathered similarly, like someone removed, someone collecting data. She recognizes his manner, one similar to a colleague she has known. His face reads as one familiar to her but not because he is celebrated like the others here. She remembers him from previous acquaintance, but he is out of context. She locks too long in his direction and he takes notice of her. He shies back into character as one of the fawning assembly. He shifts his stance to position himself away from her observation. He knows she knows.

"In moments we will begin the process," Carpenter says. "Our stewards will assist you with your accommodations and then we shall begin the transformation. In preparation, you should be aware that what you are going to experience is essentially a death of its own, restructuring your body at a molecular level. You will be placed in a trance-like state for what is typically a three-day timespan, and then return in peace. You will only know of sleep, a long deep sleep, and when you arise, the transformation will have already begun. You will encounter the bliss of perfection, at first only briefly, but as the body continues towards full transformation, that sense will become all you know."

The stewards begin to stir preparing to assist the gathered. The one Raines recognizes looks briefly into her eyes, verifying his own recognition of her. He disappears into a doorway to the service area. His name is still a blur. She is vexed.

Forty
Present Day

It must be something in the government-issue coffee, she concludes. The diuretic effect is always twice the norm when she commutes back from her instructor duties at the FBI forensics training academy, a gig she accepts to stay tight with some Bureau contacts. Patricia Hamer navigates the wobbly aisle of her commuter train with tightrope balance for the third time. By her nature, she scans the passengers with more keenness than most. Hers is a reflex inherent to her breed, cataloguing faces and postures, hairstyles and jewelry. Some faces are familiar, fellow commuters living the same pattern of life, acknowledgement nodded and returned.

One lone face, is worn bleak, disconnected and ashen. He is oddly familiar, but out of context. Arriving at her row of seats, she remains standing. Compelled, she glances again to recapture his image. The second viewing sends a chill down her spine. The recognition is complete. He was the subject of a video shown to her by Ivan Myer on a foggy pier, Myer's "Jumper."

"Can I help you?" the man asks, abrasive and emotionless.

"You... I've seen you... You are... you were," Hamer stammers.

"I am sure you are mistaken. We do not know each other," he responds coldly to dismiss her curiosity.

"No, I have no doubt, now," she challenges, "You... you should be dead." Hamer feels an odd respect for the man, one who stumped even her brilliant forensic mind. She also takes note of his age. He is probably in his thirties, but his empty visage projects a wearier age.

The man's face grows serious and challenging. "You are speaking nonsense. You should return to your seat now, ma'am," he barks back.

Hamer disobeys and takes an empty seat opposite the man across the aisle, perched sideways to face him. The nearest passenger is well beyond earshot given the rattling of the train. She presses further. "I saw you. It was definitely you. You were in pieces and walked away three days later."

"Ma'am, you are clearly mistaken and disturbed. Please leave me?" His irritation is staunch and palpable.

She tries a softer tack to pierce his defenses. A "good cop" strategy may work, she thinks. "How do you do it? Honestly, I won't tell anyone."

"There is nothing to tell. You are confused."

Hamer is more certain now than ever. His body language is clumsy with denial. "How can I become like you? Can you help me?"

His eyebrows raise. He squints to look into her to gauge her sincerity.

She presses, weaving her yarn of trust. "There are rumors out there. I have heard people like you exist. And, I think maybe you will help me. I know you are one. You cannot deny that."

The man turns away to look out the window at the rapidly passing landscape. His countenance softens. "It used to be like that... life... You know, flying past me as my days got shorter and shorter, knowing there was an end. But now everything is glacial. When there is no final curtain, when you know you will always be, the mind adjusts. Life is no longer a slave to time. What you do on any given day doesn't matter to the next or the next after that. Without finality, without a border to one's existence, one fills the space with pointlessness. Free time is just that, it is free... valueless."

"I don't follow you, sir."

"When you pack your bag for a vacation, whether you have two weeks or twenty minutes, you will pack the same regardless. You make the task fit the time and when time is irrelevant, it never gets done."

"I think I get that." She leans in closer. "Then why try to kill yourself?"

His demeanor relaxes, as if he wants to finally tell someone. "When I was made... you know... Eternal. It became instantly apparent I was an infinite being trapped in a finite existence, a fish out of water. We all know, our souls inherently know, even our cells know. We are meant to die, to progress, graduate as it were to a greater existence in the unknown. We always fear that change even though it is meant for every one of us."

"So, you try to kill yourself to forget that?" Hamer presses.

"No." He turns back to face her, his face filling with an odd sense of enthusiasm and joy. "I kill myself to be part of the greater infinite. This existence has become tedious and binding at the awareness that these three dimensions are my permanent residence. My immortality has merely revealed to me the bars of the cage. The first time I died, it was an accident, a mere tumble down a flight of stairs. I learned that when the body is badly broken there are a few seconds where the soul is set free, as it was designed, to occupy a greater space, to roam in nature's expanded realm. For a brief moment, I could swim in the ocean where my soul was begun. Those few seconds when I leave my shell are blissful beyond belief, weightless and unbounded, closer to... God, maybe."

Hamer is grateful but surprised by his candor. "So what you're saying is there is an afterlife?" Her mind of science can offer no other response but to disavow his witness. "Sir, science has proven that the near death experience is merely the action of the brain dying, a cascade of chemical responses."

His face clenches as he takes umbrage mixed with a sort of pity. "Pardon me, ma'am. Are you telling me, *you* telling *me*, there is no afterlife?" Hamer shifts herself in her seat aligning herself more to the front of the train than at the man. She musters the courage to continue the conversation.

"Presuming the afterlife exists—"

"It exists."

"Fine. Why can't you stay there? Why don't you die?"

"My body has been perfected. It has become a flawless machine of replication. I don't know the exact science. All I know is, no matter how badly I am destroyed, eventually I reconstitute and my soul is yanked back. The two are connected at our conception. If one lives, both must remain as one. Believe me, it isn't a painless process, either. One still experiences the shock of death and the agony of recovery. In my state, the body stitches itself back together cell by cell, molecule by molecule, and I feel every last measure of pain."

"How did you come to be this way?"

"I was there at the beginning, one of the original few."

"When was this? Where?"

"The nineteen-eighties. Look, you must leave me, now. I know where this is headed and I refuse to aid you in your request. I do not possess the means, anyway. And if I did, I could not in good conscience do that. I am certain, in time, it will come to you anyway. It will come to everyone. If you want it, it will be yours. You don't need my help."

"Who are you? What is your name?"

"My name is Marcus Chandler."
Chandler retreats to his stony-faced distance, staring out his train window. Hamer returns to her seat, content to let the man be. Her head is swirling with enough unfathomable information to keep her dazzled for a good while. She is dumbfounded which only intrigues her more.

The train stops. She turns to wish him luck but sees an empty seat. Through the far window she spies him on the platform. Her eyes meet his. Smiling, he walks toward the edge of the platform. He nods to her and then suddenly leaps out, floats down, and is swept from mid-air. The 5:17 northbound train arrives to deliver him to his destination of temporary bliss.

Screams and howls erupt from the platform. Hamer cringes at blood spatter on her window, his blood, a murky membrane shrouding her from the mayhem. She shudders at a touch of cold brushing across her hand. He is gone. His mangled body lies on the ground before her, but she also knows, in three days' time he will rise from his hospital bed, and walk out into thin air leaving behind a baffled hospital staff and a monumental mystery.

Forty One
April 9, 1980

"I told you Nicaragua was a huge mistake," rails Brody Markham at his younger cousin. "Some dog-shit third-world stink-hole damn near cost you your life because you thought you had a fool's chance of *enlightening* the reeking masses to rise up against the dictator du jour." He peers over his glasses with scolding eyes. "It's no cause to die for, Theodore. I hope you've got that out of your system." Markham sips from a lowball glass and places it gently on a bar top, sixty feet in length, stretching back into the narrow space of a posh Manhattan tavern. The amber-toned lighting sets off the contents of the glass of matching hue.

"Hey, I needed to find out what it's really like. I just wanted to help," Carlisle challenges back. "Dictator du jour or not, people have value no matter where they are, and it's worth making the attempt."
"Whatever. I have decided the best way to help others is to do it from where the mother's milk flows," Markham smugly chirps his own resolve.

"Washington, of course." Theodore glances away, knowing his cousin is about to deliver a mild rebuke. "You have become your father. I predicted this. You do remember me saying that, right?"

"You are only half right. Washington is the place, but my way is not my father's." Markham fashions a smile fueled by a memory. "I had an epiphany a while back, right in my father's office. I think I kind of scared the shit out of him. You should have seen his face." He grins with more self-satisfaction than usual.

"Epiphany? About what?"

"There's too much at stake to leave the most important business to the uncertainty of legislation. The usual way of Washington is impure. The very process itself corrupts and dilutes the final product. If you need something done, you have to find a workaround. You just have to take matters into your own hands."

"Such as?"

"Earmarks, slush funds, good old-fashioned pork. And if all that fails, everyone in that town has some dark moment in their past to exploit."

"What are you talking about, Brody?"

"Don't get me wrong, the goal is always noble. The end result is to the benefit of all. But to get it up and running sometimes there is a modicum of," —Markham's smile slants slyly— "grooming the process."

"This is kind of making me uncomfortable," Carlisle says as he twists atop his barstool.

"Look, it's the new way of government. You stoke an issue, throw red meat to the base in both directions, and then fire up the rhetoric machine." Markham grows more passionate, his eyes steely and shimmering. "Once the emotions are at a peak you can pass anything, or just do it anyway. Even better, you get an executive order funding a *blue-ribbon panel* to *investigate the matter*, anything to get the cash flowing."

Theodore pulls away, discomfort brewing as his cousin muses on pushing the envelope of ethics.

"After a short while the scrutiny fades," Markham continues. "In a year or so, you cobble together some patchwork data from existing studies and proclaim it relevant. When all is said and done, everyone's forgotten about it, but the money still flows." Markham empties his glass down his throat with flourish. "It's free money and all without ever having to build a company, meet regulations, hire anybody, let alone produce a product. The best part is there is no accountability—no board members, no stockholders. It's genius."

"And you're comfortable with this?" Carlisle asks incredulously.

"The history of human progress is not one of carefully laid plans. It is more commonly made of conquest and upheaval driven by men of vision. The idea of *the collective* steering the ship is nonsense. A consensus of the supreme few arriving at a rapid path to success is, by far, the exception for progress."

"And you have decided you are one of those men of conquest?" Carlisle says, trying not to sound too sarcastic.

"I have decided I would like to give it a go."

"And what makes you think you are that kind of man?"

"Frankly, I don't think it should just be me."

"And who else is worthy of this anointed station?"

"Well, I was thinking...," Markham's eyes remain fixed on his cousin, finishing his thought with a look.

"ME? Seriously?"

"We are a perfect match." Markham lays a firm hand on Carlisle's shoulder and stiffens his lips. "I am the man of ambition and you are the complementary balance of thoughtful temperance. Every sword fashioned from the forge needs the rigid cool of the anvil to harden the steel and give it shape."

"I don't know; I just don't have a knack for big ideas."

"You don't have to. I am the idea guy. You are the methodologist, the metrics guy. C'mon, you've been managing projects since you were in middle school. Remember the Rescue Network? That whole meals-for-the-elderly thing?"

"I guess so."

"You've almost got a Master's in Business from Columbia. You are a genius in your own right. Between us, and the connections we have, we can do a lot of good things. Imagine you had at your disposal a couple hundred million dollars to craft a solution to the bloodbath you experienced in Nicaragua? You could have saved a whole lot more innocents."

Carlisle ponders his cousin's sales pitch. He knows when Markham gets a notion, it's going to happen. "I never thought of it that way. I guess I always think of government as a big waste of money that doesn't get anything done in the long run."

"That's because people like you and me aren't in charge. So, what do you say?"

Carlisle's last kernel of apprehension flicks away. He smiles, meeting his cousin's gaze. "What's the next step?"
"You tell me; you're the project manager."

Carlisle downs the last drops in his glass.

"Networking. Let's start chatting up some of your dad's cronies and associates. See what springs from that."

They raise their empty glasses to meet, the ringing of crystal like a starting bell.

"Here's to changing the world, partner."

Markham's eye gathers a gleam and, with a bit of puckish flair, he says, "Say cuz. *Markham and Carlisle*... there's no edge there. We need a moniker, a name with pizzazz like *Harley and Davidson*, or *Dukes and Hazzard*."

Carlisle plays along, feeling the vibe. "Okay, but I prefer something unassuming. Something absurdly ordinary that carries with it an air of frivolous mystery."

"I'm game. What did you have in mind?"

Carlisle smiles, shrewd and slippery. "How about, Smith and Jones."

"Oh, I like that."

Forty Two
Present Day

It is the third day since his leap into the path of an oncoming commuter train was witnessed by the horrified eyes of hundreds of onlookers including Patricia Hamer. With practiced stealth, he weaves the back corridors and basement service areas of the hospital. He reaches the exit, one he knows won't set off an alarm. Tipping his head to dodge the security camera, he leans into the crossbar and departs. The intense morning sun blinds him for a moment, reminding him of the blissful brightness he encountered shortly after his body was exploded by the force of the train.

"Welcome back to the realm of the living, Chandler," quips Patricia Hamer, deftly intercepting Chandler and killing his buzz. "Remember me?"

"How did you find me?" a shocked Chandler replies

"How hard do you think it is to find the hospital where a John Doe leaper is making a miraculous recovery? Look, if you don't want to be found out, you are going to have to find less spectacular ways to off yourself, like maybe a heroin overdose in the peaceful solitude of your own apartment. Just a suggestion."

"How did you know—?"

"You always leave by a service entrance, to avoid any lurking press," Hamer replies smugly. "I've had three days to research you. You've left a lot of video out there for curious speculation."

"I suppose I have a flair for the dramatic." Chandler off-handedly grins, his smile still missing a few teeth.

"Well, your flair for the dramatic almost landed you in cold storage in the morgue this time. You might consider less drastic means or next time, you will spend days freezing your regenerative ass off in a pitch-dark hell with no way out."

Chandler weaves to pass her. She grabs his arm firmly. He returns a fiery gaze. "Why are you here, miss?"

"You are coming with me," she commands with a burning stare of her own. "You need to tell me what's going on."

"Forget it. I told you. Your chance will come soon." He grabs at her hand to remove it but loses to her determined grip.

"Look, I really don't want eternal life," Hamer admits. "I lied to you on the train. I need to know what all this is about, who's behind it. Where this is all going."

"Never."

"Do you want me to tell the whole world who you are? There are about twelve news outlets waiting at the front entrance around the corner. You'll be hounded and your little love affair with the great beyond will be exposed along with your identity. Is that what you want?" she levels boldly with cold conviction.

Chandler's face twists and grimaces at imagining the ruination of his titillating station in the world, being the center of a rising global mystery while at the same time remaining perfectly anonymous.

"Very well, but whatever I tell you, you cannot divulge to anyone," Chandler whispers.

"I'll promise you that for now, but I can't promise you forever, especially if I think there is something dangerous going on. That's the deal, okay?"

Chandler hesitates. Hamer struts off in the direction of the front entrance cavalierly muttering, "I'm off to out you to the press."

Chandler tenses with frustration. "Stop... alright."

Behind the wheel of a ten-year-old Ford Taurus, Hamer steers both the car and the conversation as she peppers him with penetrating questions. Chandler rests uncomfortably in the passenger seat. He throws out a question of his own meant to deflect.

"Hey, I'm starving... uhh... What is your name, miss?"
"Pat," she responds. "I suppose you would have an appetite—you haven't eaten in three days."

"It's the recovery mostly; the whole process burns a lot of fuel."

"So not only do you get to go to the afterlife for a while, you've discovered a miracle diet," she wryly jests.

"Oh," Chandler shakes his head, "once you are an Eternal you never have to worry about diets anymore. The body is perfection. But resurrection is a rough process. The first time it took me almost five days to recover. I was a twisted wreck at the bottom of my basement steps for almost three of those days. The first day I couldn't move, but I was fully conscious. It was horrible, like being buried alive. But my body has learned now, it is getting used to reconstituting and now; the whole thing barely takes three days."

"*Eternal*? There's a name for it?" Hamer dishes with incredulity. "How many of you are out there?"

"At this point, I have no idea. Could be hundreds, maybe thousands."

"Thousands?"

Chandler points her to a burger drive-through.

Food in hand, she parks the car. Chandler wolfs down one burger, the first of four, chasing gulps with sugary soda. He scans the parking lot and looks at her, puzzled. He says with a mouthful, "You know we could have just gone in and sat down."

"I don't want anyone else hearing this conversation. So, take me back to the beginning. How does one get involved in a life-extension project?"

"I was the systems engineer," Chandler replies mid-bite. "I built all the incubation environments for the gene cultivation. I assisted in other things along the way, too. There were only seven of us and we all had to multi task to some degree."

"Who are the other six?"

"The guy I spent the most time with was a guy named Anders Kipner. He was an uber-genius in genetics. He died in a car crash not long after we had gotten the gene isolated and began reproducing it."

"Died? Really? I thought..."

"The transformation protocol had not been developed yet. He never became an Eternal."

Hamer's forehead launches upward in bewilderment. "How did the project get finished? Who developed the protocol?"

"Oh, that belonged solely to the project lead and queen bee, Adeline Brandt. She was also a genetics genius. She made Kipner's skills look positively remedial, and he was one of only a handful of people on the planet even capable of understanding the science she was embarking upon. She was the one behind the whole idea and drove everything."
Hamer rifles her brain for any memory at the name Adeline Brandt and comes up empty. "And where is she now?"

"She vanished not long after the whole thing was completed. The end game was managed by a couple of guys who called themselves Smith and Jones. Not their real names, and I don't know their real names, so don't ask."

"Really? Never would have guessed that... *Smith and Jones.* And these guys are scientists too?"

"No, government types, but embedded, if you know what I mean."

Hamer's expression sours at the growing complexity of the players involved. "Well, that certainly puts the mind at ease," she sarcastically unloads. "So that's four, who are the other two?"

"There was a man of the cloth, some guy from the Vatican, a cardinal. Brandt had this brilliant idea to approach the Vatican offering to authenticate some of their artifacts. It gave us a large basis of testable objects from a vast spectrum of recorded time to experiment on and dial in our process."

Hamer's confusion returns. "That doesn't make sense to me. How does cultivating genetic material help authenticate artifacts?"

"I don't know." Chandler shrugs while starting on his third burger. "I knew better than to ask those kinds of questions. I was told what they needed and I built it. Anyway, the Cardinal guy was really just a liaison brought in to oversee the cataloguing of the artifacts and our results. He took off after we were done and I never heard what happened to him. He's probably dead by now, or well into his eighties."

"So he's not an Eternal either?

"No, he disappeared before we finished. I assumed he just got the results and went back to Italy. He was essentially unnecessary at that point. The artifacts were being sent back. Plus, I got a feeling he was getting disenchanted with the whole thing."

"Who was the seventh person?"

"Have you ever heard of William Reader?"

Hamer's spine stiffens. That name returning, too odd to be coincidence. Before she can ask, Chandler answers. "Look, I know this is all blowing your mind, but I have no idea what transpired in his life over the last thirty-plus years."

Another connection occurs to Hamer. "What does James Carpenter have to do with this?"

"You mean the spiritual guy?" Chandler looks back quizzically. "Nothing. I'm sure he wasn't even born yet. We did this project back in the early eighties. Carpenter can't be much older than thirty-five. Look, if you're asking why Reader tried to kill him, then I don't know. Reader was an eccentric. He was also a tad paranoid, especially after we all disbanded. He was given a chance to be an Eternal, but refused."

Hamer pauses, an inconsistency needling her. "I find it more than interesting that, given the chance to never die, it appears out of the original six under Brandt, only you have chosen to participate."

"Well, we didn't all get the chance, but I see what you mean. I was one of the first, a guinea pig. This was version one-point-oh and maybe they just wanted to wait and see. I'd bet dollars to doughnuts that Smith and Jones are Eternals—they were funding the operation—and I'm certain Adeline Brandt is one. It was her baby."

"I suppose. Look, I know I will have a lot more questions I haven't thought of yet. How do I get a hold of you?"

"I will contact you," Chandler declares. Hamer glares back. "Seriously, I will," he reassures her. "Look, this sounds weird but this has been kind of therapeutic for me. A confession thing, I guess. I've been living with this for decades and it feels good to finally tell someone. I trust you, Pat. I believe you will keep this to yourself. As long as we have that arrangement then I will continue to give you anything I can remember."

"Thanks, Marcus." She smiles. "I suppose in a spirit of goodwill I should tell you my bona fides. I am in forensics but have a background in molecular biology as well. I work with the FBI mostly. But, for now, this is going to stay confidential."

She pauses to process the density of the last few minutes. "Okay, one more." Hamer looks up and locks on Chandler's eyes, "Why? Outside of the obvious—eternal life. Why'd Brandt do it?"

"There are a million answers to that, but the one most clear to me is, why not? Wouldn't you if you knew how?"

Forty Three
Present Day

"Over here, Christy. I want you to meet some more of our honored guests," Carpenter hails from across the haute café that services the attendees of The Carpenter Institute. Raines arrives, with camera crew in tow, to a table seating a half dozen persons. Carpenter stands above and behind the six guests. They all rise to greet her.

"Please everyone, return to your seats. I hope you don't mind my video intrusion," she asks shyly while taking a seat. Carpenter remains hovering above.

"Everyone, this is Christy Raines, international television personality and journalist extraordinaire, though I'm sure no introduction is required. Let's start from the left. This is..."

"Basil THORNE," Raines gushes. "I am very familiar with your work in astrophysics. You theorized that the Big Bang was the result of a tear in the boundary between this universe and another."

"Why, yes, that is essentially correct," he patters with British flair. He straightens his lithe form and runs a hand through his gray, tousled hair convinced it will make a difference in his appearance. "Of course, it is much more involved than that, but that is the abridged version."

"As I understand it, the matter of this universe is simply some leaked in from the other," Raines recites.

"Again, essentially correct, Miss Raines."

Carpenter gestures to the left of Thorne. "This is Tanya Sulkoloff, legendary mathematician from the Ukraine."

The square-jawed woman in her mid-forties offers, "My English not good. *Kheh-lo*, Miss Raines." Their hands clasp.

"Moving on, these are Purvinder Patel, Matilda Bosch and LaVetta Jackson, Nobel Laureates all. And finally, Angela Stonebreaker. You may know her from... "

"Winning the decathlon in consecutive Olympic games, of course," Raines beams and extends an eager hand. "I feel so humbled."

"You mustn't downplay your achievements, Christy," Carpenter champions. "You are no less important here. You are here to tell the story of this journey, to serve as a window to the rest of the world." Carpenter ambles a few steps to gain an angle to address the table. "Christy is here to document this evolution. She will be the messenger of the good news we have waiting for all the world when the time is right. She, and all of you in our initial graduating class are going to be the ambassadors for a new age."

A steward arrives at the table to clear dishes and pour coffee. Raines realizes it is the same man she recognized earlier. The mystery of his identity nags and pokes. She forwards a question to the group to allow herself more time to scour her memory. "What are you all hoping this process will bring to the people of planet Earth? And, please discuss amongst yourselves."

The steward moves quickly, avoiding eye contact. Abruptly, he leaves his work without finishing. Raines whispers in the cameraman's ear to carry on. Without indicating her urgency, she excuses herself. A quick scan of the seating area shows no trace. She presses into the kitchen, popping her head into nooks and bending casually to look under counters and tables.

"Over here," a whisper beckons from a darkened pantry. "Quickly, get in and don't let anyone see you."

Raines slinks in to the pantry and leaves the door propped enough to allow a little sliver of light to paint the identity of the man whose name she now recalls: Ivan Myer. "Times are tough, Ivan. I hope the tips are good, at least," she whispers back.

"Hilarious, Christy. I'm on assignment."

"I expect nothing less. For whom?"

"Well, me actually." Myer replies softly but intensely. "This whole Carpenter Institute gives me the willies. There is something really out of sorts going on here, and I am going to get to the bottom of it. It's my latest obsession." "Ivan, you, obsessed? That's not at all like you," Raines mocks. "What do you mean *willies*?"

"I mean, something doesn't add up. It's all too... too... *altruistic*."

Discordance stirs in her. Myer's past, she knows, was often spent chasing conspiracy theories but, he has never gone so far as to embed himself this deeply. "Explain that."

"C'mon, Christy, where's your reporter's instinct?" Myer bristles. "A guy has found the fountain of youth and he's *giving it away*?"

"Why is that so hard to believe, Ivan?"

Myer's face blazes incredulity at her apparent lapse of objectivity. "Really? You actually said that?"

"Look, Ivan, sooner or later someone is going to come along in this world who is not fully absorbed with greed. It's just a mathematical reality. There are good people out there."

Myer looks deep into her eyes trying to detect any sense of the woman with whom he is familiar. "Christy, has this guy got to you? Just put on your investigator hat for a second and think with me. There's an angle. There's always an angle. He's after something. He's got all these brilliant elites here and is going to make them permanent residents of planet Earth. Then, supposedly, he's just going to hand out the secret to the rest of the great unwashed and it's all going to be hunky dory, peachy keen... all, like kumbayah—a grand, grab-ass, love-in of happiness and bliss?"

"You can make anything sound like a conspiracy, Ivan," Raines scolds.

"Please, just think about it," Myer pleads.

She waits a beat, registering his level of conviction. She nods while saying, "Okay, I'll give it some thought. So, how do you plan to unmask this *villainous cabal*?"

"I am still figuring that out," Myer responds, stroking his chin slowly. His eyes widen at an idea. "You might be able to help."

"How?"

"You have access, right? He's given you free reign of the Institute."

"Right, I have a high level of trust here. You're asking me to betray that. I don't feel right about that."

"Aren't you even curious? I've never known you to accept anything at face value."

"Maybe I've changed, Ivan," she ponders out loud, not just to him but to herself as well. Her allegiances wage a struggle again: Carpenter versus her professional ethic.

Myer detects her dilemma. "Okay, Christy. I'll make you a deal. You help me out and if I don't find something in forty-eight hours, I walk."

She places her hands on her hips. "You'll just trust there is nothing nefarious going on here and hit the road?"

"Yeah, I'll hang up my busboy apron for good."

"Just what is it you want me to do?" she asks, unconvinced of Myer's sincerity.

"Find a break in your schedule, get me into some of the more secret levels here."

"And what do you think you're going to find?"

"I don't know, maybe I find he's on the up and up. But ask yourself this. If he's so pure, why all the secrecy?"

She pauses to allow Myer's doubt a chance. It is persuasive and rekindles her curiosity. "Look, there is some time set aside for meditation and reflection tonight after hours. He wants us to *visualize the future*, an endless one. It's part of the mental preparation for the transition. We are encouraged to roam and explore our inner thoughts. Meet me at nine thirty near the fountain. You better have a game plan though. It's only a ninety-minute interval and then a bed check."

"Bed check?"

"Rest and relaxation are apparently essential to the process. It eases the physical shock, they say."

"Seriously, Christy. Doesn't that freak you out? It's just amazing how casual you are about this living forever thing. It's kind of a big deal."

"It is Ivan, but honestly, is it really hard to comprehend? All I know is, I will be able to achieve all I ever dreamed of, be the lead for the most impactful story since opposable thumbs, and never have to leave this earth to abandon the ones I love. Isn't this what humankind has always dreamed of?"

"I can think of a few nightmares that could come of that as well," Myer soberly counters. "Maybe you should ponder those awhile?"

"I'll see you at nine thirty, Ivan," Raines tersely pops back.

Forty Four
Present Day

"Alex. I am very pleased the note found you, and I am deeply grateful for your discretion." The words pass through the shadowy barrier of a confessional booth in rich Hungarian tones. "It is probably unnecessary to be so secretive, but I think we should take precautions. I hope the location does not put you off. I could think of no more secure place than here."

"I am so glad you found me again, Cardinal. The timing was perfect, Reader's video really shook me up. I think it wise to be careful."

"I do too, my son." Kovacs responds, an air of empathy wrapping his words. "If I may, I want to ask you some things, learn of your nature. I do not know why Reader has chosen you, but it seems he left it up to me to uncover that mystery."

"Chosen me for what?"

"That is unclear as well. But perhaps if we converse, over time the answer may arise."

For the first time, Kovacs is doubting William Reader's sanity. In his years in Tibet, Kovacs often wondered who Reader would find to be *the one*, or even *the several.* He trusted Reader's skills and genius, but remembers the man was always a bit off center. Kovacs expected Reader would choose a man of influence, or at least one armed with inherent knowledge or some familiarity with such matters of grand consequence, Marcus Chandler, for instance. He expected someone more aware of the details. Kovacs had known an outsider was likely, but never thought his good friend would neglect to inform Traeger of the gravity, dangers, and facts of the task at hand. Kovacs has been left to bestow all that. He decides Reader must have seen something in Traeger. He must try to view Traeger with Reader's eye, learn what is in his heart. It would be so easy to just tell it all to him. But, he is not ready.

The cardinal asks a seminal question. "Alex, do you recall me asking if you are a man of God?"

"I suppose my answer is still that I don't know," Traeger answers plainly. "I grew up going to church with my mother off and on, but as I got older, I grew out of it. It all just seemed like stories and fables. As life becomes more serious, I guess finding relevance in what happened two thousand years ago becomes unimportant."

"Believe it or not, I can fully understand your point," Kovacs states reassuringly. "If you would indulge me: pretend you are God. How would you do things differently?"

"Me? God?" Traeger answers with a skeptical snicker.

"Yes, just suppose. What would you do to help this world, to become relevant again?" Kovacs posits earnestly.

"I am not really sure… I guess I would not allow evil to exist."

"So, you, *the man* Alex, believe there is evil, that there is a malevolent force whose sole purpose is to do harm?" Kovacs carefully guides the questioning to bring Traeger to thoughts rarely pondered without steering his answer in any one direction.

"I suppose I do. There seems to be plenty of evidence of that, more than there is of the existence of God. We see the effects of evil every day whether it be at the hands of humans or just random tragedy."

"So, if you were God, would you regale the world with your presence and stamp out evil before it has a chance to do its bidding?"

"Sure, that's sounds about right. I would protect the innocent."

"So, it seems you believe there is some force of goodness as well, then. The source of this *innocence.*"

"Yes, I do, but there is no apparent origin that I can see, no solid evidence. People perform great acts of kindness every day, but those are people, not God."

Traeger's openness encourages Kovacs to submit a larger question. "Suppose God exists, what do you think would be the nature of God, his composition?"

"Well, he… or she, or *it,* is the ultimate being. At least that's what we are led to believe. If that isn't the case then I guess it's not God we are talking about. God must be all knowing. Everywhere all at the same time, all powerful."

"*It.* You referred to God as possibly an *it,*" Kovacs replies raising his pitch on the last word.

"Yes, I'm sorry."

"No apology needed. God transcends any definition of human form being neither male nor female. There is no pronoun to describe that." Kovacs is encouraged by the sense of a growing bond with Traeger. Across the veil he senses a man filled with undiscovered grace. "You see, God being so immense, is incapable of inhabiting our limited sphere of existence. If he... or *it*... were to dwell among us, his mere presence might prove harmful. This finite universe could not completely contain the fullness of his infinite, perfected condition, like a grown man trying to fit into the clothes of a child."

"What's your point? God made us but he can't be with us?" Traeger asks, confused"

"Essentially, yes. Maybe more accurately, God's creation created us," Kovacs continues. "Some believe our existence was a surprise, unexpected to God."

"You're saying something happened that God didn't expect?" Traeger asks, somewhat perplexed. "The all-knowing God didn't know *we* would happen?"

"Ours is a dimension of free will. God set that in motion intentionally on the very first day and, given that, had to relinquish complete control and be apart from it."

"Why even do that? Why create something imperfect?" Traeger's confusion reaches through the veil to find Kovacs.

Kovacs examines the cubicle he inhabits, a mere booth, confining but ruled by a code of privilege, one where he must remain. He and Traeger are separated by a thin veil, and separate they must remain. The cardinal senses something greater and purer within himself, his own spirit filled with renewed purity. "Alex, scripture tells us we are made in his image—but perhaps only a blurred reflection of his true nature. Maybe we can learn something about God by looking into ourselves."

"I'm not sure I understand that."

"Humans are curious and adventurous. We question our existence, we push beyond our boundaries as creative, inquisitive beings."

"So, you're saying God possesses all of these things too?"

"Exactly. But if you are God there is nowhere else to go. All of creation obeys you, every thought and idea has been considered countless times. Infinity and perfection to an infinite being results in a stifling existence."

"But you are saying because God is like us, curious and inquisitive, God has a constant desire to be more than God?"

"Go back to where we started. You are God. Are you happy knowing you are all you will ever be, that you live in a box, a perfect box, but a box nevertheless? The infinite is bound by the absolute certainty of everything."

"You mean God can be more than all-knowing and ever-present?"

 "Of course; God is God."

"I guess any being, especially God, could feel trapped by an inability to progress," Traeger agrees with a nod.

"So what do you do, God-Alex? Imagine it yourself. You are a creator, in fact an architect by profession."

"I suppose... well... maybe I would create something that was independent of me? A place of... umm"

"Free will?" Kovacs finishes Traeger's thought. "Maybe set in motion a universe unto itself, one that would determine its own course, one watched over by you, but one you pledge in your staunch perfection to allow to grow of its own impetus, one of uncertain determination."

"So, we are just left to be part of a random creation and subject to all manner of randomness while God watches from above?"

"Yes, and he is aware of our joy and pain. He rejoices and also suffers with us."

Traeger's growing frustration brings a more forceful response. "Then why not do something to end the suffering, Jonas?"

"God did. He..."

"I know, Cardinal. He sent Jesus Christ..." Traeger fires back at the simplistic bromide he knows Kovacs is about to preach. "This is where it all gets very *Star Wars* for me, God becoming man."

"I understand," Kovacs softly returns. "But think again about what I said before about God being a reflection of ourselves."

"I... I guess I don't follow. What do you mean?"

"I will answer that with a question... a riddle, if you will. Remember, God is driven by curiosity and a need to grow as well, right? So, given that God is all-powerful, all-knowing, and ever-present, there is still one thing God cannot be. Do you know what that is, Alex?"

Traeger strains to gather an answer. He can only muster, "No."

"My son, it is here I must disappoint you. You must learn it. You must find the answer to that question on your own."

Forty Five
Present Day

"Mr. Traeger?" a sleek male voice delivers from above.

The architect is seated at his office desk, nose buried deep in the bane of most every profession—legal documents. Eyes still affixed to his reading, he replies, "Yes, I am Alex Traeger. How can I help you?"

"I need you to build something for me."

"You've come to the right place." Traeger raises a hand to pause his guest. "I'm sorry, I need to finish this or I will have to start over, and legal gymnastics are not my forte," he replies as he scans the small print on eleven-by-seventeen pages.

"I can wait."

"Thanks," Traeger responds, his eyes stiffly riveted to the page. He mumbles, "Ugh, it's no use. I'm lost. So, what can I do for—" Traeger's speech fails as he looks up, arrested at the sight of the man before him.

"Hello, my name is James Carpenter," the stranger greets with hand extended.

Traeger rises halfway, in slight shock and extends his own hand. A whirlwind of emotion arrives, a turbulence of discord at the man standing before him, too much to consider. He forces a response. "Mr. Carpenter, what an honor. Please take a seat." Traeger's tension and caution remains veiled but William Reader's message from the grave pierces his thoughts, stirring further unrest.

"What... what can I do for you, Mr. Carpenter?"

Carpenter smiles at Traeger's state of disarray. "Tell me your schedule." Carpenter smiles larger. "What are you doing for the next two years?"

"Two... two years?" Traeger repeats, stunned and incredulous.

"Yes, The Carpenter Institute will be facing very rapid expansion in short order and we are in need of a much more capable facility; facilities, really." Carpenter smoothly leans back and swings one leg over the other. "We were very impressed with the praise your restoration work received and think you are the visionary we are looking for."

"You want me to design the new facility?" Traeger struggles to not sound too surprised. The offer is huge, but the coincidence of circumstance pokes caution at him. "I am flattered, but I must ask, why me?"

"Indeed, it is not a project of the scale you are used to. But, I have to tell you, the decision at the Institute was unanimous when reviewing a lengthy list of candidates. We have great faith that you can deliver what we are looking for." Carpenter looks firmly into Traeger's eyes to offer reassurances and put Traeger at ease. "You see, our facility is not just a scientific venue. It has spiritual meaning, and we think you can bring unique artistry to those aspects. You will be designing the aesthetic, the grandeur and splendor of the Institute as well as many satellite locations. Ours will be a place for renewal and personal growth, and that is your specialty."

"I don't know what to say. There is a lot to discuss, as I am sure you know."

"Of course," Carpenter calmly responds. "I merely came today to see if you had interest and if we could count on further discussions. We do need to move quickly, though. Can we set up a time early next week to get into the details?"

"Let me check my schedule." Traeger summons his day planner from his laptop for show, already knowing there is no conflict. "Okay, how about Tuesday?"

"That sounds perfect. Eight a.m. Here is the address." Carpenter rises and scrawls on a loose paper from Traeger's desk. His eyes seek Traeger's and lock them firmly in place. "Alex, let me be clear. We want you for this. We are prepared to offer you a sum more compensatory than your usual rate including a retainer to cover some early expenses. Will this be enough?"

Carpenter scribbles below the address, and rotates the paper for Traeger to view. It takes all of his strength of will to not scream with joy, but he maintains composure and coolly replies, "I'm confident that will be sufficient to get something off the ground."

"Very good, Alex. I will see you Tuesday."

"I look forward to it." Traeger stands and walks to Carpenter's side of the desk. "Let me show you out."

At the doorway, Carpenter closes the gap and embraces Traeger, holding him closely as a father might. Before releasing the hug, Carpenter meets his lips to the architect's. Traeger's reflex causes him to stiffen.

Carpenter smiles. "I'm sorry, Alex. I suppose I should have warned you. I am a bit European in that regard. I hope that does not offend."

"Not in the least, Mr. Carpenter."

"Call me James, please."

Carpenter departs. Traeger quietly pumps his fist. The advance alone will cover his office rent for two more years, pay his own salary, and retire the legal fees from his ongoing divorce. It is a godsend, but the distant voice of William Reader still echoes in his ears. Traeger's glee is doused by a greater sense of enormity.

Forty Six
Present Day

As soon as it ends, it begins again. True resurrection at a cellular level. Death, then spontaneous rebirth. By mere observation, it appears simple, effortless, magical, even. Under a microscope the transformation unfolds like the fluid moves of a dancer gliding from pose to pose. A performance unbelievable, yet undeniable. Cells seem to die and then un-die, the living joining to the lifeless, reanimating them. Time shifted into reverse. Her eyes witness death like any other of natural means, but a death interrupted by the unexplained. Somehow, it is undone. The lifeless cell reclaims its existence, then whole organs, then all of it, reconstituted from crude finality fully intact.

With each observation comes a host of new questions. Each time the subject individual dies only one subject returns. When individual organs are set apart from one another they all begin regenerating until some undecipherable, critical point when one wins out, growing whole again to leave the others to wither away, never to return. The location of the brain seems to command that, but what happens if the brain is set apart? What happens if the brain is *blown* apart? How would life re-spin from that obliteration? These are questions too precise for here and now. She is certain, in time, if this is truly the future of humankind, that others more brilliant and with thicker skins will emerge to brave such questions. For her, for now, she is simply resigned to observe and absorb the mystical process through her deep understanding of science. Before heeding a call to embark on a career in forensics, Patricia Hamer chose a path in molecular biology, earning a PhD at Stanford. Soon after, feeling too far-removed from the fray, she yearned for more visceral, real-world engagement. Investigative science of a high-minded nature became her happiness.

The deal she made reluctantly with Marcus Chandler was a Faustian bargain indeed. This precious data now in her possession was paid for at an unthinkable price. It is an uneasy business for her to unravel, one that leaves a mark. She soldiers on, relying on unrefined analytical tools and dated equipment, but the conclusion is unmistakable. Within the humdrum of genetic ordinariness, she spots the introduction of some foreign marker, interceding DNA of unspecific origin. Identifying and mapping it is beyond her ability, but it is undeniable. At least it gives her a basis rooted in concrete science that the Eternals phenomenon is real. How it is made real is the question that remains. Establishing the source of the DNA is the new benchmark. It is a good question for Chandler when next he recovers.

Peeling blue latex gloves from each hand, leaning back in her roller chair, Hamer pulls in a cleansing breath. The research at an impasse, she is left to confront the ugliness, the reconciliation and penance of the deal she had to accept to enjoy the privilege of such rare knowledge, the balance sheet of ethical compromise versus scientific understanding.

The idea seemed insane at first, incomprehensible to Hamer's way of being, one so incongruently macabre and inhumane as to turn her own stomach. In her storied career as a forensic scientist, she has encountered mutilation and horrific death at least two hundred-fold, consulting dutifully on untold homicide cases, wading hip-deep in unspeakable acts. But she had never considered the possibility that she would be the one administering the deed.

After gaining Marcus Chandler's trust and gleaning deeper information about the origins of the Eternal class, he proposed a symbiotic exchange. She would gain invaluable scientific knowledge, but in return she must act as executioner, not just once, but again and again. Like a craven addict seeking a greater high, he would enjoy his moments of posthumous bliss by her own hand. He would be murdered, but not really murdered, it being a condition of temporary effect.

It was his idea, pestered persistently, seven times over five weeks. The last time had been met with hollow protests as Hamer convinced herself that the scientific opportunities were too great to pass up, most of which were unprecedented to the known realm. She could observe and record vitals and brain activity during death and resurrection, document the beginnings of the afterlife, if there was such a thing. The failsafe was that there was no danger of losing the patient. In fact, the goal was to *actually* lose the patient—many times over. Her objections eventually stood no chance against her needling scientific curiosity. But built into the contract was the bitter knowledge that this study was fueled by the same impure appetite that spawned Chandler as he is today—unchecked, ethically bankrupt science. Something anathema to her own conscience.

To get the full spectrum of data, she had to devise the cause of death—
causes, really. She had to don the skin of a serial killer, an assassin cloaked
in cold, clinical purpose. She performed the "clean" deaths—suffocations
and drug overdoses. Drowning seemed a good option, but all these methods
took too long. The introduction of drug overdoses tainted the brain data.
The pair also discovered that prolonged death, or sustained arresting of the
regeneration effect, only resulted in a harrowing experience to the subject,
one similar to being buried alive, not physically, but even worse, spiritually.
The exhilaration post-death apparently has an expiration period. Chandler
pleaded to never be left in that agony again. In order for the journey back to
be sublime, the duration of death and subsequent regeneration had to be
natural for it to be humane.

With the previous attempts behind them, the two have arrived at a pure
form of death, one that will accommodate the greatest opportunity for
research but also result in an organic return. Prepared for the task, she
steels her wits again convincing herself this is all for the furthering of
science. She reasons away the ethical incongruity with placating thoughts
that she is actually bringing joy to another.

The venue chosen for the research is perfect for a dismemberment, a
remote location in northwestern Virginia, a rustic cabin used for hunting
and fishing excursions, one built by her grandfather. The garage was
designed to double as a site to process deer kills. In fact, she'd whetted her
interest in forensics helping process the carcasses as a child. Unlike other
youth, she was rendered immune to blood and guts. Not even the smells
bothered her.

Chandler lies adrenalized on the processing table, one perfectly suited for
the task, purchased by her grandfather at an auction of items belonging to a
decommissioned military hospital. Dressed in autopsy gear, she places a
gloved hand on his bare chest. Instead of the usual chill of a cadaver, she
feels warmth and a heart thumping powerfully in his chest. Chandler's eager
eyes signal he is ready.

In order to allay the torrent of pumping blood post-kill, she begins with a thin spike hammered through the skull. The crunch of bone twists her own insides and brings a gasp through her surgical mask. His pupils grow into black saucers, the breath leaving his body like a punctured air mattress. The EKG flat-line signals his death. Brain activity fades to nothing. It is done. She administers three long cuts to his torso in the shape of a Y, then pulls the skin back. Working quickly, trying to steady herself, she snips through the rib cage to reveal Chandler's vital organs still glistening, warm and pink. Her hard exterior is crumbling. The reality of her deed is oozing in past her scientist armor. The accumulation of repeated killing presses down. Instead of surgical precision, she begins slicing and hacking connecting tissue. She is faltering, desperately fumbling to finish the chore. The organs are quickly placed in surgical pans for later study as the regeneration progresses. The heart, the liver, the kidneys, the spleen, one by one. All are removed until Chandler is hollowed out.

Tears well. She has become an abomination to herself. Chandler has his wish. But from this point forward, she proclaims, he will have to find another to carry out his executions. Checking that the video feeds and the data recorders are engaged, she retreats to the cabin and showers, eventually finding herself sobbing on the shower floor. Seated, she clutches her knees to her chest until every drop of hot water is exhausted.

Dried and clothed, she pours a glass of wine, white. Red is too much in her memory. She chases it with a shot of Wild Turkey from a bottle left by the hunters. When he returns, Chandler will be on his own. She cannot oblige his lust for the love of death any longer.

Forty Seven
Present Day

"Hello, sir?" Traeger hears from behind him while fumbling in the darkness of his front stoop for his door key. The day has been a long grind and an unexpected visitor is an unwelcome interruption. Traeger turns to see a man approaching up the steps below.

"Sir, I'm sorry to bother you this late. Are you Alex Traeger?"

"Yes, I am."

The stranger reaches inside his overcoat, produces a folded document and hands it to Traeger. "Alex Traeger, you have been served."

Simultaneously, Traeger's heart sinks and his mind whirrs at the possibilities. Through the door, he randomly deposits his coat and satchel on the nearest surface. His first thought is a subpoena for loose end to the William Reader investigation. After reading the first few sentences, he wishes it were that. His heart sinks further. Once again, his ex-wife has found a new way to exact pain upon his soul.

He begins a text message and stops. He dials his lawyer and hangs up, words of reason escaping his grasp, drowned in despair. He falls into his couch, numb and hopeless. He reads the document again, trying to digest the legal-speak while blurred by a turbulent fog of putrid emotion. She has assumed temporary, full custody of their children with a motion to gain permanent status on the grounds that he has violated their custody agreement. The violations are ticked off one by one in the document: missed school events and teacher conferences, recitals and ball games. He even missed mid-week visitations. The most stinging rebuke is they are all inarguable. His work schedule is the culprit, but they are commitments of necessity to keep the child support payments up to date as well as his own Spartan existence. And it isn't just the work itself, he is bound contractually by Carpenter to remain silent about the true nature of his work.

He wants to cry, but ire prevents it. Reluctant resignation swoops in. He thinks that, in some way this bitter moment was inevitable; the burdens and responsibilities born of his obligations made it impossible for him to come out the victor here, or to even play in the game. And he is well aware that, for Valerie, it is indeed a game. Her goal has always been to paint him out of their lives. It's her nature to find sustenance in shadowy triumph. He allows himself a morsel of self-forgiveness, but still the weight crushes down, breaking his spirit once again. He starts another phone call.

"Hi, Alex. I was expecting you," Traeger's lawyer answers.

"Hi, Jim, sorry to bother you so late. I just got served and..."

"Yeah, I just got back to the office and saw this. I am filing a motion tomorrow. But I have to be honest with you, this is quite a laundry list of violations against the settlement terms. I wish you would have given me a heads-up a long time ago. We could have headed this thing off at the pass. Now it's an uphill climb. We could be tied up for six months to a year with this, maybe longer." He pauses, expecting a reply. Silence is the only sound, Traeger too frozen from devastation. "Alex?" he mildly asks.

"Yeah," Traeger sighs.

"Look, sorry to be so blunt. You know me, I'm not going to blow smoke up your ass. I just wanted to prepare you for what's ahead."

"I know. See what you can do. You know Valerie, though. We can't count on any mercy coming from her direction."

"Alright, Alex. I'll let you know."

The conversation over, Traeger sits stunned, feeling more alone than he can ever remember. Pushing past his own reflex to recite a litany of excuses to himself to rationalize his dilemma, he rapidly acquiesces to the inevitability that his own actions brought this on. But, to be sure, Valerie's own appetite for false vengeance has played a role. The cold aloneness enveloping him is his to own, but he thinks she could have approached him before taking the legal route. The thought occurs to him that maybe one can never be fully divorced. 'Til death do us part is indeed just that.

Forty Eight
Present Day

All around her the tired timbers of the cabin creek weary, the sound of worn wood struggling to bear great weight from above. Despite it being three days ago, she still feels the prickly sting of slicing a living man into chunks and pieces. The images remain seared as fresh wounds in her psyche. Sleeping has proved jagged and raw. Closing her eyes brings vivid images of healthy organs being ripped from their moorings. A steaming cup of chicory, the only grind left by the hunters, is weak refuge.

Outside, birds call to each other in the crisp morning air. The songs are familiar, ones known from childhood, but the species escape her. Her grandfather knew them all, painstakingly schooling her on their names and vocalizations, wisdom imparted decades ago, misplaced somewhere in the space between innocence and the present day. She curls herself tighter in the chair and brings another sip of the bitter brew to her lips from a pottery mug. A surrogate chalice cupped by her delicate, slender, butchering hands.

"Would you like a warm-up?"

She lurches, spilling down her sweatshirt. Chandler's ragged frame looms over her zombie-like.

"Is there enough for me to have a cup?"

"Christ, Chandler, you could give a girl a heads up. You almost gave me a fucking heart attack, and in case you forgot, some of us don't rise again after we die." Unable to look away, her eyes remain riveted on Chandler and his resurrected form.

"Sorry. I thought you heard me come in. You looked pretty deep in thought, though."

"Yeah, there's plenty, help yourself."

"Don't worry, Patricia. It isn't like the coffee will come shooting out of my wounds like the Bellagio fountains," Chandler quips on the way to the coffee pot.

"By the way, Chandler. You look positively radiant for a guy who was blue a couple days ago."

Chandler pours his own cup and adds five teaspoons of sugar to the mug. He shuffles to a wicker chair opposite Hamer near the hearth. She stares at him in awe both to marvel and to observe. He is ashen and disheveled. His movements come off a bit jerky, as if his brain is still reconfiguring the wiring.

"I guess you like your coffee on the sweet side."

"During the recovery, the body craves sugar carbs. In a few hours it will all be about protein replenishment. You remember me telling you that."

"Yes, who can forget the sight of you shoving four hamburgers down your gullet? Look, Chandler, I can't do this anymore. You're going to have to find a new way to... "

"Don't worry about it. I saw your face after your spiked my forehead. You looked pretty horrified."

"Saw my face? How did you see my face?"

"When my spirit rose out of my body. I was above you."

"Stop, Chandler."

"Whatever, Pat. You will find out soon enough. Anyway, I had an inspiration during my return to the living. I'm going to start a community to pair Eternals with people who crave the kill for sport. A match made in heaven." He grins at his own brilliance.

"As long as I'm out of the picture then go for it. Do you know how massively perverse that is? Just saying, Chandler."

Chandler sips from his cup, a leftover from a pick-me-up bouquet reading "Rise and Shine". He stares into the distance, perhaps contemplating the birth of his killing club.

"Marcus, while you were… *reconstituting,* my research revealed some rather unexpected findings in the tissue data. It looks like some foreign DNA was introduced, melded to yours. What do you know about that?"

"Is that really a surprise?" Chandler replies, almost irritated. "The whole thing back then was about DNA, and my role was strictly to create environments to culture the raw product, not obtain it. So, I don't know jack about that."

"I know, but it doesn't appear to be anything cultured in a lab, or native to your own. I was expecting some sort of synthesis, like a made-up gene or something, but there is a distinct strand of genetic material that has been introduced, spliced in. And, by the way, the equipment you loaned me was immensely helpful."

"Yes, Brandt's rejects. I knew they'd come in handy someday." Chandler adopts a more understanding tone. "Look, I don't have any idea about the DNA, though. You may be right, but I really have no idea."

"I guess what I am asking is where it came from. What is its origin?"

"Hell if I know."

"Think, Chandler," she buzzes with slight irritation.

Chandler ambles back to the kitchen for more chicory. He empties the pot, turning to Hamer and raising the carafe. She responds by shaking her head. Chandler spoons in more sugar. At the third spoonful he pauses. "How do you know it wasn't cultured?"

"There are hallmarks to it. It's not constructed like GMO, at least any I have ever seen. It's too arcane to go into. The strand is evolutionary, not manufactured or welded together, at least not the way I would expect it. It's hard to explain. I could if you had eight years of genomic forensic training, a PhD in molecular biology, and seventeen years' experience in the field."
"Well, whoop-de-doo." Chandler rolls his eyes.

"Trust me, Marcus."

Chandler reclaims his seat. Hamer continues.

"Look, this whole business with the cardinal. You say it was an opportunity for high-profile PR and a means to test the process on a large database grounded in historical context, right?"

"That's what Brandt sold us."

"What if the whole scope was just to gain access to a vast archive of genetic material? What if the test was really the target?"

"I don't follow, Pat."

The momentum of her accelerating thoughts pushes her to the edge of the couch. Her eyes fix directly at Chandler. "Just hypothetically, we are assuming the whole Vatican thing was some outreach to draw positive attention. What if the relics were truly what Brandt was after in the first place?"

"Again, I'm lost here."

Hamer rises from her chair. Feeling more centered in herself, her ears detect a familiar call. "That's a tanager. Do you hear that? The rapid chirps?"

"I guess. I hear a lot of birds out there. What's your point?"

Hamer turns back to him. Her eyes move past him and lock on a sturdy timber standing robust among the weathered others. "Marcus, we are assuming the end game was something new and innovative, an advancement, a leap into the future. But what if the grand prize wasn't that at all. Maybe it was all about collecting something ancient, some secret genetic Rosetta stone."

"Pat, as I understand evolution and genetics, *old*, at least by our standards, is still new in evolutionary terms. The Vatican stuff wasn't even human DNA; we're talking about relics and objects. There isn't any human DNA in any of the artifacts that we tested. We weren't even testing the DNA of the artifacts; we were after things like pollen and insect remains attached to the objects, things that would indicate a time and place. The authentication was based in determining context related to the item, not in the actual item itself. It was all about establishing a timestamp to the relic. I think you're barking up the wrong tree, my dear. The Vatican thing was a beta test."

"So, this Adeline Brandt, in the course of your time with her, what got her excited?"

"Nothing, I think she was asexual," Chandler returns with a crooked smile. Hamer shames him with the tilt of her head. He capitulates, accepting the scorn. "Her work got her excited. She was single-focused on whatever her end-game was. And she managed to get that accomplished without any of us really knowing what the final goal was, it seems."

"Eternal life, presumably."

"Yes, we know that now, but our tasks were compartmentalized. As far as I know, only she knew where it was going. She never made any overtures that reached my ears that she was taking us down the road to immortality, at least not during the project. After it was done, she just included me in the Eternals class, and I have no idea how she put that together."

"So, when the items from the Vatican arrived what was her reaction?"

"She was ecstatic."

"Because?"

"I don't know; because it was old and she finally had fodder to test her method."

"Exactly. These items. I mean, the Vatican archive is a documented, catalogued library of objects. There isn't another entity in the world that has that kind of archive, and if the relics were to draw worldwide attention, then why go dark after that?"

"I don't get it, Pat."

"Your project was authenticating artifacts that had preliminary historical context for the end-game of gaining global attention for your genetic chops. Why then, after doing all that, did she disappear?

"Good point." Chandler's eyebrows rise.

"It just makes more sense that the Vatican archive is the real target." Hamer's pace quickens. "If one is searching for ancient DNA, then the hard work has already been done. If she was after something specific then she would know exactly what to harvest."

"But we harvested and tested everything they gave us. She didn't select or prioritize anything."

Still standing, Hamer turns to look out the window again, casting her eyes on the denseness of the woods. "But that's what one would do to cover their tracks. She's a smart woman. You test everything to disguise the fact that you are only after one specific thing. I don't suppose you have a detailed list of the items you guys tested lying around anywhere."

"No, and again, woof-woof, wrong tree, my dear."

"Chandler, my Bible knowledge is sketchy. But in the Old Testament there are references to people living to be hundreds of years old, you know, Methuselah and the like?"

"But that's all myth," Chandler responds smarmily. "You really don't believe they lived to be..."

"Ok, maybe not nine hundred years, but maybe a whole lot longer than anyone else in that age, or older than we can live now. Maybe there was a regenerative gene that somehow went dormant or evolved out of our gene pool several thousands of years ago. Maybe Brandt was after that and then found it, then perfected it."

"I don't know, Pat. That sounds a tad far-fetched."

"Says the man who can never die."

Forty Nine
Present Day

Without the presence of a bed, the room would be unrecognizable as a bedroom. A twenty-foot ceiling supported by roughly hewn timbers makes the space more suited for a gathering lodge. The furniture appears small in proportion despite being custom-crafted as oversized, chunky natural wood in western chic. The knotted pine planks of the floor wear skins and furs from rare animals. A massive picture window looks out over a lush valley spreading far into the distance. A lifting fog still pillows green rolling hills. Morning rays of light peek in, painting streaks across silken white sheets tangled among two perfect bodies. A woman rests her head on a man's toned chest, long raven locks snake down his chiseled torso. Her hand roams his taut abdomen, fingers tracing each rigidly defined feature of his firm mid-section. Cradled in one arm, her hair slithers between the fingers of his free hand.

"Tell me about your dream, James."

"It was striking and vivid. The colors and the images, almost real. No, *more* real than real. I was atop a mountain looking down upon the world. Below me were the good people of the earth so thankful and grateful."

"Grateful for what? You, James?" she whispers admiringly from her perfect lips.

"I believe that to be so."

"Grateful because you have saved them from death? For the good works you have bestowed upon them? For the promise of a world in peace?"

"It seemed that's what it could be," Carpenter ponders aloud. "I have always felt at the core of who I am, I've been called to being just that. We have talked of that before, Marianne. And I thank you for reminding me when I need to be."

She raises her head slightly to capture his eyes with hers. Her hand finds his chest and then glides down by the tips of her fingers, carving rows in the dark curls with nails lacquered in deep, regal purple.

"Yes, my dear. Soon we will reveal the blessing of eternal life to all, and you must be ready to accept your greatness with no indecision. There will be many who will challenge you. With power comes jealous resistance from others." Her soft tone dissolves giving in to one more forceful and determined. "You are the one. They are devils who would try to steal from you your rightful place. And once they realize the fullness of your greatness, they will try to usurp your reign."

She looks deeper into him. She tugs his chin to bring his eyes directly into hers. "Remember, most of those who currently hold power and knowledge are now committed because they know they will retain their position indefinitely. But it must also be made clear that they answer to you. You have given them this gift and they must never forget it."

He nods. She is calmed and her head returns to his chest, rising and sinking with each breath he takes. Carpenter clutches her closer and whispers in her ear. "You are my strength, my love. Without you, these things could never be. Together we are stronger than armies, stronger even than God."

Fifty
Present Day

"You do know if we get caught, Ivan, that it will literally cost me my life. If we are found out, I will be out of the Eternals picture here, and have no professional future. My career will be over and eventually so will I."

"It's okay, Christy. If stopped, just say you misplaced your badge and I will take the hit for us both. Now go back to your room. I'll get you your badge back in the morning. I'll find some work to be done in your guest wing."

"Oh no you don't. I need to see whatever you discover first-hand. I'm not leaving subjective details up to your vivid imagination."

"Are you sure? I can handle it by myself."

"I'm going with you or you're not going," she proclaims.

"I don't suppose some of this is driven by your investigative curiosity, hmmm?" Myer grins at a return of the woman most familiar to him.

"Of course it is, but that doesn't mean the rest of what I just said doesn't matter either," she reiterates with emphasis.

The quarter moon makes silhouettes of their faces. A slight breeze whistles through tree branches mixed with the odd rustle of bat's wings.

"So, Christy, this is important," Myer says, his playfulness retired. "You need to walk behind me and stay close. I know where the cameras are located and where the dead zones are in the array. Do you understand?" She nods. "Alright, from now on speak as little as possible and do as I do."

Myer leads her through an invisible labyrinth of motion-sensitive security, sometimes crawling, squatting, or pressing their bodies against walls and sliding past. Eventually, they make their way into a concrete service stairwell going down.

"This is where we go in. As soon as the door opens, go hard against the right wall then down on your stomach, then swim to the right across the floor," Myer whispers below a whisper. "At the corridor, take a right and then you can stand up."

Raines looks concerned. Myer reads her.

"Don't worry, dear. This place is a lab; there's not a speck of dust anywhere. You're more likely to make the floor dirtier than it is now when you slide across it."

Myer removes a tablet device from his pocket.

"What's that, Ivan?" Raines asks warily.

"It's a remote pad to the security system. I got a guy to program the reader as if it's in a different location, but it's timed for an eight-second reversion. It has to be temporary or the system will eventually detect it. You should know it's going to show as the entry to your living sector in case you are asked about it, but you won't be. Ready?"

Twisting and turning, they traverse a darkened hallway to thick metal double doors. He pushes on the left door. The soft whoosh of a vacuum seal being broken greets them. The Carpenter Institute lab stands before them. White coats hang next to work stations loaded with precision equipment. Cooling fans gently hum amid scattered bluish lighting, the apparent night mode of the lab.

"Ivan, with all the security around here, and you're telling me the lab has no entry fob or key pad? It's not even locked."

"There are no cameras either, Christy. I was down here once before to service a lunch for the staff. I wandered down here and found that out. It's really what got my curiosity going. It made no sense until I realized they are doing something here they don't want any visual record of, even for security purposes. They don't trust their campus security people enough to even do the security here."

"But what about the people who work here?"

"I'm guessing they are loyal to the cause. The best security is knowing the people who work for you are doing it because you hold their future in their hands. If you can promise eternal life, then who's going to steal from you or give away your secrets?"

"Why only here, though? Raines whispers confounded. "Why not just be that way on the whole campus?"

"Apparently, there are only a chosen few in the inner circle. When I hired on, they never promised anything but a paycheck and some nominal benefits. General staff is merely the hired help; they're told this is a spa and spiritual retreat."

"When you served lunch down here, how many was it for? And why do they let the hired help serve in this location?"

"Maybe a dozen diners, and we were told this is where they develop spa retail products," Myer curtly responds, wishing to get back to the search. "We should start looking around. We need to get you back by the end of the meditation period. Why don't you start over there? I'll work in this area."

"What are we looking for?"

"I have no idea, really. And try not to move anything."

Myer monitors his movements, gently, deliberately placing each step across the raised tile floor. Desktops are bare, no computers left about, no phones, family pictures or tchotchkes. Even name-plates are absent.

"Ivan, come over here," Raines whispers intently while waving him over. Myer obeys.

"Over there, Ivan, see that big chrome tub that looks like a ginormous soup pot or pressure cooker? That's a cryonic freezer. During the bird flu scare I did some NIH coverage and they had several just like that. They used it to store dangerous strains of viruses for research."

"There's a bookshelf over there that had some binders titled *Viral Genome Trials* something or other. What would viruses have to do with genes, Christy?"

"Everything living deals with genes sooner or later, I would think."

"I'm going to check out that corner office." Myer tilts his head to look. "The boss always has the corner office no matter where you are."

He cautiously opens the corner office door. He spies a picture on the wall. "Yep, this is the boss's office." Raines joins him. "You know it's the boss—it's the only personal photo in this entire lab, the only photo period, and of all the photos to pick. Who do you think that guy is?"

"The nameplate says *her* name is Adeline Brandt. Ever heard of her, Ivan?"

"Never, and I think I would remember that face."

Fifty One
Present Day

"And this, Alex, this is the Great Hall." James Carpenter plays tour guide for his Institute's prospective architect. "This is where it all begins for those entering the Institute, their first impression. This was the centerpiece of the original structure, a place for dignitaries to meet and plan the future of the world. Unfortunately for them, those hopes were never realized."

"Yes, James, the original structure was commissioned by J.P. Morgan in 1903 as a retreat for Theodore Roosevelt. But that never materialized. It was two years in the making, but Roosevelt never set foot here, preferring the western United States for his adventures," Traeger follows with his deeper knowledge.

"You've done your homework. I'm very impressed." Carpenter sends his approval with a grin.

Traeger strolls inquisitively but reverently, drinking in the majestic room on his way to the center of the hall. He gauges the immensity of the space, soaking in its stately prowess. He rotates with focused deliberation to view the three walls and down the corridor opposite the huge hearth. "These windows are new, though. The original design did not have floor-to-ceiling glass. They were windows of awesome scale for the era, I'm sure. But the technology did not exist for floor-to-ceiling panes."

"Correct, those were added in the early seventies when it was renovated for Hugh Hefner's Playboy resort," Carpenter contributes.

Traeger chuckles a bit. "I seemed to have missed that tidbit. Fascinating." Traeger turns to engage Carpenter. "You see the space here, the four directions? Do you grasp the brilliance of the concept?"

"I don't have any idea what you are talking about, Alex."

"The four elements are represented here, each at one of the four directions. It couldn't be a coincidence." Traeger nods admiringly to his architectural predecessor. "See here, the wall of glass to view the Earth, to actually bring it into the space, the water feature over across the way covering the entire wall, the expansive hearth for fire, and down the corridor, air, open space. It's marvelous."

"More research on your part? I don't ever recall anyone pointing that out."

"I didn't research that. It's a practiced eye. Buildings of this magnitude always contain structural metaphors of mythological scale. Given the profile of the fellow who funded the project to begin with, I would expect features like this." Traeger lectures as a spontaneous professor patiently strolling his classroom. "They are always built into the architecture. Elites like being immersed in grandiosity; they deign to allow themselves to consider their own Olympian importance. This room is a reflection of that. The sheer size of it alone does, but then there is the virtual harnessing of the elements, the self-permission to rule over them. You can't escape it being in this room, surrounded by them residing at each point of the compass. They are symbolically beholden to the occupier of the center. Orbiting, like planets around the sun, as if you are God himself."

Carpenter joins Traeger in the center of the room and takes a look around to experience the view first hand.

"Yes, Alex, it is as you say; such an insightful observation. If I may ask," Carpenter approaches to request something more intimate. "Do you hold any disdain for such grandiosity, for people of that *realm*, ones who consider their own importance?"

Traeger ponders the nature of the question briefly. Perhaps it is a test, he thinks. He decides to answer frankly. "No, not really. I don't understand why, but, I feel some are born to it. We owe many of the great achievements of humankind's progress to individuals with visions of expansive scope. Individuals like that are vital to progress."

189

"Do you think it is born of arrogance and conceit? That people cut from such rare cloth are unworthy to assume power equal to their vision?"

"I guess it's not my place to judge them. I suppose they have their reasons. As long as they don't interfere with my life in a negative way, then they can do whatever they want." Traeger smiles a cautious grin. "Within reason, of course."

"Would you consider myself to be one of those people, Alex?"

Traeger is taken aback at Carpenter's directness and desire for candor. "Yes and no…, you clearly have a knack for envisioning change at a global level and are very successful at achieving it." Traeger meets Carpenter's eyes and speaks from the heart. "You seem different. You seem genuine in your concern for the betterment of the planet. If the world is a better place for it, then I see no reason why you shouldn't enjoy the rewards that blossom as a result."

Carpenter wraps an arm around Traeger. He exhales a sigh of relief. "Very good, Alex." The embrace over, Carpenter smiles and says, "We should continue our journey. Follow me."

Carpenter shows off the entire Institute to Traeger on an hour-long tour via golf cart. The final stop is a flagstone courtyard area shaded by a sprawling awning that resembles a right-angle sail for a catamaran or some other modern vessel. A fire pit glows across the way. Wading pools and surrounding lounge areas dot the expansive patio. Carpenter chooses a private spot at one end, but near one of the larger pools. Two attendants materialize to bring fruit, cheese, and small loaves of warm bread. One pours vintage red wine into two large crystal goblets. Carpenter raises his glass in Traeger's direction. Traeger returns the gesture.

"Salut, good sir. I do hope the tour has left you duly impressed, Alex. I want you to understand the level of our commitment here. We seek those Olympian heights, to use your term. We want to reach even beyond that."
"Honestly, Mr. Carpenter…"

"You've forgotten. I'm *James*, Alex." He casts a friendly smile to Traeger.

"*James*. I can't imagine why you need me at all. This facility and the additions you have made are state of the art. I believe I would be superfluous. Whoever designed all this is surely more capable than I am."

"Yes, that would be Lenholm Whittier. He is booked for the next two and a half years. Besides, his specialty, although brilliant in its own right, lacks a measure of depth." Carpenter swirls his wine and sips looking for his next thought. "He crafts soothing environments, ones with efficiency and economy of accoutrement, ones of seamless continuity for multi-use spaces." Carpenter leans in, his eyes more intense to express a bold thought. "But in the next phase, we are looking for something to define the ensuing evolution of spiritual awakening for the planet. The Carpenter Institute has always stood for greater awakening of the collective of humanity, but it has always been limited to the present, the here and now."

Carpenter lays one hand over Traeger's. "Alex, over one-hundred years ago, J. P. Morgan had a vision for this building and its surroundings to make a statement equal to his stature. We are looking for the same thing, but for a vision that will have unending impact."

Traeger pauses, realizing the level of ambition Carpenter is professing and coming up short on how he himself can add anything to that. He knows the job is his, but he is unsure of why Carpenter insists that he take it. "That's really quite ambitious, but I guess it leads me back to my original question. Why me?"

"I know your work, Alex. You can look at a structure and read its soul. You understand the spiritual footprint the structure assumes, the connection it has with those who use it and the community it represents."

"If I may," Traeger penetrates past polite vagaries. "What is it you will be doing here that is different from today?"

"We will be expanding our current operation, not just here but through other venues across the globe. We are expecting millions, perhaps billions of followers in the next few years, so we will need a standardized venue that can be duplicated and adapted to varying conditions."

"Billions?" Traeger's eyes betray some creeping doubt. He wonders if the man is being honest with himself. "That *is* ambitious. So, will the functionality be the same there as here?"

"Essentially, but on a much smaller scale. The research side will all be handled here. The standardized venues will be communal vessels, gathering places capable of bringing forth the good word of our movement and where the community of followers can congregate. It must also be able to continue our physical wellness programs. So there will be some need for a clinical capacity too. We will get more into the details of that as things progress. Does any of that seem out of bounds for you and your architectural prowess?"

"Not that I can see," Traeger boasts past his own internal doubts of his abilities. "I may need to bring in technical experts depending on the nature and complexity of the clinical aspects."

"We will also be expanding this venue in a way that lends more emphasis to being a... a mecca of sorts, for lack of a better phrase. As we expand, we want the satellite venues to be remote projectors of the activity here at the Institute, guiding the followers with a consistent, universal vision. As the movement becomes more unified in message, we will bring the focus more and more to the activities and thoughts professed here. So, the evolution of thought must be reflected in the structure itself. It must be dynamic and forceful, grand in scale and..."

"Olympian, yes. You are describing a cathedral, James."

"Perhaps." Carpenter strokes his immaculately trimmed beard, appearing to grow more agreeable to Traeger's description. "I never thought of it in that way. If that's the concept that gives you a starting point, then, so be it."

Carpenter gently falls back in his chair, gazes to the blue sky, and sips from his goblet. "Kevin," Carpenter addresses the closest attendant. "Can you plate some of this fine fruit and cheese for our good friend?" Carpenter leans forward to clutch one of the mini loaves of bread. He tears it in half and hands one piece to Traeger. "To our long friendship, Alex."

"But we really haven't made any decisions on—"

"Start something, bring it to me in...?" Carpenter looks to Traeger to fill in the blank.

"Three weeks," Traeger replies, following with a bite of the loaf and a sip of wine.

"Very well, I will see you in three weeks. In the meantime, do not hesitate to come to the Institute and wander about for inspiration. I will provide two site assistants to support anything you require. They will contact you in a day or two."

Traeger, sensing the work portion is over, leans back into lush white cushions. He sips generously from his glass, drinking in the lush atmosphere with the wine. As the sun fades, leaving the warm day to gently succumb to a cooling breeze, he decides he could get used to luxuriating in the surroundings and importance of this place.

His eyes wander shut, leaving his ears to detect a distant splashing, a gentle movement from the pool beside them. He eases his eyelids open. His vision beholds the emerging silhouette of the most perfectly fashioned woman he has ever seen. Bit by bit, she rises from the pool as if the water was taking human form to rise up as Eve herself. The pool's gentle tapering sides, more like the shore of a lake than a swimming pool, bring her out gradually. Her glistening form floats to Carpenter. He leans his head back to meet her lips. Traeger rises from his chair at her arrival.

"Alex, your manners are impeccable but completely unnecessary. I'd like you to meet my savior. This is Marianne."

"Please ignore James' dismissal of manners." She smiles playfully at Carpenter and then looks to Traeger still smiling. "Chivalry never gets old. A lady always appreciates a pedestal."

Traeger is trying to remain composed, but he is stunned at her flawless beauty. Black hair, made silken from the pool, drapes to the small of her back. Her figure is impeccably curved and postured for allure. Her seductive, black eyes seem of infinite depth. He reaches across and meets her hand with his. "I'm honored, Miss...?"

"Marianne is fine, Alex," spirits from her plump scarlet lips. "We are so glad to welcome you as a member of our family."

Fifty Two
August 23, 1986

"Professor Reader, I thought I owed you some one-on-one time. Let me apologize for leaving you in the dark for so long. Now is a good time to enlighten you with some context," offers Adeline Brandt to her project colleague.

Seated in her ubiquitous roller chair behind her desk, she towers over Reader who is sitting across from her. Reader's left leg is bouncing on the ball of its foot, a nervous, unconscious tic venting unprocessed random thoughts. Involuntary detox for the genius mind.

"I was becoming concerned," he returns, showing some relief. "Smearing slides was not my expectation going in. Honestly, I know lab interns who do more important work."

"First and foremost let me assure you, I am fully aware of your brilliance. You bring an extraordinary mind to the mix, a counterpoint perspective. The primary reason I brought you here is because of your body of work. If I may ask, why do *you* suppose we added you to this team?"

"I could only speculate."

"Please do."

Reader glances at Brandt to measure her sincerity and decides she is genuine. "My work is in cultural theory, grand scale human interaction. As far as I can discern the scope of this project, it has thus far been dedicated to establishing some sort of baseline to a further end. You and Kipner are geneticists, Smith and Jones are the money, it seems. Chandler is the engineer and Kovacs the conduit for the artifacts." The roster completed, Reader shows some weariness at the remedial recitation of the obvious.

"Yes, correct, but what about you?"

"Again, I have no idea."

"Doctor Reader, your theories," she professes in reserved admiration. "I want you to contemplate something. Do you ever imagine that you will survive to witness firsthand the fruits of your work borne out in the real world?"

Brandt's query whets Reader's innate curiosity. "I am not sure I follow. Could you be more direct?"

"Every scientist and every great thinker has the dream that someday their life's efforts, and the benefits they bestow, will unfold before their very eyes, fleshed out from the theoretical realm to live and breathe in concrete reality."

"I suppose. But, in my estimation, it will take humanity a full century to catch up to the ideas I have constructed. Mankind hasn't evolved to the point where, even if it were possible, the change would be a positive one." He pauses to observe if Brandt understands. He decides more explanation is required. "The process cannot be sped up. I have studied this at great length. Forcing social models into existence where society is not prepared to accept them leads to chaos or even tyranny. I am resolved within myself that I will never see the germination of the seeds I have planted."

"What if you could, though? What would that be worth to you?

"But I can't, so there is no further discussion to be had."

"But..." She adds some implication to her expression. "What if you could?"

Her question pierces Reader's veil of stubbornness. He hesitates, reluctant to expose any vulnerability. Nevertheless, he capitulates. "It would be worth a great deal to me, if you must know."

"Doctor Reader, I am going to confide in you to a greater level than I have with any of the other members of the team." She leans back in her chair, more relaxed. "I know I can trust you to keep this confidential." She pauses for a response.

"Yes, go on."

"Even then, I am certain if that is not persuasion enough, the knowledge I am about to impart will ensure you will remain loyal to our confidence here."

"Very well." Reader sighs, again growing impatient at the slow unfolding of information. "If I may say, Doctor Brandt, you can ramble a bit. Please get to your point."

She forges ahead past Reader's over-frankness. "When we are done cataloguing and processing the artifacts, I believe I will have isolated a means to extend life well beyond our current limitations, if not bring immortality to the brink of reality."

Reader's face wears a wary smile of skepticism. "With all due respect, I seriously doubt that. But, let's just say you can. What do you need me for?"

She leans in, mustering greater conviction. "Let's say I can, Professor. Speculate, if you will, on the impact to the cultural landscape?'

Reader's leg begins bouncing in double time. His head rolls back slightly to gaze at the ceiling as he drills his full, trance-like focus into the question. He exhales in staccato bursts. "The change to society is too immense to ponder so as to arrive at a succinct, momentary response to that scenario. But, the impact would most certainly be tectonic social upheaval. If everyone were not included in the opportunity, then the critical dividing line would be immortality itself, the ultimate *have* versus *have-not*."

Reader pulls his eyes from the ceiling and looks directly into hers. She flinches a bit at his intensity. "If all were included, then it might lend one to initially conclude that a freer society might develop, but I could imagine that the lack of finality to one's existence might bring about a complacency among individuals who have no further incentive to progress from one day to the next. Indeed, many might regress to a state of frivolity, leisure, and stagnation." She tries to interrupt, but his momentum overwhelms her. "Scarcity would develop as a result of greater population. Although, many might choose to forgo traditional families as the centerpiece of society. There might be a counter to the innate desire for procreation as people become less dependent upon others, dissolving into greater isolation and developing a fierce independence to the cost of all else. One must also consider—"

"Professor," she finds an opening to interject. "I appreciate the thorough analysis but now *you* are rambling a bit." Brandt punctuates her parry with a grin. "The point is, Doctor, I do not take the consequences of this lightly. The shock to the system at a global level is monumental. Now maybe you understand why you are critical to the team and the project as a whole. I plan to pursue my objectives, but I want you at my side to consider the ramifications and to advise me as the project unfolds."

"I can do that, Doctor Brandt," he avows, firming his posture, now more emboldened. "I see now that my role is actually more important than anyone's on the team." Reader looks deeper into Brandt, his brilliant mind spinning its analysis. "Doctor, your goals seem noble, but you are most certainly aware of the concept of the road to hell being paved with good intentions."

"I have heard that expression, but I don't believe in hell."

"I don't suppose I do either. So, if I may, exactly how does a collection of artifacts from the Vatican bring you a means to eternal life?"

"Lest I be thought a fool, Professor Reader, I will reserve that information for myself until further notice. It will be revealed at the proper time.

Fifty Three
May 4, 1988

The news from the bomb shelter was a moment of triumph. The theoretical made real. Adeline Brandt celebrated the breakthrough moment alone in the Spartan surroundings of her cell-like efficiency apartment. Her libation, crème de menthe, the only alcohol on hand, was purchased years before for a holiday dessert recipe and now sipped from a thrift-store juice glass.

Since that celebratory breakthrough day, nine months of frustration has reigned. Adeline Brandt remains convinced that the sample from the bomb shelter labelled "471K8D" is destined to change the world. But divining a method to deliver the findings to living humans has so far eluded her. Follow-up experimentation has confirmed the gene is real. The science is sound. All that stands in the way of full success is to cobble a way of stabilizing the regenerative effect.

Each attempt at fusing foreign human tissue has met with failure. Some trials yielded promise but eventually disintegrated, as if the process collapsed under its own weight. She suspects ordinary human cellular makeup is too fragile to accept the robustness of the infused genetic material and simply rejects it. Her impression as to what is causing the process to arrest, although unscientific, is that the new material is somehow too refined, too disconnected from its origin, as if its point of reference is uncertain.

She decides the new DNA must be brought forth whole, not introduced. It must have a universe of its own where the DNA has been cultured from whole cloth. She must make it flesh.

Pacing her apartment, her elevated intellect churns for a solution. She knows it will not fail her, it never does. Pride pours through her, every nerve firing at peak efficiency. There is an otherworld clarity she assumes in these peak moments of building brilliance as the answer gestates within. Abruptly, her own reflection from a window robs her of her moment. The dark night beyond allows her illuminated form to stare back at her across the room from a rippled, distorted pane. In the course of her life, she has taken great care to remove all reflective surfaces from the spaces she inhabits; her own appearance stirs distress.

Seeking comfort, she turns her thoughts to further glory and her next breakthrough. She imagines Chandler could build an incubation environment, one to bring the DNA to greater fruition, cultured beyond mere replication. Would it be enough, she wonders. The thought of it enlivens her being with vitality and purpose.

The reverse image leers back again. Her blocky, troll-like, frame shames her. God's curse for some undeclared sin. Pain lingers from childhood. Cruelty, rejection, and isolation run her through. It is a shame wrought merely of random genetic misfortune. Even her own parents shunned her. They could not hide their disappointment as they watched other children make friends and bask in the warmth of mutual acceptance. They lamented being overlooked by other parents, excluded from the camaraderie of school functions, dances, and dinner parties. Even Brandt's own brilliance was isolating, not just from peers, but from her own parents who floundered in intellectual normalcy. Throughout her childhood, she was shipped off to camps set aside for the genius and gifted. By the time she was fourteen, her intelligence well surpassed that of her mother and father, resulting in even greater distance between them. She looked away, turning to science as refuge. It has become her eternal savior, her truest friend.

Like a whisper from beyond, something tickles her intellect. A solution exists, but not yet apparent. The whisper grows. It is nearly palpable, her genius shaping the clay, chiseling the marble in her mind. Deeper into the window, she stares at the reflection. Out of character, allowing some measure of grace to arrive, she awkwardly tries, daringly, to love what she sees, to embrace the person in the uneven glass. Innocently and genuinely, she searches to adore herself with no idea what that could even feel like. She realizes she has never loved anything and no one has ever truly loved her.

The fullness of her loneliness and loathsome existence instantly unleashes a wave of brackish despair accumulated over a lifetime. Aloneness crushes her. Tears flow unrestrained, bringing her to her knees, then to the floor where she lies on one side, helpless. She desperately wraps herself in her own arms, knees tucked close. She cannot hold tight enough. The emptiness is winning. The darkness grows.

The whispering voice arrives to rescue her, now speaking with full throat. In a single moment, as rapidly as it fell upon her, tears of sadness become tears of delight. Glee and hope abound. A sense of utter joy shoots through, like a spirit sweeping through to remove all the shadows. Love abides now, or so it feels. How would she know if it was? It brings with it an epiphany of utter purity. The riddle is solved.

She will bear the child.

It is perfect. She will create the life, a replica, a clone. She will love it unconditionally with equal love returned. A child to usher in a new age, one to heal the planet, one to heal herself. A child born out of desperation and conceived to wear a crown of hope to all.

Fifty Four
Present Day

He's late. They agreed on nine o'clock, but Ivan Myer has yet to arrive. Fifteen minutes isn't a long time, but given the circumstances, the clandestine mission the night before, Christy Raines is beginning to worry. Thoughts of the worst begin to churn. Myer's plan included reliance on third parties introduced to the conversation with the leading phrase, "I've got a guy." She is well aware his instincts are always spot-on, but his application of common sense is sometimes lacking. She takes solace in the fact that she would have been escorted from the grounds by now if Myer's espionage had been discovered.

Her phone vibrates. A chill rattles her spine. It's a text from Carpenter instructing her to come to his office immediately. Her heart grinds away in her chest, sweat beads at her hairline. She tries to imagine Carpenter angry. It doesn't seem in his nature. She supposes she will learn the truth very soon. She walks the final ten strides down the corridor of his office as if stepping to the gallows.

"Christy, good morning." Carpenter greets her with his customary kiss on the lips and embrace. She gasps out unexpected relief. "Goodness, Christy. I can feel your tension. What's the matter?"

"Oh… I don't know… I … I just…"

"Look," Carpenter interrupts to allow her a moment to calm herself. "I want you to bring the crew to the lab with me. You need to meet our brilliant staff and have them give you the details on our science here. If we want to spread the good news, people will need to know exactly what we are doing. We want to be as transparent as we can about our operation."

"But… I'm sure that's all secret and proprietary, right?"

"Christy," he cheerfully responds. "You aren't checking your journalistic integrity at the door are you? When your documentary airs, it needs to be

201

your story. You telling it in your words. We want to project total transparency."

"Well, okay." She smiles. "Sorry I'm just not with it today, I guess," she admits, mustering a tense laugh.

Carpenter chauffeurs Raines to the lab via golf cart with the camera crew behind in a second. She snickers silently to herself at the image of the ninja moves she and Myer affected to dodge surveillance, now rendered moot and ridiculous twelve hours later. Inside the lab, Carpenter turns over the tour guide reins to his lab director, Leo Hartmann.

Cameras rolling, Raines begins the questioning. "So, Director Hartmann, there really is only one question, the most important one. How do you do it?"

"I presume you mean how do we extend life?" Hartmann answers through thin, naturally tensed lips. His eyes bounce back and forth in their orbits as he thinks of each thing to say. Thinning wisps of his reddish hair quiver in the air conditioning. "It is really very simple. Inside all of us lies the key. Our bodies inherently have the ability to regenerate. It is happening all the time. In fact, every seven to ten years or so our physical selves have completely regenerated a whole new set of cells. We are a new person, literally. The problem is that each time we regenerate there is a very slight degradation. The result of this is what we call aging."

"So, how have you perfected this replication process?"

"Early on in our lives, in fact at conception, our cells are being created for the very first time. There is no degeneration occurring at that stage, the original development of our first self. Here, in our labs, we have traced the genetic path back to cell-one and are able to reactivate the body's innate ability to continue actual growth, not replication. Instead of your body replenishing itself from a process of facsimile, it is now re-growing itself from new original cells. The body actually clones itself."

"That sounds almost too simple," Raines responds with an eyebrow raised. "It makes me wonder what took so long for someone to discover that."

"In fact, Ms. Raines, the knowledge existed on how it could happen, but the technology did not. I guess all of us here were fortunate enough to be born in the right generation," he finishes with a yellowish, toothy smile.

"So, what is the actual experience for someone undergoing this treatment?"

Carpenter interrupts. "Actually Christy, Director Hartmann is not part of that aspect. He merely cultivates the material."

"Okay," she says slightly disappointed. "I'll rephrase. What is your role in making me, for example, immortal?"

"Well, at the beginning of the transformation, your core DNA is extracted. We receive it here and begin the origination protocol. The tracing back process I mentioned that locates your original genetic material. Once that is complete, we merely reactivate it, basically turn the switch back on, and then reintroduce it to your body."

"Again, that just sounds too simple, Director. You are dumbing it down quite a bit, I suspect."

Hartmann smiles at her directness. "Yes, you are right. It is way more complicated than that, but it is essentially correct."

"You said *turn the switch back on.* Is it possible that maybe nature has a reason for keeping the switch off?" Raines presses.

"Ms. Raines, there are more things in heaven and earth..."

"Yes, an elegant reference, but Shakespeare was not a scientist altering DNA."

"Correct, but we are, and it is sound science. Trust me." He smiles wider with unblinking eyes.

"So, Director Hartmann, why wait so long? Why not make it available decades ago? How many have died needlessly? And you are certain, any unintended consequences have been worked out?"

Carpenter answers for Hartmann. "Yes, Christy, they have."

The tour of the lab continues, Raines carefully sneaks glances to see if there is anything new or different from the night before. Only one thing stands out. The picture on the wall in the office, the only picture in the entire lab, is no longer hanging there.

"James, this office. Whose is it?" Raines queries from the doorway of the office where the picture hung.

"It belongs to Director Hartmann."

Fifty Five
May 30, 1985

"So, it has begun. The young Kovacs journeys forth knowing not what lies ahead," Cardinal Rodriguez reminds his fellow cardinals Vincenti, Monihan and Grant.

"It is for the best. There is no need to cast unnecessary doubt now," Grant chides. "This is for the eventual benefit of all mankind. In this, we have all agreed."

"Yes, we agree, but I alone have cautioned against it. Must I always play the devil's advocate?" Rodriguez interjects "I fear it is reckless, selfish even. It is not our right to create life in this manner, and especially the life that will result here. That is God's domain and his alone."

"Stop. There will be NO MORE of this," Grant rebukes loudly to bolster his presumed authority. "Look, Cardinal Rodriguez... Carlos... we have prayed together endlessly about this. The consensus is that this is God's will. It is his way to remind the world of what came before, the chance to—"

Rodriguez returns the volley. "Cardinal Grant, there is still much we do not know. There may, no, *will* be unintended consequences."

"Please, brothers." Vincenti interrupts to assuage the brewing tension. "I must intercede before words are uttered that cannot be unsaid. We must agree to leave this in the hands of God now. Table your discontent. The Lord guides us and ushers Cardinal Kovacs to be the unknowing vessel of God's will. No more need be said. All that is required is continued, steadfast prayer. The hand of the Spirit will ensure that only good will come of it."

Seeking to dispel further friction, the Cardinals flutter off to farther reaches of the room to collect their thoughts, to make peace with themselves and pray further. Consequences formulate as possibilities now. Gaseous mists of the previously imagined take solid form in the tempering chill of stark reality. There is strength in the whole, but individually the reservations find a foothold in the newly exposed weakness of their frail humanity. Is it caution or fear, they wonder?

The gravity of uncertainty pulls them back to each other. Cardinals, in black, flocking together like a murder of crows. Monihan breaks the silence with a hopeful thought.

"Gracious Fathers, we must unite as a brotherhood. Of the entire planet, we are the only four who have been entrusted with these most precious of treasures, the manifest, physical markers of the greater spiritual existence. We are the custodians entrusted with the rarest of treasures, the physical leavings of the vast, divine realm of God. In these glorious relics the perfect intersects with the imperfection of the physical world."

Monihan raises outstretched arms. "Dare I admit it, to believe in my own heart, that our doubtful questioning here is itself an intervention of the Almighty? It is not a mere accident that we are gathered here today, much like the day when we were joined together to fulfill our duties as the trustees of the archive. The four of us placed here to do as we see fit with the artifacts reveals to me that what we have set in motion is indeed the will of God."

He tilts his head upward to look into the heavens. His eyes fix on the ceiling adorned with an image of a gray-bearded God floating in clouds. "Otherwise, the means to do so would not have been provided. It is clear that *we* did not set it in motion. It was set in motion *for us* to complete. We are the instruments of God, the mere implementers of God's great plan."
"Yes." Vincenti adds his support. "I understand what you are saying. The Lord's hand is at work within us, within our circle of four. His will is clear to me now. What we have begun is God's desire."

Rodriguez makes it unanimous. "Very well, we are the agents of God. It is agreed." He smiles at their concordance. "Tell me brothers, I am curious," he utters while peering into his own imagination. "Will we ever look upon his face? Will we ever know what will become of him? We are old. We will surely be gone before—"

"There may be a way," Grant interjects. "I sense Doctor Brandt has a deeper purpose in her request. She confessed to me that there may be other secrets to be unlocked in what she has yet to obtain from our archives."

"What are you saying?" Vincenti queries eagerly.

"I am saying the artifacts may harness powers locked within, not yet known. The joining of the divine realm with the physical may have led to a kind of divine physicality."

"What do you mean by that?" Rodriguez asks, shocked.

"I am saying there are possibilities we may have never considered," Grant professes with pronounced gravity. "It may be true that God's power, and the essence of Christ's divinity, may still remain within the artifacts themselves."

Fifty Six
Present Day

"You betrayed me, Christy. I gave you my utmost trust and openness and you took advantage of me and my goodwill," James Carpenter scolds from his chair behind the massive redwood slab that serves as his office desk. His anger gives life to her darkest fears, electrifying her. She scrambles to make a case. "Mea Culpa, James. I guess my reporter's instinct got the best of me. I merely accessed some areas that really weren't even secured. I know I should have asked. It won't happen again," she confesses with tears welling.

Carpenter places his forearms on the table and leans toward her with glaring eyes. "You went behind my back. I personally guided you through the facility the very next day, unaware you had been through it on your own the night before. I told you at the beginning we have no secrets here. I gave you full run of the entire grounds. My only demand was that you simply make a request. You failed that. The trust is broken. This is an irreparable breach." Carpenter leans back in his chair, tight lipped and looking down his nose watching her unravel."

"So, what does that mean?" she stumbles out, trembling with desperation. "What about the documentary?"

"Because you have so brazenly overstepped, I have no choice but to exercise my rights in the written agreement." He pauses for her to grasp the implications of the statement.

"Wait… James," She pleads, her voice catching on the words. "You mean the whole series? Over this? James, please be reasonable."

Carpenter pulls away adopting a tone of cool legality. "You and the network surrender all rights, all footage, and the gag rule is in full effect. It is clearly stated in the contract."

"James, please. I beg you," she desperately forces past tears. "This will be the end of me. This was my Renaissance project. You can't do this. I will be forced into retirement. My life will be over."

"It is done."

Head in hands, the horror burrows in. Her career is lost. Even more devastating, the endless life she imagined crumbles to dust. She will be deemed unfit for the process, her final punishment, fate sealed. She thinks to ask of Ivan Myer. There is a sliver of a hope he was not found out. Silence seems the better course for the man who risked his own safety for her benefit.

"It is time to go now. We have escorted your crew from the Institute. Go with these men and join them." He gestures to two men in security gear standing outside the open doorway. She rises uneasily, a ghost floating from the corpse of her bleak future. She is led to the perimeter of The Carpenter Institute grounds. A short distance further she sees her production crew. They will be full of questions. Another flogging to compound her humiliation.

***

"Look, Christy, we went over it line by line. It's iron clad. We've got no case. You really stepped in it. Stepped *over* is more like it, over a cliff, I mean," Pete Kilgore admonishes his longtime colleague as gently as he can.

"There's got to be something. They always build in a back-door clause," she pleads grasping for any hope.

"Nope. An hour ago I had two Ivy League suits in here confirming that."

Raines grudgingly peels her body from the chair across from Kilgore's desk. Her journey lasts four steps where she crumples into a couch. Kilgore continues.

"You do know the rest of it, don't you? I don't have to spell it out for you?"

"What? You can't be serious," she sighs, tightening up her slumped frame.

"Seriously, Christy? We discussed this before the whole project began. This was your last hurrah. It was hard enough selling the project to the board then. Now, it's an impossibility. I can't justify your contract for any project going forward. There will be no more. You're officially a has-been."

"C'mon, Pete," she grovels to try and ward off the stinging rebuke of his assessment.

"If I go to them now, they will can me too." Kilgore explains, already resigned to the situation. "I look bad enough as it is. We've got almost two hundred grand invested in this thing and nothing to show for it. I'll be lucky if I get past this unscathed."

Kilgore's words stab at her, each inarguable point piercing further into her deflated spirit. He senses her despair and tries to bolster her with consolation. "To be sure, you'll get a good send-off. Mostly to preserve the network's image. As far as the public, your reputation is intact. It's just best if you fall on the sword with a smile. You're still loved by your fans. They don't know any of this happened. Go out and sell some beauty products on the shopping channel or something. The hours are better anyway," Kilgore pitches with an empty smile knowing it all rings hollow.

"What?" she groans. "Sell beauty products to the twelve remaining women who will need them?"

"Sorry, I'm just trying to soften the blow," Kilgore burbles apologetically, realizing his short-sightedness. He fishes through a lower desk drawer and approaches the couch clutching two coffee mugs in one hand and a bottle of scotch in the other. He flops down next to her and pours a good measure in each cup. "I know the time isn't exactly right for this, but I don't know if there will be another. Here's to you and one hell of a brilliant career... minus the last twenty-four hours."

Their mugs tap. He sips, she gulps. Kilgore thinks out loud. "I guess we will be able to meet Zarabeth's contract demands now."

"Good lord, Pete. Now you're just piling on," she returns wearily, too spent to be angry.

Kilgore has one more itch to scratch. "Seriously, Christy. I love you to death, but you've got to admit, rookie mistake."

"Yeah. No more, okay? I've hung on this cross too long."

Fifty Seven
Present Day

"Three weeks ago, The Carpenter Institute issued a press release promising answers to *big* questions certain to put to rest years of rumors and conjecture on a subject matter of *deep importance*," Stewart Waverly broadcasts around the globe with news-anchor seriousness adorned in a British accent. As soaring news-intro music builds, he resumes. "The release was worded with provocative descriptors such as *breakthrough*, *seminal* and *world altering*. Given James Carpenter and his Institute's legendary track record, full attention has been brought to bear since then." He pauses for the final musical flourish. "Good evening, this is 'World Headline News' and I'm Stewart Waverly."

The Lazarus Chain

Waverly sits at a studio news desk. A monitor behind his left shoulder shows an empty podium resting before the great room panorama window at The Carpenter Institute.

"In the three weeks since The Carpenter Institute's announcement, rumors and supposition have escalated into a whirlwind of speculation. For years, conjecture and circumstantial accounts of ordinary people rising from the dead have grown in stature. Legion conspiracy theories, supported by supposed eye-witness claims, have cultured a variety of notions lending some credence to it being a *real* phenomenon. But, skeptics have countered, and successfully thus far, that no individual has ever come forward to claim they are indeed one of these *Eternals*. Today, it is rumored, James Carpenter will shed light on this subject, perhaps even bringing the matter to rest. It appears Mr. Carpenter is approaching the podium. Let's have a listen."

The broadcast shifts to a camera view directly in front of the podium. Without ceremony, Carpenter strides boldly from off-camera past a side curtain to take the podium. With earnest fortitude he looks through the camera lens into every eye watching on. Speaking from his deepest beliefs, without tele-prompters, or even notes, he delivers.

"Imagine there's no heaven..." Carpenter continues on, reciting the song's lyrics in somber, almost prayer-like reverence, ending with, "... And the world will live as one." Carpenter then pauses, the moment needing to resonate.

"Good people of planet Earth, I bring you glorious news. The immortal imaginings of John Lennon are soon to be living reality. Decades ago, science began to uncover the secrets of life, the building blocks of human existence comprising the human genome. As the science progressed, it became clear that there is an unlimited, untapped potential within all of us." He pauses to savor the rush of the culminating moment, and the landmark revelation ready to leap from his tongue.

"In the fledgling days of the Institute, I was drawn to a calling to advance further research and shepherd breakthrough science by employing the greatest minds available to combat a myriad of scourges vexing humankind. It is now, with great pride, that I can report to all: these scourges will soon be a distant memory. Moreover, we have adopted a pledge and a philosophy that affirms that the science of our origins belongs to all of us. Furthermore, the secrets therein belong to everyone as well, and shall remain unattached to any selfishness of personal enrichment."

Carpenter pauses to allow the global audience to assess the enormity of his words. He breathes in more conviction, energizing his being in the next moment, one to alter the course of humanity.

"A decades-long effort of unflagging determination has defeated the one fate destined to afflict every man, woman, and child to ever set foot on this earth. Until now, it was only a promise. Today, it is a reality. Of course, I speak of the curse of death itself."

Carpenter pauses again, overcome with emotion knowing the world as it was will never be the same again.

"Dear friends, I know you all have many questions and perhaps even doubts. But I assure you, what I speak of is real. This is our gift to planet Earth. In the coming days, months, and beyond, our team will be providing further information for what lies ahead for those who choose to join us. All who desire to participate will be accepted. We ask nothing in return. Soon, we will make available the means to live on uninterrupted and do so as your greatest self. Yes, your *greatest* self."

Carpenter leans back to allow his good news linger.

"Not only have we reversed the specter of death, but the body you inhabit will transform into the one it was intended to be, one perpetually operating at its most perfect. Soon, we will unveil the full details. Until then, we ask that you begin to imagine your life as one where all dreams can be had in a world living in peace. Until then, good evening fellow citizens of village Earth."

Fifty Eight
Present Day

"I was thinking there might be more time for us, but I fear there is not. The Spirit has advised me that I should speak to you now, tell you what you need to know. I sense my enemies are quickly closing around me," Jonas Kovacs confesses to Alex Traeger from a chair across from Traeger's office desk.

Kovacs is disturbed and agitated, absent his usual reserve. "The Spirit? Advised you? How? Like a vision or something?" Trager asks.

"No, nothing so grandiose. The Holy Spirit is not given to spectacle. The spirit speaks in soft tones and subtle gesture, but it is clear to me that the time is now or it will never be."

Traeger swivels nervously in his office chair. "Tell... Tell me what?" He sees Kovacs' stern, troubled visage and it delivers to him even more concern. Kovacs rises from his chair, randomly scanning and pacing the office, hoping for a distraction, something to offer a few moments more to avoid the subject. He is left wanting. Slumped, facing the far wall, he drones, surrendered: "Alex, I have committed a sin, a sin like no other, a sin committed only once before—by Judas himself."

"I... I don't follow." Traeger, showing worry, rises and approaches Kovacs.

"I have betrayed our Lord, handed him over to the clutches of evil."

"How could that ever be true? Does this have something to do with what happened thirty years ago with you and William Reader?"

"Yes! Oh, God forgive me!" Kovacs turns to face Traeger, tears flowing down his ashen cheeks. "I believe in the forgiveness of Christ. I am a true man of faith. But I see no way that I cannot spend eternity in the fires of hell in a circle reserved for the likes of me and Iscariot alone."

Traeger tries to calm the cardinal's fears. "Look, Cardinal, I haven't known you very long, but from what I can tell, a man of your makeup is incapable of such an act, at least not intentionally. What happened back then?"

Kovacs paces, pushing through surging emotions locked away for so long, now unleashed. "Brandt... She had it planned from the very beginning. She shrewdly put together a team for one purpose and one purpose only. The Eternals, it was the reason for all of it. There was never any serious effort to authenticate the Vatican archives. She did that to bolster a facade, but the whole scheme was to get at one thing."

"And what was that?"

"It is so obvious now. How could I have been blind to it then?" Kovacs sobs frantically. "I was a good soldier. I didn't question my superiors. But it never occurred to me, not even once."

"I don't follow. Was it something in the archives she was after? How could anything in there provide what she needed to reach the goal of eternal life?"

"She wasn't after *something*, Alex, instead... *someone*."

"Again... I don't..." Traeger sighs at a growing frustration with Kovacs' cryptic ramblings.

"Her field of expertise, Alex? What is her gift?"

"Genetics, and so... wait... you don't mean..."

Kovacs buries his hands in his face and begins sobbing again. Traeger gently strokes Kovacs' back, learning of the true frailty of the man beneath his baggy thrift-store clothing.

"Yes, Alex, it is true. She made a copy of him."

"Who?"

Kovacs raises his head, his somber, shattered eyes meeting Traeger's. Traeger stares back into tortured orbs wearing the strain of abject horror, shame, and guilt. Kovacs' soul wordlessly spills out the answer to the architect.

"Oh, my god, she cloned *Christ*... Jesus Christ? Cardinal. How, how can that be? In order to clone you have to have... "

"His flesh... the nails driven through my Lord left the traces of his body deep in the cross. And not only the wood of the cross, but the garments from the tomb, the tunic laid upon him after his lashing—It was all in the archives. She somehow found a way to make him whole again."

Traeger slumps at the sight of Kovacs despair. He leads Kovacs back to a chair and returns to his own, the weight of standing too much to bear.

"But, Cardinal, it really isn't him. He's a clone, something else," Traeger counters, trying to comfort Kovacs who is now semi-catatonic with grief. The caged secret kept inside thirty years is set free, leaving him withered.

"I think they meant well," mumbles Kovacs.

"Who?"

"The four who sent me, my brothers at the Vatican. They knew the plan from the beginning. They had to. They must have seen it as a chance to gaze upon our Lord, to learn of him and see who he was in person. To have him live among us again. They were men consumed with history and the ancient church. They only wanted to be among him. But, you see, in their zeal they forgot the true nature of Christ."

"Which is?"

"You know that. What made Christ what he was?"

"He was God made into man."

"Exactly, Alex. He is *God* incarnate, but the replica consists only of the human shell, a creature of the Earth alone, not of the divine."

"So, why is that bad? Does it make him necessarily evil?"

"Hopefully, no, but a man... *just* a man, one wrapped in the body once belonging to Christ, more likely than not a wolf in sheep's clothing."

"Why must it be that?"

"I believe that God chose Mary as his mother for many reasons," Kovacs relays, his emotions quelling somewhat. "God's wisdom chose a bloodline of superior nature. From scripture, we know Christ as a man possessing natural charisma, a born leader. His physical presence was commanding and virile."

"So, Cardinal, this clone, he must walk the earth as we speak. Do you know who he is, where he can be found?"

"Yes, and so do you," Kovacs' intensity pushes back. "You know him well, Alex," Kovacs alerts with stalwart eyes.

Traeger's face twists while he searches for an answer, one soon found. He whispers the name with an exhale of resignation. "Carpenter."

"Even his name gives him away," Kovacs adds for emphasis.

"How?"

"*James*, a biblical name beginning with *j* and ending with *s*. Christ even had a step-brother named James. And the last name—"

"Carpenter…" Traeger interrupts. "Jesus was a carpenter by trade."

"People are drawn to him like his predecessor, and not just for what he can give them. Soon, they will worship him. But, he is a false god, a man living in another's mansion."

"Cardinal, I trust you implicitly, but I am with him almost every day. The man I know is not evil."

"My dear Alex, I have one more thing for your consideration. If Carpenter is not the true Christ, then what else would he be? Is he not a pretender? He has stolen what belongs to God and lives with the inherent belief that his being is divine. So, if he is not Christ, and not divine, then he is…" Kovacs pauses looking for Traeger to finish the thought.

"I have no idea."

Kovacs rises and looks deep into Traeger, his eyes burning with unfaltering conviction. "ANTICHRIST." The word spits with contempt from his mouth. "He can be nothing else—and *you* have been sent by God to stop him," Kovacs proclaims.

"Wait a minute, Cardinal." Traeger raises his hands to quell Kovacs' storm. "Look, just because William Reader threw my name out there—"

"I see William's reasons now." Kovacs states with unbridled conviction. "I know, without a doubt, that you are the one called to stop him."

"Let's just, for a moment, pretend that's true." Traeger tries once again to diffuse the intensity. "How am I supposed to *stop* him?"

Kovacs takes two powerful strides away from Traeger's desk. With his back to him he fires out, "I have no idea, Alex." Kovacs finds the door handle and slowly turns to Traeger. "I fear I must go now. The Spirit is calling me away. I do not wish to put you in danger. I wish I had more for you. I commend the matter to the hands of God. Goodbye, my friend Alex." Kovacs flies away through the door.

Traeger sits frozen and quaking. To steady the tremors, he clutches the arms of his chair. His breath rattles abrupt and staggered. His chest is tightened like a vise. Before he left, Kovacs commanded the impossible, transferring his own burden to Traeger. Another moment passes. He musters the will to elevate and walk unsteadily to the window. He spies Kovacs walking in the distance, down a sidewalk as fast as his aged legs will carry him. A moment later, he thinks to go after him.

Before he can act, he sees a white, windowless van roll up behind the Cardinal and slide to a stop beside him. Two men in suits swallow him up and rudely toss him into the van, disappearing behind a cloud of dust. Traeger clutches his phone to call for someone. But whom, the authorities, maybe? Caution overtakes him. If there are shadowy forces at work in all this, it is best to leave Kovacs' fate in the hands of God. He suspects it is what Kovacs would choose anyway.

He considers, maybe any moment now, that the van will come to fetch him, too. He waits, tempting God to allow that. The moment never arrives.

Two Years Later

Fifty Nine
Present Day

The boulder provides cover from sight but not from sound. Somehow, he must seat the arrow and draw the bow without the slightest noise or the advantage of surprise will be lost. He might get one away clean, but it must be a kill shot, or a shrill warning to others will immediately follow. This deep into enemy territory, he would rapidly be engaged from all directions. There is no margin of error. Crouching, he eases a gold-tipped carbon shaft from a leather quiver strapped to his thigh. He tempers his breathing to prepare for a steady release. Rising slightly to see above his cover, he marks his prey. Thirty yards, maybe, but facing away, head angling, the would-be victim is listening for any disturbance, oblivious that solace has only one moment left. A distant crow caws as if on cue. The distraction seals fate.

A whirr from behind, followed in a millisecond by the shattering of wholeness. No air remains for even a gasp. Falling to his knees, the prey spots the arrow glistening, his own blood and viscera extending more than a foot from his chest. No strength remaining, he tumbles backward, folded over. Pressure applied by his own dead weight to the shaft of the arrow brings a hell fire of pain to his entire being. Urgent, synaptic firings to flee are lost on the way to their destination. The network is unavailable. His blurring eyes are frozen, staring at the trees pointing upwards to the heavens. A form steps between him and the firmament. The bow hunter laughs, posturing victorious.

"You owe me five hundred bucks, Childress."

Childress, the prey, tries to utter something through the pain, but there is no air. The hunter grasps the bloody arrow shaft with a gloved hand and steadies the soon-to-be carcass with a planted boot. He pulls the arrow through the rest of the way. Childress winces and then relaxes with the pain lessened, beginning the numb descent into expiration. The hunter draws another arrow back. The gears of his bow wind, building the tension. "Let me put you out of your misery, buddy." An arrow tip vibrates four inches from Childress' drifting left eye, which reflects back both fear and gratitude. Childress' failing hearing detects a thud, then another louder, larger one occurring on the ground beside him. A gloved hand falls across his torso and groans of agony find an ear. "A fucking crossbow bolt, GOD DAMN YOU, MARTIN!" Childress' drained face finds enough strength left to form a vengeful smile.

"Childress... I'll... I'll see you in... in the office Tuesday," The newly dying man offers with professional cordiality through thick spits of blood. "Don't forget... ahhgh... I need the Townsend numbers by close of business... Frrr... Friday."

A crowd of footsteps arrives. Another bolt thuds into the fallen mass of the now late bow hunter. Childress hears a voice through the fog "Childress, bummer, I owe you. Should have had your back, man. Let me end it for you."

Another thud, then darkness.

***

"It's so needless. She's so young. Take away the grime and she was probably really beautiful."

"C'mon, Underhill. You've been at this, like me, for almost twenty years. What's with the rookie remark?" Patricia Hamer chides her colleague, crime scene photographer Steve Underhill.

He replies while angling his lens from a squatting position. "No, I mean now that there is no reason to die like this. A short drive up the highway and, in a weekend, she could have lived forever."

"Yeah, she could have lived in squalor on crack *forever*. That's a dream come true," Hamer slides out bitterly while lifting a crusty, stained couch cushion up with a blue-gloved hand, scattering cockroaches.

"Who's to say, Pat? But I guess now she'll never get the chance," he finishes with a pant after rising back up. "I'll tell you, I'm seriously giving it a thought myself. These old bones could use a refresh."

"And then you could do this through eternity."

"Not necessarily. The wife and I were talking to a financial guy. There's a way to taper off the employment track. Eventually your money works for you and you never have to work again. It's pretty iron clad."

Hamer widens her eyes in disbelief. "Based on actuarial charts that... oh wait, *never* existed because no one could live forever before," she scolds "It's all a big guess, Steve."

"With the cost of end-of-life healthcare removed, the whole equation shifts dramatically," Underhill counters. "So, maybe I have to work now and again." He shrugs. "I'll try different things, jobs that interest me. I'll be a chef or a painter and be virile and have the energy to do it."

"Where's Murphy? He was supposed to be here two hours ago," Hamer snaps out.

"I think he's pulling extra duty on the social transition task force," Underhill answers.

"So, what? Were supposed to do all his work now, too?" Her usual patience is wearing thin. Hamer's agitation, stuffed below the surface, is finding fuel in the rapidly changing landscape of daily life thrust upon everything.

"No, it's not like that. He's still on his way; it's just with homicides on the wane... well, you know why." Underhill stops himself rather than give voice to the obvious. "They want to use him, and eventually all of us, for other stuff—to get prepared for the new world ahead."

Hamer's form deflates slightly. The thought of someday never having to visit another scene like this one ought to be something to rejoice. She knows in a matter of time, the need for her skills will dwindle into obsolescence. She scans her phone for Murphy's number but pauses before dialing, seeing the name below Murphy's—Ivan Myer. A brief moment that replays a lifetime of memories freezes her. She wonders again, for maybe the thousandth time, what became of her friend. She used to call but the number went out of service six months after he disappeared. All of her investigative expertise and access to government databases have provided no clue of his whereabouts or fate. At a familiar mental dead end, she returns to duty and dials Murphy.

A phone rings across the room. A man answers. "Hello?"

Hamer spots the answerer facing away, a man clearly not the form she expected to see. She marches over, building for a confrontation. Her suspicion is that some cub reporter has gotten too clever for his own good and *borrowed* Murphy's phone to gain access to the scene. She grabs the man's shoulder and turns him around, then snatches the phone from his hand.

"Ok, smart guy. You are in BIG trouble. What's your name?"

"Pat, it's me. Murphy," he chuckles back, noticing her disparate irritation. "What the FU—?" Before she can finish the last word, she realizes why he looks nothing like his old self.

"Chill, Pat. Don't look so surprised. My lottery number was picked. I couldn't wait." Hamer marvels at Murphy's chiseled, vibrant form. "You know the bum ticker and all. I wasn't ready to move on."

She hands the phone back in a daze. Seven weeks ago the man was thirty-five pounds heavier with sallow skin and yellowing eyes. Now he is practically an Adonis.

"Hey, what do you think of the ponytail, Hamer?" he crows, shaking his mane from side to side. "I always wanted one. The ladies are loving it."

***

"I don't know. There's some bluish tone in the upholstery fabric that is setting off the drapes all wrong. I called the designer to discuss, left a message. I think she's avoiding me. It's been over three hours and not a word back."

"I'd Yelp-smash that bitch into next Tuesday," Barb Wagner replies to her friend Cindy Bonham, taking glee in her smarminess. The two sit opposite one another with their mutual friend Jennifer Tweed between them as they while away a girls-day lunch at the posh eatery Vendome. Tweed silently nibbles a Cobb salad through a smile at the humor.

Cindy picks up where she was interrupted. "Honestly, I think it's something about the light coming through the picture window. We've had the room painted three different shades and it still isn't right. Randall is bitching about the cost and inconvenience. What else is new? But it can't stay the way it is. I'm too embarrassed to have anyone over in the state it's in now."

Jennifer breaks in to change the subject, still chewing but daintily covering her mouth with her fingertips. "Did you hear about Jim and Diane?"
Barb follows the opening. "You mean the separation?"
"Yes," Jennifer confirms while leaning back in her chair. "If you ask me, it's that treatment thing she had done."

"It's more than a *treatment,* it's the makeover of makeovers. Surely, you've heard of the Eternals thing, Jen," Barb tilts her head with incredulity.

"Of course I have. Are you saying that's what she did?"

Cindy breaks in. "Yeah, I thought everyone knew."

"She told me she did some spa retreat thing," Jennifer injects, surprised. "You know, total cleanse and daily wraps and skin peels."

"Well, that's what she is saying, but there's no spa that can make you look like that, ever," Cindy boldly asserts. "She had it done. She entered the lottery and her chance came up. It's the only explanation."

Barb sips from her Chardonnay and swallows quickly to get the floor back. "She looks like she could be Jason's sister now. It's kind of disturbing when you see them together."

"Well, some of that is because Jason has grown up to be a handsome young man. He's not a child anymore," Cindy slips in, her manner meant to provide more than just observational insight.

Barb resumes her narrative. "I wouldn't blame Jim if he left her. I think the separation is because she finally must have, you know..."

"*Cheated*, the word is *cheated*, Barb," Jennifer bluntly blurts.

"Well, there is no proof, but not long after she did the change, we were at a charity auction and I saw her there. She was certainly enjoying the attention she was getting from the males in attendance."

Cindy interrupts to add her own grievance, "She even openly flirted with Randall. She was kind of downright slutty, if you ask me."
"So, does anyone know if Jim is going to follow suit?"

"Not so far. Either way though, I think the marriage is over. It just has that look."

The women end the subject to digest it all with a few bites of food. Jennifer hesitates to spill a twitching thought in her head. The unspoken code says lunches are not a place to broach such deep subject matter. Still, it pokes at her relentlessly until she can't bottle it in any longer. "So, what about you two… are you going to…?"

They look up from their plates surprised but now gratefully permitted to add voice to the same thought gnawing at them.

"Randall and I have discussed it briefly," Cindy confesses, trying not to sound too eager. "We did conclude that whatever we decide, we will both either do it or not."

"Don't hate me," Barb mouses out. "I kind of want to." Barb's tablemates pause mid-chew, forks clanking to their plates.

Resuming composure, Jennifer eases out with both judgement and empathy, "That surprises me Barb, but we all have our reasons. I haven't seriously looked at it and I still don't know. We are all still young, so it's not so pressing a thing. But then I think that I could die in a car accident tomorrow and I kind of panic." She stabs another bite of salad, then sets the fork down. She allows a rare moment of depth to peek out. "I sometimes think about what the world would be like with everyone living forever and it just seems strange. Everyone would look the same age. Would the idea of age bringing wisdom continue on? Maybe in that world people just never grow up because they don't have to. The parents would look like the kids and everyone else. The creepiest thing is that the change is for free. Nothing is ever really *free,* so I'm skeptical."

"True," Cindy breaks in. "I agree with everything you just said. But, I look at my mom and her last years with Alzheimer's. I can't bear the thought of that being me. I'm not sure if I am ready to live forever, but I know I am not ready to die anytime soon…" Cindy stops herself, realizing the conversation's weight is imposing on her *light* lunch. "Well, who knows?"

"I think you should do it, Cindy. Maybe then you and young Jason could finally hook up," Barb barbs. She and Jennifer snicker at the jab. Cindy ponders a moment on Barb's proposition, locates a tender morsel on her plate, skewers it, and devours it with gusto.

***

"That's it?" Dr. Rajiv Patel looks with surprise at his practice colleagues, Dr. Mary Singleton and Dr. Colin Linwood.

"Fifteen minutes? We are done so soon again?" Singleton asks incredulously.

"Face it, Mary. These are going to get shorter and shorter and eventually disappear altogether," Linwood answers, surrendering to inevitability.

"I guess I have been lying to myself that this new life-extension thing was just a hyped-up pipedream," Singleton submits. "Do you suppose this could really be upon us?"

Patel replies while stepping away to raise the lights and dim a projector. "It's very real, at least in the short term. I've had two patients I referred to hospice walk into my office six months later to,"—he pauses to find the right words—"sort of gloat that they are now cured. Not only that; I didn't really even recognize them. They looked so much younger."

"But is the science sound?" Linwood asks. "Does anyone really know if the effect is truly lasting or, perhaps, even detrimental?"

"I don't think anyone can know that yet. It's only been out there for a few years, and only a few months broad spectrum. I just can't believe we can determine that the whole thing is truly a godsend yet. It might be one of these be-careful-what–you-wish-for things," Singleton points out.

"True, but it is exciting," Patel adds with a nod.

"Look, the prospect of all major disease and malformation being eradicated from the planet is something I can get behind, even if it does mean we are out of a job," Linwood admits. "The idea of no one dying of diabetes or AIDS gives me a great sense of pride in the human race. It is truly a day to celebrate when it is all absolutely confirmed. To never see a child with a cleft palate or distended belly in some far corner of the globe is the reason we all pursued medicine in the first place. I know you both whole heartedly agree."

His colleagues nod.

"But, again, has any of the science been peer tested or reviewed?" Singleton restates her caution.

"I would surely hope so, but I have not seen any data in that regard," Patel responds.

"Well, by the looks of things, we should all have plenty of time on our hands in the near future to do our own research to find out," Singleton dryly admits.

***

"Look, don't get the wrong impression here. Everyone in this room is extremely grateful that you included us in the game plan and jumped us to the front of the line. Because of that, we will all benefit greatly. But the rapid change you guys and Carpenter have set in motion could spin out of control very quickly unless we address some of the tectonic shifts to the world economy and society at large," cautions Committee Chair Rance Dennison across a twelve-foot-long conference table.

One of two bald men, Smith, adjusts his black tie and leans in. "I thought that kind of stuff was your job—you know, what you were elected for in the first place," he replies smugly to Dennison, although loudly enough for the other twenty-two ears around the table too.

Another committee member takes over. "Look, we aren't wizards. We yield a lot of power, but what you have unleashed may seriously jeopardize that. The leverage we had with programs like Medicare and Social Security have now been turned on their head. A country full of free spirits fearing almost nothing, especially their government, not only overturns, but explodes the apple cart."

A third member, a woman senator, jumps in. "Yes, and industry sectors like insurance, healthcare, retirement planning and mortuaries all face ruin. All told, we're talking trillions of dollars in uncertainties."

The second bald man, Jones, reaches in his suit pocket and removes a cigar. In the pregnant silence, he expertly snips the tip and slowly lights it, bringing wide-eyed scorn from the assembly of lawmakers. He looks around and smiles. "What? It's not like anyone here is going to die from this. Anyway, I thought smoke was mandatory for this kind of backroom skullduggery."

"The entire Capitol Building is a no-smoking zone, Mr. Jones."

"So, shoot me," he replies with a snicker.

"Then there's the whole matter of overpopulation, which brings environmental conditions and food supply to a crisis point pretty rapidly when you look at the numbers," the woman resumes.

Smith responds for Jones who is in mid-puff. "I assure you, that will not be a problem."

"Why not?" she challenges.

"It just won't be."

A smoke trail snakes its way through the conference room, wafting up to the thick, intricately crafted crown moldings and oil renderings of powder-wigged predecessors peering on blankly.

Dennison retakes the floor. "I don't know what that means. I don't think I want to know. But all the other matters are huge and potentially catastrophic on a global scale."

Jones takes to his feet and begins pacing around the table. "If you all are anything like my father when he was here, I know what your greatest fear is. It has nothing to do with anything you just voiced. It always boils down to retaining your status." He glances around to spot any disagreement. As expected, he sees none.

"This is how it lays out. It's the only way, so you'd better get used to the idea. The god you worship—power—will still be yours. You will, however, not be the top of the food chain anymore. But you all knew that going in. You will enjoy all the trappings of your position, which will put most of you at ease, I'm sure." Jones adopts a baby-talk tone. "So, don't put on your sad faces." He smiles at his mockery. "Order will be retained, and you will all have a grand old time."

The Chair asks with slight confusion, "How *will* you manage that?"
Jones puts a hand on the questioner's shoulder. "Rance, put your hands together and cup them."

The man does as asked. The cigar hovers over his hands and, with two gentle taps, ashes are dislodged into the makeshift human ashtray. "We just will," Jones answers with dark confidence. "You seriously think we haven't thought of all this? One of the great minds of the study of culture and human behavior gave us the road map and so far it's been spot on. It's kind of insulting that you all really think we got this far without considering a way to deal with little messes that might crop up."

Sixty
Present Day

"We are actually ahead of schedule, Alex, and a great deal of credit goes to you," James Carpenter compliments his Director of Global Venue Development, Alex Traeger. Carpenter sets his pad device on the glossy surface of his desk, a three-inch-thick slice of petrified sequoia trunk. Nearly fifteen feet in diameter, the smooth, polished surface reveals rings of time from thousands of years ago. The rings are shadows of the living tree that once was, a ghost of former glory represented by mud turned to stone.

"James." Traeger postures humbly. "You know the force behind the success is you. I am only herding the felines."

"And quite a fine job of herding indeed." Carpenter's praise resonates his respect, reflecting an almost brotherly bond. "With your stellar performance, we are on the brink of surpassing a metric that will bring the Eternals process to nearly triple capacity, meaning one hundred percent availability in only eighteen months, a truly global footprint."

Traeger nods affirmatively with bright eyes. Carpenter takes notice, smiles, and rolls his own. "Well, yeah. Look who I'm telling this to. Next time, stop me before I ramble on about something you *actually* designed."

Traeger smiles, enjoying his camaraderie with Carpenter. "Is that all, James?"

"I think so, for now."

Under Carpenter, Traeger has found a true home. He is trusted with a wide berth of responsibility, a challenge he relishes. More so, in Carpenter he has found a true friend, perhaps even a brother.

"James, if you don't mind, I'm going to leave a little early," Traeger says somewhat shyly. "I have a dentist appointment. If not, I can postpone. There aren't many patients to compete with anymore. They kind of want you to stick around and shoot the breeze for a while. They get lonely, I think."

Carpenter, seated across the desk, raises his eyebrows and grows a pursed smile. He looks as if he has something to say, then shrugs it off. "Please, go to your appointment."

Traeger takes one step. Carpenter changes his mind. "You do know what I was about to say, right?"

Traeger rubs his hands together and answers with an apologetic air. "I know; here I am in charge of the temple development and still not an Eternal."

"Exactly. I still don't understand your hesitation." Carpenter seems almost hurt by Traeger's ongoing resistance, but once again he withdraws his true emotions. "I have promised not to pressure you. It must be one hundred percent your choice, just like everyone else."

"Yes, I do know. It's hard to explain. I'm not entirely sure myself. There is nothing really stopping me. The process has proved to be safe and without unexpected secondary effects. Some of my best friends and, of course, many team members here at the Institute, have completed it and swear by it. For some reason, I have some anxiety about something so... permanent."

"Death is permanent too, Alex."

Carpenter approaches and places his hands on either side of his architect's shoulders, gazing into Traeger's eyes bearing deep concern. "Do consider it, my friend. We'd hate to lose you to some unfortunate accident. We can't do this without you." Carpenter pulls him into his chest and embraces him for a few moments, then delivers his customary kiss. "Now go. I'll see you tomorrow."

Sixty One
Present Day

She must find the roots or they will never die. The vines tangle slowly into the beds, choking off the flowers, then steal the bounty of the soil. They creep patiently from the forest lining the back edge of her property. This time, she is determined to locate the source and eradicate the scourge.

Gently, she untwists the intruders from flower stems and vital tendrils. The innocent freed, she clutches the vines and pulls upward being careful not to rip the captured marauders free of the main strand. She needs them to betray the origin. Pulling up reveals even more vines leading her inward, ten feet, then fifteen. The forest surrounds her now. She knows she is close.

Between pulls, she hears a faint voice, a mere whisper. It sounded like a breathy utterance of "Patricia." She halts. It finds her again, but from no discernable direction, so faint it might even be in her own head. Rustling follows, but she can't determine the source. Her adrenaline fires.

The sound of breathing needles her ears. It is her own running apace. Her neck throbs with every heartbeat. More rustling from her right, it seems. She squares up to face it.

Her name floats to her from deeper inside the sylvan maze, now decidedly not hallucinatory. Carefully, she steps toward the voice. She summons her combat training from years before. The rustle again, from behind a tree eight feet away.

"Okay, show yourself!" she commands.

"Patricia? Is it you?"

She peeks around the tree to spy part of a human form sitting, facing away, propped up against the far side of a maple trunk directly ahead of her. Legs extended out. An arm hangs limp. She proceeds no further, still unsure.

"Come out, NOW," she barks.

"I... I can't. Help me, please."

Her instincts warn her to go back to the house and call the police. Instead, curiosity compels her. The figure ahead appears frail and unthreatening. She moves closer.

"Please, Patricia."

She tramps the final few steps to find a zombie of a man. He strains to lift his head and look up at her.

"Marcus?"

"No." The figure tries to angle his head upward even more to establish eye contact.

She bends down closer and then gasps through her hand, snapping her head away. Mustering courage, she cranes her neck back slowly to look again. Her face clenches at the sight.

"Ivan."

Myer's bulging eyes relax, followed by a sigh and a grateful but struggling grin.

***

"There, I think you're stable now. I thought I was going to lose you," Hamer gently reassures her new patient, Ivan Myer, as he rests peacefully on her guestroom bed.

She carried him inside by herself. His diminished form and her energized state teamed up to get him to comfort and care. He is a shell—weak and pallid. By sight, he should be dead. A sight so wretched as to compel her to look away. She, a woman who has witnessed hundreds of corpses in every unimaginable state. Apparently, it is more difficult to look upon the face of death while still alive than after the fact.

"And, oh by the way, where the hell have you been, you son of a bitch?!" the newly drafted nurse booms, losing her bedside manner. "You fell off the face of the earth and I honestly thought you were dead."

"I... I..." Myer reaches down for breath.

"This better be good."

"I escaped."

"Escaped? From where?"

"The Carp..." He gasps for air to finish the rest. "The Carpenter Institute."

Hamer timidly slides back further in her chair, confusion washing away her anger. "Escaped?"

"They were holding me."

"Why?"

Myer gathers more energy, tilting his head to look directly at her. "I was investigating the place, undercover. I embedded myself in the staff at the Institute. They found me out and have held me ever since."

"Since when? Two years?"

"Two years and four months give or take, I think."

Confused, she asks, "They imprisoned you?"

"A prison of a sort."

Hamer's anxious energy compels her to begin tidying up. She stows the emergency care gear she used to stabilize Myer. "What does that mean? *Of a sort*?"

"They made me an Eternal."

"What? Then why do you look like... pardon me, Ivan... like death warmed over?"

"I know I do, but I am."

"What happened? Did it not work right on you?"

"It worked fine, unfortunately. I didn't want it, but they did it anyway."

"Against your will? That doesn't make sense. So, why do you look like hell?" she presses on.

Myer's face strains. His fists clench. "Oh, God!"

Hamer returns hastily to her chair and resumes her bedside manner, taking Myer's clenched, fused hand in hers. "What's wrong?"

He turns his head to hers. Through his watering eyes she views abject horror. His whole body is rigid in seizure.

"What is it Ivan? What did I say? Tell me how to help you."

After a time he bursts out, "Stop!! It's in your mind, Ivan!"

"Ivan, what is going on?"

He begins to calm. His hands release. His eyes relax slowly.

"Ivan, please," Hamer pleads to understand.

"The prison is not one of their building, but one of your own," he manages through his return.

"Will you stop speaking in riddles, God dammit!" she implores.

"It's part of being an Eternal. There are no free lunches, Pat."

"Again, riddles." She throws her hands up.

"The protocol, it's an ongoing process, ongoing forever."

"What do you mean by that?"

"You live forever, for better or worse. If you continue on with Carpenter's protocol, it's all peachy keen. But, if you don't continue with the maintenance plan, there is hell to pay, literally."

"*Maintenance plan*? You mean it's not a silver bullet?"

"It's a lot of silver bullets, infinite bullets, really."

Hamer rises up again and paces, wheels spinning. "So, let me get this straight: if one becomes Eternal one must also keep up on... uh... booster shots or the whole thing takes a crap?"

"Essentially."

"That doesn't make sense."

"Just look at me, Pat. It makes perfect sense."

"No, I mean, when you were off mowing lawns, or waiting tables, or whatever at The Carpenter Institute, I was working off-line with one of the original Eternals trying to deconstruct the regeneration phenomenon. This guy never needed boosters or replenishment of any kind."

"You, working off-line? I guess we both have our secrets," Myer slyly spills with a raspy tone and crooked smile. "You of all people working off the grid. I have a newfound respect for you. I didn't know you had it in you." Myer itches his face. A scab dislodges, refreshing an open sore. "As far as my experience, boosters are essential."

"What did you mean by *hell to pay*?"

"It is quite literal, you"—oh shit!" Myer's body clenches again. He flails and writhes in seizure, eyes rolling back. Foam spills from between his twisting lips. Hamer too is paralyzed, frozen in helplessness. Unconsciously, she wanders backwards into the farthest corner of the room, the spectacle too dreadful. Myer furiously utters something unintelligible through clenched teeth, as if speaking in tongues then slowly returns.

Hamer snaps to her senses to test his vitals, calming him until he is himself. Myer chuckles, shaking his head at his absurd circumstance. "You see, Pat, quite literally."

"Why do you keep seizing?"

"Life as an Eternal is bliss, unless you decide to go it on your own. Then it is a trip through hell."

Hamer's face twists with more confusion. Myer is undoing every firm conclusion she took away from her days with Chandler. "I don't understand. I'm really trying to."

"Look, I don't know if it's intentional on Carpenter's part, but if you stay on board with the Institute's plan, it's all beer and skittles. You know, buy into the *vision*, drink the Kool Aid. If you don't, then eventually the demons catch you."

"Demons?" she asks, chilled.

"Every worst nightmare as real as life running through your head, through your soul, really." Myer's tone grows haunting as he relives dark moments. "First, you are the murderer or the rapist, and then you are the victim." He waits to muster the words as he reimagines the ugliness. "Aloneness and despair befall you in rushing torrents. Love and hope are extinguished, over and over, hundreds of times a day."

"How do you know it's the Eternals process causing that?"

"They know how to stop it. I assume they know what causes it."

"And your body, too? Is that why you are dying?"

"I am not dying. I feel like I am in every moment, but it never comes. I may even go into a coma, but I will never expire. The best I can hope for is suspended animation. At least the pain and the torment will stop. But I fear the nightmares won't and I will be stuck there, damned for eternity."

Hamer speculates. "The protocol must do something to partially alter the brain in a way similar to schizophrenia or that of a psychotic event. I would need to test you to try to learn more."

"Look, you know me. I may be a bit impulsive, but I'm a practical man. It feels like more than just a chemical imbalance."

"What then?"

"It feels like..." Myer's eyes grow large he turns his head again to meet her eyes. "Like real demons."

"What?" She shakes her head to dispel any such notion.

"Like actual demons, like I'm possessed."

"Ivan, you can't..." Her voice trails off. Her denial has no fuel behind it. Her reflex is to dismiss any conjecture, but the image of his pain and the horror in his eyes trumps her impulse to argue against his claim. When he first seized, his eyes reported the level of torture in his soul. She can offer no rational counter to the anguish visited upon him. She changes the subject. "How did you escape? Did they leave the cell unlocked?"

"There is no cell, no walls." Myer shakes his head. "They simply withhold the maintenance. For most, once is enough. Once one goes into that abyss, you never want to go again. But after more than two years, I decided living a lie was just as bad. I couldn't take it any longer. I finally trained myself to weather the episodes. It's still hell, but I have found a way to fight it. Three days ago, I walked away. I came to you because you are the only person I trust to believe my story."

"What did you find out while you were investigating?"

"Ironically, not much. I never found any hard evidence of anything nefarious, but the whole place has an unsettling energy. Behind all the touchy-feely-we-will-all-live-together-in-harmony bullshit is something really creepy."

"But you have no proof."

"I don't know why they made me an Eternal. Doing that brings more suspicion on them. If they had just kicked me off the premises back then, I might have said good riddance."

"Not likely, Ivan," Hamer grunts. "We're talking about *you*. Who knows? Maybe they wanted a guinea pig to beta test the maintenance protocol." Hamer's processing is complete. Her uneasy emotions are tamped by her keen intellect. "Look, I might be able to quell the demons with some meds. And, I also need to call a guy and get him over here. I hope I can still reach him. It's been a while. Try to get some rest. I'll check in on you from time to time and get you some food. When did you last sleep?"

"Sleep?" Myer snorts.

Sixty Two
November 7, 1987

"I see you discovered some items with matching human DNA among the Vatican archives. What do you make of that, Doctor Kipner?" Adeline Brandt dribbles out with suspicious curiosity.

"Well, Doctor Brandt, at first it seemed an impossibility, so, I cross-referenced the object codes with the Vatican item roster—and that's where I found the commonality."

Her face screws. Rising from her creaky chair, she approaches Kipner and shakes the printouts of his findings in his face. "I told you *never* to cross-reference; this is double-blind research. You may have tainted the whole study."

"Doctor... Adeline." Kipner returns a knowing grin. "I am not a novice at this, surely you can't think I—"

"NEVER!" she commands. Kipner recoils at her coarse rebuke. "Do you understand?" Brandt reiterates with raised eyebrows while towering over her fellow geneticist.

Kipner squeezes his lips together and thinks to nod but knows she wants a verbal response. "Yes, I understand," he mumbles in Austrian-accented English.

Brandt returns to her seat. Kipner turns to hide his seething face. He looks out from her office window to the research area of her beehive and speaks to the glass. "You have other motives here, don't you, Doctor?"

"You are dismissed, Kipner," she answers abruptly while eyeing more printouts.

"The items bearing DNA, they are most important to you, yes? Items most rare."

"Kipner, you have much to do, I suggest you—"

"I fully expected to find no positive matches for the items labelled by the Vatican as *wood of the cross*. After all, in the ancient marketplace for holy treasures, what could be more priceless than a sliver of the instrument of death? What a marketing coup for a parish or cathedral to have an item such as that. So, if I were an enterprising young cleric, circa fourteenth century, in search of a congregation, I might resort to brazen forgery. Who would know the difference with no science existing to prove otherwise?" Kipner turns back to face her with one eyebrow elevated and puffed full of the bravery that secret knowledge affords.

"With that kind of demand, and very little supply, fakery would be rampant and quite profitable. There is no aversion, even among the anointed, to propagate bald-faced deception to bolster one's cause, especially when coupled with the rationalization that it is all in the name of saving souls. But, interestingly, my results found only eighty-seven percent of these items to be from other chronologies and geographic regions than where we would expect to find the wood of the cross."

Kipner places his hands behind his back and approaches her. "So what of the other thirteen percent? How curious is it that items scattered all over the globe happen to have been stained by the blood of a single human male?"

"Yes, that is curious, Kipner. Do tread lightly," Brandt replies, containing her ire.

"Could it be that there is some truth to the myth of the divine nature of Christ? To some, but I'm sure not to you, Doctor; you are a scientist. I suspect your understanding resides in rational thought and reason. I think maybe instead, you would entertain the possibility of genetic anomaly, a mutation perhaps?" Kipner leans in closer to her from across her desk.

"That is a quantum leap, Kipner. It only means there was a crucifixion and one party sourced the artifacts from a single sample. Who knows, the seller probably used his own blood."

"But the carbon date and associated flora are consistent with Christian-era regions and time period for the matches."

"It means nothing. The Romans crucified thousands; there is no evidence it was even from a crucifixion. Where is your science, Anders?"

From Brandt's desk, Kipner picks up a model of the DNA double helix. "But what if I'm right? It isn't so outlandish to imagine that somewhere in the course of human evolution a mutation event could randomly stumble upon solving the regeneration problem, one perfecting the process of cellular restoration." He looks through the model down at her. He points to a section of the model.

"For example, the mere altering of just a small percentage of the origin genome has led to the development of conscious human beings from the slime of the swamp in a relatively short time. Why couldn't there be an event to create a perfect being, one who will never die, or at least to greatly outlive the rest?"

"Kipner, you should hear yourself," she sputters out with a feigned chortle. She snatches the model from his grasp and returns it to her desk.

"Such a person, knowing of his unique ability to conquer death, could fashion a tall tale of being God incarnate."

"Then why didn't he? If you are implying what I think you are, then why didn't he rise and conquer rather than fading into the scenery? If I read your meaning correctly."

"Perhaps his ability was imperfect," he replies coolly, as if the question was expected. "Look, Brandt. I haven't known you long, but I have learned enough to know you are too brilliant to be wasting your time on authenticating religious artifacts. You have an agenda here and it's a big one or it wouldn't interest you. Your secret is safe with me. Tell me if I am right, Adeline. You think there is a chance that the whole Christian myth is built upon a genetic fluke. I think you imagine that, if you can get your hands on the DNA, you can uncover a fountain of youth and topple an entire religion as a bonus."

Brandt simmers stone-faced. Kipner continues, sensing no capitulation on her part.

"Very well, have it your way, but you know I am on to something; and I want nothing out of it except that if I am right, I want in. None of the others have to know either. It will be our secret."

"There are no guarantees," Brandt tersely replies. "There is no shred of evidence that it even exists. You should leave now, Kipner."

Sixty Three
Present Day

Dawn breaks as a sliver between theater-sized curtains separating the picturesque view of Maryland hills and the expansive sleeping surface of James Carpenter and his companion Marianne. The sliver paints a streak across the floor, rises up the bed, and finds the contour of two perfect, naked bodies.

Carpenter gently commands, "Let there be light." Darkness gives way to light, the curtains slowly parting at his behest. She is cradled in his right arm. Her head makes a pillow of his taut chest to take in the newborn dawn, wrapped safely in his perfection.

"The date is set, James. Three weeks from next Tuesday," she imparts in a whisper. "We fly to New York to meet in closed session and finalize the resolution. Then a full session where the official announcement will take place. At last, the dream of a world living as one will become reality," she concludes, lifting her head to look back into his eyes between strands of her flowing black mane.

"And the resistance encountered before? Has that..."

"Yes, Smith and Jones report that those with objections have been *convinced,* and there will be no further resistance. The path is cleared."

"You are so persuasive, my dear," Carpenter returns admiringly while running his fingers through her hair and kissing the top of her head. He pulls her in closer.

"It is easy to persuade when they know there is a movement underway," she gently speaks the words across his body. "The people of the world are awakening. Their leaders now understand your nature and have accepted the superiority of it. They understand that you are the one who will lead in peace and bring us all together."

"A *movement*, really?" he asks thinking it too big a word.

Her head raises up to find his eyes. She smiles, now as mentor. "My dear James, sometimes your naiveté is adorable. You consume yourself so much with the daily business of things that you miss the big picture." She clutches the sheet to her sternum and leans up, raising her free hand toward the landscape unfolding before them in the rising sun. "The people of the world are out there and behind you more than their own elected leaders. They understand your vital purpose. You are an unstoppable force. The old guard will fall in line or be removed. All are beholden to you."

"But some have chosen to be apart from us."

"Yes, but most will join. Those who don't will eventually take nature's course," she replies softly as she returns her head to his chest.

"It's a shame any choose not to be with us," he laments. "I suppose we must understand there will be those blind to the vision we offer them."

"It's unfortunate, but they have made their choice, James. Perhaps they will change their mind before it is too late."

"After they hear my speech at the UN, they will be persuaded."

"Yes, James, the truth will be undeniable. Greatness is embedded in who you are. Soon, your vision will be the only one that has meaning, a vision of the people of this world all living for each other."

Sixty Four
Present Day

"Today marks the most important day in the history of humankind. A day when all have truly come together for the benefit of all, a day where the arbitrary borders of both the physical and philosophical have been torn away," James Carpenter decrees from the podium of the United Nations general assembly. Robust applause meets his final word. His eyes behold a chamber vibrating with acceptance and gratitude.

"No longer will there be a place for war. No longer a place for social and economic injustice. Disease and hunger will soon be ended," Carpenter proclaims, his chin proudly raised, "With our differences and fears abandoned, we can now work to free humankind from the physical limitations once imposed on us by our own imperfect nature, as well as the ones we have inflicted upon ourselves through ignorance and selfishness. Today, the citizens of the world, in unanimous accord, have agreed to the framework that will, once and for all, dissolve our differences and adopt a common governance. As we move forward, our newfound unity will bring with it a set of principles and tenets that will define who we are as one, unified village of planet earth."

The full assembly rises, bringing with it a thundering ovation. Carpenter steps back slightly to acknowledge and absorb the honor. As the furor quells, he postures again, firm behind the podium. "I am at the same time humbled and honored to have been offered the role of Secretary-General, but for here and now, I must respectfully decline." Some murmurs of surprise are sounded. "My path, and my purpose is one of guidance and counsel. I seek not the title of king and ruler. Therefore, I leave you to your work. I will remain an important voice in this transition and always at the ready should the need arise. But, I leave the role of leader in your hands to decide on another. One more eager and worthy for the challenge."

***

"So, tell me again how this works?" asks Smith of his colleague Jones, holed up together in a posh hotel suite near the UN building.

"It's called puppet master 101. How is that so difficult to process? We've been over this."

"I know, I just wanted to hear it out loud again. Of course I grasp how this works," Smith chirps through a Cheshire smile from his desk chair. "And once the final phase is complete, you and I are free to do as we please," he trumpets.

"You know I know that, so don't keep saying things to *hear them out loud again*," Jones returns, irritated.

"Marianne, what is the schedule for full deployment?" Jones queries her while she lustily admires the view of the Washington skyline, arms folded behind her like raptor's wings.

"Once the majority of remote sites have been completed, then we will have the capability to deliver the ongoing protocol in great numbers. According to Traeger, the window is less than six months. Nearly two-thirds are already queued for immediate implementation of the ongoing process once we are at capacity."

"Marianne, you can be straight with us. You know we are fully committed. James can't really sit back behind the scenes for too long. We know he will have to step to the front sooner or later," says Smith.

Her head swivels to gaze ardently at the questioner. "Why does that concern you, Mr. Smith? You two are immune. You have only your very glamorous, powerful, and endless lives ahead of you. You have done exemplary work, been loyal to our vision since the inception. Do not worry about things that don't concern you."

"We're not *worried*, just curious," Jones interjects. "We've spent a great deal of time, our whole lives really, around people who seek power. James is instinctively equipped for that kind of role. In fact, we've never known anyone more equipped,"

Smith chimes in, "But James *will* have ultimate power whether he is in the forefront or not. When they choose a leader, a mere figurehead, we will still control the strings because we control the means of life in heaven or hell on earth. James will be the true leader, not one of office or mandate, but because we control the process. He maintains the vaunted role of guru rising above the fray, not the uneasy life of a king."

"Look, Smith, and you too, Jones. In the many years we've spent together have you ever known me to operate in any other way than on a need-to-know basis?"

"No," they voice in unison.

"Then you have your answer. Now, you boys just enjoy your view here, keep the natives in line, and take your jet for a joyride once in a while. Leave the planning to me. It's all going to be just fine."

Sixty Five
January 3, 1989

She used to loathe the sound. The shrill shattering of the order of things meant only to draw selfish attention. She often mused that Homo sapiens should have failed as a species given that its brood so brazenly announces its whereabouts and utter vulnerability to predators nearby. Such a great risk to simply revel in its own self-importance. But now, with each helpless cry of her own newborn, Adeline Brandt's clinical observation from earlier days crumbles to dust.

"Baby James, are you okay?" she burbles in loving, childish tones. Lifting him and cradling him in her ample arms, she rocks the boy to a calmed state while tiptoeing to find her favorite perch, a bay window overlooking a small, serene lake near her modest escape in upstate New York.

"You are my miracle, James," she whispers into his tiny ear. The phrase passes her lips more often than even she can believe. Each time, it comes from a different place than before. Sometimes she thinks it is a thing a mother should say. Sometimes she says it to hear herself say it, as if taunting her own disbelief in the very idea. And sometimes, to her surprise, it means the exact thing. Until the birth of the child, *miracles* to her were merely the bedazzled glorifications of willful ignorance pitched by purveyors of myth and fantasy. The refuge opiate of those too lazy to seek factual truth. In her experience, science eventually prevails, snuffing out the superstitions and mysticism belonging to the previous age. But the birth of this child has raised fresh questions, applying a stiff jolt to her own paradigm.

What has her puzzled isn't that the live-birth experiment worked in ways she never expected, but that for the first time, she doesn't really care. She is consumed with joy at the life she has created. As the child lies wriggling in her arms, finding content purchase in her confident grasp, she is enrapt in exuberant delight. Her scientist mind reminds her that some of this is natural mother-child bonding, simple evolutionary programming. But throughout her life, she has always found herself immune to these sorts of impulses. She is at a loss to divine the power of her feelings. Feelings themselves are strangers to her makeup, but ones of such magnitude she has never encountered. "Dream your magnificent dreams, James," she whispers softly as she lays him in his crib.

His name, James Carpenter, was chosen as mocking homage to, as she calls it, *the ancient messianic fairy tale*. The child will never know the reason she chose that name. It is a name ordinary enough, a commonplace moniker designed to not attract interrogative probing or curious mischief should an occasion reveal his lineage to be suspect. His name serves another purpose, though, it being a perpetual reminder bolstering her certainty that the proclaimers of a divine presence are just so many fools. "The Christ," she concludes, was falsely believed to be the son of God in a time when no other explanation could serve. For now, the child shall be her secret. No other can be trusted with such explosive knowledge.

She returns to unfinished business, sorting out the details of the experiment that yielded the child. From her humble work-space in a far corner of the main living area, she ponders the impure variables introduced during the process that may have altered the fundamentals. Foremost, she surrendered all control of the clinical culturing environment to the autonomic stir of her own body. Ordinarily, she might blanch at submitting so much to randomness. But her newfound happiness has overruled any second thoughts about scientific purity. At the very least, she is most certain that natural gestation and live birth were vitally important to foster the organic beginnings required to stabilize the genetic material after numerous laboratory attempts failed.

Soon, when the analysis is complete, she knows she must disappear. She must vanish into the ether to raise the child and observe the ongoing experiment under her sole, watchful eye. The treasure trove of genetic possibilities, resident in the infant, are too important to be left to any but herself. Her path is clear. She will approach the Vatican contacts and pronounce the project complete, provide them an accounting and maintain distant connection with her cofounders, Smith and Jones. Kovacs' contribution is complete and he has apparently fled. Reader is too curious and full of inconvenient questions. He will be written out, as will Chandler. Anders Kipner, warned, but too concerned with his own flamboyant importance, has been dealt with.

Sixty Six
Present Day

Thunderous beats, two a second. The space itself like its own ornate drum. The sound grows up like an army readying for battle. In this case, the drum is an exercise treadmill, the mallets are running shoes. Pulling deep breaths, Marianne pushes forward, striding ever on but gaining on nothing. Her destination is the same as her beginning on a journey of forty-five minutes.

The pace slackens, the beating resolves, the battle apparently won. She blots her brow with plush, bone colored terry, then continues down the length of her nape across the front of her supple neck, finding momentary rest over her thumping jugular. The one drum that is still furiously beating.

Her colleagues Smith and Jones appear through the massive, finely carved oak panel doors. The exercise gym resumes its primary function as Marianne's office and sanctuary. The daily morning briefing, always 8:00 a.m. sharp, is now underway. Jones fishes a bottle of spring water from a bowl of ice and extends it to Marianne who cradles it with the end of the towel, now draped around her neck like a vestment sash.

"Gentlemen, your faces wear more concern than usual. Tell me this is only because your supply of century-old Armagnac is running low."

"It's Traeger." Smith comes directly to the point.

"Yes," she acknowledges. "Are we going to have this conversation again?"

"Yes, we are," Jones returns as brashly as he dare.
"And what great, unproven conspiracy is he presently concocting underneath our noses?"

"It's… it's…" Smith sputters.

"Let's have it, man," Marianne fires out exasperated. She twists the cap from the bottle of water, slaking her thirst shy one drop which escapes the edge of her mouth to traverse her chin, landing to mingle with newborn beads of perspiration.

Jones takes over for Smith's failed attempt. "We don't trust him. It's that, plain and simple."

"Look, the whole reason he is part of all this at all was to find out how he is linked to Reader and Kovacs. That was your reasoning anyway," Marianne reminds him.

"Right; keep your enemies closer."

"Exactly. And that's what we have done, but Traeger, an enemy? That seems a far cry. In fact, he has been extremely helpful, invaluable really. James thinks the world of him, and for some reason James tolerates that he hasn't become an eternal," she says in tones meant to caution them against any distrust.

"He knows something. I am sure of it," Jones proclaims. "Remember, we found traces of some files from Reader on his computer, and we know he met with Kovacs several times. He searched the internet for both names in the same search. No one on the planet has ever done that, then or since."

"I find that hard to believe—the planet? No one? Ever?" she queries.

"You forget our NSA connections, Marianne," Jones answers confidently.

Marianne glides to her office armchair and lands softly in the cushion of her tall wingback dazzling with bold burgundies and grand golds. Settled in, she continues. "Look, we've had this conversation many times over the years. I'll ask again, and if you have nothing more than your own fear, I want to never hear of this again. What sinister plan do you imagine he is brewing while spending seventy or more hours a week immersed in the temple projects? It's been almost three years since that Internet search. Doesn't loyalty count for anything?"

"I don't know. But, to your point, he has befriended James and is a trusted advisor for his most prized endeavor. I don't know how he coincidentally did that, but he did," Smith postulates "Maybe it's Kovacs' doing. In my mind, that is of concern. It's awfully convenient... too convenient."

"Christ, Smith! It's our doing! We brought him on to do exactly that. You two are wasting my time, and kind of pissing me off," she blasts back.

She turns in her chair to face them one at a time as they stand meekly across her desk. Her eyebrows raise and smug disappointment washes over her face. "I am beginning to think this is all too much for you. Do I need to worry?" Throwing her gaze upward, she mocks them with their own words in melodramatic cadence. *"We need to bring him into our circle, Marianne. We need to see what he knows."* Returned to her own voice, she furthers her case. "He's been with us a *long* time. I have personally spent many hours with him. I have dined with him, spent weeks on the road in his company. He's an ordinary fellow through and through, harboring no guile and no agenda. From where I sit, he can be trusted in the utmost. I acknowledge your concern, Smith, duly noted. But I feel there is no concern to be had. Look, if anything starts appearing suspicious, we will just make him go away. It's as easy as that. That has never stopped us before. James will understand if that time comes. He knows what I decide is always for the best."

Smith and Jones fidget, simmering in a sense of control lost, rapidly imagining viable possibilities of how an overlooked, thin thread of their own weave could cause it all to unravel. She continues. "Truly, if he found something Reader left behind then it's probably rantings. And Kovacs only preaches his single-minded orthodoxy. Perhaps they pitched their wares, and Traeger, being the smart fellow he is, chose to dismiss their buffoonery. I see no threat posed by either." She plants her palms on the desk and rises.

"But, do continue to monitor his movements and communication. I'm sure that instruction is unnecessary. Thank you, both."

They begin their exit. Smith turns back around. "Marianne, can I ask you a question?"
"Sure."

"Why do you exercise? It's pointless. Your body maintains itself at peak condition on its own."

She pauses to examine her reasons, his point being a flawless one. "I don't know. It feels good, I guess. Endorphins perhaps. I couldn't do it before, and now I can, so..."

Smith nods in acceptance. He and Jones continue towards the door. She offers one more instruction. "Oh, gentlemen. Let's be absolutely sure of one thing. Traeger and Kovacs are never to meet again, correct?"

Jones responds confidently. "There is no way he will ever find Kovacs."

"You are sure?" Marianne contends.

"No way. Only four people have access—the three of us and James."

Sixty Seven
Present Day

"Good God, he looks like death warmed over... I mean, over and over and..."

"Chandler, he can hear you. He's right here," scolds Patricia Hamer.

Ivan Myer musters a sly, bony grin in response to Hamer's attempt at stifling Marcus Chandler's discourtesy. Myer's gaunt, twisted form lays on a single bed in the cabin where, several years earlier, Hamer repeatedly slaughtered the man with whom she is now carrying on a conversation. It has been a week since she found Myer's withered frame in the woods behind her townhome. Thinking Myer would certainly be sought after, she pulled some things together and rushed him to the most remote location she could imagine that still offered a quality of life. Given her past association with Myer, her townhome would surely be one of the first places to be watched. The cabin is off the grid, untraceable back to Hamer.

Hamer takes Chandler's forearm in her fingertips and guides him towards the door. "We'll be right outside, Ivan," she softly says. Myer blinks acknowledgement. Hamer douses the lights and leaves the door an inch from closed.

"You got anything to drink around here?" Chandler tosses out callously. Hamer stiffens at the seeming dissonance of his request, but obliges the ask.

"Check under the sink. There's usually a bottle of Wild Turkey under there."

Chandler pushes aside a flower-pattern window curtain beneath the sink. "Jackpot," he exclaims as he snatches two juice glasses from another cupboard.

He plops in an armchair while Hamer takes a seat on the couch. Chandler pours a couple fingers for each and extends one her way. She ignores the offer. He gently shakes the glass to disturb her stare into the far wall. Her hand disobeys her determination for staunch seriousness and grasps the makeshift tumbler. She sips, nose crumpling at the burn. She sips again.

"Thanks for coming, Marcus. I didn't know where to turn, and frankly, you are the only one I could have asked to come here anyway."

Chandler is tilted back in his seat, one leg over the other at the ankles, posed as if he is sunning at the beach. "No sweat, Pat."

They both sip again. Hamer firms up and coolly stares at Chandler, eyebrows lifted. He tilts his head as if to ask "what?"

"Well, aren't you going to say something?"

"What's to say?" he cavalierly answers.

"What do you make of this?" she presses, incredulous at his indifference.

"He's in a world of shit, Pat."

"So that's why Brandt chose you for the team, your keen observational skills," Hamer returns with terse venom. "*WHY* is he in a world of shit?"

"Dammit, Pat. I'm an engineer, not a bio-geneticist." Chandler guffaws at his silliness. "You see what I did there with the 'Star Trek' thing?" He pours another two fingers for himself and shows the bottle as an ask for a refill to Hamer. She answers with piercing eyes which snap his attention to her urgency.

"Look, seriously, I am an engineer. This isn't my bailiwick. But maybe after Brandt disappeared, the level of scientific expertise left with her." Hamer simmers with disappointment. He offers more. "Maybe it wasn't perfect in the first place, some corruption in the inserted genome. It's all a big guess." Hamer leans forward, clutches the whiskey bottle and refills her own glass. "But look at you. You are one of the first Eternals ever and your genetic alteration is flawless. So, what changed on the way from processing you to Ivan?"

Chandler returns blank eyes and shrugs his shoulders. The bigger unanswered question injects a claustrophobic stirring within him and pulls him from his chair, whisking him up and away. "Did you do any work up on him?"

"Yes."

Chandler ambles to the cupboards again, opening doors, searching for something else. "You still have my data? Anything different in the comparison?"

"Yes. As far as I can tell, the two of you are essentially genetically the same, at least where the regeneration aspect is concerned."

"Have you figured out what is different about us compared to ordinary humans?"

Hamer turns in her seat on the couch toward the kitchen and Chandler. "When you decide to come back, grab me a couple of ice cubes on the way." Chandler nods while still searching. Hamer resumes. "I have observed two functional genetic differences that could explain why you are eternal, but not necessarily how it came to be. Both you and Myer have cell structures that have overcome the two main causes of aging. First, somehow apoptosis has been completely arrested and second, the telomere chains are perfectly reproduced during cell generation."

"Again," Chandler replies. "I'm an engineer. Dumb that down for the novices in the room."

"Apoptosis is cell death. Over time, human cells are naturally programmed to self-destruct. It's thought this is to keep time-damaged DNA strands from reproducing and corrupting the whole. Somehow Brandt, or whatever gene she found, has overcome that programming."

"Really, so nature has us all programmed to die?"

"At least when it comes to individual cells," Hamer affirms. "Try the cupboard to the right."

Chandler searches again. "And the telo-whatsits?"

"Telomeres. They are located at the end of each strand of DNA, sort of like leader tape on the beginning of a tape reel. Each time a cell divides it loses some of this leader tape, and when the leader is gone, the vital DNA is itself exposed to fraying. Eventually the cell dies or becomes dysfunctional when the original DNA strand is compromised."

"So, what is different about me and Myer in this regard?" As Chandler asks, he finally finds what he is looking for—food. It is a can of peanuts, but ones well past their expiration. "I guess these will do," he mumbles to himself. He pulls open the top, sniffs the can, cautiously munches a few, and heads back to his couch with the can and a small glass with Hamer's ice.

"Based on my study of you and Myer, it seems Eternals produce an abundance of an enzyme called telomerase," Hamer continues. "It's the fertilizer for restoring telomeres, so the fraying never occurs in them. Cell splitting is perfection. Normal humans lose the ability to produce telomerase over time, but you two don't. Somehow, Brandt found a way to perpetuate telomerase generation at a constant level... and then," she pauses in resigned reverence for her next utterance, "there's the strand of mystery genes she found somewhere."

"Presumably from the Vatican archives," Chandler replies between peanuts.

"And despite all that, it doesn't get anywhere near the universe of how dead people can rise again. I saw it happen before my very eyes at a cellular level under a microscope and I can't begin to explain it. Sure, I get how some genius could tweak apoptosis and telomeres. How she got it to auto-jump-start after the death of the subject is beyond comprehension," Hamer utters breathlessly with admiring frustration.

"Did Myer tell you anything about the process he underwent?"

"He said something about... umm... *maintenance.* He said that without periodic refreshes, the perfection wears off. You still live forever, it's just life in hell... tortured thoughts and pain, deterioration but no death." Her face grows grim at reliving the memory. "He was convulsing and paranoid, but I found a drug cocktail that seems to limit the horror."

"Not the case for me. I just go along my merry way. I haven't had any booster shot or anything," Chandler adds.

"Exactly."

Chandler's brow twists, eyes scanning upward as if chasing a butterfly and then return to level viewing. "Maybe the process isn't flawed at all. It's just another person's idea of perfection," he calmly posits, his brain finally kicking in.

"How's that?"

"Well, it's perfect if you want to keep an order of things. Unfettered Eternals prancing the planet doing whatever the hell they want could be quite a mess. After all, people being free from risk or mortal danger could get a tad chaotic and rebellious."

"You mean they built in a stick along with the carrot?"

"Sure, let's call it that. They incentivized it, uploaded a law enforcement component. You get out of line, you get to live in your own personal hell for a while. It's brilliant, actually."

"Yeah, law and order, but according to whom? Whose laws? Whose idea of order?" Hamer darkly contemplates.

"I would think most likely according to James Carpenter."

Hamer nods in undeniable agreement. "So, if Carpenter possesses the key to the gates of heaven or hell, and if all the world's leaders become Eternal, then who would you say is really in charge?"

"You don't really need me to answer, right?"

"So, somewhere along the way there was a handoff, or a hostile takeover of Brandt's process by Carpenter," Hamer contemplates. "Isn't that the way it always is? Some scientist finds a breakthrough and the powerful find a way to corrupt it," she pontificates, alcohol lubricating her commentary.

"I wouldn't go that far, Pat. Look, Brandt was brilliant and everything, but she was no saint. She loved playing God. When we worked together, sometimes she would send chills down my spine with her lack of consideration towards the ramifications of her discoveries. She was a purist in that sense. She considered herself just another force of nature."

"Point taken. Like opening Pandora's Box and then disappearing from the face of the earth."

"Yeah, sort of like that."

Sixty Eight
Present Day

"Don't you see? It's perfect, Pete. I won't be covering Carpenter. I will be examining the effect of the single most impactful event to ever face the people of this planet," pitches Christy Raines to her former managing editor.

"Every man, woman and child, every race, color and creed will have to decide on living forever or letting nature take its course and come what may. Every day, more and more people are joining the ranks of the never-dead. Many more have not." Raines' pours out her passion, selling a winning formula for a hit news series. "Why do some choose to and others not? In order to make the decision or bolster the one they've already made, undecided viewers will want objective information, and we will be the broadcast leader in providing that. It's a no-brainer of a news series."

Kilgore twists and squirms at the possibilities as he weighs her argument. His head shakes for no apparent reason, an eyebrow raises. He hoists a thirty-eight-dollar Reuben sandwich from his plate to buy a few more moments to ponder and quell his grumbling appetite. A hearty bite later, he garbles, "Look, I'd have to have the legal guys look at your agreement with Carpenter again." He swallows and wipes his mouth. His diction fully restored, he continues. "My instincts like the idea, but you not anywhere near it."

Raines motions to jump in. His hand raises to interrupt her interruption. He plucks two shoestring truffle fries from his plate and bites them in half, then finishes them off. "But there is some serious juice in your audience appeal and the fact that you are not on the Eternal track yourself, and no one really needs to know why. Carpenter will never out you on that because it would raise inconvenient questions and, de facto, release you from your gag order. It also cloaks you in a sort of unquestioned credibility about the matter. But, I still don't know."

"Pete, look, I've already done some preliminary investigation. Carpenter is fudging the numbers." With eyes charged with purpose, her words come packed with self-assured intensity. "He tells a story of gradual, global conversion, but my sources estimate almost fifteen percent of the world's population is already Eternal or will be in short order. He's got the accelerator pushed to the floor. There are now rifts and disenchantment growing within all the major religions and new ones cropping up. There's even a sort of grass-roots Carpenter cult growing."

Riveted to her monologue, Kilgore mindlessly chomps bite after bite. She soldiers on. "There are death clubs and cannibalism, really sick shit, Pete. People need to know this is going on in the dark corners of our global culture."

"I'm eating here, okay?" he protests in corned-beef-muffled tones. He swallows. "And hasn't that always been going on?"

Kilgore is not the only one casting aspersions on her subject matter. Patrons at nearby tables glare silent disapproval. She thinks maybe one of Manhattan's most opulent bistros was not the optimal choice for a production pitch of such raw content, but she had to sweeten the offer enough to gain an audience with Kilgore. She knew he couldn't refuse if she could get in front of him. She tones down the volume, but not the heat.

"It's like now that death and damage don't count, every seedy impulse has this unquenchable drive. All the darkness below the surface of the collective human psyche now has license to go on an endless, guilt-free spree of debauchery. Paintballs have been replaced by real bullets. The new form of selfie is a snuff video. And no, none of those things ever went on right out there in the mainstream."

Kilgore leans back in his chair. He spots a colleague leaving at the other side of the restaurant, smiles and waves. "Look, I get it, dark stuff. Is there any good stuff coming out of it? Have you found anything to balance the slimier side of things?"

"Sure, there are ongoing discussions about long-distance space travel and the overthrow of a number of tin horn dictators who are quickly losing their leverage to dispense genocide. There are the terminally ill becoming whole in three days while they and their families rejoice... and the fact that Carpenter does all this for no charge." The last comment slithers out with an acid bite of sarcasm attached which Kilgore easily detects.

"So, Christy. I have to ask. Given what happened... your experience with Carpenter. Seriously, what's your angle?"

Raines obscures her angst-pursed lips with a sip from her wine glass, then responds. "C'mon, Pete. I'm a professional."

"Yes, you are, consummately so," he seconds with obligatory resolve. He leans forward and squints his eyes slightly. "But no one could taste the humiliation you did and be able to blindly cover this story."

"Pete, I..." She knows she is exposed.

"I know what you're going to say, so leave it." He pauses her with hands in the air. "Just hear me out and I won't judge you. Off the record, *what's... your... agenda*?"

She sighs and slumps, deflated by the moment she'd hoped to avoid to win the deal but knew would most certainly arrive. "He's not who he says he is. I see that now. When I covered him all that time, he worked me. He crawled under my skin and danced with my soul. No one has ever done that." Her eyes glare unshakable conviction. "He is up to something, Pete. You know it all too well. I've interviewed scoundrels and all manner of murderous devils. They come and they go like so many bad winters. But he... Carpenter is of a make like none I have ever seen."

"So, because you met your match, he's *up to something*. Sounds like the fury of a woman scorned to me, Chris."

"Nice try, Pete. I'm not biting," she retorts abruptly without blinking.

Kilgore slumps back, his play rebuffed. "Okay, I had to test you. And now you're kind of scaring the shit out of me. You said that like you truly believe it."

"I do. I've had years to reflect. I've watched him and studied him. I understand him now. It won't happen again. I know why it scared the shit out of you, too. The truth is, I know how Celeste is and I am sure she is pressuring you. How much have you spent trying to soothe her anxiety about every last wrinkle and roll?"

Kilgore smiles dry at her parry. "At least a hundred grand," he drones out as he hoists his martini glass up for another sip. The sting of gin mingles with the sour of the kraut. "I forgot how good you were at this," he smirks. "Yes, Celeste can't wait. She wants to live forever. I have apprehensions, and believe me, it would be great to see her looking like she did thirty years ago, and possibly even better. She'd be so much more relaxed."

"And if you don't go along?"

"She'd dump me for sure. Not right away, but it would be a foregone conclusion."

"The *'til death do you part* thing in the marriage contract is probably out the window for everyone, now," Raines adds.

"I get it. It's all too clear. All of her friends are planning to do it when their number comes up, and she won't be left out. Funny thing is, I know these people. Once they are all looking fabulous, virile, and at their peak, marriage won't mean a thing. It's going to be a free-for-all." He washes his words down with the last of his second martini. "Okay, where do we begin?"

"I think you just wrote our first episode," she champions.

"Well done. I really missed this... *us*... doing *this*, Christy. By the way, mea culpa. Zarabeth is a complete idiot, but you probably knew that. You should have told me," Kilgore deadpans. Raines breaks out in full laughter, Kilgore responds in kind, then offers, "Why don't we head back to my office and do some further brainstorming, maybe put a pitch together to the network."

She signs the credit card receipt and they begin their departure. His tone changes to caution while donning his jacket. "Let me throw this into the mix, though. Most of the network cronies are either friendly to, or will eventually be, Eternals. Some are even friendly with James Carpenter himself. We have to watch how we angle the lens on this."

Outside, the bitter cold of a January afternoon rudely greets them. Walking past him, she utters, "I have the perfect take. It immunizes me and paints Carpenter in a corner."

Standing alone together in the chilled air, Kilgore questions, "What do you have in mind?"

"The whole premise of the series is that I am thinking of becoming an Eternal."

"But you can't be. He won't allow it."

"As you said yourself, no one out there knows that."

"Right." He nods. "Brilliant. And as the series progresses you gain popular favor, and then you have the leverage on Carpenter. If you say yes, then he can't say no. If he did say no, it would bring about suspicion."

"Exactly." She smiles with bright eyes, her reporter's edge now fully restored. "Now let's get a ride before we become the last two people on the planet to freeze to death."

Sixty Nine
Present Day

"I don't know why I didn't think of this before."

"Because you were too focused on the next glorious way you wanted to die, Marcus," Hamer volleys back. "Have you found anything?"

"I think so; at least there are some files in here. I'm trying to recall her naming system, and what the file extensions mean," Chandler replies while tapping on a keyboard. "If I can, then maybe I can whittle down the files worth looking at. But let's not get ahead of ourselves. It's iffy that the software is even intact."

The *her* Chandler evokes is Adeline Brandt. After a couple of Wild Turkeys, inspiration struck. During their macabre research two years ago, Chandler supplied Hamer with some of Brandt's discarded technology. It still resides in the shed adjacent to the cabin, physically and emotionally too much for Hamer to disassemble since then.

Decades ago, as Brandt began her exit and eventual disappearance, Chandler absconded with the precision equipment. Most of it he had crafted out of whole cloth as the project progressed. His work was unique, his own form of art. He didn't want anyone else to reverse engineer it, or worse, warehouse it into obsolescent obscurity. Ultimately it was more about pride than anything else.

Before she disappeared, Brandt wiped any drives clean of her research data. But her cutting-edge method of purging the data was the 1988 version. With modern methods, restoring the scrubbed data turned out to be a routine task for Chandler. The drives were well-preserved, state-of–the-art hardware at the time they were employed. Evolved from his work at NASA, they were designed to operate in extreme climates and varying gravity, let alone thirty years in temperature-controlled storage in western Maryland.

"I might be able to tap a resource at the Bureau

"No," Chandler interrupts. "No outsiders. I'm pretty sure I can get most of these running. Some of these programs I actually authored. After a while, she had me writing code to keep things in-house and off the grid. But mostly because the programs she needed didn't exist."

"What exactly is this machine anyway?"

"Among other things, this was our data farm. But it also housed the operating system linking the other equipment together."

Chandler types in commands and lines of code then exclaims. "That's it! Okay, I should have some options for you soon. I just had to remember her encryption method."

"That was quick, Marcus."

The unit itself, is comprised of khaki-green panels. Inside the unit lie rows of circuit boards, connected by patch cords. There is a single nine-inch green-screen monitor. Chandler continues typing, perched atop a rustic bar stool. As he types, lines of code and commands rapidly scroll by, released from their slumber. Finally, a list of files appears.

"Booyah!" he shouts with a pumping fist.

Hamer, peering over his shoulder, says. "Where do we start? I hope you know what the file names mean. Is there some rhyme or reason to those?"

"Yeah, I'm a bit rusty, but if I recall, the 'Q' files are mostly data tracking, progress reports, etcetera. The 'J' files are journaling—her notes and such. And the 'Z' files, well, those were used to catalogue the Vatican artifacts. What strikes your fancy, Pat?"

"Journal files?" Hamer lights up. "I want to know what she was thinking."

"A word of warning: they are bound to be cryptic. Most uber-genius types are hyper-protective of their work, so she probably had some sort of secret code structure to her documentation, something known only to her, a la DaVinci."

Chandler taps out a command opening a "J" file. Hamer's eyes eagerly scan the text. The entry shows a sequence of numbers as a header with words beneath.

"The numbers have to be some sort of date reference or sequence number," Hamer posits.

"Most likely. But from entry to entry the numbers don't appear sequential."

"She may have scrambled them. I'm sure they are encoded, too."

"And the text entries themselves make no sense. What's this mean? *Dancer yields plus remains shoes in place of top hats.*"

"My point exactly."

"Lord," Hamer deflates. "This will take a while to cipher out."

"If it is even decipherable. Good luck."

"Here, open a Z file," Hamer requests, pointing to the screen.

The file opens, scrolling unreadably fast. Chandler leans back, surprised. "Okay. Wow." He strokes his chin. "This is all main frame batch compiler crap. Damn, I forgot about this." He rubs his face with his hand in disappointment. "I recall now. The data got so encumbering we moved it to a main frame environment because the PC processors kept crashing. All these 'Z' files work together and cross reference with the 'Q' files. It was just easier to drop it in here and run reports than try to manage it in the clumsy, limited spreadsheet programs of the day."

"So, can we get reports out of here?"

"We could, but we would be flailing in the dark trying to connect reference points." Chandler rises and crouches behind the unit. He examines the back panel, looking for any sort of porting assembly. After a few moments and wordless comments, he barks, "Okay, I think I can do this. Look, I need to run to my storage unit and grab some stuff. I might be able to get all this transferred to a laptop. Then I can craft an emulation program and it will go much smoother to link it all together. Once organized, we can see it, sort it, and search it."

"How long will you be gone?"

"Maybe six hours, depending on how long it takes me to find suitable hardware and connection cables among my outcasts."

"Can you give me a quick tutorial on the commands? I want to try reading the journal files while you're out, get a head start."

"Look," Chandler cautions urgently. "Be very careful; these old programs don't give you much warning about when you are queued up to delete the lot."

She nods and places her hands on his to offer reassurance. "Believe it or not, I have worked on some of this type of thing before. It's been awhile, though. I just need a refresher."

In ten minutes, Chandler has Hamer up to speed. He snaps a couple cell phone pictures of the unit's rear panel and then crashes out the front door. Hamer pulls up the stool and plops down before the green glow of the monitor.

"Major resurgence of McArthur status on blueberries. Hard mustard – green beans," she reads out loud as if that will give more clarity to the confusion. "Christ almighty, I must be crazy to think I can make heads or tails out of this mumbo jumbo." Hamer sighs but charges ahead undaunted.

After nearly an hour of reading files, she decides to abandon the cause. She hopes that, if Chandler can truly transfer everything to a laptop, she can attack the Journal files as a whole. She stretches, unwinding frustration. Outside, the day has turned to night. Back down the hall she peeks in on Myer. Finding him asleep, she leaves him to his peace. At least in slumber he appears undisturbed by the demons.

Seventy
Present Day

"Killing has replaced sex as the ultimate high. With the stigma of murder removed from the equation, there is no longer the moral dilemma. The first recorded sin of man against man in the Bible is that of Cain offing his brother Abel. One wonders, if Abel had reconstituted three days later, would it have been cut from the early drafts?" entrepreneur Conrad Weeks pops out with an Australian accent and a self-satisfied chuckle. "The once greatest mortal sin is now the recreation of choice for many who have chosen to live forever."

Christy Raines churns to formulate a follow-up to the entrepreneur's flip statement, one so implausible—unthinkable—just five years previous.

"You do realize how absurdly ironic that sounds, Mr. Weeks," she pokes.

Weeks smirks confidently perched in his armchair opposite Raines and her production crew. "You mean that those choosing life have opted to make a sport of death? Of course. It's not as outlandish as it may appear, however, since there is no such thing as death for these people. In fact, it's a celebration of life. These pastimes are the issuing of a sort of middle finger to it." Weeks laughs again.

"I suppose I can see your point." Raines pauses to reload. "But humanity has been given a gift from Mr. Carpenter to evolve beyond such frivolity. Don't you think we as a species should simply discard death, remove it from the menu and focus our energies on life and the living of it?"

Weeks straightens in his seat. "That is a question for someone else. At Forbidden Adventures, we are merely providing a gaming experience never available to any before. Our role is simply to organize and fulfill fantasy. We are not in the business of judging the merits of the individual choice. We are just glad we can provide that service. After all, we all need our diversions."

"But is it only that? Some argue, many celebrated psychiatric scholars even, that what you define as *diversion* might be leaving a lasting stain on our intellectual makeup," Raines counters. "Harvard's own Harold Green states, and I quote, 'Even when no ultimate outward harm comes of it, the act of murder is summoning the darker side of the deeper human spirit. There is damage done and we don't know the extent of the long-term effect, especially over the very long term.'"

"Again, not my place to judge others," Weeks deflects from her pensive delving. "We are providing a service for consenting adults that seems to be in great demand. If it wasn't us, there would be at least a dozen more following to offer it themselves. It is happening already as we speak. It's a growth industry."

"Very well, Mr. Weeks. I guess only time will tell." Raines moves on past her own skepticism. "So, can you give us a rundown of the services you offer?"

Weeks raises his right hand slightly and clicks a button. A large television monitor behind and between them animates, projecting a promotional video. He narrates as the images fly past. "What we don't offer is what any old Joe can do—turn on a helmet cam and jump off a bridge. We are providing the thrill of whatever experience you choose. It really isn't about killing; it's the drama and juiciness of the thrill that is the true fantasy. We have skilled technicians and a corps of brilliant role players to provide a full, grandiose life experience for our patrons. We recreate historical scenes from the past. If you want the Roman Colosseum with gladiators and lions, we can make that happen. We are currently in negotiations to acquire the *actual* Colosseum in Rome to recreate the past for a broadcast event. More on that later... "

Raines watches intently, occasionally jotting a note or two. Weeks pushes his ideas further.

"If you want a true manhunt you can have it, war games, medieval dungeons, vampire cults, you name it. These make great corporate team-building exercises. Or perhaps, imagine"—Weeks' eyes grow large "Shakespeare... Hamlet and Romeo and Juliet... where the characters *actually* die at the end."

"So much for taking a closing bow, I suppose," Raines jokes, then seizes another opportunity to probe her subject. "So, where does this all lead, Mr. Weeks?"

"Lead?"

"Yes. I mean, is this the new shared experience? To see by how many diverse means one can expire and then share them on social media like vacation pictures?"

"How people choose to share or not share is up to them. But, if they want to share, we will be there to give them an experience worth sharing. One they can't wait to share," he delivers smoothly, gleaming with pride. "Tell me, Christy. I want to host an adventure for you. What would you choose? Any time period, any place?"

"Let me get back to you on that," she returns only half-serious.

Seventy One
Present Day

"Stewart?" Christy Raines says, surprised at the unexpected sight of her news counterpart, Stewart Waverly. "What brings you to New York?" She spotted him alone in a conference room on her way to Pete Kilgore's office.

"I'm here on business, but I thought I'd stop by and see some colleagues I haven't seen in years." He rises to shake her hand. "We're headed to lunch soon; would you like to join us?"

"I'd love to, but I've got a production meeting."

"Oh, you're producing now?" he asks with a raised eyebrow.

"I'm wearing many hats now, but I'm working on a news series. Our third installment airs Sunday."

"I'm sorry, I had no idea. What's the subject matter?"

She thinks it would be best to answer in generalities, but her competitive pride gets the best of her. "We're examining the brave new world of Eternals. Frankly, what other story is there?"

He nods back. "Most assuredly."

She continues on, despite being unasked. "We're taking a deep dive into the societal upheaval that the planet and humankind are facing, not just the big picture things, but focusing in at a granular level."

"That sounds marvelous." Waverly's curiosity pokes at him and he asks. "Such as...?"

"There are shockwaves to all religions, population concerns, environmental—"

"Of course," he interrupts with patriarchal dismissal. "But isn't everyone doing that story, my dear?"

"Not so much," she parries back with a smile. "First, we are asking questions about the science of it all. Everyone seems to be conveniently ignoring that question. We're discovering some unforeseen cultural consequences playing out. For example, many who have spent a lifetime preaching an afterlife are giving strong consideration to becoming Eternals. There appears to be a growing societal stratification of Eternals vs. non-Eternals, the former detaching from the latter. Families are being torn in two..."

Waverly nods, unintentionally showing admiration. "Fascinating."

"You just have to ask the right questions and..." She stops herself. "But look who I'm telling this to, the one and only Stewart Waverly." She smiles craftily, offering feigned admiration. "You said you were here on business, if I may ask..."

Waverly pauses, thinking of how to delicately phrase it. "Tomorrow, I'm going to Maryland." He leaves his response to hang in the air.

It takes her a moment, but Raines makes sense of it. "Oh, I see."

"I assume you will be joining the Eternals class soon, as well?" Waverly asks.

A dose of harbored shame from two years before assaults her insides. "I haven't decided."

Astonishment covers his face at her response. He assumes an air of counselor, albeit patronizingly so. "You know, Christy, if you plan on continuing your career, there really is no option." He smiles at something only he knows. "There are, of course, other benefits to eternal life besides career."

"I know," she answers, still hiding her darkness. "Look, I'm late. I need to run, but it was really nice to see you. Good luck, Stewart."

Seventy Two
Present Day

He knows it is there, a trigger stone in the floor, or a catch release hidden in the wall. If the latter, there would probably be some telltale grime or wear in the critical spot. None is revealed. Traeger is left standing, staring at a wall, waiting for his imagination to decipher the riddle.

Always the faithful researcher of his architectural enterprises, he discovered some nuances in the original drawings of the main building now housing The Carpenter Institute. More than two years ago, as he sought insights and inspiration for his temple designs, he hoped the design notes and layouts of the initial construction might reveal some. He learned that the majestic, core structure came complete with its own lore and mysteries.

Designed for grandiose purposes, the original mansion was an anticipated retreat for a larger-than-life man, then-president Theodore Roosevelt. While paging through some of the documents tucked away in an architectural library, Traeger found obscurities. When examined by his learned eye, he discovered indications of voids and unexplained spaces, mostly in the excavation beneath the main structure. Traeger never gave these discoveries much thought at the time, but recently, for no particular reason, their existence has churned some curiosity in him.

Led there by the original architectural drawings, his journey to the wall began outside the grounds in the woods. A mound with no outward telltale features deftly concealed a screw hatch door not unlike the one to a bomb shelter or a submarine. The entry was well hidden by a lifetime of accumulated debris and flora. The hatch opened to a steel ladder depositing ten feet below ground level. Inside, Traeger's flashlight revealed a damp, dank corridor, but one well built, one anticipating disaster scenarios only imaginable at the time of construction. The passage floor is roughly hewn granite resembling cobblestones, but larger. The walls are supported by muscular beams, most likely railroad ties, reinforced by steel joins all coated with a tarry, black waterproofing compound.

He chuckles at himself when the thought of using magic words as the solution to entry occurs to him. Reason, not hocus-pocus seems a better course, he decides. He thinks of the original architect and the esprit of his era. He is a man whose life and work Traeger briefly studied in engineering school. In the time of its construction, building a castle-mansion meant the employ of forged metals and the conquering of bedrock granite. The design was meant to reflect the rise of industrial superiority and the muscular subduing of the natural environment for the purposes of man.

He examines the wall again, this time imagining himself as the architect. The surface is comprised of stacked stones blended in with the native hewn rock. He runs his hands carefully up and down all of it, making a brief connection with each individual stone. Several passes later, he fixes on two stones about four feet apart, knee high and both equidistant from the floor. He pushes and tries to twist them with no success. He pulls instead and they reluctantly submit swinging outward on cranky, hidden hinges. An iron oval handle is revealed behind each. He yanks the handles. The sound of a mechanism releasing on the opposite side echoes through the passage. The wall swings ajar, now a door. Easily pushed inward it reveals a further passage.

He sends the flashlight beam down. The sparkle of damp cobweb threads, sparse but randomly weaving through the darkened square of passage, awakes his caution. The waft of mildew drifts to his sinuses, an odor he expected and fortunately the only smell to greet him, no noxious gas or rotting anything. Traeger proceeds forward deciding it is safe, noting similar construction with timber beams anchored firmly on the sides. There is no indication of crumbling or deterioration, let alone a cave-in. This passage had defined purpose and was constructed to survive indefinitely. He suspects this was a sort of escape route or hiding place should the president need one in a time of crisis.

Across the threshold, Traeger treads gently, more cobblestones layered with a thin coating of dampened dust. He notes the path ahead is undisturbed and concludes he is the first to walk here in a very long time. Arriving at a T, he stops and pulls a folded piece of paper from his back pocket, his makeshift hand drawing of the network of passages culled from the documents. He glances at it and shines the light down the passage to the left then the right. He scans the map again and proceeds down the leftward direction.

His target destination is the largest hidden room he found on the drawings. Cobweb strands, now more comfortable with their visitor-friend, eagerly grab at his clothing. A skittering sound reaches his ears from behind. A rat, he presumes, he hopes. His thoughts comfort him, reminding him that places like this will have such things in residence. He spurs himself onward, not lingering on what else may take notice of his presence. In less than twenty steps, he arrives at a dead end. The passage has found a wall, one of human construction, but this time he stands at the backside where the locking mechanism is in plain view. A strip of faint light is breaking through the gap on the floor below. A scan with the flashlight finds an iron lever not unlike a crude handle to an old-style slot machine. His right hand clutches the lever and as he begins to tug downward, he pauses to wonder why there would be light coming from a room unknown for over a century. He releases his eager fist from the lever.

Seventy Three
Present Day

"I think I've got it now, Marcus. It's starting to make sense," Hamer bellows to Chandler from her usual place on the couch in the main room of the cabin.

"How so?" he asks from the kitchen while screwing the top back on a jar of Dijon mustard.

"It's as simple as just understanding these bizarre notations as locations and not prose."

"Hang on, I'm almost done. It will be much easier if I can see it."

For four straight hours Hamer has been working on unlocking Adeline Brandt's encryption method. Chandler found the cabling and hardware needed to transfer the data from the old mainframe environment to a laptop. An hour later, he had applied a mainframe simulator and completed the data transfer. Since then, the laptop has been in Hamer's unrelenting possession.

Chandler loads a wooden cutting board, a make-do service tray, with freshly made sandwiches, fruit, and some cans of beer. He deposits the sustenance on the coffee table by Hamer and sits on the couch.

"Here," Hamer motions for him to scoot closer on the couch. In one move, he grabs a half sandwich and a beer, takes a bite and receives the laptop from Hamer.

"So, what am I looking at?"

"It's a three-dimensional spreadsheet."

"Three-dimensional?"

"That's her twist to it all. Back in the day, it was only possible to use such a thing if one could emulate the third dimension in one's head. A pretty foolproof encryption device for 1987. But, now I can actually build it for us to map out her journal entries," she finishes during a lunge to procure her own sandwich and beverage.

"I think we can add the *brilliant* label to you, Ms. Hamer."

Hamer smiles and pauses. "Holy shit, Chandler. That's the nicest thing you've ever said to me. And it was downright sincere. I could kiss you right now," she utters through the muffle of a large bite of sandwich.

"Uh, maybe later." He grabs a napkin and wipes her mouth of sandwich leavings.

"So, how did you figure this out?"

"You mean besides being brilliant," she boasts as much as her humble nature allows. "I realized she used a lot of colors in her descriptions along with objects, famous names, inseparable word pairings such as *green beans* and *garden gnome*. I was making it much more complicated than it really was. I came to the conclusion she needed to have a method that she could decipher on the fly like knowing another language. She was managing an immense amount of data and it would have been clumsy and inefficient to refer to some decoding key, or run some script each time she needed to use the database," Hamer chirps.

"Makes perfect sense to me," Chandler returns. She resumes in stride.

"Each entry had to have five things. Basically the five simplest questions. Where, what, why… etcetera. The *what* is the item from the archive. It's the numeric value at the top of each entry. We thought it was a date. It matches one of the original Vatican catalog numbers if you strip the first and last number and reverse it. I won't bore you with all the spreadsheet variables, but I mapped them all out. What really broke it open for me was the epiphany that she had a Z axis as part of the construction." Hamer pauses to catch her breath and swig some beer.

"Okay, what was she mapping?"

"That's the last piece of the puzzle. Each entry had some sort of evaluative comment like *positive* or *unremarkable*. I am certain these aren't code words at all. She used a lot of words, but the degree range of positive to negative was only about a factor of six levels by my own extrapolation. I color-filled and valued the results, then added them to the data."

"So, we should be able to sort the data and maybe understand what she found, or at least what was significant," Chandler contributes.

"We *should* be able to because I *already did*," Hamer booms boastfully, punctuating her bravado with another hearty swig. "Take a look and see if you can understand the correlation. The more intense the entry is on the red scale means it was a high value item." She completes her tutorial with a ballsy belch.

Chandler dives in, mumbling entry text to himself and finishing off his sandwich. Hamer heads to the kitchen.

"It's all wood fragments and fabrics. I don't get it. What value is that?" Chandler muses.

"Does it say where the wood and fabrics came from?" a third voice mutters wearily from another direction. Myer has emerged like an apparition from his room to join them.

"Ivan? Is everything okay?" Hamer dashes over to assist his frail, draping form. She helps him to the couch. Chandler sits stunned at finally seeing Myer's drained appearance standing on two feet.

"I'm fine, Pat. Go to the Vatican documents and compare her description of the items to theirs. I think you will find she omitted something very vital from her entry and did so on purpose."

"Why would she do that, and how do you know that?" Hamer asks.

"You'll see. It's the key to all of it. She left it off as a failsafe so no one else would know. In fact, it's all you need to know."

"It's not that easy, Myer," Chandler jumps in with a brash tone of denial. "We worked for almost two years on this. There is no one simple thing, okay? First item. *St. Barnabus 1542, W-O-T-C.* Second item. *Jerusalem Chapel, 287 AD. W-O-T-C.* Third item, blah blah it says W-O-T-C too. What does that mean, *W-O-T-C*?"

Hamer looks incredulously at Myer. "How did you arrive at this in your semi-coma in there and I've been immersed in the data and didn't see that?"

"Intuition I guess, Pat, and…" Myer pauses, realizing the next thing he wants to say will come off as insanity.

"And what," Chandler probes, irritated.

"I don't know." Myer is compelled to proceed. "All these voices gnawing at me, and, it's like in some way I have access to what they know. It's hard to describe."

"Myer, come on. It's just the random ramblings of your darker subconscious. That's all," Chandler dismisses to ground the conversation.

Myer reluctantly capitulates. "Very well. What are most of the items assigned that label?"

"Wood," Chandler answers.

"Every descriptive phrase has an article or two thrown in there, sooo…" Myer guides.

"On the… on to," Chandler thinks aloud.

"Try *of*," Myer leads on. "Wood of the…"

"CROSS," Hamer finishes. "Wood of the cross."

"I still don't get it," Chandler admits.

"What was Brandt's field of expertise?" Myer continues.

"Biogenetics," Hamer answers.

"What happened on the cross?" Myer asks professorially

"Jesus died," Hamer answers again.

"Yes, Jesus died a horrible, agonizing, bloody, *flesh-ripping* death," Myer says with finality.

"Of course," Hamer accepts in dulcet resignation.

Chandler's face flushes. "Wait, are you saying she found Christ's actual DNA and somehow utilized it to bring about the Eternals?"

"That's exactly what I am saying," Myer's raspy voice musters all the conviction it can harness. "And you and I have that DNA circulating in our bodies as we speak," he finishes looking straight at Chandler.

Chandler gently sets down the laptop and falls back surrendered, into the couch. He scans his hand and then his arm with new eyes. Two fingers raise to his neck to feel his pulse. "Fuck me," falls from his astonished lips where no other words can find form.

Seventy Four
Present Day

The investigation is as thorough as he can muster for one requiring absolute silence. With an ear to the door to listen, he hears nothing. Stooping to look through the gap between the wall and the floor, he sees the light still there, but too faint to give any clue of origin. Traeger's better judgment says to walk away, forget this. But brazen curiosity pesters him. Proceeding seems foolish; it gains him nothing except scratching an itch of his own imagination at the cost of possibly everything. Opening the door to the secret room beyond could explode his world in a thousand ways. Scrutiny would lie heavy upon his character should the door open to a common area like a delivery dock or a lab space. The secret he kept from James and Marianne would be his undoing and grave consequences would surely follow.

He has mapped it all out in his head, though. He knows he is at least twenty feet below ground and far from any significant area on the grounds of The

Carpenter Institute. That conclusion leads to even greater mysteries. The light creeping under the door into the passage means there is some purpose to the room for someone. If that someone is James or Marianne then he may be opening a door to knowledge he didn't bargain for or ever want to know. Still, his hand, with a mind of its own, wanders to the lever. Commanding its own agenda, it grips tighter. His breath quickens, gulps of blood from his pounding heart thump his temples. Before he can arrest the impulse, his arm engages.

The lever barely moves, fused in place from decades of idleness, too rigid in its resolve to cooperate. But noises were made. The element of surprise is lost. Approaching panic, Traeger goes all-in with both hands; rising up on his toes, his entire body pulls down. The mechanism surrenders with a weighty, metallic clunk. The door teeters open, the room now visible through a small sliver. He pauses to listen and is met with silence. He carefully pulls the heavy door, eyes darting, searching for danger. But the view is unremarkable. A faintly lit room lies ahead, but one more resembling a cave than a finished construction. Stone and concrete, some of it man's work and some nature. A chill greets him with the faint smell of kerosene—perhaps the fuel for the faint light.

He hears a groan, one of human origin, a moan of mild agony. Traeger spies movement from a darkened far corner. A figure moves on the floor, one wrapped in a blanket. The figure rolls to face him. Traeger stiffens. It speaks. "Leave me, Satan! This place is blessed and sanctified. You are forbidden to dwell here."

The admonition is bracing, at first. But Traeger's spirit eases with recognition. He knows only one person who would even say something like that. He hurries over. Closer in, the flashlight beam finds a very old man. The man raises the blanket to block the light, as a vampire might block the sun with his cape.

"Cardinal, is that you?" The blanket lowers. The man's face lights up, then twists with confusion.

"This is yet another false vision. Lucifer, be gone!" the man commands.

"No, Cardinal, it is me, Alex. Why are you here? What is this place?" Traeger asks urgently, bending to one knee.
"Whatever you are, you must speak more softly," Kovacs instructs pointing to a passage off the main room, one blocked by bars across the opening.

"It is me, Cardinal, Alex Traeger."

Kovacs raises his head and squints, then brims a big smile. The smile turns to weeping, a grateful wail. "Praise God, my prayers have been heard."

"Cardinal, quickly, I can get you out of here, but we must hurry."

"I cannot leave here."

"That makes no sense. There is no reason to stay," Traeger pleads.

"My disappearance at this time would cause great harm to many. I must remain here. It is for the best. How did you find me?"

Traeger is bewildered at Kovacs' insistence to stay but answers anyway. "I wasn't looking for you. I found some hidden architecture. I was exploring. Who is holding you here?"

"The Devil is with permission from God. He has assigned to me this penance to repair my soul, sparing me the damnation of hell. Here, there is at least a presence of the Holy One. God lives with me here, and now you being here brings hope that all is not lost. God's plan is still underway. He has listened."

Traeger is reminded of the Cardinal's propensity for grand proclamation, but he fears that maybe Kovacs has slipped deeper into his own thoughts living alone in this cold, forsaken place. "Why are they holding you?"

"I am too much of a threat. My knowledge of the past could bring them down. This is the only reason I can imagine."

"Excuse me if this sounds insensitive, but why don't they just kill you? To be honest, I had decided that had been your fate soon after the last time I saw you so long ago."

"I have wondered myself, Alex. It would be the rational thing to do. But they have done the opposite, in fact. They have made me Eternal."

Traeger spends a moment in stunned silence. "You? That makes no sense. And who has made you Eternal?" Traeger says as much to ask himself as the Cardinal. Kovacs' appearance is as someone not Eternal.

"Carpenter and his succubus Marianne."

Traeger takes a seat on the floor, wheels spinning. James and Marianne holding a harmless man hostage? There is no equation for that or for the skeleton of a man before him. Traeger's heart sinks at the sight of a man he considers his good friend.

"I am an amusement to them. Mostly for her. A ranting zealot kept as an exhibit for their personal zoo. But, it is much more than that. I am the proxy of God, in their eyes. They use me as a finger to poke the eye of the Almighty. They enjoy taunting me and testing me, trying to break my faith. But, they only make me stronger."

"But they don't believe in God. Why do they need to taunt something they don't believe in?"

"So they say. Their actions betray their words. If one wants to poke a finger in the eye of God, one must first accept there is an eye for the poking. They made me Eternal so I can never live in the place of God's full love. They have trapped me in this life so that I might never know the other, the place of utter bliss."

Traeger takes to his feet, then paces while contemplating the new knowledge. After a minute he turns to Kovacs. "But they plan to make everyone Eternal. That seems like something good to me."

"It is not, especially if the bargain is made with the Devil." Kovacs waits a moment to collect his thoughts. "You see, Alex, the human soul's natural habitat is not one of corporeal existence. Our spiritual being was conceived in heaven. Our time here on earth is meant to be temporary. When it is complete, our spirits continue on to a greater glory, eventually residing in the presence of God."

"And if we stay on earth forever—"

"The soul is trapped for all eternity. The natural spiritual order will never be restored. Eventually, a jealous God will return to collect those he claims as his own. The rest will be left to live in a godless world."

"You mean like... hell?"

Kovacs nods back, satisfied Traeger understands. "But there is more to it. The Devil is the Devil. His unquenchable thirst for false glory, his insatiable longing for praise and worship, would mean all live a life in service to the dark master. Those who remained would exist only to serve him to the exclusion of all else."

"...and for all time," Traeger finishes, trailing off as he slumps in grim realization. "And to accomplish that, he might build a network of global temples," he adds despairingly.

"You know of a plan to do this?"

Traeger's head sinks down. "I'm the project director, Jonas," he sadly confesses.

Kovacs' eyes grow gloomy. Traeger returns to the floor to meet him at his level. "You are working with Satan, Alex. You must be very careful. He will read you. Should you have any doubt, if your thoughts remain alive with anything we've discussed here, he will know it. I fear our conversation may have put you in great danger."

Kovacs sits up and peers urgently at Traeger. "How are you not Eternal, Alex, being that you are so much a part of their operation?"

"I have had personal reservations, but lately Carpenter has been applying pressure."

"You must not. It is still my belief that you are the one that can stop this. You were placed here by God."

"Yes, I recall that. It just doesn't feel that way."

"Don't forget it. There will be a time and a place where God will open the door and whisper at you. Be aware, this is all he asks."

"I will. But I am very deeply imbedded in their business. I may never get that chance."

"What better way for you to have a chance than if you are deeply imbedded? You should go now. They will be coming soon to check on me. Come again and we should talk more. Do so in the early hours of the morning. They never visit me then."

"Are you sure there are no cameras or listening devices here, Cardinal?"

"One can never be sure, but I do know they want no others to know of this place. There is no reason for any of it to be here."

"I will visit you again in a short time." Traeger rises and takes a few steps back to the passageway door. He stops and turns, asking the one unasked question. "Cardinal, if you are Eternal why are you still so weak and frail?"

"I do not know how, but they clearly have a way to apply a lesser degree of what they possess. As I said, they want me to suffer. Be safe, young Alex."

Traeger disappears. The door closes behind him with a sound of metal grabbing metal. The door once again becomes a wall.

Seventy Five
Present Day

"Why would you stop there?"

"I'm sorry, Pat? Me stop where?" answers a puzzled Chandler.

After their chilling discovery in the data files of Adeline Brandt, the trio of Hamer, Chandler, and Myer dispersed about the cabin to their own sanctuaries of thought. The sobering revelation required deep reflection given the enormity of consequence at such a staggering revelation.

Chandler, seeking respite, trespassed into Hamer's space on the main couch to borrow from the bottle of Wild Turkey perched on the coffee table. The chiming of swirling ice mingling with Kentucky mash broke the silence, allowing her tacit approval to ask something out loud.

"Not you, I mean Brandt. Here she is, way back then. She has presumably carved out some DNA that may or may not be divine and found a way to splice it into anyone to make them invincible. Then she just calls it a day and disappears?"

"Well, it's undeniable she disappeared, so maybe."

"But c'mon. You're one of these genius types. You worked with her. Do *you* just decide one day, 'I'm going to turn off my intellectual process and go sit on a beach'?"

"I kind of did exactly that, but now that you put it that way, it would not be like her," Chandler agrees. "But, she didn't totally shut it down. She apparently worked in the shadows somewhere coming up with the policing mechanism."

"Policing mechanism?"

"You know, the difference that makes me free as a bird and makes Myer a prisoner in his own body. I assume there were other things she had cooking as well. But there isn't a lot she could do completely on her own. It's just logistically impossible."

"You knew her and her method; postulate her next move. She has this fountain of youth in her possession, this Lazarus chain of DNA. So, what was her ultimate goal? What did she plan to do with that kind of power?"

"Lazarus?" Chandler asks

"It's in the Bible. He was a man, I think a friend, who Christ returned from the dead."

"She always had an immense ego and delusions of grandeur," Chandler resumes, "But, one could argue they were justifiable given her immense talent. I never asked her, but assumed she was, or was planning to be, Eternal. She must be out there somewhere."

Hamer throws her head back onto the top of the sofa cushion in frustration. She stares at the ceiling, the rows of timbers one after the other, all the evenly spaced apart by a sealant of gooey, black tar. Chandler walks a few steps to peek into Myer's room. He is resting on the bed, managing unconsciousness despite occasional involuntary fits and jerks.

Hamer spies an abandoned wasp's nest tucked into a roof timber and a cross beam above. Its delicate structure briefly draws her attention away from the subject matter. The paper-mache-like walls of the comb captivate her. Each individual chamber is exactly the same. It is the creation of insects not consciously aware of the purpose or the design, but driven by a compulsion programmed by natural selection. Hamer's thoughts blend together.

"Marcus?" Chandler returns from checking on Myer. "Did she ever mention pushing the experiment further?" Hamer asks.

"Not sure what you mean by *further*. But never, not to me at least. The whole thing was mostly about harvesting and compiling the data. We did have some grow operations going for sure, though."

"Grow operations?"

"Genetic reconstitution. Anything organic we found, she had us attempting to make viable again. She explained it was to try and identify lost species and DNA that might be useful in other research. She showed her hand a few times that there might be some profit in identifying new compounds for use in research and to obtain grant money."

"And what did you think of all that at the time?"

"I thought it was a good idea, but nothing ever took. We never got anything to reconstitute fully for long. It always just blew up."

"And who controlled the DNA samples in these experiments? Did you know what you were trying to grow?"

"I wasn't charged with growing anything. I just created the incubators and isolation environments according to her specifications. But she was the only one who knew what was in each trial. The samples were all coded. It's standard procedure to rule out research bias."

"So it could have been anything," Hamer states with inquisitive resolve.

"What do you mean, *anything*?"

"Maybe all these trials weren't for a lot of things; maybe they were all one thing."

"Such as?"

"Human reconstitution."

Chandler twists his face, trying to imagine where she is taking the conversation.

"Hear me out, Marcus. Pretend you are Adeline Brandt. You have a savant-like relationship with genetics, probably the top mind on the globe, and you're an ardent disciple of the scientific method. You are also steeped in the culture of the day. You have familiarity with a myth—or is it a myth?—of a man, no, two men for sure, who apparently rose from their own death almost two thousand years prior."

She pauses to load her next thoughts. Chandler prods. "Go on."

"In fact, one of the gospels, I think Matthew, mentions that after the resurrection of Christ, large numbers of souls began rising from the dead, walking from their tombs, and many bearing witness to it. If you are Brandt, and you have DNA from that era, Christ's DNA even, do you stop at growing strands of DNA? Isn't there something you just want to try because now you have a new Everest?"

Chandler squirms a bit as if some buried, blinded intuition from decades before is rising from dormancy. "You know, Pat, I want to not believe you, and I've been trying to be a devil's advocate here." His face gradually lights up into excitement, his mind changing. "But I think you're probably on to something. Maybe that's why she disappeared. Had she wanted to pursue what you're suggesting, it would have been scientific sacrilege even among rogue cowboy scientists. It still is. No one would back her on that or work with her. They would have been outcasts from then on, a total career killer, not to mention probably something illegal. She would have been outed for sure."

"So we're in agreement. She would have tried to create a clone, and knowing what we know about her, would have not stopped until she was successful."

"Agreed," Chandler affirms raising his glass as further acknowledgement. "But I do know engineering, and in my opinion, the technology of the day would have made it impossible. There just weren't stable enough environments back then. If she got it done, it's a wonder how she made it happen."

Seventy Six
Present Day

"Alex, I greatly appreciate you visiting me. I trust you are exercising all due caution," Kovacs gently implores. "I fear for your safety, my son."

"Trust me, I have, Jonas. After I left you, I had a lot of thoughts about what you said. I am very confused and I needed to talk to you." Alex Traeger sits attentively, cross-legged on the cold stone floor with Kovacs' facing him. After his last visit, he was shaken to his foundation at the thought that he might be an unwitting pawn in the demise of humankind at the hands of James and Marianne. He seeks more answers, more guidance from his elder friend.

"Confused?" Kovacs asks.

"Well, I know you have very strong feelings about James Carpenter, about him being, well…," Traeger struggles, the words heavy on his tongue. "You called him the Antichrist once… Satan."

"Yes, I believe that he is."

"But he has helped so many." Traeger's face wears a look of being torn at the contradiction. Kovacs' stalwart conviction is challenging the goodness he has witnessed in Carpenter. "His work has ended disease, and death. The idea of war, and soon, the very memory of any war, may be over. How are these evil things?"

"They are not, at least not on their face. They improve the human condition and that is good. The question remains, why does he do it?"

"Does it matter?" Traeger's tone rings more insistent and mildly challenging. "Life on Earth is going to be better than it ever has been. Every great social mind, philosophy, and creed has sought what he is delivering—a utopian existence; freedom from the limitations of our fragile bodies. I think even Jesus would approve."

"And with life on Earth an endless experience, what will become of our souls then, Alex?" Kovacs responds calmly but directly.

"We will be free to think and be whatever we want to be. Our souls will flourish."

"No, I speak of our *souls*, our truest and eternal self."

"I... I don't follow, Jonas."

"You understand the concept of a soul, don't you Alex?"

"Well, sure. We talked about that some last time. It's like our ghost. But... what do you mean by *truest eternal self*?"

"Our soul is the purest essence of who we are. The physical body is merely a temporary container for our brief stop along the way to other realms and experiences, and eventually to being one with God in true perfection."

"Other realms and experiences? You mean like heaven or purgatory?"

"Yes, and those are names of convenience simply assigned to dimensions we can't possibly comprehend. We must consider that there may be realms of other composition with physical properties beyond this limited existence."

Traeger's forehead wrinkles, more confused than ever. Kovacs reads his befuddlement and assumes a more empathetic approach.

"I understand your skepticism, Alex. That may not be as farfetched as you think. Remove the religious labelling and it all seems more conceivable. Science has long pondered the existence of other dimensions and parallel universes. As we learn more and more, we do not come away with the sense that someday we will know all there is to know. Quite the opposite. We are overwhelmed with an unfolding of even more questions, not fewer. To conclude that limiting the whole of everything to only those things we can see and know of in three dimensions, is akin to proclaiming the Earth is flat."

"But what does that have to do with *souls*?"

"Let me put it this way. If our true self is found within our soul, then it seems to me we are more suited to a reality not constrained by time or physical limitations. A soul in its natural habitat is formless."

"I'm so lost, Cardinal," Traeger chuckles. "So the whole idea of Saint Peter and the pearly gates somewhere up... there," Trager's eyes drift upward as he finishes the last word. "It all sounds too fantastic. To really think that when we die, we float off to some... I don't know. It just seems like something made up to keep people believing in something greater than this life. You know, the 'opiate of the masses.'"

"I understand, Alex, I truly do."

"And to be frank, Jonas, when given the choice of life here, living forever in what we know is real, or a promise of something glorious but unproven— can you expect anyone to allow themselves to expire, to give up this life? I think more people will choose to go with what they know."

"I fear you are right." Kovacs nods in somber agreement. "It is forged into us by millions of years of natural selection to survive at all costs. We are bound to this physical world by the nature of our flesh. It wins out over our soul, which languishes beneath the compelling urge of primal demands and the diversions of whimsy and desire. But, when one transcends beyond the demands of our physical nature, the body is just so much cosmic dust arranged for a time for our brief visit on this speck in the universe called planet Earth. In the entirety of our journey, life in this world is a mere blink along the way."

"But if there were only proof, a message or sign from beyond, some way to demonstrate it truly exists, then everyone would know without a doubt. The discussion would be over."

Kovacs' conviction and faith begin to swell within him, raising his withered body from the floor onto his feet. "But there was one," he replies reverently. "He was God himself delivered in human form." The words bounce back from the granite walls of his prison as if the ancient stone is adding its own voice of confirmation.

"You mean Jesus." Traeger stands as well. "I have heard that over and over and it makes no sense. Why wouldn't he just come as God, end all doubt?"

"It would seem the most direct way, wouldn't it?" Kovacs smiles at Traeger's practicality. "And maybe the best, at least at first glance. But God chose to come as one of us." Kovacs turns to Traeger, his eyes clear and brilliant. "What if God wanted more than to make his existence known?"

"You mean to *die for our sins*. The whole notion of God becoming man to *save us*. Can't he just save us from where he lives? After all, he is God. Can't you see why it sounds more like fantasy to most people? Father, I'm sorry, but it just does." Traeger's frustration returns. "If God exists, why doesn't he just make himself apparent to everyone? Instead, he hides in the shadows, away from us."

"Because God understands that the power of living by passionate belief outshines mere knowledge."

"But if we knew for certain that God truly exists, we would all follow his way."

"Would we?" Kovacs waits a moment to allow his question to linger. "Concrete certainty leads more to acceptance and capitulation. When confronted with incontrovertible fact, one is resigned to it, not transformed by it. There is no allegiance, homage, or worship attached. It is merely acknowledged without question with no further discussion."

"But at least we would know."

"And God would be relegated to being a *fact*, no longer a thing to be passionately sought after. The vibrant fuel of human passion is the quest for truth and knowing. Once something is learned to absoluteness, it becomes cold certainty. God wants most to be the spark of our deepest passion, the thing we seek with relentless burning in our hearts, to grow beyond ourselves in ways we could never imagine."

Kovacs, despite his depleted condition, is filled with bold passion. He wanders his prison, no longer seeming caged. "Alex, absolute knowledge is a wonderful thing, but unwavering, unshakable fact is static, a realm bound in the absolute. Something is or it isn't, true or false, off or on, one or zero. Knowledge might even move you, at times, show you something you never imagined. But no matter how astonishing, the heart is never engaged. Knowledge is a realm of the mind and the mind alone."

"Then what is it God wants from us?" Traeger asks.

Kovacs approaches Traeger, eyes aglow. "Love," he whispers out with fervor.

Kovacs wanders again, his thoughts needing more space. "Love stands greater and above knowledge, and despite there being no proof of its very existence, it is something we crave and ache for every single day of our lives." Kovacs' eyes well with joy, then a smile shines from within, "And so does God."

The Cardinal raises his gaze. "The funny thing about love is, there is nothing certain or guaranteed about it. It is a leap of faith all its own." Tears of passion stream down Kovacs' cheeks. "It is the same for God as well. God loves us with no promise that it will be returned. The great all-knowing God has no certainty he will ever be loved. In this way, we are made in the image of God. In our quest for love, we understand his anguish to be exactly the same as ours."

Traeger is moved at seeing his friend's passion spilled out. But another nagging thought spawns a question. "Why did God create a universe outside of himself?"

"You mean why do we exist apart from God?"

"Yes."

"God wanted to create a universe of uncertain outcome and free will."

"Why?"

"Some speculate that it was to create something that continues the creation of its own volition."

"I don't understand."

"Every idea we have, every feeling we experience, continues the creation. Each thought and feeling being the first ever to be imagined by that unique human soul, the first ever of its kind in all the universes. Creation continues. God marvels at our lives and how we go about living them and wants to be part of our experience."

"But, God is all-powerful and all-knowing. How can he marvel at something he already knows? There can be nothing beyond an all-powerful, perfect being. Right?"

"Unless that being wanted it so," Kovacs answers raising an inquisitive eyebrow.

"Why would God ever want or need that to be?"

Kovacs postures firmer, eyes commanding Traeger's full attention. "Alex, a while back when we met in the confessional. Do you recall me asking you a question?"

"Vaguely, but I don't recall the question."

"I stated that God is all-powerful, all-present and all-knowing. The fullness of everything is known by him and he is everywhere all at the same time. But, despite that, there is still one thing that God cannot be. Do you know what that is?"

Traeger looks about the cavern as if it will be written on a wall. He shakes his head imploring Kovacs to provide the answer.

"You almost stumbled onto it just now, son."

Traeger shrugs his shoulders again, signaling Kovacs to answer for him.

The Cardinal's eyes glow. The answer leaves his lips wearing earnest resolve. "The one thing God cannot be is… *not* God."

Traeger falls back into his thoughts to let Kovacs' revelation take hold. After a moment, he asserts, "Well, I guess I can't argue that. If he is God he cannot also be *not* God. But there is no way he cannot be God, so…"

"He found a way." Kovacs charges fully into his element again. "Imagine you are God yourself, all of everything, a creature with no limits, but now you see there is a way to be more by being less."

"How?"

"Become human."

Kovacs' words fade boldly into the stillness. Traeger asks, "You mean Christ?"

"God wanted to know what it was like to *not* know. So, instead of observing his creation from a distance, he decided to become part of it, to leap into the unknown. The infinite God found a way to grow beyond infinity by becoming finite, to live an existence of ambiguity and doubt instead of abject certainty. He wanted to experience a life of seeking to become more than what he was the day before, to burn with the passion of wanting to believe something as only a human can, to live as we do."

"It still makes no sense to me. If one is God, why lower yourself to our level?"

"So you can live it. To be subject to frailty and submission, the anguish, doubt and fear. To live as both natures at once, divine in one and human in the other. To struggle each day as a fragile human experiencing the pain of being removed from the unswerving love of God."

Kovacs, once again, wanders the dark cavern, a man driven by a strength beyond. "He knew he would find a greater love of humankind by understanding all of it in the way that we do, and then to die as one of us in utter aloneness. On the cross, Christ cries out 'My God, why have you forsaken me?' In THAT moment comes the full realization of fragile humanity. God is no longer God, instead, a man in darkness torn away from God. God instantly became more than God, a being capable of accepting the imperfect—humankind—because now he too has been stained by the knowledge and permanence of death."

Seventy Seven
Present Day

The click of designer heels tramp a deliberate pace ricocheting off cold, hewn granite and pierces Kovacs' weary ears. His frail frame stirs beneath a single wool blanket, his only defense against the dankness of his cage deep beneath The Carpenter Institute. The heels trek nearer. Kovacs twists and strains against stiffness to spy past the bars. A shadow crawls the polished floor from the other side, angled and stretched out of proportion, one unmistakably identified by the hour-glass form. His question answered, he turns away and braces himself for another chill soon to arrive—this time, one for the soul.

A beep, then the gate swings open. The shadow paints over him. The light beyond is eclipsed by her presence. Above him stands a silhouette. It is only her this time, no accompanying "muscle"—as if that was ever needed, he thinks, bringing an ironic smile to his lips.

"I'm really not a horrible person, Jonas. I don't wish to cause anyone suffering, especially you," Marianne begins with stark sincerity. "Please know you have been kept here to bring you to an understanding of what pure, brutal loneliness feels like."

"And yet, you don't understand, I am never alone. God is always—"

"Spare me the platitude," she scolds. "When will you learn that your insistence on living a delusion is your real prison, not this place I keep you? Once I feel you are convinced of this, you can walk free again, having been made whole and strong."

Her face relaxes, appearing almost hopeful. "I have much in store for you when you are ready. You would be a valuable member to our team. We would work well together as we did before. I know you think I am a monster and despise you, but I actually admire you," she admits. "Men of utter conviction are rare. In all my years, I have known very few. Well, at least none without any agenda of personal enrichment as their motivation. You have always been yourself and unshakably so," she finishes with a nod of esteem.

Kovacs' insides clench at a chilling realization. "What do you mean 'work together as we did before'?"

Kovacs ponders the words followed by a dawning, disturbing awareness. He gathers his energy to pull up his stick-figure form, quaking at the weight pressing down. He stands before her, face-to-face, his own now frozen in frightened disbelief. His eyes strain to see behind hers, angling in the sparse light to find confirmation. Familiar eyes peer back, perched above a smile all silky and smooth. Astonishment overcomes him. His breath leaves him and he gasps to catch more. An unwelcome pall of dread arrives, mixing bitter with sudden confusion and horror. Tears, ones sorely miscast for the moment, find his eyes. Their appearance brought on by some measure of greasy atonement. Breathless, he pushes out a name from long ago.

"Brandt?"

"It is I."

His legs begin to buckle. She clutches his arm to keep him upright. He clutches back to find anchor.

"Come with me, Jonas. Be free. Let us walk through the gate together and in three days you will feel strength and clarity," she proclaims with uncharacteristic compassionate urgency. "I don't wish to see you this way. You can once again feel the sun on your face, strength in your being. We will feast together and forget all our differences."

Kovacs stares at the open gate and sees the light shining from beyond. An eager foot turns to point himself in the direction of freedom.

Her toughness temporarily discarded, she offers, "I always considered you an unwitting dupe in all this business. We all used you. Your superiors betrayed you. I lied to you throughout. You deserve a chance to live freely. To be made whole. I have only kept you here to help you understand what it can be like to be so very alone and to realize your true purpose. Walk, please, let's just walk," she implores, still supporting him.

More tears find his eyes, painful ones bursting with his own unshakable truth. He turns to meet hers. She tries to read his anguished stare.

"If you cannot walk, I will carry you. Let us leave this horrible place."

His expression remains unchanged. She understands now: it is his faultless conviction. Her own face sours and she thrusts him away, his bony back thudding against the unrelenting stone wall. "You contemptuous old man, FOOLISH old man," she rails, towering over him, compassion burned away.

"You don't even understand the gift I have given you, the gift I have yet to give you. I am trying to thank you," she bursts out, infuriated. "I am trying to reward you for delivering the perfection of DNA that will save the world from the waste of death. It should be yours as well. At the very least, I have spared you from demise. It is time for you to be fully restored and join the living."

Kovacs props himself up just enough to meet her eyes again, his arms quivering to keep him there. The words struggle out. "You think you offer life, but it is death just the same. You see this place you keep me, a lonely cage. It is what you offer the world, shackles of endless physical existence where the soul remains trapped in a prison of the flesh."

"Jonas... Cardinal." she volleys back with methodical resolve. "There is no God. There is no life beyond this. I know this with all my being."

"And I know only the opposite."

"And you call yourself a *man of science*," she sneers. "You are a disgrace. An entire universe, and theorized universes beyond that, and yet in all that we know, this *omnipresent* being has left no trace of its own existence."

"Marianne... Adeline," he answers, matching her conviction with his own. Calmly but forcefully, he declares, "It is everywhere if you look with open eyes, if you seek with your heart. The limitations of the physical realm cannot contain an infinite being. But, the *trace* of God is clear to see. It is simply... love. A thing transcendent of all science. Tell me, Brandt, how does science explain the existence of love?"

"This love you speak of. I see nothing of it."

"You choose not to see it. You chose a long, long time ago, didn't you, Adeline?"

She turns away, stepping a few paces deeper into the darkness, standing rigid. Kovacs braces one arm against the cavern wall and rises to his feet, shaking, pushing through his weakness. Careful steps take him just behind her. "You were born with all the hope and glimmer of any other child, gifted beyond explanation, a mind that only a handful of others could compare to." He moves in closer. His voice has softened with knowing sympathy. "But the gift was a curse setting you apart from everyone. Your awkward appearance only served to make it worse. Even your own parents rejected you. I can see why that young girl might wonder if such a thing as love could even exist. You learned very soon that love, like so many other things, was for others to enjoy. Isolation brewed into bitterness and even hatred, hatred for a God that could allow this."

She pivots on her heels, eyes simmering. "How could a *loving* God allow that? This is my proof that no such thing exists. And yet, tell me, Jonas. You believe in him. Your passion is unwavering. Tell me why your *loving* God can allow you to suffer as you do. Why doesn't he just swoop down and pluck you from your misery?"

"God's plan is one greater than either of us can imagine, than even the whole world can conceive. I am beholden to his will and the path he has chosen for me."

"He chose no path," she scoffs. "The path you are on is one of my choosing, now. If you believe God has a plan, then you must believe that he brought you to me, believe that years ago he delivered you on a platter to carry out what I have given to the world—eternal life."

Kovacs slumps, the weight of his consuming guilt returning, a shroud upon his shoulders. "That... that was my indiscretion alone. I should have listened to my own truthful voice. What I provided you was no gift of God. Instead, the greatest sin of all." Gravity too much, he finds the stone wall and slides to the floor. She approaches, looming over him again.

"And all these precious souls you speak of, they belong to *me* now, never to be in the presence of your God. What was his is now mine, forever."

His eyes lift upward. "At least you understand the enormity of my sin, now." Kovacs looks away. Tears stain the bedrock beneath him.

The clicking heels march away. The gate slams in steely surety behind her, leaving Kovacs to wrestle again with his own darkness. "My God. Why have you forsaken me?" escapes his lips.

Seventy Eight
Present Day

"We have a problem, Marianne," Smith reports to his superior with grim certitude.

"What now, Smith?" she sighs, eyes looking upward from behind Dior sunglasses.

"Seriously, Marianne. You need to have a look at this," he presses through stern lips.

Her lithe, oiled frame scoots up in her poolside chaise lounge. She gestures to another chaise beside her. Smith walks around and sits sideways to face her. "It's Traeger."

"What's Traeger?"

"It seems the good architect has been exploring," Smith says as he angles a tablet screen. It shows an aerial photograph. "One of the drones caught this image. It's located to the far west end of the Institute grounds roughly a half mile from the building proper."

"What am I looking at? I just see a blur."

"It's an access tunnel. Something part of the original structure."

"How do you know that's what it is?"

"I checked it out. It must have been an old escape route."

"Escape from where?"

"The Mansion. It leads to the bottom level. There's a hidden door and past that a system of tunnels."

"That end up where?"

Smith's turbulent eyes lock onto hers. "The Keep."

"The Keep?" Her hand finds her forehead, fingers gently stroking and pulling together through a slick of tanning oil. She tugs her glasses halfway down her nose. "How do you know it's...?"

Smith stretches the image to unmistakably reveal Alex Traeger.

"Do you think he found...?"

"I'm pretty sure. I questioned Kovacs. He denied it. But he's not a very good liar," Smith confirms.

"So now we have to assume—"

"That he knows we snatched the Cardinal and have been keeping him prisoner all this time," he finishes her thought.

"But he hasn't confronted any of us. He's still working as hard as ever. Why would he do that if he knew about Kovacs? Do we have any surveillance from the Keep? Any proof Traeger really found him?"

"We never put any surveillance down there. It was *impenetrable*, remember?"

Marianne falls back in her lounger and removes her glasses. "Yes, I do," she vents with exasperation. "But who foresaw a *secret passage*. Christ! It's like a god-damned episode of 'Scooby Doo.'"

"We have to maintain a watchful eye on Traeger and assume he talked to Kovacs. I verified there are no further access points inside and I've sealed the passage both at the access point to the Keep and the outer entrance. I am also authorizing some video surveillance inside, unless you object," Smith informs.

Marianne chews the end of her sunglasses earpiece. "I have no objections. I will have a talk with James, too. Traeger is overseas right now, but when he returns, I think it's time we insist Mr. Traeger be one of us. If he is on board, he will accept. If not, he will refuse. I think once he is made Eternal, he will see things more clearly."

Seventy Nine
Present Day

"Jonas."

A delicate whisper reaches the ear of Kovacs. His eyelids lift heavily. His cheekbone rises slowly from the tormenting granite. Scanning his dungeon, he sees no one.

"Jonas."

Softly the word arrives from the direction of the barrier of bars standing firm between him and freedom. He pushes himself up as far as he can. A speck of vivid brightness, floating, suspended, piercing the darkness as if a nail of light was being driven through from the other side.

"Jonas."

The light flickers with the sound, then grows.

"Rise. Find your feet. The time is upon you. Your journey awaits."

Kovacs takes his feet with surprising ease, one not known since he can ever remember. A glow of warmth and strength pour into him. Breathing is no longer a struggle, instead cleansing and revitalizing. The light grows to fill the room. Kovacs shields his eyes, seeing his own arms in front of him, full and strong as if someone else's. He stands tall and rigid.

"Who are you?" Kovacs implores.

"I am known as Gabriel."

Kovacs falls to his knees, subjugating his unworthy gaze to the prison floor.

"Jonas, rise. The time is here. The moment is upon you. You must make haste."
Kovacs cautiously obeys. He dares to look upon the being. His pulse is filled with glorious grace and thumping adrenaline. The magnificent one is standing before him, the very one who proclaimed to the Blessed Virgin that she would bear the Savior. He stifles another impulse to take to his knees. Through the liquid haze of joyous tears he peers closer. Momentarily, he dons subjectivity to satisfy the curiosity of the inner scientist named Jonas. The being has form, but one not human. It bears a certain similarity but, he thinks, maybe one adopted temporarily for his sake. Perhaps the form is the only possible one for this being of uncounted dimensions to occupy a universe of only three.

His contemplation is doused in a wave of epiphany. Kovacs has received his purpose with unflagging resolve. Words are no longer needed to reveal his calling. The being bears a knowing, reassuring smile of a sort, stepping aside from the bars behind. The cage door has swung wide open. The form raises an arm, or its equivalent, gesturing to the path beyond the gate. Kovacs takes a step and then another. He is free of his captivity and free of all doubt. He knows with certainty that his path will not be intercepted by the enemy. The calling is clear. The method not so much. There are others to find. Ones who possess gifts other than his. Together a solution awaits.

Eighty
Present Day

"He's gone," Jones yells across Marianne's rotunda office, bursting through the entry.

"Who's gone?" Her face clenches at the possibilities.

"Kovacs."

"How is that possible? she bursts back, head shaking in bitter denial. "The man can barely stand!"

Jones paces back and forth in front of her desk. Furls in his hairless scalp betray a sorting-out process beneath the surface.

"He had to have help, Jones," Marianne fires urgently. "Now would be the time to tell me if anyone else besides James, me, you and Smith have access."

"No one else. Getting down there, let alone opening the cell, is way beyond anyone's permissions."

"And yet Traeger found a way in. Are we sure there is no other egress?"

"None. We sealed the secret passage and did sonar scans of the walls around the Keep. They are solid granite."

Marianne reclines in her office chair to stare upward into the ornately gilded dome above her. A thought shoots her forward again. "You said 'let alone opening the cell.' You mean the cell gate was opened?"

"Yes, it appears he just walked out."

She leans forward to gain some eye contact with Jones through his fevered stare at the floor. "So someone must have opened it for him, Jones," she harshly suggests with dense implication. Jones glares back, meeting her intensity.

"Look, Marianne. Put the kibosh on any conspiracy theories right now. We don't have time for a witch hunt. I've checked all the reader logs, and no one, repeat *no one* was down there. We suspected maybe a malfunction or some sort of hack into the system, but there was none. We did regressions and full audits and there was nothing sent to the device."

"So, it just failed. Simplest answer is always the right one," she drips out sarcastically.

"There was no failure. We got no alarms from the device. We just now reengaged it over a hundred times and it continues to operate as designed. Besides, you said it yourself. Even if the lock failed, he was a physical specter incapable of getting down that hallway, let alone evading all the security... God DAMMIT," he forces through clenched teeth.

"Look, I'm sure he's still in some dark corner of the campus. There is no way he got very far."

"I don't know, Marianne. I have teams scouring the premises. But this just has a really weird vibe. It gives me the chills."

"You? The chills?" She laughs and rises.

"I don't think you get it, Marianne. This couldn't happen. It is an impossibility. And there's the footage..."

Marianne's moment of levity evaporates to concern. Jones taps furiously on his tablet. "Here, look at this. Tell me what you make of it. This was recorded by the camera outside the cell. It's the only image we have of him. No other camera picked him up on the premises, and we used facial recognition searches through every frame of all our security footage."

Jones angles the tablet for Marianne to view. Greenish-gray images taken from higher up in the hallway show the cage bars release, then swing slightly inward, leaving a gap. Moments later, a form emerges through the opening and walks past, just beneath the camera. "As I said, it's all we have. There's no other angle."

"That wasn't Kovacs. He's moving at normal pace and his hair isn't even gray."

Jones cues up the video again, then pauses when the man walks by the camera. "Look at him. I mean really closely."

Marianne squints and scrubs the video back and forth, looking at the image in regular speed and then pausing and repeating. "You're right."

"So you get it now," Jones says, reading her face "Our old companion Cardinal Jonas Kovacs, as we knew him thirty years ago."

"How on earth?" Her mind spins, pulling data from long ago to solve the unknown. A sick feeling pours through her, an oily black fear. The unexplainable towers over her, casting a wide shadow of grave doubts upon decades of immutable certainty. She stammers, "Something about him, or the process... No, it's just impossible," she mumbles, furls of her own finding a place on her forehead.

"And we found something else," Jones interrupts. "Right here, right before the gate opens. You can't see it at normal speed. It's only in one frame." He taps three times on his tablet. "There," he points to the screen.

"What is it?"

"We don't know. It could just be an anomaly. I've had it analyzed. It's probably some trick of light or digital noise. But anything we could think of would last longer than one frame," Jones advises.

"Could that be related to some tech intrusion? Like an energy beam or something directed at the lock mechanism?"

"See the tiny shadow on the floor? It indicates a physical location of its own between the bars. That's what is so puzzling. If it was any of what you suggest, there wouldn't be traces of it really being there. It's something that happened right there, not an artifact."

His frantic energy sets him off, pacing randomly. "If it were some type of EMP it would have to be very powerful to get down there. It would have interfered with the video stream, probably taken the camera out altogether, not to mention most of the electronics on the compound."

Marianne again uneasily assumes the throne behind her desk. "Well, keep analyzing, but top priority is that we need to find Kovacs. He can't be allowed to get out to tell anyone what has happened or what he knows. It would end everything we've worked for. At the very least, it would be a major setback to our goals."

"Agreed, Marianne. I've had teams underway as soon as we discovered it."

"Tell me you have more ideas than just that, Jones. After all, you are the man with the world at your fingertips."

"I'm way ahead of you, Marianne."

Eighty One
Present Day

The murmur of cable news from the tube television in the front room of the cabin competes with the succulent sizzle of bacon in a pan. The salty hickory cure serves as an olfactory alarm clock, stirring Patricia Hamer from her slumber. She teeters on fawn's legs to the kitchen. At the sound of her door opening, Chandler began service for her morning quaff and now delivers the steaming brew to her waiting hands as she arrives.

A grumble meant to imply "thanks" spills from her lips, her words still trying to catch up to the rest of her slow return to consciousness. Chandler urgently clutches the remote, and dials up the volume on the broadcast.

"... If you see this man, please notify authorities. Do not try to approach or engage him. He is believed to be armed and dangerous," jumps from the portable television speaker.

"My god," Chandler wavers breathlessly.

"What?"
He raises a finger. "Hang on."

"... I repeat, authorities have issued a call for anyone seeing this man, Felix Cardonez, to contact them immediately. Please do not engage or approach him. If you see him you should notify the authorities immediately."

"What is it Chandler?"

"I don't know," Chandler ponders out loud. "It doesn't make sense."

"What doesn't? If you are going to say things out loud at least try to include me in the conversation," Hamer grunts still half asleep.

"Sorry, it must be a case of mistaken identity. Some newsroom screw-up. But, if so, it's a doozy."

"You wear me out, Chandler." Hamer tops her coffee with more cream and wobbles to her place on the couch wearing a plaid flannel robe. She assumes her usual pose, knees pulled to her chest as she sips the potion of wake-me-up steaminess with two hands.

Chandler plates some reheated coffee cake, piles bacon strips over it, and joins her in the seating area.

"All I know is, that guy ain't Felix Car... Car..."

"Cardonez," she finishes his sentence into her coffee mug.

"Right. At least that picture isn't Felix... not that guy."

"How do you know?"

"Because, I know the guy in the picture... well, knew."

"From where?"

"He was on the team, one of the seven, the Vatican guy."

Hamer shrugs off any remaining sleep, Chandler's revelation too colossal to ignore. "He was the go-between for the archives, right?"

"Exactly, and that picture on the news is one from over thirty years ago. It was actually Kovacs' security badge photo."

"So why would the news guys have it?"

"I guess it was given to them by the police."

"And how would the police have it?"

"No earthly idea. All that was internal to the project. It was kind of superfluous anyway. We all knew each other. There was no need for badges, but Jones was obsessed with security and oversight."

"Jones?"

"One of the money guys." Chandler's face morphs through several phases of bewilderment as he searches for any good reason a thirty-year old picture of Kovacs would be broadcast as part of a manhunt. "This makes no sense. It can't be an accident. It smells intentional."

"But by whom?"

"It would have to be one of us from the team. Kovacs wouldn't do it, and he disappeared decades ago. Reader and Kipner are dead. I'm here. So that leaves Smith, Jones and Brandt."
"Or all three."

"Interesting thought, but I'm banking on the first two."

"The bigger question is *why*, Marcus. If you answer that, then you will know who."
"The only *why* that makes sense is that one, or all of them, believe Kovacs is alive and in the vicinity," Chandler posits before jamming some coffee cake in his mouth.

Hamer's wheels start spinning at full speed. "And they want him found at all cost. You know, this kind of thing isn't easy to execute. To get something of that gravity on the air, especially if it's a fabrication, you have to have some incredible pull or leverage on some pretty important folks."

"Smith and Jones do. It has to be them."

"By themselves?" she asks. "And when was the last time you saw those guys? How do you even know they are alive?"

"They are Eternals."

Chandler's kinetic energy pulls him from his seat. He makes an errand of it to refill his cup. Hamer raises her mug above her head and he obliges.

"So, again, *why*, Marcus?"

"Kovacs knows a whole lot, and grew to be suspicious to the project. As time went on, he figured out that Brandt deceived him. After Kipner died under dubious circumstances, I think he figured he was next and got out of Dodge."

"Why would he come back?"

"He is a man of bold conviction and passion when it comes to his beliefs. He would only come back if he felt he was *called by God*."

Hamer floats a theory. "So, consider this. Once the Eternals process was brought mainstream, he caught wind of it and decided to do something about it. If Brandt really did manage to reconstitute Christ's DNA, Kovacs would see that as utter sacrilege, right?"

"I'd buy that. I wish I knew where he was. I'd love to pick his brain. Plus, he's a good man. I've never known a man so committed to his beliefs."

"Or a woman so committed to hers as Brandt."

"Well said, Pat."

Hamer sips deliberately, intensely focused. She decides it might be time for a little help, something she doesn't take lightly. "Look, Chandler. Maybe this is the time we can bring in another resource. Maybe we can find him before they do."

"What are you suggesting?"

"I have some very trusted contacts in the Bureau. At the very least, I can get one of them to tell me what they've heard about it and if it's for real. At best, I might be able to tap some resources to let them know who this guy really is, or even intercept him before this Smith and Jones can get to him."

"Trusted?"

"Very trusted."

"Do it, then."

Hamer picks at some coffee cake while her brain searches. "So, why use a photo of him from 1987?"

"Maybe it's the only one they have."

"Or maybe he still looks like that," she firmly posits.

Chandler stops mid-sip. "Kovacs an Eternal?" he waits a moment to consider, then dismisses any doubt. "Never. He believed in eternal life, just not on a hell-hole called planet Earth."

Eighty Two
Present Day

"Alex, my brother, welcome home." James Carpenter shoots up with open arms and marches around the sequoia desk. Traeger is swallowed in the embrace and returns the gesture. Carpenter presses his lips to Traeger's, then steps back. "You have been missed. I know we communicate every day, but it's no substitute for the real thing."

"Likewise, James. Ten weeks is a long time to travel, and then with not more than three days at any one stop. Well... it's exhausting to say the least."

"I am sure it is. I can only imagine for someone not Eternal," Carpenter smiles to soothe the jest. "I can't wait to hear all the progress from around the globe. I appreciate you taking so much time away. We have much to cover, things I thought best to address in person."

"I have cleared my schedule for you, James."

"Before we get to business, if you will indulge me for a moment. I have a surprise for you," Carpenter says with a knowing grin. With sparkling eyes he speaks into thin air. "Candace, please bring in our guests."

A large slab of the wall at one side of the room opens, revealing its dual purpose as a door. Traeger's jaw drops as his family dashes through the door. "Valerie... Jason... Melissa. Welcome," Carpenter embraces the three in one hug and multiple pecks. Traeger's children rush over to hug their father. He meets them halfway, his chin quivering with emotion.

"Mr. Carpenter, we are so honored to meet you," Valerie gushes, her eyes locked on to Carpenter.

"I think the three of you may know my Executive Director of Global Operations," Carpenter gestures to Traeger.

Traeger is swarmed with bittersweet emotions. His children are a glorious sight. The presence of his ex-wife brings with it a blunt anxiety. More so, the timing is suspect. The moment seems calculated beyond the primary purpose, perking up Traeger's suspicion that there may be a second shoe to drop.

"Alex, you work for Mr. Carpenter?" Valerie's pitch raises in genuine surprise.

Carpenter looks at his architect with unbelieving eyes. "Alex, please tell me they know where you work?"

Traeger looks to his shoes.

"I think the architect's stalwart humility has left us in an awkward moment." Carpenter pauses, cupping Traeger's shoulders in his hands, then slips his arm across his back to pull him in to his side. "Valerie, children, this man has brought so many of my dreams to life, given shape and artistic form to my vision in more ways than I can imagine."

"James, I took your confidentiality oath quite seriously," Traeger humbly explains.

"And yes, of course you *would* do that," Carpenter surrenders with a grin. "I am grateful for that. But, I think family should know. So, now they know." Carpenter crouches to look the children in the eyes. "Kids, your father is a very talented and important man. He is helping me change the world for the better."

The children look up to their father with new eyes, although not completely sure how to understand the meaning of Carpenter's praise.

"Alex, honey... I... I am so proud of you." Valerie stares with new eyes of her own, ones filling with tears.
"I try to tell him how important he is, but he just brushes it all aside," Carpenter says in feigned protest. "Do you see, Alex? Let your family confirm for me what I have been trying to tell you for so long."

Traeger savors a moment and then another longer one to bask in some vindication at his ex-wife's admiring glow. Her vindictive play for full custody is first and foremost ladled thicker with uncountable repetition over the last several years of reprimands for his absence in their children's lives. Recitals, birthdays and ball-games missed to work at the pleasure of James Carpenter and all the while unable to explain why. He included her in his financial gains, but "thank you" was uttered far less than the rebukes. His stir of emotion calming, he catches Carpenter's eyes to reflect his silent gratitude at being untethered from the bonds of his oath for those so close to him.

Carpenter gestures to a lanai outside his office overlooking the lush landscape beyond and directs them to some sofas and loungers. The afternoon light stretches across the landscape as the sky readies for the evening. A long column of gas flame emerges from a river rock formation at the center of the group, the growing chill of the evening air now staved off by the gentle warmth. Stewards arrive wispily to offer wines, juice refreshments, and hors d'oeuvres. Small talk spent, Carpenter leans forward and engages the Traeger family members.

"There is something I want to make known to all of you. I have been a very patient man. You must admit that, Alex. Here we are; we have been together almost five years now." Carpenter rises and stands behind Alex, laying his hands on his shoulders. He looks more intently at Valerie and the children. "Millions are with us now, and still, my right hand man has not partaken in the salvation we offer." He walks around and takes a seat next to Traeger, looking him in the eye. "You are now the sole holdout here at the institute. Your hesitancy is a mystery to me. I have asked and asked, but now, I think I must insist. It is time to stand together as one. And yes, I am guilty of bringing your family here as a further means to persuade you, but I need you Alex. The world needs you."

Carpenter pauses, building some angst in Traeger. The moment is unavoidable, it would seem, but too many doubts linger, most notably the harsh treatment of his friend Kovacs.

Carpenter breaks the heavy silence. "Indeed, the offer is extended to all of you. Of course, eventually everyone will be offered eternal life, but I wish for all of you will join me as soon as possible. I will not rest until I know you are all safe from any harm, living in true salvation. And do know, with me as your advocate, you will be considered part of my own close family, assured of an elevated place above all Eternals, for the rest of time."

Alex shifts in his chair, growing uncomfortable despite Italian leather. "Jason and Melissa are only children. They should be allowed to grow out of childhood," he implores with hopes to delay.

"And they will," Carpenter calmly responds. "The process does not pause growth; it merely perfects the body's natural processes of regeneration. The growth from childhood to adulthood is a natural process and it will continue to be as it was programmed by nature."

"Mr. Carpenter," Valerie says.

"Valerie, call me James, please."

"James," Valerie corrects herself while almost blushing. "For me, I want to do it," she busts out almost lustfully. "And Alex, I think it is only right to have the children do so as well. We deserve... all of us deserve to enjoy the great life James is offering us."

Traeger again twists in his seat. Carpenter interjects, "Look, I know you all need to think and talk about it amongst yourselves. We have prepared a dinner for the four of you in the private dining room." James fixes his gaze on Valerie, capturing her. "We also have accommodations here at the Institute that I am sure you will find luxurious. I am going to finish up some work and then retire. I will see you in the morning. Good night, all."

Eighty Three
Present Day

"They fell right to sleep. They were exhausted," Valerie whispers to Alex. "I think I would be too if I wasn't so full of adrenaline."

Four stories closer to the moon than the night wildlife, Alex and Valerie share the balcony off her suite. The crisp air adds sharpness to the darkness beyond. She leans against the railing, trying to find the perfect casual pose. "Look, I know why you couldn't say anything, now. I feel so embarrassed and I am dreadfully sorry. Please accept my apologies, Alex." She gently lays her fingertips on his forearm.

Attention elsewhere, he stares into the dark night. A response forms, one forged from conversations rehearsed in his imagination many times before.

"I have to admit it was difficult and painful at times," Traeger reveals, his emotions pulling him in all directions. There is a relief in the truth revealed, but there is a sense that things are stirring in the shadows. He is untrusting of Valerie's motives. Even his friend James seems out of character. First and foremost, he worries for his children's wellbeing. "I know from your point of view, it probably looked as if I was just being a selfish workaholic, or avoiding you and the kids intentionally. I hope you know I would never do that. This work, it's the opportunity of a lifetime."

"Yes, Alex." She smiles. Her eyes begin to moisten. "A lifetime that doesn't have to end." She swirls her wine to distract from a charge of emotions. "Look, maybe I'm just caught up in the moment here, but we have a chance now to give everything a fresh look, to reassess, well... " Her eyes soften and her hand moves to capture his. "… us. Now that we will have nothing but time, the pressure is off. We'll be financially set, have the world at our beck and call, and"—she weaves her fingers into his—"and it never has to end."

Alex angles to look into the night again, lost in other thoughts.

"Alex, what is it?"
"Look, Valerie." He turns back, firm conviction relaying deeper concern. In whispered tones he breaks the solemnity. "There's something going on here."

"No, you have to trust me: I still love you, Alex."

"No." He shakes his head once. "I mean here at the Institute. This whole Eternals thing. There's something… well, unsavory about it. There are some things that just don't add up, things I have learned that are a little scary."

"Scary?" she echoes back with bewilderment.

"It's too much to say now. You'd think I was quite insane," he submits in dampened intensity to quell alarm. "I'm afraid to voice it here." His cadence ramps up more caution. "Maybe now isn't the time to discuss this. Just trust me."

Concern grows on her face. "I think you need to tell me."

"Not here, not now. In the morning, okay?" Inside, Traeger is burning with suspicion. Others could be listening in and he is still not sure where her allegiances lie. "Tell Carpenter you need some more time. Tell him you'll get back to him soon. Then meet me, uhh…" He scans his memory for a perfect rendezvous. "Where we had our first date, nine o'clock. I'll tell you everything then."

"Okay, I trust you." She squeezes his hand more firmly, bringing her gaze to find the depth in his eyes. "I'll see you then."

Eighty Four
Present Day

Traeger nervously rummages his desk and bureau—busy work straightening and discarding of the unimportant. He is killing time before his offsite meet with Valerie. A scramble of thoughts and worries crowd the anxious mix. Will she understand what Kovacs has shared? Will she even believe Kovacs is real? He knows Valerie and her appetites better than she does. Asking her to postpone eternal life in physical perfection will be a monumental task. It would be for most anyone—but he knows she is intoxicated with the idea. His nondisclosure to her of his job details was only partially due to his confidentiality oath. If he had disclosed his employer to her, she would have been unrelenting in her pursuit of the process as soon as she could get it.

But she is not his primary concern; the children are. If Kovacs is correct, they would be subject to an eternity of dubious outcome. But then again, maybe not. There is too much uncertainty to make a decision on something so permanent and irreversible. The clock reads eight-thirty. He grabs his satchel and steps to the door.

"Where are you off to, Alex?" Marianne guards the threshold—an appearance too much for coincidence, he thinks.

"I'm… I'm meeting some old chums for coffee," Traeger stammers nervously. "Just a quick catch-up before my meetings back here."

"This will only take a minute." She swishes into his space, makes a few coquettish turns, and lands herself a tense foot away from Traeger. "Alex, I spoke with James. He says you gave him the impression you have reservations about joining us as Eternals, especially concerning you and your family. This is puzzling to me."

Traeger stands frozen, hoping his demeanor conceals his urgency.

"It is time, Alex. I understand you are a cautious man by nature. It is an endearing quality, attractive even. But, it is time."

His shoulders slump in defeat.

"What is your worry, Alex?" She stretches the sound of his name out, playing with it on her ruby lips. She eases even closer. "I've often pondered what you'd look like in your full perfection, young and virile."

"Marianne, what... what are you doing here?"

"I'm looking after our communal interests, and indulging myself a little," she draws out while patiently circling around him, a prowling panther.

"Seriously, this is confusing." From behind, he feels her warm breath on the nape of his neck, then traveling to find his ear inches away.

"Let me be perfectly clear, so there is no confusion left in you. You see, we are entering a new age of thought, Alex. The prudish conventions of the past no longer apply. I want you to be with me anytime we choose."

Her fingers snake around his upper arms, a caress and then a gentle squeeze. "What do you mean *be with me*?"

"Alex, are you really that naïve?" she teasingly scolds, sliding before him all liquid and supple.

"But, James?"

She smiles and begins to laugh. "This was his idea," she says, eyes burning of desire. "He told me a long time ago I should be..." She pauses to find the right expression. *"Rewarding* you for all your hard work. He likes you, Alex, and so do I." Her lips move in again bringing the rest of her with them. Her curves brush against him. Any remaining sense of self he had is now untethered and strewn. "Complete the process, my dear. Let me see you in all your glory, strong and blazing."

She strikes his paralyzed lips with hers, arms slithering around his back, hands wandering. He disappears into a blur of sensual chaos. Too much for him to assimilate. She uncoils and smiles into him. "This can all be yours too. There is more than enough, in an endless lifetime, for you to share in anything you please."

She leaves him to his thumping madness as she swishes out the doorway. He sees the clock again and scoops up his phone to send Valerie a text that he is on his way. Instead, there is a message from her.

> *Alex, I had a good talk with James. He assured me there is nothing to worry about at the Institute. The kids are waiting for a bit. They want to make sure it's okay with you. I am sure once they see I am fine, they will join me. I think you should too. Luv you, V.*

Eighty Five
Present Day

I had a good talk with James.

What on earth could that mean? What had she told him? Traeger wonders if she mentioned what he divulged to her the night before. And, why the seduction by Marianne?

He assured me there is nothing to worry about.

She must have told him. Why else would she say that?

A bolt of panic strikes his core. He needs to leave, get gone somewhere, save himself. One hand takes firm grip on his satchel handle. The other has a different idea, anchoring him to his desk. The safety of his children is paramount. And what of Kovacs, still trapped in the dungeon? Traeger is trapped in a tug-of-war between base instincts—survival versus protecting loved ones. He negotiates a truce: self-preservation in the immediate and rescue as soon as possible after. The second can't happen without the first. He pushes himself to his feet. Just as quickly, his children flood his thoughts again. They may already be lost. If he leaves, they certainly will be. A hot blade of dread slices his being. He could try to make it to the guest quarters, but they may not be there. Carpenter would expect that. He would never make it out and the children would be lost anyway.

The decision made, a means of escape eludes him. How to get out undetected? There is no immediate right answer. He submits a request, an asking to anyone who might be listening along to his silent turmoil. A prayer, he decides. He asks for a delivery to safety, and to stand guard over his children. He implores to keep the Cardinal close to his God or send him guardian angels, if there are such things.

Reflexively, he picks up his phone, then sets it back down as if it were aflame. It would betray him. It must be left behind. The icy realization arrives that now he is adversary to the collective of technology and its masters Smith and Jones. Everything will betray him. He will be found; it's only a matter of when. He will share a fate of eternal wasting with his friend Jonas.

The heart of a hummingbird beats in his chest. His stomach folds over. Through the dark fog, a cool breeze of clarity wisps through him. There is a way, something he remembers from his research. Knowledge of the original estate design will serve him now. He must be cautious, but a way exists.

His memory guides him with perfection. Freedom is at hand. Two stories down by way of rarely travelled stairwells, then a left and a corridor. There is a janitorial supply closet. They never lock it as they should and today is no different. Behind an unfinished wall and beyond the bare framing, there is access to an abandoned coal chute, one of a dozen belonging to the original structure. Traeger makes the small climb out of the chute window and laying before him is a forgotten, underground rail tunnel used for coal delivery to the estate over a century ago. A mile of tunnel rises gradually to ground level and ends at the main coal house. From there begins a larger feeder rail line. He will walk beside the rusted track for a little over five miles to a small town whose name eludes him. From there, he hopes grace will bless him with clarity again.

Eighty Six
Present Day

The man staring back at him is one he knew long ago. He was a man of hopeful conviction, a man driven to serve witness for God's will, possessing strength of both body and spirit. He was a man afraid of nothing, shattering conventions, but a man once gone astray where once was enough to cancel the rest. Jonas Kovacs stares into his own eyes in the back of a diner spoon to see the face he wore over thirty years before. Now, with wiser eyes, ones privy to what eventually befell the younger, the seasoned Kovacs possesses the perspective of steadfast experience. The man he beholds is one youthful and vulnerable, idealistic and unaware. He is a tender fellow who had no idea the breadth of force wielded by grandiose circumstance. Most of all, he sees a man who needs his forgiveness.

"Have you decided yet, sir?" a waitress asks. Kovacs notices the unopened menu on the table before him. He scans the diner for inspiration and points to a table. "I'll have what he is having."

"Oh, the Salisbury steak, our house specialty. You'll love it."

Too submerged in his own moment to respond, he reflects on the impossibility of his here and now. Waves of disbelief crash over him with only time enough to catch his breath and dive down again beneath the surface to dodge the next charging whitecap of onrushing thought. His youth restored, but how? Brandt altered his DNA, but for the worse. Could it have reversed on its own somehow? He unexpectedly grapples with the idea of a miracle. Why grapple? Why not a miracle? His understanding of things allows ample room for such an event. It is not only possible, but essential to his faith. Instead, he is uneasy to conclude as much, left puzzled by rational doubts. The skeptical man of science that shares his being is searching for lucid explanations. But, the Cardinal counters, *we witnessed the archangel Gabriel. We had a conversation with him.* The physicist responds. *It was a hallucination, a companion effect to the physical transformation.* The Cardinal redoubles, *how do you explain the gate opening? And then to simply walk from The Carpenter Institute unnoticed and unharmed.* How does the physicist explain this, blind luck? A mystery it must remain, they decide. The debate is tabled, for now. He is here, however it came to be. He is here and it happened.

His spine finds the back of the booth. Time to take some further inventory. What an abundance of gifts he has been given. The archangel not only bestowed freedom and strength, but a parallax view of now versus then. To carry forth, Kovacs knows he must embrace his mistake, but no longer with the side effect of paralyzing guilt. God forgives and he must do so as well. A shroud falls away revealing the sublime simplicity of God's truth. What good is God's forgiveness if we do not permit the same of ourselves? The greater sin is to stand in the way of God's absolution. God forgives. So should we. Kovacs resolves he must forget, be done with the gnashing and wailing. Be the man he once was, but one also wearing the armor of knowledge he has acquired along the way. Once again, he must become the sturdy instrument, a soldier ready for battle.

Nearly forgotten is the Good Samaritan. After safe passage from his prison and emergence from the woods to a roadway, a motorist stopped to lend assistance. Now clothed in thrift store attire and with cash in pocket, Kovacs waits for his first hearty sustenance in years. Knowing the stranger could be in jeopardy if found with him, Kovacs lied that he could call a friend from a nearby diner and sent the stranger on his way. Kovacs closes his eyes, thanks God for the intervention and asks blessings for the stranger.

The feast arrives. Hunger subsiding, the steps forward become the subject of inner conversation. He is free. But God, as he so often does, has chosen not to provide a to-do list, no blueprint or step-by-step instructions. And what would those be for a task of saving the world? A few more bites and at least the first stride is revealed. He was brought from his sanctuary in the Tibetan highlands by his friend William Reader to find one man, Alex Traeger. He shall find him again.

His senses shift from inner thoughts to the noises surrounding him. One especially catches his interest. A television above the service counter tuned to cable news now displays the image of Kovacs' face. The same one he became reacquainted with on the back of his spoon. Kovacs arrests an impulse to bolt. The diner's occupancy is a scant few. He sees no one else's attention is drawn. The next item of news replaces Kovacs' image. The meal finished, he pays and calmly exits the diner. The sun will be down soon. He decides if a more fragile version of himself endured the dungeon of The Carpenter Institute, the younger self can withstand a cool evening in the nearby woods. Tomorrow he will set his bearings on finding Traeger. It is a task made more difficult given Traeger is usually found in the place from where he just escaped.

Eighty Seven
Present Day

"What do you mean you can't locate him? Déjà vu, Jones. It's Kovacs all over again," Marianne barks at the image of Jones staring at her from a monitor. She turns her head to look incredulously at James seated beside her in their limousine.

"Not exactly, it's not like we were holding Traeger," Jones corrects.

"No, but I did ask you to track his movements. And, well, now you say you can't find him."

"He left his cell on his desk. We were tracking him via that," Jones replies.

"He had to take one of the vehicles, Jones. Trace that."

"No, he left on foot. We are still not sure how he left the Institute grounds. It wasn't by one of the standard exits. We would have caught him on camera."

"So, it sounds like we have another breech in our perimeter. How does Traeger know these things and you don't? What good are you?" Marianne's tone coarsens.
"Well, if I can remind you—"

"It was a rhetorical question," she blares, then ends the communication.

Marianne slams herself back into the plush leather seat and sighs. Carpenter gently lays his hand on her thigh. "He will be found. Alex will return. His children are with us. He loves them too much."

She softens. "I know, James." She places her hand on his and finds calming sanctuary in his eyes. He smiles. "It's just that I am concerned. We don't know what he will do out there. Whom he will see and what he may tell."
"What can he tell? Whatever he has to say, the world will not believe."

"How can you be so sure, James?"

"Because the world wants what we offer. They will not stand for a spoiler. He will be a pariah, not a messenger."

"Right—he would be perceived as disgruntled and delusional. You are so wise, my love."

Carpenter pulls her close, wraps her in his arms, and kisses her head. "Alex has his own questions and doubts. He will work through them and return. We will accept him back without judgement or rebuke and his loyalty will be unwavering."

She pulls away to gaze at him longingly. He smiles again.

"But if you think I should cancel my trip, I will."

"No, James. I've got this."

Carpenter pulls her even closer and gently strokes her hair. Her eyes meet his. She sees his eyes radiating with resolve and behind them an inferno fed by the understanding of his reason for being.

"Marianne, I need to tell you something. I have been thinking about it a great deal." He pauses to collect his thoughts from the fury within. "Please don't think I ever doubted you or wasn't aware of what you were laying out for us. I see how much you have sacrificed and labored your entire life to bring us where we are today."

Sensing a shift, she pulls from his grasp, pride raising her up in her seat. "Go on, James."

"All these years you have put together what we are now on the brink of realizing. You have mentored me, prepared me for the future that is now upon us. You have raised me, cared for me, given me life itself."

"You have thanked me before, Love."

"Yes, but never with the full appreciation that I feel within me now. The scope of what we are meant to embrace is clear to me—it is the entirety of everything. I am ready now, ready to lead, to take the throne. I will raise the world and all its citizens up to the highest ground."

Tears roll down her perfect face. The man she created has stepped full-stride into his destiny. She sees Carpenter's inner being filled with a presence more than just himself, a frame now fleshed out in its full potential.

"Marianne, the world belongs to us," he proclaims, steely-eyed. "We will steward on the greatness that has been so sorely unfulfilled in all of history. All will see the vision to achieve beyond what was ever possible, no longer as fractured segments pursuing their own interests. We will fuse the collective of humanity to build a great society, one directed by *our* wisdom. None will doubt us. All will follow."

"Oh, James, you *are* ready," she flutters out admiringly. "They *will* all follow. They will praise you and proclaim your greatness. It is undeniable. You have given them eternal life and they will gratefully give their lives back to you."

Eighty Eight
Present Day

"Yeah… Okay… Yeah, I know. Just maintain a distance. Keep yourself safe, but if you hear anything… Okay, thanks. Bye." Patricia Hamer taps her cell phone to end her call.

"Was that your contact?" Chandler asks knowing the answer.

"Yeah."

"Well?"

"He said he knows what we know. He has dug into it as far as he can and says the man is known as Felix Cardonez and has connections to Columbian cartels."

"That's BS, Pat."

"Well, he kind of hinted he was forming the same conclusion. He said there is no history of any kind for Cardonez. If he was a cartel guy, there would be a file. So he's curious to say the least."

"What can he do about it?"

"Not much. I told him I might have further information on who the guy really was but was reserving revealing that until I could *confirm*. That will keep him looking. In the meantime, he'll let us know if there is any progress made in the manhunt. So far, he says they have nothing."

The front screen door opens behind the two. "If you ask me, you are looking for the wrong man." Ivan Myer shuffles his sallow form out to join them on the front porch of the cabin. He finds refuge in a rustic chair made of a twisted fashioning of tree limbs, his frail form almost blending in.

"Why do you say that?" Hamer responds doubtfully.
"Well, this Kovacs may be important, but there is one fellow who could tell you everything."

Chandler squats down to look at Myer face-to-face. "Who?"

"Pat, do you remember when Carpenter was shot, you interviewed a guy who had a strange connection to Reader?"

"Refresh my memory, Ivan."

"The architect, Traeger."

Hamer's wheels churn. "Right, there was some cryptic connection to Reader, but it didn't pan out."

"Or maybe we missed something. The cryptic nothing was some notation Reader made about Traeger in his address book. Traeger only knew him as an acquaintance, but ask yourself why now the good architect is one of Carpenter's closest confidants."

"What do you mean?"

"When I was undercover at the Institute, I saw him there all the time. It seemed like they were always together. I wanted to approach him, but I know that would have exposed me. So I just had to observe from a distance. There was something about him. Carpenter adores and trusts him. He just knew how to talk to Carpenter."

"Wait... wait," Chandler jumps in. "I've never heard of this guy, and you say he knew Reader?"

"They both did some work at the University. Their paths crossed briefly. But, I find it an extremely odd coincidence that this guy who knew Reader, no matter how well, is in tight with the man he shot," Myer pronounces like a prosecutor making final arguments.

"Yes, that is quite a coincidence." Hamer falls deeper into her own thoughts, her detective mind activated.

Myer continues, "From what I could tell, Traeger was in charge of some project of global proportion. Carpenter had him overseeing the construction of satellite locations connected to the Carpenter Institute. They were rumored to be gathering places of some kind, like temples or something."

"Why would Carpenter need temples?" Chandler wonders aloud, still trying to keep up.

Hamer says, "The first thing that comes to my mind is maintenance outlets."

"Somehow *maintenance* and *temples* don't seem to square up."

"No, but delusions of grandeur and controlling the masses do." Hamer's intellect begins piecing the puzzle together. "If you repackage maintenance as *worship*, then it all makes sense."

"Right, if maintenance is required then why not turn it into a kind of ritual," Chandler adds. "If you want to keep the masses connected, then wrap a philosophy or community around something, make it a cause. Paste some deeper meaning on it."

"Well, that's pretty insightful, Marcus."

"That ain't me talking, that's all a William Reader thing. You triggered a memory. Looking back, knowing what we know now, Brandt was anticipating a world of Eternals with possibly no philosophical anchoring. This is why Reader was on the team. He brought that dynamic to the table. You know, future shock theories and deep knowledge of human social systems."

"But how does the long-lost Adeline Brandt's knowledge base find its way to Carpenter?" Myer asks.

"Well, he's got her science, why not the notes to go with it?" Hamer answers.

Chandler rubs his chin and says. "And that's the big question. How are Brandt and Carpenter connected? There is no trace of her. Hasn't been in decades."

"I have to say this, though," Myer adds to tie his thoughts together. "Traeger always gave me the impression he wasn't all in. He worked for Carpenter on some really important stuff. But he wasn't a zealot, if you know what I mean. He was passionate about his work, but he had an air of caution around him. He wasn't an Eternal either."

"Really, how do you know all this? I sense some embellishment on your part," Chandler argues incredulously. Myer glares back and then twitches a bit, holding the continuing inner torment at bay.

Hamer jumps to his defense. "Marcus, look, Ivan may enjoy weaving a good yarn, but his observations are always on point. I've known him for over twenty years and his intuition is second to none."

Chandler backs off. "So, again. Why do you think he would help us and turn on Carpenter?"

"Well, I didn't quite say that." Myer angles his eyes out to the forest beyond. His demeanor finds a distant place. He almost answers but hesitates. "No, you will laugh."

Hamer walks to her friend, lays a hand comfortably on his back, and rubs gently. "No, Ivan. Anything helps. Why would we laugh?"

"It's silliness. It's all just a feeling."

"Please, Ivan," Chandler capitulates.

Myer pauses. His face grows serious and grim. Facing the inner darkness he battles always brings the fear that he will succumb if he lends it his awareness. "Without Pat's help I would be living in a literal hell. She has managed the cacophony of demons with whatever cocktail she uses. I am grateful for that." His fists close and his shoulders slump. His eyes grow wide and his voice falters facing the inner ugliness. "But I still hear them. They are at a distance, but they are quite clear. Something changed with them very recently. Their ire has grown." He looks up to Hamer and Chandler with dreadful eyes. "They are afraid, but cover their fear with bold shouts of venom and disdain. The focus has shifted. They curse him. They speak true evil and Traeger is the one they curse now. There is something about him they despise and they want him gone."

Chandler and Hamer stand frozen for a bit with too much to say. Hamer looks at him empathically. Although his torment is real, she still resides in objective skepticism. "Ivan, I really want to believe you, but," she stops before saying something that might seem insensitive.

Myer reads her doubt and mumbles. "I know, I told you, you would laugh."

Eighty Nine
Present Day

"Gentlemen, we are at a critical juncture and there are too many loose ends. The time is upon us; James had a breakthrough yesterday," Marianne announces to Smith and Jones who sit rapt in their sofa seats in the retreat area of Marianne's office space. She paces around, circling them. "Our patience has paid off. James has reached the pinnacle and is ready to lead."

"I thought that was a foregone conclusion years ago," Smith returns, puzzled.

"Until now, he was merely the student learning as he must, but now…" She pumps her fist and smiles wickedly. "He has embraced the fullness of his nature. His kingdom awaits," she announces as if speaking to every ear on earth.

"Does this mean we are nearing the final phase?" Jones asks to confirm a step hatched long ago.

"It is upon us." She nods triumphantly. "I will finalize the delivery mechanism for the maintenance virus immediately." Her eyes beam satisfaction at the culminating moment of a lifetime's effort.

"I think a review is in order for the sequence of events for the post-viral phase," Smith states in a business-as-usual tone. "Present company excluded, all other recipients of the Eternals protocol have received the modified version containing the maintenance sequence in a dormant state. Once released, the trigger virus will unlock that sequence and initialize the necessity for maintenance."

Marianne nods.

"And we are assured this will go undetected by the hosts through any physical symptomology, correct?" he queries.

"Correct. Some may experience a slight immune response. That is to be expected across any diverse population, but it will be of no consequence," she answers plainly.

Jones chimes in, "Is this absolutely necessary to maintain order?"

"We know this from Reader's research," Marianne counters with self-assured bravado. "It takes only a few intent on discord to disrupt the many. Chaos will be managed. It is the mechanism for progress. People will have eternal life. They will soon learn of the necessity for an ordered existence."

"And should they choose not to, they will find life rather difficult," Jones adds with a half grin.

"If I may say, Marianne, I am so often overwhelmed by your brilliance," Smith slides out admiringly. "The long-sought quest for a society with purposeful structure has finally arrived."

"Gentlemen," she says standing firm and tall, chest puffed out, "I could not have done it without you."

Ninety
Present Day

A stripe of sunrise through branches and trunks of alder and oak nudged Jonas Kovacs from his sleep. Morning songs of thrushes and wrens announced to him a glorious day, a day of freedom and renewed purpose. Whatever stirrings are wont to happen in the hidden places of slumber where sub-conscious and soul mingle, have left him an image, and a sense, to return to his first destination upon his arrival from Tibet—Mount Calvary Catholic Church. No better place to meet with God, it occurs to him, than in God's own house.

The early months after his arrival served him with a keen knowledge of navigating the Baltimore area's maze of public transportation. It once again delivers him to safe haven. Again, he thinks, upon arrival at the church, that he was aided. More angels sent to deflect any recognition of him by strangers. He sits safely now in near darkness, communing with his Lord in the peaceful anonymity of the clergy side of a confessional. Welcome isolation from his abrupt return to a random world full of people.
The peace is too soon startled away. The confessor side of the booth's door swings open. A troubled soul seeking salvation sits across the barrier. A bolt of concern shoots through the Cardinal—but it is quickly calmed. It is years removed but, he decides, he is still well suited for the task. A timid but urgent voice reaches out. "Father, I... I don't really know how this works, but I have something I need from you."

"How may I help you, lad?"
"I have done something unthinkable. But... but I had no choice. Can you ask God to help me?" the stranger pleads.

"The grace of God allows you to ask him yourself," Kovacs comforts.

"But, I would think you would have more... more... *pull* with God than me, Father. I am not a practicing Christian. I just think it would help if, well, you know."

"I will pray with you, my son."

"What do I say?"

"The words are yours to choose. Talk to him as if he is sitting here in my seat. Say it to me, if it helps."

Silence reigns for a moment. And then, "God?" the voice asks. "I have left my family and a good friend in danger. I need you to watch over them and provide them a way to safety. If you were there, you'd know I had no other way."

Kovacs cautiously acts the divine role in which he has cast himself. "Son, are you responsible for the danger? Did you abandon them when you should have remained?"

"I saw no alternative," comes back in shaking tones. "I need to try to bring them to safety, or for God to show me how I can." The confessor's tone of grief increases to desperation. "Please, tell me how."

Kovacs pauses, reaching for a moment to think of any way to add greater guidance, but there is something else his attention is drawn to as well, nagging at him. No form comes to it, more a sense of déjà vu. "What kind of danger and why did you leave them?"

"It's a long story, Father. My family doesn't even know the danger they are in. I tried to tell them, but..."

It's the voice, Kovacs realizes, the voice of a friend. "I think God may have answered your prayer before you even entered here. He has answered mine for certain. It is you, dear Alex. It is you!" Kovacs exclaims as loud as one should in a confessional.

"I... How do you know my name, Father?"

"I am also known as Cardinal."

"Jonas? Traeger pauses, incredulous. "How...?"

Both doors swing open. Eyes meet. Kovacs reaches to embrace. Traeger pulls away, his face showing confusion and fear. The man before him looks like another.

"Jonas, what did you do? You have joined them!"

Traeger turns, panicked, and dashes to the door at the rear of the church. Kovacs pursues, catching him by the coat collar. Traeger wriggles in disbelief to find release.

"Alex! Alex! Please! I am not against you." Kovacs releases Traeger and steps back with arms raised. Traeger remains flexed and defensive. "How did you find me?"

"I didn't. You found me."

"You had help. This smells of Smith and Jones," Traeger sneers.

"Alex, how can I assure you?"

"I don't think you can. You are now healthy and young. There is only one way that can come about. You turned. You have sold your soul and are with them. Admit it," Traeger challenges with a rebuke of disillusionment.

"Alex, when you saw me last I was already Eternal, and you knew my disdain for them first-hand," Kovacs pleads.

"Then how...?"

"How am I myself at half my age?"

Traeger nods in a twitch.

"I was visited by the Archangel Gabriel. He brought me to safety."

Traeger's face projects disheartened disbelief. "What? Archangel? Do you know how ridiculous that sounds? That doesn't explain anything. I am not a fool!"

"I have no explanation for my renewal," Kovacs tries urgently to convince. "I woke this way in the dungeon. God's power manifest in the angel transformed me. I am youthful, but also free of the bondage and the malaise brought upon me."

"Or they broke you and released you to find me." Traeger's scorn turns to disgust.

"It is nothing of the sort, Alex. And how am I to not think the same of you for me? Perhaps you were commanded by those devils to find me, to go to the places we met before. To corral me into further bondage?"

"Cardinal, I ran from you."

"To lead me out the door where they are waiting to subdue me? You see, Alex. I am the one who should be running from you."

Traeger's pose unwinds. The stalemate apparent to both, Kovacs then asks. "Why are you here? Why have you left them? Is it true what you said about your family?"

"James is using them as leverage. They are probably Eternal by now. I have failed them." Traeger slumps in despair.

"There is always a way with God. I am standing here as living proof. He has brought us together so you may save your family and the rest of humanity."

"*All* of humanity? Me? No pressure there." Traeger issues an ironic and panicked laugh.

Kovacs smiles knowingly. "Forgive me, I have been accused of phrasing things in rather..."

"...Biblical proportion?" Traeger finishes with eyes rolling.

Kovacs beams bigger and nods. He reaches out his arms. Traeger takes lingering comfort in the embrace of his friend and his newfound safety. Grateful tears wet the Cardinal's thrift-store jacket collar.

"How did you catch me, Jonas?" Traeger groans.

"I ran track in seminary. I may still hold records. Perhaps now I should go see if I can best them," he says with a warm smile.

They share a laugh and another embrace. From behind a column, a figure appears. "Is everything okay here?"

They both nod. The figure, a man, approaches a few steps. He is no less suspicious, looking them up and down. Traeger replies. "We were just leaving."

They turn to find the door. Traeger whispers "You know, you are all over the news."

"I am aware of that. I think our friend is aware as well. Come, we must find another place in the shadows."

Ninety One
Present Day

"Here. That's what he looks like," Myer says to Hamer while handing a tablet device forward. "There are other pictures of him in there too," he adds from the back seat.

"Where did you get this?" she asks from one side of her mouth, craning her neck back to look him in the eye over her sunglasses.

"It's from my cloud site. Every day I was at The Carpenter Institute, I took tons of shots and uploaded them. Those are a few years old now, but I'm certain he doesn't look much different."

"Okay, I remember him now. That's definitely the guy I questioned about Reader," Hamer confirms.

From behind the steering wheel, Chandler breaks in. "So now we are just supposed to wait until he pops out in plain sight, recognize him in that brief moment and say, 'Hello, Mr. Traeger. We're here to rescue you?'" he sarcastically asks.

"Something like that," Myer replies in kind.

"Well, this isn't a fool's errand by any stretch," Chandler pops back with simmering eyes in the rear-view mirror. "Can't you call your guy at the FBI again, Pat? See if he can help us out on this?"

Hamer glares back to Chandler.

"Ok, I'll give this one hour tops," Chandler proclaims. "We'll drive around downtown aimlessly and hope we find Waldo, then I'm out. This is a supreme waste of time, just my two cents."

"Hey, I get it, Marcus. It's a long shot, but it's all we have. Next time, it's your call," Hamer returns, trying to ward off frustration at the likely futility ahead.

Twenty, then thirty minutes pass. The three snake their way around downtown Baltimore in silence, heads swiveling like sentry prairie dogs. A notification tone sounds from Hamer's tablet, breaking the quiet.

"I think someone is pinging you, Pat. Maybe it's your FBI friend," Chandler suggests, hopefully sardonic.

"Not on my tablet, he wouldn't. I have no idea what that was for." Hamer examines the screen. "No idea."

"Hand it to me." Myer commands. He taps away on the screen. "He's near Mount Calvary Church. It's about eight blocks from here. Turn right up here, Chandler."

"Nice work, Myer," Chandler praises.

"Oh god, Ivan. I don't want to even know," Hamer gasps in disgust.

"It's an open-source facial recognition platform. Very hush-hush," Myer blurts fluffing his plumage at his own cunning.

"And you just thought it would be okay to use my ISPN to tap into that probably illegal activity," she scolds.

"Well, you wouldn't have let me if I told you."

"Damn right about that." After a moment, she sighs with a tone of resignation. "Where do we turn next?"

"Take a left in two lights, then jog over and keep to the right. I'll let you know."

"I suppose you put Kovacs' picture in that search too, right?"

"Yeah, why not?" Myer asks rhetorically. "But nothing so far. There was only the one picture of him available, so the 3-D rendering is less precise," Myer explains.

A sign in the front offers confirmation, but there is no mistaking a church among the towers of commerce, conspicuous by its contrasting lack of size.

"How should we do this?" Chandler asks. "You want me to get out on foot and you guys drive around? Maybe I should go inside."

"That sounds like a good idea," Hamer agrees. "How accurate is the radius on that recognition, Ivan?"

"Precise within about a city block. The positive ID happened twelve minutes ago. It was a street camera northwest of the church."

"Just a thought here, guys," Chandler interrupts. "The church seems like it would be a Kovacs thing. Why would Traeger be near the church? Doesn't that seem overly coincidental?"

"I would agree," Myer says.

"And still no recognition of Kovacs?" Chandler asks Myer.
"Nope."

"It is odd, to be sure." Hamer makes it consensus. "We have the unlikely Traeger-Reader connection. Then the Traeger-Carpenter connection. Could there be a Traeger and Kovacs connection, too?"

"Or, has Traeger been tasked with hunting down Kovacs and he is staking out churches?" Chandler posits.

"There, on the streetlight. I think that's the camera." Myer points ahead.

Chandler double parks the car. He and Hamer swing their doors open simultaneously and exit. As if practiced, she slides in behind the steering wheel. Chandler stuffs a Bluetooth earpiece in and dials Hamer's number while walking. "And now I have no idea where to begin," his voice spills from the car speakers.

"We're going to circle. Just peek your head in all the shops. Maybe you'll get lucky," she answers as she pulls the car back into traffic.

"Because he probably wants to get in on that sale at Old Navy while dodging The Carpenter Institute," Chandler thickly quips.

"Look, Marcus, unless you have a better idea—"

"It just hit again!" Myer breaks in. "Same camera."

"I'm heading back... Wait... I think I see him," Chandler whispers.

"We'll be around in another minute," Hamer says, her voice ecstatic.

The man who might be Traeger surfs through the city bustle and turns into an alley. Chandler arrives moments later. He sees no one. The alley leads to a loading area surrounded by the backs of buildings. "Crap, I think I may have lost him. I'm in an area behind the church," he whispers again. There is no time to wait. He takes cautious steps deeper into the alley, peeking behind dumpsters and delivery docks. He stops to listen, but there is nothing to listen to. A chill finds his bones. This place between the towers is a stranger to the sun. He pulls his jacket collar up to defend against the cold.

The man must be here, he decides. There is no other exit besides alarm-tripping emergency doors. Chandler steps slowly, crunching bits of glass and grit. The waft of restaurant grease and diesel finds his olfactory. "Marcus, where are you? I think we're in the wrong alley," Hamer's voice shocks the taut silence in his ear. He holds his response to maintain silence, still hearing no other sounds.

A ruffle comes from the far corner. Chandler sneaks in, but nothing. Closer in, he hears another sound of more human origin. "Hello?" he offers to quell any concern of threat. He is greeted with no reply. "Mr. Traeger?" Nothing but city hum returns. "My name is—"

Cold concrete finds his cheeks. His arms freeze in place. A sturdy body behind him glues his own against filth-slathered brick and concrete. "Your name, sir, is Marcus Chandler," fills his unbelieving ears, ones dulled by the fog of impact with the wall. *How could Traeger know my name*, he wonders.

"Mr. Traeger, I want to help you," Chandler offers.

"You seem to have mistaken me for another, Marcus," the voice behind him chides.

The fog clearing, a trace of memory sparks, something about the accent adorning the phrases.

"Kovacs?"

"It is I."

"Jonas, let me go. I'm trying to help you. You're in danger."

"This I already know, but last I saw of you, you were thick with Brandt and her minions Smith and Jones. Now, when they are hunting me, you suddenly show up. And you seek someone named Traeger, not me. Maybe I should kill you just to be safe."

"Do you promise, Jonas?" Chandler cracks dryly.

Headlights spray the darkened alley. The car stops to a skid. Hamer jumps out. "Let him go, Kovacs," she warns behind the barrel of a gun.

"You can shoot, but I won't die," he shouts back defiantly.

"Are you certain of that?"

Kovacs releases Chandler and raises his arms. Hamer walks in closer to decrease the range. "Marcus, check him for weapons and electronics."

"I don't think—"

"Just do it, Chandler."

Chandler gives his former colleague a terse patting down. Hamer moves in even closer. "You know the FBI is looking for a man who could be your twin brother. His name is Felix Cardonez. Do you have any idea why that might be?

"I do."

"Would you care to enlighten us?"

"Because there are those who do not wish me to be a free man."

"Because?"

"Because my free existence is a threat to their dominion. If I may be so bold, Miss...?"

"Hamer, Patricia Hamer."

"Miss Hamer, is there any authority which gives you the permission to point a gun at just anyone for no reason?"

"You were assaulting my friend."

"I'm your friend now, Pat? I am truly touched," Chandler gibes hoping to bring calm to the moment while dusting himself off. "It's Kovacs. There are no two ways about it. It's okay."

Hamer reaches behind to holster her weapon. "We are surprised, but glad to find you Cardinal." Kovacs looks back with surprise. "Yes, *Cardinal* Kovacs. Marcus has told me much about you. We think you could fill in some knowledge gaps for us, and maybe we can shelter you from detection in return."

Kovacs juts his chin and postures firmly. "And why should I trust you, a strange woman? One who threatened to kill me seconds ago partnering with a man of dubious loyalty?"

"Because we are all you got," she boldly asserts. She puts her hands on her hips. "I'll give you two days max before the FBI or worse, someone else finds you out here. If we found you, they can."

Kovacs' posture loosens a bit. He peeks behind himself in the direction of a darkened corner. "Who is it you think is after me?"

"James Carpenter. Marcus here seems to think you might be at odds with him and his agenda. We have much to discuss. But I think it best if we take this conversation elsewhere. We have a safe place. Please come with us."

Kovacs looks to the darkened corner once more. A figure warily emerges.

"Please join us, Alex. We are among friends," Kovacs implores.

Traeger slinks out from the dark submissively, looking frazzled. "Hello, my name is Alex Traeger. We need your help."

"That's what we are here for," Hamer submits, extending her hand for a shake. "So we meet again, Mr. Traeger."

Traeger returns a puzzled look.

"I questioned you about William Reader a few years ago. You seem to find yourself woven into the fabric of many interesting circumstances, don't you, sir?"

"It would seem so," Traeger concedes.

A whirring crawls down the building walls to find their ears. "That's a drone, people, and not the peek-at-your-nude-sunbathing-neighbor kind," Chandler announces.

"He's right," Myer seconds. "It's Carpenter's. I'm sure of it."

"Everyone in," Hamer commands. "We need to get the hell out of here."

Ninety Two
Present Day

"This view is from directly over the church area now." A flat-screen displays from drone's-eye view.

"Are you sure it's the right church?" Smith asks blithely. Jones' eyes stab back with disdain. Smith offers a note of optimism as an olive branch. "At least we're looking for *two* needles in the haystack, and have a pretty good idea they are together."

"They could be in a building, on the subway, in a car. We are just going to have to trust technology," Jones submits. "The Kovacs ID and the Traeger facial rec happened within ten minutes of each other. It's a miracle Kovacs got this far without getting picked up. We'll get another hit on Traeger soon, too. It's only a matter of time. I'm sure of it. We just have to be patient and ready."

"Where would they get a car?" asks Smith.

"Steal it, where else?" Jones' frustration returns as condescension. "We got the list of thefts in the last forty-eight hours and put them in the recognition database. Enersteen is keeping an eye on that and will let us know if any pop up."

"Brilliant move," Jones lauds. "Have you heard anything from Marianne, today?"

"Well, just that we'd better find them." Jones pauses at an unpleasant thought. "For the first time, I think she has really lost faith in us. We've never been in this position with her and—to be totally honest —it kind of scares the shit out of me. I do know this, we'd better find them or we could be in a hell of our own."

"After all this time do you think she'd turn on us? Even if she did, what can she do? We're Eternals, and not subject to the maintenance," Smith offers as reassurance.

Jones abruptly swivels his chair from the wall of monitors to face his cousin, wearing an anxious look. "And you don't think she has some way to change it all in a very short time? Have you ever known her NOT to have a backup, a plan B through Z?"

Smith slumps. Jones grinds on. "You saw what she did to Kovacs and that Myer guy? Just look at her own transformation from being clunky Brandt to temptress Marianne. She can do anything she wants to our DNA and we can't do a damn thing about it. She invented Eternals over thirty years ago. It's not like she's been knitting in the corner in a rocking chair ever since. I can't even imagine the possibilities." His face goes grim. "I don't want to even consider them."

Jones rotates back to the monitors, his face drained and sullen. Smith fills his lungs and spins his brain as fast as he can, churning away to think of some avenue they might have overlooked, then dryly directs, "Look, both of us in here isn't doing much good. Why don't you call NSA and see if we can borrow a satellite for a while. Maybe we can link the recognition tool to a larger landscape. I'm sure those guys have something, after all we did for them. You might suggest what's at stake, too, without giving away the farm."

Ninety Three
Present Day

"After Brandt disappeared, I bounced around doing contract and consulting work, built a comfortable nest egg and have lived modestly off the interest ever since. I learned to exist as a nomad. Thirty years ago being an Eternal was a liability. If you stayed anywhere too long, people started to notice you never changed, or got sick, or got a pimple," Chandler recounts for his former colleague Kovacs as they catch up on their lives since they last saw each other years ago. Hamer listens intently, the three seated in the main living area in the hideaway cabin. The day too much for Myer, he has retired to his room to find rest.

Kovacs asks, "And the gift of immortality did not open your soul to the world of possibilities before you, to consider the larger questions in life?"

"I suppose not; I guess when tomorrow is a certainty..."

"You can always wait another day." Kovacs finishes Chandler's thought. "Popular opinion might suggest, without the burden of limited time, we would find the motivation to reach above ourselves. But, we are only human; we lie to ourselves about our higher nature. So much more could be ours, we think, if we only had the time. Yet, with no limits, the opposite occurs—stagnation and idleness, not growth."

Kovacs smiles, suddenly reminded of the late Professor Reader. "It was something our old friend William was very adamant about. He used to warn Brandt of that danger, and she ignored him. It was all too clear to me, though. The certainty of death as our pursuer, and a journey into the unknown beyond, compels us to our own greater callings."

"I wouldn't say you've done nothing, Marcus," Hamer inserts as preamble to a jab. "You've explored myriad methods to kill yourself, if not only temporarily."

Chandler almost frowns. "That's a little harsh."

She expected a parry to her poke. "Sorry, Marcus. I guess I still have scars about that whole business," she concedes, surprised at her callousness.

"It's okay." Chandler nods sympathetically. "I know I made it seem like recreation, but there was another reason."

Hamer tries empathy instead. "Curiosity, right?"

"Not exactly. It's just... there is a moment... just after death and before I return." He tries to find words for something almost indescribable. "There is... a... a bliss."

"You mean the euphoric chemical effect of the brain after expiration," Hamer recites like a text-book.

"No, I know what you are referring to. You mentioned that before, but it is more than that. I mean it isn't that. It's hard describe. It's like..."

"The grace of God," Kovacs sublimely submits.

Chandler meets Kovacs' eyes to acknowledge his awareness, then turns to find Hamer's to relay what words would fail to express. Hamer sees transcendence in his eyes, the effect of knowledge known only to him. She is frozen for a moment in a depth beyond words.

"You see, Pat," Chandler's tone softens as he plumbs his inner thoughts. "I know there is no convincing you, no way to prove it to you, or anyone. But there is something after this life, something glorious. I never used to believe that." Chandler's face assumes a warm, knowing smile. A calm fills his being. "I've always required proof to believe anything about anything. In order for me to accept something, I had to see it myself. I had to be there. My curse is, now that I have my proof, I can never be there. I can only experience it for a brief moment after I die, then my Eternal state yanks me back." His calm wavers slightly as he confronts his dilemma. "I understand now that life continues on. It's meant to be endless, or maybe just boundless. Earthly human existence is only a step along the way. Eternal physical life isn't necessarily evil. It's just that living *here* forever is kind of like... well, a life forever spent in preschool."

"So, there is a heaven?" she asks, intrigued.

"I don't know if it is *heaven*, but consider this. We are scientists here, even Jonas. Science is about probing new concepts and theories, pushing our imagination past boundaries and then proving it. We feed on possibilities when it comes to alternate universes and the curving of time, black holes and the enigma of quantum physics." Chandler takes to his feet and walks the room, energized by a cascade of notions. "We so casually discuss traveling through wormholes to who knows where, or who knows *when*. Hell, we really don't even know what gravity is. We know what it does. We can record its effects. But how does it even exist or work?"

Traeger, detecting a seriousness in the conversation, quietly moves in and finds a seat next to the others. Chandler, too filled with the enormity of his thoughts, fueled by an energy too charged to be contained, orbits his audience. "And in all that we observe and consider, science simply dismisses any possibility that human beings are more than a mass of cells somehow conveniently pasted together. All they see is Homo sapiens puttering around in our preprogrammed quest to redistribute our unique DNA to the next generation before we expire. And yet, we are the only known species possessing full awareness of ourselves, learning and advancing as we go, contemplating our nature and our purpose, having a discussion like this one. Science so easily considers the existence of the infinite, but never considers that we may be as limitless as all the other stuff."

Chandler's thoughts are moving faster than he can speak. He sorts through the cascading watershed, an expression of long dormant theoretical bits finally finding form. "As science sees it, the very fullness of the human race on planet earth, alpha to omega, all of it will happen within the wink of the universe's eye. But there is little, or no, scientific attention given to the thought that some portion of us is as boundless as that which created us. Call it a soul, or a spirit. Call it the *collective unconscious, the passions of all of humankind*, whatever the name. There seems to be more to us than just physical matter."

Chandler pauses briefly and lands next to Hamer on the couch, taking the moment to breathe. He looks powerfully into the others' eyes, lingering, one after the other. "Is it unreasonable to suggest that we are all connected to this vast complexity in more than just our physical form? Maybe the basis of who we are, at our fullest expression, is a much greater being. Perhaps our time here is merely a chapter, game level one, where we find brief physical form. Could we just be formless souls stuffed into a fleshy suit for a time as a stop along the way? Then, we move on to another existence beyond anything we can imagine?" Chandler nods as self-affirmation. "There is more than this. I have seen it, and it is magnificent." Abruptly, his face morphs to a chilled despair. "And I fear I have trapped myself here forever by my ignorance of thirty years ago when I thought I had lucked into a jailbreak hack over death."

Chandler's eyes go lost somewhere behind a teary glaze. Silence reigns again. Hamer lays her hand on her sorrowed colleague's shoulder and stares at the floor, trying to digest Chandler's dense philosophy, one she never thought would ever be served up by the man she has known now for several years.

Kovacs, smiling, gently rubs Chandler's other shoulder in fatherly pride or perhaps priestly admiration.

Hamer manages a mumble. "Well, for my sake, I hope you're right. I'm still planning to exit the old-fashioned way."

"I am right," Chandler's voice charges back. "I've been there dozens of times. And, if what I have just told you is true, we need to find a way to end the Eternals process."

Kovacs voices a concern of his own. "My good friends, just as important as Marcus' concern, the future of mankind as a species is at stake as well. In a world of Eternals, the process of life and human evolution will cease."

"How so?" Hamer pulls confused eyes from the floor to meet Kovacs'. "It would seem to me life would continue on indefinitely."

"The *living* would continue on, but not *life*," he asserts. "Our path as a species would be trapped in a cul-de-sac."

Traeger, taking in the discussion, is silently sinking. The bursting realization that he has contributed firsthand in such profoundly grim circumstances has him tumbling in disillusionment. He expresses a desperate measure of hope. "But that isn't so. Procreation *will* continue. Children will be born. Life will progress."

Kovacs looks sadly and sympathetically at his friend. "In all your time there, they never told you?"

Traeger sinks further, anticipating Kovacs' next words.

"She told me herself, and with great pride. She has disconnected reproduction in Eternals. There will be no new souls brought to life."

"She? She who? Wait, did Brandt resurface?" Hamer asks with alarm and slight confusion.

Kovacs looks demurely at Hamer. "She never left. She is now Carpenter's companion, Marianne."

"But she looks nothing like Brandt based on what Marcus has told me," Hamer responds, even more befuddled.

Chandler mutters in grudging admiration, "One more testament to her brilliance, I would think."

"Yes, she is his partner. There is more," Kovacs continues, his voice growing even dourer, disgust building on his face. "She is his consort, his lover, but she is also his *mother*. She conceived him and now..."

"Oh, god." Traeger shudders. He leaves the couch and steps away from the group to work through a flood of repulsion and inconsistencies. The two of them, his friends, all this time harboring a massive lie and secret existence.

"Yes," Kovacs continues. "She not only conceived him, she inseminated herself, a virgin, with Christ's DNA. It is an unthinkable mockery of God's own, true virgin miracle. The sacrilege!" he growls, his full ire on display. "She even changed her name to usurp that of the Blessed Virgin."

Chandler needs more persuading. "How do you know this?"

"When they held me captive she confessed it to me. She is so proud of her creation. Sadly, I think that is all he is to her, not a man, just a living monument to her brilliance."

Hamer jumps in with greater urgency. "We will see what we can do. We should know something soon once Jonas' DNA results are ready, I will do some comparison between Chandler and Myer. The three of you are all Eternals, but by very different means and in different composition. Hopefully, some clues will emerge and provide a solution."

Ninety Four
January 12, 1988

"I don't know how someone so smart can be so stupid," Anders Kipner launches at Adeline Brandt, no longer able to contain his contempt.
"So, you admit there is something you don't know," Brandt bitterly volleys back.

"I know what you're up to," he roars at her, leaning in and above her, his hands nailed to her desk. "You think you have found some special DNA that you can just weld in that will cure all the ills and imperfections that millions of years of evolution somehow overlooked. It won't work. This, I promise you."

Brandt leers at him, stone-faced, seated behind the desk. Kipner presses his challenge further. "You think genes are just building blocks, some Lego set you can snap together and make into anything you wish. It doesn't work that way, and I can't figure out if you are merely ignoring this fact or truly believe this is possible."

"It is possible, Kipner; that's how it all works. It's nature's design, you know that. The very moment of human conception is exactly that."

"Yes. But the how and why remain riddles. There is nothing known about the force that compels the bond. I'm not talking about the proteins, just the deeper sophistication of it!"

"Genes don't know. They have no inherent intelligence. They are compelled to bond and merge because it is their reason for being. My process will work, Kipner," she snorts back, her face projecting less tolerance with each successive rebuke.

Kipner calms himself, his usual arrogance stowed away, his cause more important than simply winning an argument now. "That it may," he replies gently, "but you are forgetting genes are not fixed things. They have an interaction that we don't understand. They are not components of a system. They are the rulers of the kingdom. They ARE the system," he pleads. "Genes are dominant and recessive. They skip generations. They mutate. They are the operating system and we are the RAM."

"Spare me the undergrad lecture," Brandt rolls out condescendingly. "I was formulating my theories long before you were playing with *actual* building blocks and Legos. My methods are sound." She glares at him. "Please don't make me have to say it again."

"With all due respect, Adeline. The first version of anything never works right. You are monkeying with the delicate placement of millennia of natural selection. It is foolish to think you can outsmart all that."

She sits unmoved, glaring him off, her limit reached. Kipner gives it one last go, albeit softer in tone.

"Just please consider it. I beg you. We must never lose sight of the fact that the purpose of genes is not to construct beings to live lives for their own purposes. Genes don't care if we are happy or sad, or have meaningful lives or love one another. They exist solely for the purpose of continuing their own existence." She opens her mouth to speak, but Kipner talks over her in one last desperate hope. "They developed carrier vehicles called *species* as an end to those means. We exist at their behest and their mercy. No matter what you do to try to alter that, they will find a workaround to do as they please."

Brandt's eyes burn deeper. "I am beginning to have doubts about you, Kipner. Your ability to operate within the scope and spirit of the project seems to lack resolve and commitment, not to mention a growing pattern of disloyalty. Forget all this nonsense and stick with the program. It will work. I have no doubt. Consider yourself the carrier vehicle for *my* purposes. Now, leave me and do what I ask."

Ninety Five
Present Day

"Well, thank you Adeline Brandt," Patricia Hamer hails triumphantly.

"Why Brandt?" Chandler asks, perplexed as he peers over her shoulder, one of an audience including Kovacs, Traeger, and Myer. With three versions of Eternals at her disposal, Hamer dusted off her biomedical background and began a deep dive into the differences in their DNA. With Chandler's help, they converted the slaughtering shed into a space of more positive effect, a place for testing and study.

"It was her log notes that led me to the precise areas to look in the genome. I was able to compare the three of you and discern the differences. You get a strong assist, Marcus. The tools you put together back then are second to none, even thirty years removed."

"What did you find, Patricia?" Traeger asks.

"So, here are the three maps." She points to a monitor displaying three separate windows horizontally. "The top sample is Chandler's. He's the baseline, pure, original gene-craft, the Eternals template. Second is Myer's." She points to the monitor. "Don't ask me how it works, but the differences right here are what must be the *on* switch for the *living-in-hell* option." She clicks on her mouse. "The blue line is Kovacs'. As you can see, it seems to retain some of what Myer has, but it appears to be overwritten, if you will. It shows us that Jonas had the same deteriorating changes applied, but ones modified again in some way."

"How?" Myer asks.

"I wouldn't know the specific genetics involved, but—"

Myer breaks in. "No, I mean can we tell how it was introduced?"

Kovacs follows with a lilt of impish frankness. "You mean, can we detect if it was brought forth divinely?"

"Not really saying that," Myer answers, "but sure, why not?"

Hamer offers a quip with a raised brow. "You mean is there some trademark logo etched in the strand that reads *all rights reserved, Archangel Gabriel*?" She pauses for effect. "Sorry, Ivan. We can't determine the source, or when it was introduced."

"You said *overwritten*," Myer presses.

"That's just an assumption on my part."

Chandler probes further, eyes intently locked on the computer monitor. "Can you isolate the difference itself? The full strand that restored Kovacs?"

"Not sure," Hamer answers. "But it might be good to know. And by the way, I don't think it is Brandt's work from then or now."

"Why not?" Kovacs asks at the behest of both his curious inner scientist and clergyman.

"The obvious answer is why would she do that, and the second is, it just doesn't look like her work."

Myer, Chandler and Kovacs simultaneously begin a murmur building to the next, obvious question. Hamer holds up a hand to quell the tsunami. "In my experience, the work of savants always has a detectable, unique signature. It's hard to put it in words. I guess Mozart versus Beethoven. Jobs versus Gates. I've spent enough time profiling in my life to conclude it's not hers."

"So, whose is it?" Traeger asks.

"The scientific answer? Hell if I know," she answers shrugging.

Chandler digs deeper into his memories. He considers a possibility or maybe a nagging belief resurfacing from many years before. "So, you *are assuming* it was introduced *after*?"

"Yes. It only makes sense since Kovacs began like Myer, then changed. But I'll play along with a theory if you have one." She pivots to face her audience standing behind her. "Do tell, Marcus."

Chandler turns to Kovacs, gleaming. "Jonas, do you recall as things progressed, there was a good deal of tension between Brandt and Kipner?"

"Tension? It was palpable confrontation." Kovacs nods. "They were not even speaking by the end."

"Yes, and then, all of a sudden Kipner just chilled out, ended the feud. I always assumed that the alpha dog finally broke him." Chandler's theory takes form in his thoughts, generating a sly smile. A clever intrigue plays out in his memory. He wags a finger and says, "But what if something else transpired?" He pauses to play it over again in his head.

"Out with it, man," Myer pleads, sniffing a juicy conspiracy.

"Kipner's complaints were lodged from a sort of future-shock position and the no-brainer point that playing God was dangerous. A viewpoint supported strongly, if not introduced, by William Reader. It had good merit on its face. But, despite that, I always felt that Kipner's real motivation all along was his own interest."

"He was only about himself. With this I can agree," Kovacs affirms.

"So, just like with every good software developer or security analyst or pyramid builder, there is always a back door, a secret way in, or perhaps a doomsday switch." Chandler pauses to see if anyone is catching on but is met with baffled stares. "You know these types. Delusions of grandeur and all that. For means of sabotage or blackmail, or just because they are in love with their own ingenuity, they leave a secret access point."
"So, you think this Kipner guy did that?" Hamer asks, leaning towards agreement.

"Yes, I think he left some latent DNA behind as some sort of unlock mechanism or means of sabotage in case Brandt decided to write him out. She eventually did, but before Kipner could activate it."

"Left it where?" Traeger asks.

Chandler waits. He slowly turns his head to find Kovacs. Kovacs returns a surprised look and replies, defensively, "He did nothing to me. I wouldn't have let him. I did not trust him."

"You trusted Reader, though…"

Kovacs raises his gaze, staring into space to allow the current conversation to mingle with distant memory. He concludes, "I suppose it is possible, but it was without my permission. But, how could they introduce that without me knowing it?"

Chandler recalls something. "Jonas, do you remember they were always taking blood tests?"

"Yes! They said it was to monitor our health. Something about avoiding contamination. That was always suspicious to me."

"So, at some point, Kipner could have introduced his DNA into your bloodstream during one of these routine tests," Hamer adds. "It's probably the same way Carpenter introduces the whole Eternals process. Viruses are really just random bits of DNA. They can be customized and retrofit to deliver non-random DNA too."

"Then why have a process at all? Why doesn't Carpenter just create an airborne virus and deliver it to everyone?" Kovacs asks.

"Because there is a specific genetic mutation." Hamer replies. "The Eternals sequence must be delivered to an exact location in every cell through a gene-editing process. I would imagine an airborne virus isn't precise enough. Or maybe she just wanted more control of the delivery targets."

"How can she be sure the gene editing will take place automatically and in the way she wants?" Traeger asks.

"Gene editing is pretty commonplace today. The most prevalent is called CRISPR. If she used that, though, she was a generation ahead of everyone else. It's a remarkable feat of genius given the limited tools she had at the time."

"How does this CRISPR thing work?" Traeger inquires of Hamer.

"It uses a specific protein to determine the exact location, then it snips the strand and splices in the gene."

"How does it know where to cut?" Traeger returns.

"Some guide DNA is present with the enzyme," Hamer explains. "The guide DNA contains certain sequences that find like sequences in the genome. It lines up the strands and then the protein does its thing, dropping the new strand where the old one was. It does this throughout the organism wherever it finds the matching strand."

Traeger replies, "So, it can be a precision insertion or a universal one. It just depends on what you tell it to look for."

"Exactly, Alex." Hamer says, impressed with his acumen. "You're a quick study."

"Okay, Marcus, assuming Kipner planted his stealth DNA in Kovacs, why only him? Why not Reader or himself? Why not you?" Myer asks, his curiosity now fully engaged.

"Maybe Kipner was using Jonas as a test subject, thought he was more expendable than anyone else." Chandler answers nodding to Kovacs as an apology of sorts. "Perhaps he never finished before he was killed, or he just introduced it into Jonas as a beta test before going all in. Maybe they did have it and never went Eternal, so it never kicked in."

"There is no way to know," Hamer interrupts. "It doesn't really matter who, or how, just that we have it." She looks up with a relieved smile.

"Why then did it take thirty years to take effect?" Kovacs asks bewildered. "And why did it not only reverse the debilitating version? I became fully Eternal."

Hamer concludes, "Who knows? Maybe Kipner's version was built for a slightly different cultivation of Brandt's strand, maybe one before the policing modifications were added. Perhaps it takes an archangel to switch it on." She smiles reverently to Kovacs. "What we do know is, we have a starting point to maybe dismantle the whole process altogether. Once we isolate it, we will know for sure."

Ninety Six
Present Day

"I don't know how much longer I can be your producer, Christy," Pete Kilgore confesses to Christy Raines while waiting for his street-vendor hot dog. "I just think it would be a huge conflict of interest."

"I can't believe you are going through with this after all you know about Carpenter and how much your gut is telling you there is something seriously wrong here," she says.

"I know, but Celeste is pretty much all in. It's at an ultimatum stage."

"Have you talked to her about it, shared your concerns? You've got deeper information than most." Raines asks before an eager first bite into her Sabrett hot dog.

"She's having none of it. She's convinced James Carpenter is like a god, you know, the second coming. Not literally, but she's read all his books, seen all the talks online. He's a prophet to her. She wants to be Eternal. She's made up her mind and now she's pressuring me to use my connections to move us up in line." Kilgore must punch the last few words to rise above a city bus roaring by. "It's hard to argue against a guy whose track record includes curing almost every major disease known to man, ending widespread hunger, and bringing mortality to a halt. I'd have to have some pretty convincing evidence he was basically the devil incarnate to change her mind."

Raines swipes a napkin across her mouth and pushes a response past her second bite, still in mid-chew. "We need to find something fast, then. It's not just you and Celeste I'm concerned about. We're talking millions, if not billions of lives here."

"There is one thing that is really odd to me about how this is all going down." Kilgore stops himself. He lowers his voice while scanning for eavesdroppers. "Looking at his website, I'm thinking his long-term outlook isn't just improving everyone's physical status. He's putting together a movement, an organized philosophy, doctrinal stuff."

"I would expect that," Raines says with a nod of confirmation. "Without the normal fears of the consequences of death, I would think things might begin to spin out of control from a standpoint of orderly society. There always has to be a cause, an *ism*, a tribal icon to glue society together or it falls apart pretty rapidly."

"Yeah, he's got this whole one-world vision of unity. That's always been his play. There is something between the lines, a vibe, a disturbing mojo." Kilgore takes another bite and pauses the conversation with a raised finger. After a few chews he continues. "You know his type, we've even worked for a few of them, calculating and duplicitous. There is some ulterior motive to his whole agenda. He's spent a great deal of time and money building these centers all over the world, too. He says they are gathering places for the *New Freedom*, he calls it."

"Right, it's community building, a cohesion tactic. Once everyone has eternal life, any adherence to the doctrine might be abandoned in short order, I would think. The centers would serve an anchoring purpose." Raines pops the last bit of hot dog in her mouth to punctuate the thought.

"You see, that's what I was thinking. Carpenter can't possibly think that the great masses will just follow him like sheep out of some loyalty. He's smart enough to know that without any leverage everyone will scatter."

"I think calling them *centers* is a bit understated," Raines adds while looking at her phone. "Have you seen this? It's from Carpenter's website." She angles the screen for Kilgore to view. He peers through freshly donned reader glasses. "I don't get it, Chris."

"Looks more like a church or temple than a community center, if you ask me."

Kilgore peers closer. "Nooo, that seems a little farfetched. What are they going to worship?"

"Carpenter, of course. It fits perfectly. You are forgetting I spent time with the man. It sounds like Celeste is well on the way to worship herself."

"But there's no incentive. Why follow him let alone *worship* him?"

"Maybe he's got an incentive, Pete."

"I can't imagine what could have more leverage than a fountain of eternal youth that he's giving away for free."

"Nothing is ever free, nothing, Pete," she professes with stern eyes. "I think there is another shoe to drop, some edge here, a method of control. I mean, after all, once you've gone Eternal you've given a stranger the key to the most important lock of all, your very physical being. No one has ever really vetted the process or done a thorough analysis of what actually happens to the genetic code during the conversion. The method is known, but the materials are still in his hands. I don't think anyone except Carpenter and his cronies *could* vet the process. It takes extremely rare knowhow."

"And now were talking about a potential cult like atmosphere surrounding it all," Kilgore spills forth somberly.

Raines gently clutches Kilgore's forearm to ease his growing panic at his personal dilemma. "I'm going to check with some of my sources," she reassures. "I'll get back to you."

"Quickly, please. I don't know how much longer I can stall Celeste."

Ninety Seven
Present Day

"It's really quite ingenious," Patricia Hamer declares to her fellow cabin mates from her seat on the sofa. Her conclusions reached, she summoned them for a review.

"How does it work?" Chandler queries.

"Kipner utilized a retrovirus as a delivery system for his own designer strand of DNA."

"A retrovirus?" Kovacs asks from the kitchen area.

"It's different than a standard virus."

"Different how?" Traeger asks.

"A standard virus merely attacks cells and adds its genetics to the existing DNA of the host cell, but a retrovirus actually mimics the DNA of the host cell altering it to become a hybrid cell and hiding it from the immune system. It is tricked into thinking everything is just peachy, which allows the retrovirus to replicate as a wolf in sheep's clothing."

Kovacs, now seated, furls his brow trying to use his physicist's brain to work out the biology. He asks, "But, surely the immune system eventually will detect it, right?"

"To one degree or another," Hamer responds. "Retroviruses also evolve, continually morphing and disguising themselves over time. When an organism is infected it can never completely eradicate the infection."

"Is this something new?" Traeger asks.

"No, common retroviruses are chicken pox, Epstein-Barr, and HIV."

Chandler jumps in. "So, I think I know where you're going with this: he used a retrovirus because it would alter Brandt's genetic edit and if any further replication of her process were reintroduced, it wouldn't take because Kipner's version would continue to operate indefinitely as well."

Hamer smiles. Chandler's summation validates her own conclusion. "That is correct. I am sure of it." She nods approval to the shrewd intellect of Anders Kipner.

Kovacs takes deeper interest in the details, his future now dependent on Kipner's science. "If Brandt used a virus, wouldn't the immune system eventually attack it?"

"All forms of viruses aren't necessarily harmful. In fact, most aren't. They have just evolved to where they can live symbiotically within the host. Besides, she only used the virus to deliver the DNA. Once that is complete, it doesn't matter what happens to it."

Chandler's ardent curiosity nags him further. "Going back to Kipner's version. The good Cardinal here is kind of the fly in the ointment, Pat. Wouldn't you say?"

"Please explain that," Kovacs asks through a growing curiosity of his own fate.

"Well, we still can't account for how you went in the opposite direction. If Kipner's cocktail was supposed to undo Brandt's business how is it you are now a man in his thirties? And why did it take over two years after becoming Eternal to kick in?"

Hamer tilts her head and shrugs. "I don't know, I've just kind of scratched the surface on all this. I understand the theoretical aspects, but the actual mechanics are very new to me. I suppose it remained dormant in Jonas and somehow woke up. Retroviruses can be very patient."

"But it looks like you finally figured out the puzzle. Fine work, Patricia," Traeger champions.

"And Kipner probably crafted his version to act on an earlier version," Chandler adds. "The deteriorated form that was introduced to Myer and Jonas is different, so it's kind of acting randomly, it seems."

Kovacs has more to ask. "Do you know how the Eternal DNA works, the perfect replication?"

"The entry point of both Brandt's and Kipner's genetic string is stem cells," Hamer replies. "It's really quite a basic thing, and I should have realized that some time ago. Stem cells are the drivers of all cell replication. They also have the ability to develop into any kind of cell in the body. They are the source of all rejuvenation. By amping up the stem cells into supercells of flawless replication, the body is continually renewed at the highest level possible."

"Eternal life explained," Chandler concludes, patting Hamer's shoulder. "Your usual excellence, Pat. Well done."

Traeger, sensing an end game, asks. "How do we isolate the Kipner version and see if it will work on general Eternal population?"

"We don't really know if it will. There is one way to get closer to the answer, though... if Ivan is up for it."

"Hell yeah, I'm up for it," Myer announces. "What do we do?"

"We give you some of Jonas' blood for starters, see if it works," Hamer pragmatically responds.

"You mean all this time the cure for me is just a blood swap?" Myer complains.

"Maybe, but you needed the right blood," Hamer answers.

"Why blood?" Kovacs asks. "We breathe the same air. Would he not have it already in his system? Wouldn't all of you?"

"Airborne transmission is not very effective for something as complex and as fragile as delivering a retrovirus. I am confident that Kipner, and Brandt for that matter, would be using blood as the means of transmission. It explains why Brandt has a process that requires the subject to be present. She probably has some reinforcing redundancy as an added layer of certainty. She may actually spin out an individual's stem cells and just culture them directly instead of increasing risk of failure by relying on the retrovirus to go to work on its own."

"How soon can we get on with it?" Myer asks, buzzing with anticipation. "I'm tired of these blasted demons in my head."

"You know this is only a theory, right?"

"Honestly, if you are worried about a negative result, could I really get any worse than I am now?"

Ninety Eight
Present Day

It is the sound that wakes him. The sound of nothing, nothing but his own thoughts. Before, the unspeakable was spoken, dark despair shouting down the better, hopeful voices—but no longer. These first moments of the brand-new day welcome Ivan Myer back to a brilliant world after a long absence. He rises. A few steps later, a face from the past greets him from a medicine cabinet mirror. "Hey, stranger. It's been a while." Glee surges within him. "IT WORKED," he shouts.

His exclamation finds Hamer and Chandler occupying their usual haunt, coffee mugs in hand. "Ivan?" Hamer hurries over with a grateful grin and welcome hug. Chandler jumps to his feet, too.

"Oh, Ivan, such a good thing to see." Hamer's eyes gleam with joy.

"It happened so fast, too," Myer gushes.

"Well." She pauses and twists her lips. "Not so much, really. It was the better part of three days you've been in there."

"Three days? It felt like just overnight."

"Well, that's good." Chandler shares relief through a smile of his own. "We were a little concerned that something had gone south."

"Yes, you weren't quite comatose, but you looked it. Three days isn't a shocker, it's typical, really. But we just had no idea given the new genetics involved." Hamer exhales a relaxed sigh.

"Well, I feel great, and thank you, both of you, really... and Jonas." He scans the cabin. "Where is he, and Alex too?"

"Kovacs went for a walk. Alex went into town to get supplies." Hamer lays a hand on Myer's shoulder. "How do you feel? Are the demons gone?"

"I feel like I am thirty again and wholly myself... and hungry." He smiles "And, best of all, the tormentors in my head are no more. Thank you so much."

"Enjoy it, you may be like that a while... a long while," Chandler quips.

Myer falls blissfully into the couch. Hamer and Chandler follow.

"Ivan, do you know how wonderful it is to see you back... back as you?" She grabs his hand. She feels him grip tightly in return, a welcome sensation compared to the frail, weak hand she held just days ago. "That day," she chokes up, "when I found you in the forest..." Rare tears begin streaming from her eyes.

Myer wraps her in his arms. Chandler gently rubs her back from behind. Her swollen eyes find Myer's. He beams back and says, "That Adeline Brandt is no match for the brilliance of our own Pat Hamer."

Hamer laughs off her sadness. "You really think so?

Myer nods and kisses her forehead. "So, what is the next step?"

"While you were transforming," she says through sniffs while wiping her eyes. "I was isolating the retrovirus and now I am culturing it. It should be ready soon and then we will have something deliverable."

"And still no idea how to deliver it," Chandler adds.

"When the others get back, let's have a pow-wow about that," Hamer submits, wearing a newfound sense of authority. "Between all of us, I am sure we can come up with a good solution."

Ninety Nine
Present Day

"I call it Homage: 'The blessedness of being'," floats from glossy ruby lips across the room to the ears of James Carpenter.

"It's beautiful, Justine... just beautiful," Carpenter replies, eyes aglow. "I know now that Marianne and I made the perfect choice with you."

"It is my honor alone, James," she returns with a nod, a blush of pink finding her cheeks. For a moment, she looks away, fearing her eyes could reveal too much. She thinks back to her beginnings, her fledgling spiritual practice in a humble strip mall in Simi Valley. Her "discovery" at the hands of some Hollywood, A-list talent who stopped in to hear her message. It was her breakout moment. Since then, the usual state of things is for her to be the object of admiration, a sort of spiritual rock star. But now, she is unsettled and nervous. She is now alone in the presence of the great James Carpenter, presenting to him her ideas for a service of worship.

"So now, with the blessings and thanks having been given, the ceremony will focus more on bringing the attention of the followers to the source of their blessing and to invoke a greater sense of purpose and awareness of being in their lives." She pauses, sensing Carpenter wishes to contribute and also put her at ease.

"I see. So, this strengthens the bond between all the followers and the collective sense of progressing the whole to another level." Carpenter crosses one leg over the other, regally postured in a high-back armchair. "So, help me visualize how this happens, you know, within the setting."

She is taken by his natural grandeur. His back is sturdy and firm, anchoring his excellent form. His face is taut and assured, determined but with welcoming, almost innocent, eyes, orbs looking forward into every next moment.

Again, a small flame ignites, one she thought she'd stamped out. Almost involuntarily she wisps her long blonde mane about and stands firm with her ample chest pronounced. "Well... um," she collects herself but only momentarily; the flame burns too strong. Her voice is racing with anxiousness. "The followers will be reminded, hearing their own voices proclaiming it, that without the gift they have received, their lives would have soon been no more." She tries to temper her pace, but can't stop panting the words. "They will acknowledge aloud that their continuing path exists only because of the goodness of the one deserving gratitude. The one who gave them eternal life is the one most worthy of acclaim."

Carpenter shifts smoothly in his seat, eyes never leaving her. She gulps and continues, no less agitated. "In tandem, a message of transcendence beyond the self is proclaimed, the arrival to a place of bliss. The giving of oneself to the wholeness of all is the most righteous and supreme state of being. Immediately following, your weekly inspirational message will be given. Finally, the act of sharing the body is administered so that all may live restored and renewed once again."

Carpenter stands, bringing his hands together in applause. "BRAVO, Justine. You have so brilliantly captured the essence of my vision."

"Why, thank you, James," she pushes out relieved but still breathless. Carpenter approaches.

"Are you okay, Justine?" He approaches and stares into her. She receives him, her thoughts scrambling and swimming.

"James, I don't know why," she chitters. "I'm just kind of overwhelmed for some reason."

Carpenter tenderly wraps her in himself. Her succulent form melts into him. He returns an easing smile. She looks away, shy and vulnerable. He tugs her chin with a finger, pulling her back up into his gaze. He presses his lips to hers. She returns all of herself with her own response. The tangle continues.

For her, the moment seems a precious lifetime. She suddenly jerks away. "James... oh no... We can't... I..." He places a finger to her lips. "It's quite alright. I chose this," he comforts.

"But what of Marianne?"

"Marianne is still herself. This is the new way. In our way, no one belongs to anyone else. All of us are free to do as we wish."

She returns a look of confusion, but only briefly. The dilemma dissolves. A luminous smile returns. "I understand, James." She kisses him again, then presses herself into him. "Are you sure Marianne won't mind? I really don't want *her* angry at me."

Carpenter laughs. "Oh, my dear Justine. She would be quite pleased at the sight. When I tell her, she will be filled with joy. Perhaps she might even want to join us next time."

One Hundred
Present Day

"Where do you suppose Alex is? He should be back by now," Hamer airs to her cabin mates.

"You're right, and Jonas too," Chandler adds with some unease as he checks the time.

She scans the landscape beyond the window pane. The serene woods show early signs of spring. The oaks push new buds past the expiring winter; tips of eastern hemlocks, chartreuse-dipped fan brushes foretell a new season ready for birth.

"It's too quiet out there," Myer voices under his breath over her shoulder, picking up on her observation.

"You know, now that you mention it," Hamer admits.

"It's Kovacs!" Chandler yells from another window. "Something's wrong, guys."

Hamer and Myer rush to join Chandler. Kovacs is dashing full sprint for the cabin and throwing his arms forward in the air as he yells: "RUN... RUN!" Behind him, emerging from the forest, dogs, and then uniforms. Faceless devils in combat gear, Kevlar, black boots and weapons of war are in thunderous pursuit.

"Let's get the hell out of here!" Hamer screams.

Frantic flight. But to where? As fast as they can, all scatter in different directions. Hamer bolts into the woods a few yards away past the slaughtering shed, weaving, jumping, and dodging. Last autumn's leaves crunch beneath her panic. The fresh growth slaps her as she passes. She hears only *her* noise, though, no tumult behind her. She peeks, still running. No one, not even a dog. It can't be that easy, she thinks. It could be a trap. She stops to listen ahead: nothing. Behind her again, the same. She stills her thoughts. There is one sound, one from above, a familiar whirr. She looks up to see a drone staring back. "Oh, shit." A wisp of air. A sharp sting fills her neck. Darkness fades in.

***

Chandler found the woods too, the ones behind the cabin. His physical perfection gets him farther in than Hamer. Ahead, he sees a break in the woods and then a clearing. He will be exposed, easy prey. He waits behind a large trunk, borrowing a jagged, fallen limb from the forest floor. Boots mangle the ground not far away. Faint whispers approach, earpiece chatter, instructions from command. They are near, very near.

A boot lands aside him. He thrusts forth to the neck under the chin. Flesh rips. One down. He grabs the gun and turns. He hears another from the other side, further away. He sprays the area, and a body falls—two down.

The forest is thumping with faster boot falls. Chandler runs again, nuzzle forward.

Shapes seem to move ahead, maybe the enemy, maybe phantoms. He fires short bursts into the forest in stride. At the very least, they must take cover. Fifty yards separate, now maybe one hundred. The footsteps behind now fainter, but he knows they will not relent. Hope sparks. A road lies ahead through the pillars of wood. Citizen traffic zooms by. He hears a different zoom... pain, great pain. His legs fail. His hands claw the forest floor. His shirt against him sticky and cold, then colder. The cool spring air finds the dampness against his body. The chill spreads from inside, now. His old friend is back. At least for a few moments he will find bliss in another place, the place he can never remain.

***

Myer's dash lasts twenty yards, stopped by nothing but himself and the sound of dogs tearing into a man. Kovacs seems like a brother now, the bearer of kindred genes. Myer, compelled, turns and chooses to rid Kovacs' terror rather than try to save his own neck. He runs as close to Kovacs as possible without drawing a beastly wrath upon himself. Hands in the air, he hurls pleas of surrender to the faceless goons. "Call them off. It's over, we can do nothing. End this, please!"

The dogs release, paused by a soundless sound. Kovacs ails and groans, writhing in dust, canine slobber, and blood. Myer bends a knee to lend aid.

"Remain standing, arms high. DO NOT move," blares shrill from a helmet-speaker, one cleansing anything human from the utterance. Eight now surround the defeated.

"Who are you? What have we done?" Myer challenges.

"This man is wanted by the authorities," returns the voice, robot-like.

"Yes, wrongly so, but you aren't *the authorities* now, are you?" Myer levels with sneering scorn.

Myer and Kovacs are dutifully rendered harmless with cable ties. A van whisks them away. Their last sight is the cabin door being kicked in. Termites with guns, Myer thinks. Sanctuary will never be theirs again.

One Hundred One
Present Day

The soulless chill is a familiar one to Kovacs. For the rest, it is the coldest hell they have ever known. Kovacs and Myer have been conscious the longest. Hamer's recovery took through the first night. Chandler seems to be coming around, fully aware, having spent the last day in and out.

"Chandler?" Hamer gasps. "He's coming around. I think he should be able to stay awake now. I've watched him reconstitute at least two dozen times," she says crawling over to lay a welcoming hand on his shoulder. "Marcus, are you there?"

"I am, Pat." He musters a strained reply. "I am, but where is here?"

Kovacs, being the foremost authority, answers. "This is their *Keep*. It was my home for nearly three years," he exhales a defeated sigh, "and maybe now the rest of my permanent existence."

"Think of the Tower of London, but instead thirty feet underground," Myer cynically declares.

"Who's *Keep*?" Chandler asks.

"One guess," Myer replies no less callously.

"How long since—"

"Three days," Kovacs answers.

"So, they tracked us down somehow," Chandler laments, staring up at the rocky ceiling.

"The drone, the one over us when we were looking for Kovacs and Traeger. It must have got the license plate, or at least they triangulated the car's position with street cameras," Hamer posits. "Anyway, it's only a theory, but they must have satellite access, and finally some recognition software found the car at the cabin."

"We should've known," Chandler groans. "What about the—"

"Before you finish that," Myer interrupts. "You should assume they are watching and listening to our conversation."

"Right," Chandler goes no further. "Jesus, I'm hungry. What about Alex? Did he get caught?"

"We have no idea. He was with the car, so I can't believe he didn't," Hamer suggests.

A beep sounds from down the hallway, then footsteps. The captives rise. Until now there has only been one visitor to bring food and remove the waste buckets. Four shapes approach the gate. The harsh hall light from behind reveals only silhouettes. One is a woman. Two appear bald. The gate opens. The captives, all standing now, brace firm.

Marianne leads, approaching on slithering steps.

"Well, now that you are all conscious, I thought it would be a good time to acquaint ourselves, introduce you to your hosts," sneers the queen bee.

Chandler eases forward for a closer look. He looks her up and down. Her captivating appearance shocks him with more disbelief than he expected. "Brandt?" he asks shaking his incredulous head. "It's really you. I could have lived the rest of my life never sharing the same space with you again. But I have to grudgingly admit, well done. Your brilliance is inarguable." Hamer glares shame at him.

"I suppose *thank you* is in order," Marianne returns "But I am pretty sure that will be the last good thing you ever say to me, Marcus."

"Alex, *it is* you," Kovacs stabs venomously into the air with surprise and terror. His form deflates, all hope evaporated.

The others follow with faith lost, hearts falling, seeing the fourth visitor now as Alex Traeger. He is not the Alex Traeger they knew just three days ago. He is youthful and striking a defiant pose.

"Oh, Alex," Kovacs sighs, emptied out, tears cascading. He turns away, palms hiding his face. "What have you done?"

Hamer shares quiet tears, devastated and defeated.

Myer boils over. "You son of a BITCH," he screams, charging at Traeger. His fist raises. Before he can thrust it forward, he is jolted in the jaw, sending him to the floor. The fist's owner stands over Myer, his naked skull gleaming. "Myer, welcome back. You just couldn't leave well enough alone. And, if I may say so, you look much better than the last time I saw you."

"Enough!" Marianne booms. "You all must know you have severely pissed me off. I don't know what you were thinking you could accomplish, but you've been meddling in my business. If you haven't figured it out, that was not a good idea. I will get to the bottom of what you know and what you have been plotting in short order, no matter how that has to be done. It will be unpleasant, I assure you. Deception will be useless. Alex here has told me everything. Now it is your turn to fill in the gaps. Enjoy what little time together you have left."

Marianne pivots and departs, her entourage in tow. The gate slams, hard steel echoing its rigid superiority.

"I can't believe I fell for Traeger's *aw shucks* bit," Myer curses, rubbing his jaw. "I should have picked up on that."

"We all should have," Chandler grumbles.

"He was so sincere. But why would he have stuck around all that time?" Hamer utters disconcertedly. "Why did he even come at all? Once they knew where we were, why wait any longer?"

"He had to learn what we knew," Myer answers. "She sent him to spy on us, to determine what our knowledge level was, to see if we were anywhere near the truth."

"Pat is right, though. Once they knew where we were, none of that mattered," Chandler counters.

"I suppose maybe she wanted to see what we knew to determine what weaknesses might be lurking in her methods," Hamer concludes. "She let us go on until she learned we could reverse her work and why."

"And Traeger knows exactly how that happened," Myer spits out, surrendered. "Once she figures out how to beat Kipner's genes, she'll cancel it out."

Kovacs glides between them, his form repowered. He has discovered some grain of hope in the darkness of the moment. "In my three years alone here, I never had my faith challenged like the last few minutes. Satan tested me. He drove daggers deep into my soul, shattering me. Alex..." Kovacs pauses, to swallow his pain. "He is like my own son. I had to look away as the man I knew died to me. But it became so powerfully evident that I was sharing a moment with God the Father. I saw him witnessing the death of *his* only Son." Kovacs raises his eyes upward. His being fills with crucial resolve. "A peace found me. The Father spoke to remind me of faith." Kovacs, one at a time, looks deeply into the eyes of the others. "We all need to calm our fears and trust instead. Have faith, my good friends. We were not led into this moment without a purpose. Put away your doubt and join me in my belief."

Myer thinks to voice more cynicism, but decides it would do nothing helpful. Kovacs, his thoughts expressed, wanders away further into the cavern, apart from the others. He leans one hand against the wall and slumps. Hamer notices and urgently follows.

"Cardinal, I will do my best. I promise. But... Cardinal?" She sees his face wincing with discomfort. "Jonas, are you okay?" she asks softly.

"I am, Patricia. It is only the wounds. They are still a bit fresh."

"You mean from the dogs?"

"I do."

"Forgive me," she grins with a spark, "but that is actually a good thing."

"How so?"

"You see Marcus?" She turns to look at Chandler who is looking fresh and revived. "He is good as new and you are not."

"I am happy for him," Kovacs replies, confused.

"No, I mean he was shot, fatally shot, and after three days he is good as new." She pauses, raising one eyebrow to see if her point has landed.

"I think I know your reasoning," Kovacs says with a nod. "I was less wounded but I am still not healed. My body is returning to its natural state. Kipner's intervention is undoing Brandt's work."

"I believe so. It appears there may be a viable way to short-circuit the Eternals process."

"I hope you are right, my dear. There is only one problem. We have no way of delivering it where it is needed most."

One Hundred Two
One Day Earlier

It was a dream, but not a dream, a place not anywhere but everywhere at the same time. He was complete in the fullness of his being, but wrapped within a sensation of being fully dissolved and undone. He awakened both exhausted and refreshed, renewed but spent. It was a journey of three days, he believes. At least, that is as long as they said it would be. The experience seemed more like a millennium. And so, it remains an enigma. The only certain thing Alex Traeger knows is that he has never known anything like it.

Three days prior, he returned to The Carpenter Institute. In order to be welcomed back, he knew the only gesture that would convince them of his loyalty would be to immediately become Eternal and to accept it unconditionally. At the core of his being he knew it was what must be done. It was time and nothing remained to argue against it. What he was unsure of was which version he would be given, the Chandler version or the Myer/Kovacs version. For the moment, no harassing demons roam his thoughts. It seems the Chandler version is the more likely candidate.

Through the blur, the hangover of three days of complete cellular makeover, he understands himself to be in recovery. Strength is fleeting. He possesses enough to angle his head and eyes. There is equipment for medical observation; pulse and blood pressure readings beep and oxygen feeds his nostrils. He raises his forearm into his line of sight to behold the hand of a younger man. He harbored no doubts it would work, but there is relief just the same.

Remembrances trickle in. The actual external administration was unspectacular. He had been placed on a bed, although one more elaborate than just for sleep, it being equipped for medical purposes. The devices for monitoring were attached, then two intravenous drips. The rest is a fog, at least where the physical is concerned.

Then it was the dream, like being turned to liquid and poured through a filter. Or maybe like a tightening of focus dialed to the sharpness of perfection, lines now crisp and razor-edged. The psyche is laundered and pressed, the impurities of doubt, insecurity and vulnerability rinsed from the fabric and swirled down the drain. All at once, each cell is vibrantly connected to the rest. Mind and body in unison and communion. The garden and the apple no longer hold sway. The fragileness of human existence, living as flawed from the outset, is no more. God is no longer a mystery or out of reach. The wholeness of everything now resides in one perfect being—oneself. It is intoxicating, God is you and you are God. The perfection of one's being, freshly made, has become the complete vessel of all that matters. Visceral knowledge is baked in with no inconvenient questions to shake the foundation. Born again. Life is yours and you are its undeniable master.

Traeger's reconstitution quickens, the scales of his coma fall away. A familiar face floats above, then another. "Alex, welcome home," he recognizes the voice of Marianne.

Another, belonging to Valerie, asks "How do you feel, Alex?" He tries to speak. He sees them smile. A hand strokes his hair. He hears, "Rest now; we will see you soon." Eyelids slide down his drifting orbs. Sleep returns.

One Hundred Three
Present Day

"Alex, I am so happy to see you," Traeger's ex-wife Valerie offers with an eager hug. "You look so fantastic," she pleasantly sighs with bright eyes. "I knew you'd come back. You've made the right decision. This is the way we are all truly meant to be, so full of life. James has taught me so much."

Traeger, now fully lucid, responded to an earlier request to meet with Marianne in her office suite. Valerie's presence was unexpected, but she glows of youth looking even better than when they first met.

"And the kids?" Traeger asks.

"I waited. I knew you had reservations, but now that we are both Eternals, I think we should go ahead with them too. After all, we don't want our children looking older than we are." She laughs.

"Of course, Valerie," Traeger smiles back.

"They are with their grandparents now, but as soon as they return, we will get them scheduled. I've arranged for Mom and Dad to get bumped to the front of the line, too."

"That's the least we could do, Valerie," Marianne interjects from behind her desk. "Now, if you wouldn't mind, I'd like to be alone with Alex? We have some catching up to do. He's all yours once I bend his ear for a while," she grins politely.

Valerie bounces her young body through the huge office doors which close behind her.

"Alex, please, join me in the retreat."

They pace the few steps into an area adjacent to the office featuring panorama windows. Alex finds a chair, contemporary white leather with no arms. She takes the matching couch, but seats herself on one arm of the sofa to face him. She throws one silky leg over the other.

"James has taken quite a liking to Valerie," Marianne boasts with almost motherly pride. "I thought I'd lend you that courtesy in case you possess any lingering feelings for her. As I told you before, James and I feel that attachments are antiquated notions. But just the same, I wanted you to know about them."

"I understand. Revolution comes in many forms. I am looking forward to my own... *explorations*," he smirks with a mischievous smile.

"That's very good to hear. Why don't you and I consider some *explorations* of our own soon? I've caught you looking before. A little forbidden fruit might be just what you need."

"I look forward to that very much, Marianne," Traeger grins slyly.
She unfolds her supple form from the sofa. "Beverage, Alex?" she offers, swaying off to a wet bar. She returns bearing two stem glasses of red wine, her visage less agreeable. "Look, I think we need to clear the air as far as your whereabouts in the last three weeks. You can see why I might want to know some details. You disappeared from the face of the earth, then rematerialized at the front gate, the prodigal son returned, begging all manner of forgiveness. James was really quite hurt when you left."

"I know, Marianne. I panicked. There was too much going on and I... I just needed some time."

"Needed time?" she asks, confused at the idea.

"Yes, I..." Traeger sits in suspense momentarily posturing firm so as not to betray his lingering doubts or thoughts overflowing with the events of the past few days in the cabin. "I just felt like I was losing my mind. I've been so consumed with work that I hadn't had a talk with myself in forever. I needed to really dig deep, to shed my skin and prepare for the change ahead. Once my old self had been dealt with, I decided it was time to move ahead. That's why I asked to be an Eternal right away. I wanted to let you know, in no uncertain terms, that I was all in."

"You do know we have extended you tremendous liberty over the years. Your stubbornness has been puzzling to us, even generated some suspicions within the organization. You understand that?"

"I do, and I apologize. I am ready to move on and I hope you can too in regards to the old Alex."

"We will."

Returned to the couch arm, she sips. Her full lips paint red on the rim of the glass. She adopts an innocent demeanor pasted over an air of suspicion. "While you were gone… wandering, as it were. How on earth did you run across our meddlers?

"They found me," he replies confidently. "Myer had some tech, facial recognition. I guess he took note of me while he was spying on the Institute. He had pictures. He found Kovacs that way too."

"They were really quite busy in that silly little cabin of theirs," she sneers, her façade of innocence now washing away to reveal a germ of contempt. "My staff has done some investigation and found they were planning some sort of sabotage. It appears they meant to overthrow all our work." Her contempt grows to scorn. "I will see that they never have that chance again. I'm sure you know I have no tolerance for enemies or anyone who might be their confederates."

She rises, towering over him. "Do you still stand by your statement that you stayed with them to gather information and report back when the time seemed right?" She stares down, fists on hips. "Think hard, Alex. Are you sure you harbor no allegiance with them?"

"None," he returns unflinching. "Marianne, if I was against you, why would I return of my own free will and become Eternal?"

She relaxes slightly, hearing the only answer that would make sense. He stands, sensing the conversation is completed. "Alright, Alex, welcome home." She calmly smiles and cradles his chin in her hands. Her lips press gently and lusciously to his. The kiss ended, she replaces her lips with a firm fist. He collapses back into the chair, stunned. The redness of blood mingles with a stain of red lipstick. She redoubles her dominance above him with eyes full of flame. "If I find out differently, you should know your Eternal life will not be pleasant. There are places in hell so dark even Lucifer won't visit. The conspirators are about to learn that soon. I would hate for you to join them."

"I understand," He responds, trying to contain the dread stirred by her threat. "You have nothing to worry about."

Dryly and callously she replies, "I am reassured."

One Hundred Four
Present Day

"The other two I don't hold as responsible as I do both of you," Marianne scolds her two former colleagues Kovacs and Chandler. Humbled, they sit atop gurneys in hospital gowns. Beyond them, past air-locked doors, a sterile medical examination chamber glows a sickly blue, fluorescent tubes casting unnatural light from above.

"Rest assured, they will have their chance to confess their involvement. You and I know they will not last as long as you. So, in the interest of demonstrating that I can be a merciful person, I will spare them a messy experience if you just come clean now."

They stare back, lips tight and eyes fixed back. Her face tightens more.

"Myer is just a snoop. I have no need of him. But, he did piss me off when he walked. He is no longer how I left him, so something has been monkeyed with," she finishes with a sneer. "And then there is you, Kovacs. What a curious thing that you are now whole and young." She pauses to glare at him. "And the woman, Patricia Hamer, I have had her checked out," she levels with dismissive disdain. "She is just a crime scene investigator, so I know she doesn't have the knowledge to approach anything of this altitude. That only leaves you two. Tell me now what you were up to." She leans in, eyes burning.

"Kovacs, tell me of your transformation. How did you escape the Keep? Who aided you? Someone from the Institute?"

Kovacs fiercely glares back, then broadcasts from his soul, "God, and God alone."

"BULLSHIT!" she explodes as anger spills over. "I am so weary of your metaphysical blabber. There is an answer, one found right here on Earth, and you two know what has been done."

Chandler breaks his silence. "Look, Marianne, it's not just Patricia. None of the four of us possess any knowledge capable of altering your process. That is the most obvious fact in all this. Did you ever think that maybe, just maybe, there is an error in there somewhere? What you are asking about is two individuals who were given a derivative version of the Eternals process. Maybe that version has some flaws."

"I have thousands in that state and none of them have ever morphed into full, unfettered Eternals. I know my work, Chandler."

"Thousands?" Kovacs exhales a pained, shadowy sigh. "Thousands who are guilty of what crime? Disagreeing with your... *Utopia*?"

"It is more freedom than mankind has ever known. The freedom to live forever and have no dream unmet."

"It is hell, plain and simple," Kovacs fires back defiantly.

Chandler breaks in to still the brewing fury. "Look, Brandt, all we did was to try to figure out why you have made this such a big secret. If you and Carpenter really are out to better the world, why not be as transparent as possible? We just went through your old research on a knowledge quest."

"You know why," she returns with irritation. "Reader was adamant that sometimes you need to guide people into accepting what is best for them in the long run."

Kovacs bristles to shame her and hisses, "You mean *trick them*. I never heard him say any such thing. Do you hear yourself, Brandt?"

Her frustration builds. "I even had to keep it secret from you. If anyone had known my plans, we would have been shut down and the future of mankind would be in grave doubt."

"Right, the Vatican would have put the kibosh on the whole thing and you would be nowhere," Chandler challenges.

"Tell him, Jonas," she commands.

Kovacs slumps, an old wound opened, stinging his spirit. He pauses to find the strength to speak something out loud that he can hardly bear to hear himself say. "They knew; they were in on it. Just a handful, but there was tacit approval from above. They wanted to witness the man, to see the face of the Son of God in the flesh."

Chandler, shocked, gapes at his friend. Kovacs sighs and continues. "The whole thing was a grotesque sacrilege. They kept me in the dark, knowing I would never be part of anything of the sort by choice. They gave me no insight as to where it might lead. Then, Brandt deceived them." He looks up at her with a derisive scowl. "After getting what she wanted, she told them she was unable to make it work and deliver their request to see the clone of Christ." His eyes widen with bitterness and umbrage. "But you made it happen. You gave birth to the child and now you take him as your lover. Such evil this is! What a demon you are, WOMAN," Kovacs furiously shouts.

Chandler interrupts again more tersely, "What did you find, Brandt?"
"Brandt is NO MORE. Do you understand?" she defiantly proclaims.

She steps away to gain distance from Kovacs' icy sneer. She adopts an academic tone, recalling her original vision from long ago. "The Bible... at least in the last couple of centuries, science has pulled away from it as so much fairy tale. I decided to consider: what if it were true. Not the so-called miraculous, but what if what is reported there really happened. Two thousand years ago, to the primitive minds of that time, the only explanation would be something called a 'miracle'. But what if, instead, a mutation occurred, or perhaps a recessive gene, or the whole strand had surfaced again."

"Blasphemy!" Kovacs blares.

"Hold on, Jonas," Chandler interrupts, raising his hand. "I know how you feel, but I want to hear this."

"She is twisting lies..."

"Please," Chandler insists.

Marianne's face lights up, now free to reveal her theory to her team members. "In the Old Testament there are stories of people living for hundreds of years. Then, at the same time as Christ, Lazarus also rose. He was a good friend of Christ's, perhaps of a similar bloodline. There are accounts in one gospel that many rose from the dead after Christ rose."

A triumphant grin grows on her face as she relives her own revelation. "It makes so much sense," she pants out. "All of these people reportedly rising again emerging from a small, ethnic population pool from one small region on the planet. It seemed there was enough merit to at least have a look."

Almost possessed, she fixes on Chandler. "Marcus, we found it. Sure enough, it was there. You and Kipner in the bomb shelter. It took thousands of attempts, but we found it and brought it back to life."

"Why did you need to bring it to term as a living human, though?" Chandler asks

"I couldn't get it to culture past a certain point. You were there for part of that. It seemed to me the genes needed... context. They needed to be reconstituted as a complete being, not as a chain of disconnected DNA."

"So, given no other alternative," Chandler gulps, "you impregnated yourself. You knew if any of us saw you with child we would be highly suspicious, so..."

"Well, Smith and Jones knew, but they can keep a secret," she clarifies.

"Because they are Smith and Jones," Chandler slides out of one side of his mouth.

"Reader suspected, but he wanted nothing to do with it. Being an atheist, he viewed the whole project as unusual, but nothing to find any major concern. He was eager to return to his work and for some strange reason I trusted him. I think part of him was curious and wanted to see where it was all going. Maybe he wanted to see if his predictions would materialize. He was good on his word until he began to become delusional."

"And you bought my silence by making me Eternal," Chandler completes the circle.

"Yes, you never had an eye for grand ambition. I knew you were going to just not think about it anymore. And Jonas," she casts determined eyes in his direction, "you just disappeared."

"You would have done to me what you did with Kipner," Kovacs stares back. "I was a loose end that happened to also be a loose cannon."

"Well, I am not sure if I would have dispensed with you. But when you disappeared, I knew you had gone into hiding. Kipner was a liability. His ego would not have let him remain silent, and he was behaving like an idiot."

"And then you transformed yourself," Chandler submits with an involuntary tone of admiration.

"I did. I corrected nature's mistake. With practice, I got even better at honing the process. These genes, the ones we found from long ago. They are like none I have ever seen. They are perfection."

"That is impossible," Kovacs argues. "Christ was physically no different than any other man. What made him the Christ is that he was God in the flesh, not some magic mutation."

"I beg to differ, Jonas. The millions walking the globe today, all living free of the ravishment of disease and rising to new life again from death—they are all the proof I need. Take, for example, the man sitting next to you. Look at yourself. Have you another explanation? One of scientific basis? Do you, scientist Jonas?"

Kovacs' head lowers. "Return me to the Keep. I have no desire to continue this conversation."

"You will be returned, but only after I have been satisfied as to what has been altered along the way. Be glad. I plan to use anesthetics. And, I'm sorry Marcus. I need answers, so you will be examined as well."

One Hundred Five
Four Days Earlier

It was maybe two hours ago, but it seems like days. Hunkered down in a position far into the woods, but still within earshot, he intently listened for any sound that might betray the slightest presence of anyone remaining.

After a time, he taught himself to filter out the traffic noise from the distant highway to give full attention to any other stirring. He imagined the sounds that might be made by lingerers, those lying in wait to trap him, or finishing up their dreadful business.

Satisfied, he charts a path sure to be under as much cover from surveillance above. His steps crunch through the forest. Any thoughts of stealth are now dashed by the leaves announcing his approach. Still, better safe than sorry, he treks beneath the forest canopy. Halfway there, the ground is painted with blood. He heard the whole thing from far away but was unsure if the gunfire was for show or to fell others. The latter wins. The dispute settled. He arrives. A quick peek in the window, then he waits, listening again. Nothing. He eases the back screen door open and enters. The violation before him sinks his heart. For Alex Traeger, no hope remains that his friends escaped. His only consolation is that there are no bodies, no splatters of blood. Into Hamer's research area, the equipment is scuttled, hard drives ripped out. Carcasses of technology remain, smashed and lifeless. Returning to the main room, he rights a chair and locates the cushions. The fabric is gashed and gutted, but there is just enough left to rest his emptied shell.

How were they found out? he wonders. It is a pointless pondering, an exercise in academics. They were found out and there is nothing to undo that. Alex Traeger sits perched in purgatory, a man without a home or a future. All chance of ending Eternals is itself extinct. His good friend Jonas is surely once again at the mercy of Marianne and her ilk. His freedom was so short-lived, he laments, and now is forever gone.

As an homage to his friend, he sends a flaming arrow of a prayer to God. If he exists, he would certainly be listening in this grave moment. He asks freedom for his friends. But, if not that, at least to be at peace. Traeger is consumed with his own uneasy liberty. He would rather have been with them, sharing their fate.

Panic surges. He feels his smallness, his hapless self, adrift on a vast, endless sea minus any current or headwind to direct him anywhere. His chest tightens. His mouth is thick and sticky. The adrenaline of panicked despair fills his veins. He has failed in every way.

He recalls Jonas telling him he was to be a catalyst, some sort of agent of change. At least that is what Kovacs' friend Reader told him. It is a laughable prediction, especially in this dark moment. Reader was most likely insane at the time, anyway. Traeger never seriously considered the forecast to be much grounded in anything except an eccentric's delusion. But he held off from full judgement thinking that, maybe, there was something to it, something that might prop up the sad, ordinariness of his own life. His heart shrivels into despair. For sure, the ordinariness is long gone, replaced by one extraordinary thing: his absolute, abject failure. He failed his friends. He failed mankind. Fate is sealed in a dark tomb never to rise again. And all this failure finds its expression in a single tear, slowly tracing Traeger's quivering cheek.

Like Nero reaching for his fiddle, he decides it a good time for a drink, to ironically toast the downfall. What lies ahead is uncertain, but at least he has this morsel of self-determination remaining. He cheers silently at the sight of the Wild Turkey still beneath the sink. A few glasses remain intact in the cupboard. And what of ice? He sends another arrow, a mocking prayer to God for ice.

Tugging the freezer door he finds the answer to his prayer. A tray rests undisturbed. Ice hits glass. Bourbon hits ice. Bourbon finds stomach. Traeger clutches the bottle.

Another pour begins but he ends it before the splash. The first pour was enough, enough to bring clarity. He sees it now. The liquor has unveiled the secret. The cubes are perfectly transparent, now. The opaque frosting has melted away to reveal they are more than frozen water.

He stops the sink, tumbles the cubes in and blasts the hot water full over all the ice. Despair melts away. Hope emerges from cold suspension. "She did it!" he shouts in triumph. She isolated Kipner's retrovirus, he is sure of it. The ice now history, the sink now holds lukewarm water and three small, sealed vials. Nothing is written there, but it has to be the cure, Kipner's retrovirus. What else would it be? Traeger fires another from his quiver, a prayer of glorious thanks.

He remembers the discussion on blood transmittal. Drinking them would be fruitless. It must be injected. A closer look at the vials reveals rubber seals over the openings. They seem the kind you pierce with a hypodermic needle to gain the contents. He bolts back to the research area and rummages the rubble, eyes shooting back and forth. His hand digs. A dog after a bone. He finds a syringe and then another still wrapped sterile then bolts back to his tattered throne to brainstorm this out.

There is one chance left, only one. It must be right. It must be perfect. He could inject Carpenter, but the task seems impossible. He could never get near him. He could never get the vials past the security at the Institute. A fool's errand. Perhaps there is another way. The fog clears. Plain as day, he sees it now.

One Hundred Six
Present Day

"As we all step into a new age for humanity, the horizon before us is endless," declares Justine Dupree, Carpenter's chief proclaimer of "The Good Words."

"For the first time in human existence, we've broken through the barriers that divide us. For the first time in human existence, we are bound together for a single purpose." She speaks as a firebrand from the stage of The Carpenter Institute auditorium to a crowd pulsing with anticipation. "All the fears we held both as individuals and as nations are swept away. Fears birthed from scarcity and distrust, fears formed in the irrational, manufactured differences defining *us* versus *them*. Now it is just us, *all of us*, working for each other."

The Lazarus Chain

A thunder of cheer rises up, wrought of the collective enthusiasm of several thousand of the Institute's most hallowed members. These well-bred elites are vital to the cause of her work, work that has led to this day of brilliant success. The declaration garnering unanimous approval, she cruises the platform, blonde mane flowing among the folds of her vestment-like gown. A messenger of vibrant hope, she is perfection to the definitive.

The tumultuous response is not limited to the walls of the Institute. It resonates through the temples scattering the globe where the event is being broadcast to all. The worldwide goal of the project is nearly complete. Today, the temples are filled with newborn Eternals taking their place among their brethren, and those soon to follow, from all countries and cultures. The "Day of Eternal Celebration" has now begun, a day that will be repeated ad infinitum as a gathering of renewal and thanksgiving. It is to be a festival of unity hailed by all as a reminder that their refreshed state of being is due to the good graces, and remarkable genes, of one man, James Carpenter.

"Today, we pledge our lives to work for the betterment of others. As mortality has been driven away, we throw off the fear of death. The space once filled with the knowledge of finality and death will be renewed with eternal thoughts of abundant life. This is the wish of the great one, the deliverer of our eternal state. The lives we lead, we lead for him. Join with me in the pledge?" she preaches with a shout to fill the auditorium. She thrusts her arms into the air, and the audience joins. The hall rumbles—the Earth shakes.

The applause tailing, she summons serenity in a softening of her voice. "And now, please join me in the renewal vow." Eyes gaze up. A screen above the stage provides the pledge. The words unfold before them, read in unison, presented in hundreds of translations apropos to the location.

My life was dust, bounded and incomplete.
In receiving the gift of Eternity, my quest will not end.
I am to be, the greatest me.

And now with my life renewed, I give of myself for the betterment of all.
I fear not death. I fear not disease. I fear not a life of want or need.
And now, today, I receive the continuance, the gift of life unending.
All praise to the one who has delivered me, the Great One.

The shared moment over, Dupree raises both arms again. "And now... the feast of renewal." One by one, the rows empty to approach the front of the stage. Their hands extend, cupped to receive. To each is delivered a pill. Embossed on the surface of each is embossed the symbol of infinity. Hands raise to the mouth. The pill, once swallowed, unfolds its magic. The Eternal within each is refreshed and revived.

One Hundred Seven
Present Day

"So, you are the man of God. I am told without you, I would not exist." Carpenter addresses Kovacs as genuine thanks, but it is wrapped in condescension.

Kovacs stands frozen, his thoughts spinning in contradictions. Before him, in the flesh, is the genetic reproduction of his beloved Lord. His fit frame stands just over six feet; dark hair is set off by smooth skin with a hint of olive tone. His eyes, a piercing brown, rest above pronounced cheek bones and a neatly trimmed beard. Millennia before, his image belonged to the savior of mankind, now it has been hijacked by a man the exact opposite. He is an impostor living in the shell of another. That which belonged to the sacrificial lamb, the forgiver of all sins, is now the greatest sin to ever walk the earth, a wolf in lamb's clothing.

"Do I frighten you, Mr. Kovacs?"

"No, you disgust me," Kovacs levels rudely, with matter-of-fact chill. "It isn't your fault, but you must know that you are merely the product of genetic tinkering, Adeline Brandt's misguided belief in a scientific fiction."

Carpenter smiles back. "Me, a fiction? I am as real as yourself."

"The fiction is the delusion that she has created you to be the great savior, that you will bring eternal life to all."

Carpenter tilts his head to one side and looks down on the cardinal. "Again, do I need to point out what is actually happening as we speak? Millions walk as Eternals because of me."

"Eternal, yes. But imprisoned just the same in their endless state," Kovacs replies. "I suppose you consider yourself their god, the one who must lead them."

"I am the source of life. It is only natural that they will turn to me for direction. Without my existence, they would face their end."

"And you take the credit for it and all the spoils of that presumption?" Kovacs' tone grows increasingly agitated.

"All species seek the alpha," Carpenter brims, self-assured. "They are naturally drawn to those who shall lead them."

"But the choice is not theirs. You have discarded free will from their decision. There is no allegiance where there is coercion. Necessity breeds loyalty, perhaps. But without the freedom to decide on their own, you have no following. Instead, you have captives. This is not leadership; it is tyranny."

"Mr. Kovacs, to the contrary, what we, Marianne and I, have given to the world is the perfect freedom."

Kovacs, perplexed, responds, "Perfect freedom?"

"Humans need structure. They need a cause, something to identify with. For progress to continue, a common direction must be established. When all eyes are focused on a solitary goal, the whole becomes greater than the parts. As individuals, humankind merely spins off in all directions. Single-minded visions result, as many visions of unreachable perfection as there are people to imagine them."

Inside, Kovacs struggles to retain his grip on faith. He feels the Devil's plan is fully formed, ready to metastasize.

"With individuality, friction and conflict breed, resulting in stagnation. We are merely releasing the burden of selfishness. We offer one vision with everyone moving in the same, perfect direction. They are emancipated from the bondage of the imperfections of their own imaginations, and clarity fills the vacuum, the clarity of being committed to something bigger than their own self-concerned lives."

Kovacs can remain silent no more. "You call this freedom?"

"Mr. Kovacs, is it not the same teaching of your belief? One must give everything over to God. You believe when one commits their life to God and puts away one's selfish existence, salvation is begun? One must lose one's life to save it?"

Kovacs stiffens at Carpenter's distortion of the grace of salvation. "Yes, but only to God, not to a charlatan." Kovacs pauses to finish a thought, then speaks it breathlessly, "What you speak of, it is the essence of evil. Do you not see that?" Kovacs answers his own question out loud. "But, of course you do not. The Devil knows only of hollow imitation and not of the perfection of unbounded creation."

"There is no such thing as evil," Carpenter volleys back undaunted. "*Evil* was invented by the peddlers of religion to foster loyalty," he proclaims forcefully. "You accuse me of making captives of all Eternals, but the followers of religion are just so many captives in their own right. They are captives of the fear of losing the promise of a life after this, one promised with no proof. At least my reward is apparent. There is no doubt what the future holds for any who decide to become Eternal."

"Yes, no doubt remains in your promise." Kovacs eases in towards Carpenter with rebellious eyes. "Life is self-contained where tomorrow promises only more of the same for the remainder of time. You offer the unfailing, dry certainty of a billion todays, each bringing the same existence in differing attire. All hope of something greater is cast away like so many autumn leaves before the coming winter."

Carpenter waits to respond. He shakes his head slightly. "Marianne was right; you are delusional, Mr. Kovacs."

"So be it," Kovacs returns undaunted. "Enjoy your false glory, Mr. James Carpenter, for as long as it lasts."

"Then you mean for all time," Carpenter smarmily counters.

"If you think God will allow you to live on, the thief of his most precious gift, you are grandly deluded yourself. He will return to reclaim what is his, and return your dark soul to where it belongs. Get behind me, Satan. You have had your fun and soon it will be over."

"You first, Mr. Kovacs. With what Marianne has planned for you and your friends, you will be taking up residence in the abyss long before you imagine I will."

One Hundred Eight
Present Day

"James, who are you?"

399

"I'm sorry, Alex?" he replies while looking through his office picture window, imagining the pristine landscape beyond going on forever. Carpenter is postured in shaman-like clothing, pure and natural in loose fitting linens.

"I mean... I know who you are. But what do you believe yourself to be? I know how you came to be, but how do you understand your destiny?"

The jumble of thoughts and emotions over the last few tumultuous days has left Traeger needing answers and clarity. Before him, he sees a man whom he has almost considered his brother for several years, one he has worked with hand in hand. In the course of bringing Carpenter's vision to life, the shared struggle has developed a brotherly bond, perhaps even love. But the man he knew is changed. Traeger has sensed a shadowy pall creeping in, and he hopes his questions will summon back the man he once knew, a man he misses.

"Marianne has told me everything, if that's what you mean. I am a product of her brilliance and I am surprised it has taken you so long to ask."

"I didn't really know until, well, my time at the cabin with Marianne's former... you know," Traeger responds, leaving some truth unsaid. "So, she has told you of how you came to be? That you are..."

"Sourced from another? Yes. She has told me. I am the second coming of a man of great influence, Jesus Christ. Many believe him to be the son of God, God made into man."

He pivots to face Traeger. "Christ was a lie," Carpenter boldly declares. "I am his genetic twin and I sense no kinship to any god. God is fiction. I am a man of superior breed, a reincarnation harvested by Marianne to bring eternal life, for all here on earth." He cocks his head and looks deeper into Traeger, almost menacingly. "And what do you believe me to be, Alex?"

Traeger thinks of many answers, none of which would be good to say out loud. He changes the subject. "I am wondering if you compare yourself in any way to the original."

"The original Christ?"

"Yes."

Carpenter paces a few steps, facing away, hands clasping behind him. He pauses then abruptly turns back, his face aflame and passionate. "Alex, it is time you should know something about me. Long ago, when I was a child, Marianne saw in me a quality like no other. She calls it, 'an understanding of the depth of everything.' Nothing is hidden from me. I see the mass of humanity in one resonant harmony. I possess perfected intuition. I can sing a note that is music to all and they sing it back to me as praise."

"James... I..." Traeger's greatest fears slither in closer. The James Carpenter he knew is clearly something darker, now unveiled. A chill stabs his spirit, some indistinct awareness poking at him.

"I know how humanity is built, it is as plain as day," Carpenter continues fervently. "As with you, an architect, you see the finished structure and know all that lies behind the walls. You know the forces at work that give it strength and what would cause it to crumble. You see both the glorious beauty and the hidden, glaring flaws. The structure *I know* is humankind, and it is far from a finished work. My abilities and vision sanction my authority to act as both architect and rebuilder. Mine is the task to bring it to perfection."

Traeger tries to conceal a sinking sense of doom and stumbles out another question. "How does perfection look to you, James?"

"All of history is marked by conquest and nation-building, kingdoms rising and falling. Empires built for their own purposes and all the while unable to recognize they were cultivating their own inevitable demise. Humanity's greatest shortcoming is its inability to act as one, to come together with a single purpose, rather than divide and conquer."

"And how will you accomplish that?" Traeger asks with cautious dread.

"You see, Alex, my genetic predecessor understood humankind the same as I. By inventing the idea of a life after this one, something larger and more promising than this meager existence, he focused the eye of humanity on something beyond itself and even past earthly existence. Humans want to believe they are part of something bigger than just themselves. It is how all progress occurs."

"I understand that, James, but..."

"Christ's greatest mistake was to embolden the *individual* to define their own existence and destiny instead of focusing on the collective. In time, without any proof of the reward, the foundations inevitably crumble."

Traeger's heart is leaping in his chest. He is overcome with trepidation. But he also senses deeper within himself a surging counter strength, one not belonging entirely to himself.

"Marianne and I have made the reward a reality, and for that we shall receive all due praise and glory."

"But, James you also control their—"

Carpenter raises a hand, then pauses to explain calmly. "Yes, humans are stubborn and rebellious. Marianne and I have decided that an orderly compliance is the best means to scuttle rogue intent. It is our right to do so. It is in the interest of the common good." Carpenter smiles, consumed in his own confidence. He proclaims, "The truest form of happiness comes from setting one's own interest aside and giving one's self to the whole, don't you think?"

Carpenter steps in closer, his form firm and empowered. "Alex, bow before your king. Kneel before your savior," he commands.

Traeger's stomach turns. Anxious turmoil pulls at him from deep within. It is apparent to him, in this one small moment, the balance of all possible outcomes hangs. The thought of supplicating himself to Carpenter's will sickens him, but he does so. Taking a knee, Traeger is filled with a strength from a place beyond. He decides, instead of Carpenter, his knee is bowed to the one true God. He gives thanks to the Almighty for trusting him with this formidable task and lending him the grace to perform it. The crucial moment has arrived, the one predicted by William Reader.

Traeger feels his lip against his teeth. The wound inside his mouth left by Marianne's fist remains unhealed, assuring Traeger that Kipner's cure is in full bloom and ready to be set free. Traeger's sanctified eyes find Carpenter's. He bites down hard on the wound, reopening it while he rises to his feet. A sting, and the taste of iron swirls on his tongue. He approaches Carpenter. Traeger lays his palms on Carpenter's shoulders.

"Here's to a kingdom without end, James." Traeger presses his lips to Carpenter's. Blood mingles with saliva. The remedy is delivered. There is no earthly guarantee, but Traeger's newfound clarity promises him that it is done.

***

Striding confidently back to his quarters at the Institute, Traeger's thoughts return to his time in the ransacked cabin. There was no other choice than to make himself the vessel for the cure. He injected himself with Hamer's serum. It was the only way to get it anywhere near Carpenter, the source of all the Eternals. He knew that once infected with Kipner's version, Carpenter himself would become the means to transmit it to all. Kipner's version will remain hidden away and passed on through the maintenance doses at the temples, working its stealth magic until all have received it. By the time its presence is discovered, with Eternals falling from their perfection, it will be too late to reverse it. The retrovirus will have spread as wildfire.

There will be upheaval. There will be a global correction to the order of things with some measure of devastation and destruction. But after any wildfire comes the new growth, greener than any. Things will pass away leaving something better to rise from the ashes—humanity restored rightfully to its flawed, uncertain imperfection.

Four Months Later

One Hundred Nine
Present Day

"Nearly three years ago, James Carpenter announced the dawning of his Eternals process, claiming nothing less than eternal life for all residents of planet Earth. Carpenter's own Institute reports there are now nearly two billion people who have undergone the transformation. All is well for most, but there are increasing reports of a growing number of individuals experiencing mixed results, if not an exact opposite effect," Christy Raines delivers from behind the prominent television news desk once occupied by journalist Stewart Waverly.

Six weeks ago, Waverly had to surrender the desk indefinitely due to an *unknown physical setback*. Raines now enjoys the limelight, and the journalistic gravitas that anchoring the world's most-watched news broadcast brings with it. Although a logical heir to a spotlight of such import, any competition to the position had severely dwindled. Vast numbers of the camera-facing community eagerly committed their fate to Carpenter's handiwork. Many apparent successors fell victim to the same affliction as Waverly. The network decided it better to assign the helm to someone less predisposed to random physical occurrences—someone not Eternal.

"World Headline News has contacted The Carpenter Institute repeatedly for an on-camera interview," Raines reports, her cadence charged with vindication and renewed confidence. "These requests have been answered with a lone statement that the Institute is looking into these claims and will comment at a further date."

She turns to face another camera. "In the field, we have our own Alain Hadjimi investigating. Alain?"

"Thank you, Christy," Hadjimi responds in smooth, polished reporter-speak adorned in a silky French accent. In the background, over his shoulder, one of Carpenter's temples stands stoic. A gathering of villagers stirs, unsettled. "Regardless of The Carpenter Institute's claims, undeniable are eyewitness accounts, including this reporter's own observations that, as we journey through South America, we are seeing many cases of a sort of *reverse* effect. You should see now, scrolling through our feed, some before-and-after images. These images show individuals who seem to have aged ten or even twenty years in less than a week's time. These are rare, indeed, although, there is some unverified data that seems to indicate the failure rate is increasing. All summed, claims of Eternal life, or even heightened physical improvement seem to be a hit-and-miss proposition. The consensus is that, early on, the process is a genuine effect delivering as promised. However, over time it seems there can be a random diminishment, which in some cases, is rapid and extreme."

* * *

"Tell me, GOD DAMMIT!" screams Marianne at Patricia Hamer, who is trying to steady her trembling fingertips to enter commands on a keyboard while unhinged rage seethes above her. Marianne's undoing is not limited to emotional turmoil. It is as much the construct of her physical being. The sultry beauty of her own manufacture is pulling away at the seams. Bit by bit, the one she hid away, Adeline Brandt, is emerging from the depths to haunt her. The genetic tailoring Brandt stitched so long ago to entomb her natural self is succumbing to the ravages of Anders Kipner's deft viral artistry. Like a moth devouring the taut weave, his genetics eagerly feed. He has his revenge, albeit one orchestrated from the grave.

Her body is a battleground, Marianne versus Adeline. Slowly, Brandt is winning, overtaking the alter ego. To the eye, she is both—some parts still

Marianne and others Brandt, a ghoulish specter of incongruity. She looks to be two persons haphazardly mashed together, some bits deformed and aged, others the empty shadow of the sleek Marianne.

Hamer struggles frantically to pull herself together. The past few months have been an ordeal of incremental terror, living day by day at the whim of Marianne's creeping demise. Observing Marianne's deteriorating state, she fears worse things may soon be upon her. Hamer decided to finally confess the truth in hopes it will lead to her freedom, either one living or one in death. Either way, she decided, at least she will be at peace.

She navigates her files and notes now, ones captured in the raid on the cabin. "Here," she points. "Here they are. Have a look yourself," Hamer directs.

"I have no time to look. Tell me what it is. What did you find?" Marianne growls.

"There," Hamer points again. "This is the genome weaponized in a retro-virus. It was lying dormant in Kovacs since some time during your project long ago. We suspect it was introduced by your colleague Kipner. Eventually it activated, overriding the Eternals chain."

Brandt straightens up as much as she is allowed by her embattled frame. Her face contorts, bringing an even more unsightly visage. She shouts into an earpiece mic, "SMITH... JONES... get down to the lab immediately." In a far corner, Alex Traeger stands rigid and stone-faced. Marianne's ire redirects. She hobbles over to administer her venom. "You... in the cabin... of course, you brought the virus here. It was intentional. We trusted you. We MADE you. You will join us in HELL, Traeger!"

She is deteriorated and broken, but Brandt's dark, vile soul stabs away at Traeger, slashing into his very foundations. Accompanying her distorted presence, an atmosphere of demonic ether hangs heavy. Undetectable to the eye, tempestuous vengeance churns wild.

Hamer sees her frightened friend, his face flushed of hope. Her own heart tumbles further into a chasm of despair.

"Marianne?" Jones asks as he lumbers in with a cane, depleted and sallow, teetering in weakness. "What is going on?"

"Where is Smith?"

"He couldn't make it. He can't walk."

"Take these two. Dispose of them in any way you see fit. The others too, they are worthless to me now," Brandt snarls.

"Him too?" Jones queries, looking at Traeger. He deciphers agreement in Marianne's face. "YOU!" Jones blasts at Traeger. "I knew all along." He angles back to Brandt. "I tried to tell you, but you wouldn't listen. You've murdered us all, Brandt."

A snap punctuates the conversation. Jones tumbles to the floor screaming bloody agony, his left leg folded back like a flamingo, the mere weight of gravity the only force needed. Marianne, indifferent to his helpless state, looms over him returning rebuke.

In one motion, Hamer snatches the laptop from the desk and slams it down on Marianne's skull. Hamer delivers another blow and another, some administered of practiced training, the remainder of pent up wrath. With Marianne collapsed and unconscious, Traeger seizes the bloodied laptop from Hamer and calms her rage with a reassuring look. He grabs Jones' security card and hands it to Hamer. With bold, determined eyes he commands, "Go to the Keep. Get everyone and meet me at the far southern end of the campus. I know a way out where we will be undetected."

"What about you, Alex?"

"I am going to get my kids. I will meet you there. On the lower floor there is a janitor's closet. Inside and beyond there is a passage to safety. Hurry."

407

Both begin the journey to their destinations. Initially, they move with cautioned stealth, but it is apparent there is no need. The Institute is in disarray. Staff is sparse. Security, in most cases, have abandoned their posts. Access is not a problem; the card readers still work.

So many signs of abandonment and chaos feeds Traeger's anxiety concerning what may have come of the only ones who matter to him. His whole world is now his children's safety.

One Hundred Ten
Present Day

Traeger arrives at the private wing of The Carpenter Institute. Since his former wife's conversion, she has enjoyed *elite* status, which has awarded her and their children first-class accommodations and rarified access. Traeger's only hope for a quick exit is finding them hunkered down in their quarters. Arriving urgently, his worries subside. Good fortune shines. His hunch was correct.

"Jason, Melissa," he sighs with swelling tears of joy. His children dash over to meet his eager embrace. Their faces wear worry and confusion. A smile seems to comfort them. "Hurry, we must leave immediately. There is no time to waste," Traeger pleads gently.

"Dad," the firstborn, Jason, implores desperately, "what about, Mom?" He points to a hallway.

"Let me go check," Traeger reassures. "You two fill your backpacks with some clothes. Be ready in three minutes, okay?"

A short, but dreadful, walk leads to a darkened bedroom. The bed holds a rumpled pile, some of which could be Valerie. Talons of distress scrape down the insides of Traeger's skin. He prepares to discover a corpse.

Muffled mumbles escape from beneath the pile. Traeger's trembling hands slowly pull them down.

"Alex?"

"Yes, Valerie," he responds, the words bearing the weight of boulders.

"Oh Alex, it is you. I have lost my sight but I know your voice. I will never forget your voice... The kids?" she forces out with as much alarm as she can muster.

"They are fine. I will look after them," he reassures her, grateful she is unable to see his horrified face. He takes pause to consider the sight before him. His eyes demand answers. Her once flowing hair is now patchy and white. The fit yoga body has been whittled to a skeletal rail draped with a fragile cloth of skin. Her form-fitting athletic wear hangs slack. It must have happened rapidly, he decides.

"Valerie... I... I don't..."

"Take the children. They shouldn't see me like this. When James fixes all this, bring them back. I know he will. He is working on it now. It will be better soon and then it will all be all back to normal. We will talk then."

It is the last he will ever hear from her. Traeger knows it. He thinks for a moment to tell her there will be no *back to normal*. But then he decides it better she die with some hope than in utter despair. A chill shoots through him as he realizes she would not be in her current condition had he not released Kipner's virus. Guilt runs thick and oily. It was her decision, but she had no idea what would come next, or that her death would be partially of his own hand.

He moves to better thoughts. Though their life together was troubled and contentious, now all the resentment melts to black and pours away. The clarity of the moment now shows him only the one person with whom he ever shared himself through times of great joy, despair, doubt, triumph and struggle. The early years were the best of their lives. Hope and future with an endless bounty of possibilities seemed theirs for the taking. For all her failings, he thinks, she does not deserve this. Thinking he may now have some greater influence, he implores God to grant her, when she is in his presence, all he wished to give her but never could.

Gingerly, he slides down to the bed. Carefully, he finds a way to pull her in close with his arms. Her brittle body relaxes. Finding her ear, he whispers words long stuck in his heart, ones lashed down for as long as memory serves, now soaring as doves. "I love you, Valerie." A gentle smile finds her lips. He kisses her cheek. A tear lands next baptizing her with grace and forgiveness.

He eases away. It is time to leave, but the bedroom threshold is made impassable, blocked by the children. "We need to go," he whispers. They remain, unyielding. Traeger sees in their faces unshakable determination, but also a newfound maturity. Silently, they convey to Traeger they are aware that this is the last moment they have with their mother and are willing to share it regardless of the horror. He motions them to the bed. A pile of four Traegers lie in silence, one last time fused together by love.

One Hundred Eleven
Present Day

"Follow me, guys. My friends are waiting for us," Traeger instructs as he guides his children through the weaving corridors of the private residence areas. Museum-quality art used to adorn the hallways; now only shadows remain as evidence of their existence. The valuables, looted by staff, are long gone. Traeger's treasures follow close behind.

A figure approaches from down the hall. "Wait," Traeger whispers urgently, silently directing the two to a darkened doorway. The children cower motionless in whatever concealment they can find. The figure nears, a man with gray hair, sixties maybe. A hallway light illuminates the face as one changed, but one familiar.

"Jonas?" Traeger chases the silence away.

"Alex?"

"Why are you here, Cardinal? Was it Patricia who freed you?"

"It was." Kovacs places his hands on Traeger's shoulders and smiles knowingly in thanks. "The rest are waiting. I told them I would only be a few minutes. There is something I must do first."

"Jonas." Traeger tugs at Kovacs' arm and sternly commands, "We need to leave."

Kovacs hesitates, then confesses. "I need to see him."

"Why?"

"I just do."

Compelled, Kovacs slides past Traeger. Despite his better senses, Traeger follows with his children dutifully in tow. Kovacs arrests his determined gait, now unsure of his destination. Traeger finishes Kovacs' thought. "That one, the one straight ahead," he advises, referring to a large double door of stately bearing. Kovacs continues forth more cautiously, reverently perhaps. Slowly he opens the door and the room spreads wide, the grand dwelling of James Carpenter.

Sullen and motionless, Carpenter lies upon a bed with white linen shrouding his hollowed form. Carpenter's face is sallow and drained, hair thinned and graying, the beard unkempt and patchy. Kovacs stands above looking down. He is petrified, the scene so perplexing and surreal. Christ depicted as a withered man suffering death is not an uncommon image, but seeing him now as a man of advanced age is irreconcilable. Only now can Kovacs allow

411

himself to appreciate the image of the man before him, the literal carbon copy of the one he hails as "Lord." What a mighty presence he surely was. Carpenter, though not the Christ, is the exact human image of the most influential man to ever walk the Earth. For the remainder of his days, when Kovacs imagines life two millennia prior, he will have a face and form to accompany the narrative. Carpenter's way, his mannerisms and expressions, were probably not far removed from those of the actual Christ. For this, and only this, he is grateful for Brandt's unthinkable pursuit.

"I fear I am too late," Kovacs breathes out to himself.

Traeger gathers Jason and Melissa. He decides they have seen enough death for one day and leads them to a bench outside the quarters. He assures them he will be just a few moments. Traeger returns to find the Cardinal kneeling bedside the bed, head bowed, hands laid upon Carpenter's head. The only word Traeger hears is "Amen."

Kovacs rises up, eyes still fixed on Carpenter. Traeger approaches. "Is he gone, Jonas?"

"If not, it will be soon. He is cool to the touch," he whispers. "We should go, Alex."

From the bed they hear, "Am I one worthy of prayer, Cardinal?" Carpenter struggles out a question, startling Kovacs and Traeger.

Kovacs kneels again. He leans in to Carpenter. "All are worthy of prayer, James. I have said many a prayer for you over time."

"You find me an abomination. You have said it," Carpenter pushes out, eyes opening to meet Kovacs.

"How you came to be was an abomination. That is not yours to own. What you grew into is a different matter," Kovacs answers.

"Am I a devil, the enemy of God? Am I a disease, a blasphemy? What do you believe me to be, holy man?"

"You... you..." Kovacs sighs, letting go any harbored contempt, leaving him with only mercy. "You are a man, just a man, a sinner like the rest of us," Kovacs replies as acceptance and absolution to Carpenter. "You are a man needing God's forgiveness through the grace of Christ. I seek only to hasten your redemption. It is the least you deserve."

"So be it then... I am a sinner," Carpenter strains to find Traeger. "Alex?"

"Yes, James," Traeger kneels.

Carpenter's eyes wear the sadness of abandonment, now a soul starkly alone and unloved. "You truly were my friend. I think maybe my only friend. For that, I am grateful. You betrayed me for reasons I do not understand. But I hold no hatred for you or what you have done." He looks to Kovacs with absolved but conquered eyes. "You were right, Jonas. God would not allow this to continue."

Carpenter's eyes wander, breathing rattling and distant.

"You should go, Alex. I wish to stay to shepherd him across," Kovacs gently directs.

"You should all leave," Carpenter forces out. "If you stay you will be in great danger. Please, this I know. Now, go."

They leave Carpenter to his finality. In the corridor, Traeger has one more request. "Jonas, I know we should really be leaving. If you will please, quickly," he points to another door, "Valerie needs prayers. Will you?"

Kovacs returns minutes later, ones seeming as hours to the Traeger family. Kovacs' eyes are somber and drained from seeing the face of death too many times. As dismissal he mutters, "Now, we must leave."

The four journey swiftly toward their freedom, corridors and stairs along Traeger's proscribed route. While climbing into the train tunnel, the final passage out to freedom, Traeger is pulsing with disquiet. He is unsure how he will be greeted after being unable to release his colleagues who spent months in the Keep. He arrives to find them waiting, released from captivity by Hamer. At first they stare coldly, but soon any remaining animosity melts at the realization their struggle is over. Smiles and hugs put the last of concern to rest. Traeger's age shows a few more years since that day, Myer even more. They push on to freedom. The deeper conversation can wait.

One Hundred Twelve
Present Day

"James, my beloved," wails Marianne. All hope lost for finding a solution, she finds her final refuge at the side of the only thing she has ever loved. "It is over, James. Why, when offered paradise, does the world spit upon it and reject it? We gave all of them a chance at salvation and endless hope, but instead they prefer death."

She caresses his chest, once so perfect and proud, now a skin-shrouded ribcage. The once-powerful shoulders now left as bony points. His face is void and blank. "You are my masterpiece, James, the greatest scientific achievement in all of history." She stares off into emptiness to indulge her grandiosity. "Of our legacy, when all is revealed, they will study all we have accomplished. The name *Adeline Brandt* will be reviled, the poster child of *unethical, dark science*, the new Goebbels and Mengele all wrapped into one. Then in the privacy of their laboratories, they will strive mightily to reproduce everything I have done. It is inevitable."

She rolls to her side, clumsy and pained, dried blood matting her hair. She lays her head on his chest like so many times before recalling tender moments, moments of bliss. It was to never end. She was the owner of time itself. She fishes her cell phone from her garments, then taps the screen a few times. "Oh yes, they will all try to reproduce what I have done so many years before, but not with *my* science." She places a capsule between her teeth, bites down, and taps the cell phone once more. In seconds, she is gone.

* * * *

Seven travelers follow the rails from The Carpenter Institute. In silence, weary and worn, they step forward to freedom. There will be a time to talk, but this moment is one too soon. For now, all thoughts are on finding a place of peace and sustenance.

The silence is broken by a series of jarring explosions, colossal and ominous, several times in chain reaction. They turn, shocked at the ferocity. Behind them, flames and debris shoot skyward above the distant tree line. A hundred feet in the air, maybe two.

"She blew it up," Chandler announces, agape with amazement.

Alex Traeger's heart clenches one more time. They are all gone for sure, now. Valerie, the one least deserving. He pulls his children, now made motherless, close to him. They are the true innocents. For a moment, he curses William Reader. He is to blame for their loss. There had to be others capable of the small thing he did. Inspiration washes over him. He recalls what he asked of God for Valerie. A deeper sense of himself is assured that the request is now granted. He smiles, relieved.

Kovacs notices his friend and asks, "What is it Alex?" Traeger looks upon his children, then deep into the Cardinal's eyes and smiles a greater smile. "Ah, yes. I understand." Kovacs smiles back.

Jason finds an opportunity in the moment to seek answers for what is foremost on his mind. "Dad, when can we eat? I'm starving."

"Yeah, Dad," Melissa chimes in.

"I know a good place not far from here that serves a Salisbury steak that is to die for," Kovacs pitches out like a local.

"Seriously?" Hamer shoots back, incredulous. "You really said *to die for*?"
"So, you're hungry, kid? Let me tell you something about being hungry," Myer quips.

All too much, the tension breaks. The weariness wears off.

"I'm buying," Traeger volunteers.

"You better," Myer throws back.

"Ivan, that's not called for," Hamer shames.

"No, no, I mean no one else has any money."

Another collective laugh fills the open field.

One Month Later

One Hundred Thirteen
Present Day

"Although Carpenter's science is still not completely understood, The Center for Disease Control reports they have one hundred percent confidence the genetic variable that appears to be affecting the Eternal population is not contagious in any way to non-Eternals, either through airborne means or even blood transfusion. Investigation continues, but the CDC confirms, and I quote, 'the variant is only viable in combination with the Eternals condition and no other,'" Christy Raines informs the world from her news desk.

"In a related story, we have Sasha Malevic reporting on the continuing losses of celebrities, noteworthy academic minds, and captains of industry as further fallout from Carpenter's legacy. Sasha?"

Ivan Myer closes his laptop ending the news stream. "It's so nice to see Christy in her element again," he says with a satisfied grin.

"You say that like you know her," Hamer returns, surprised.

"We worked together on some things a long time ago. You know me, Pat. I've worked with everyone at one time or another. Last I saw her was at The Carpenter Institute."

"The Institute? Her?" Hamer asks, even more surprised.

"I was helping her. That's how I got caught. I'm pretty sure she fell out of favor because of her association with me—*the spy*. It's probably why she never became an Eternal."

"Lucky for her."

"As it turned out."

"Have you talked to her since?"

"No... I..." Myer hesitates, some weight of culpability bearing down. "I'm pretty sure she won't ever talk to me again," he replies, fighting off disgrace.

"I think you should, Ivan. It all worked out okay."

"We'll see, Pat."

"Who's up for burgers?" Traeger announces to the gathered, the same seven who found their way from The Carpenter Institute, now assembled on his back patio.

"Dad, can we go eat in the other room? We want to start a movie," Jason pleads.

"Sure thing, kids. We have some adult things to chat about anyway... Don't forget napkins," Traeger calls out as they leave.

Hamer observes the content smile on Traeger's face. She stands and quietly says to him, "They both seem to be doing much better, Alex. It's good to see."

"Thank you. We talk a lot about it. It's still very fresh," Traeger replies contemplatively. "Losing their mom this young in life will always be with them. Jonas has been a big help." He pauses, emotion rising up. "I think you all being here helps too."

Traeger's eyes water. She takes his hand, smiling her sympathy as she says. "She made her own choices, Alex. You did what had to be done,"

"I know. But it still hurts."

Plates fill: burgers, slaw, green beans, and Jonas Kovacs' contribution, a Hungarian potato casserole. Wine and beer refill glasses. They take places around a table on the back deck.

"Thanks for doing this, Alex," Marcus Chandler pops out in between bites.

"It's my pleasure. I wanted to see you all again. You're my family now," Traeger responds as he gazes fondly around the table.

"Here, here!" Kovacs seconds, raising his glass. The others follow.

Myer's inquisitive nature and some self-concern arrive to ask a question. "Pat, you're the one who spent so much time with Brandt's documentation, so I am going to ask. Why do you think there is such a variance in the deterioration path of the Eternals? My aging seems to have stopped at where I was before I became Eternal, maybe a few years past, I suppose."

"It's hard to say without running an empirical study. But off the cuff, it appears anyone who was an original Eternal had a very rough time with it. They deteriorated very fast. Those initially given the deteriorated version seem to be like you and Jonas, returning to where they began."

Traeger asks, "Would you consider my outlook similar to Jonas since we both received Kipner's version at first?"

"I see no reason to assume otherwise," Hamer answers. "But, based on hearsay, there seems to be some randomness across the spectrum, so it's hard to know for sure. We will just have to see how things play out in the long run."

Kovacs follows up. "Do you think anyone will ever unlock Kipner's genetics, try to reverse the effect?"

"I fear a lot of things, Cardinal," Hamer replies. "No matter what happens, there are millions of people out there with the Eternals genes inside them. Some of them are very smart and harbor ill intent. My one hope is that the world has had enough of this whole mess and will reject any further dalliance. At the very least, there needs to be some strict global discussion on what can be tolerated."

Hamer's oration is interrupted when she notices Chandler solemnly staring down to his plate, his fork randomly pushing food around. "Marcus, yes, I know..." she sympathetically airs. "Don't think I haven't thought of what you must be going through now."

"It's inevitable, Pat. It's just a matter of time," Chandler drips out grimly while beginning to quake. "Retroviruses are designed to proliferate. It will find me soon enough and my fate is sealed." He pauses to clear a growing lump of angst from his throat. "It's not the death part of it, I welcome that. It's just not going to be pretty. I saw Brandt in her last days... Smith and Jones..."

Hamer puts her hand on his. Chandler's eyes raise up to her, swollen and worried. "I'm scared, Pat."

"I'll be there with you. I can make it as painless as possible. I will watch over you, Marcus. You will not be alone," she soothes with tears of her own. "Thank you, Patricia. You are an angel of the first degree."

The mood thick, meals continue in silence until Myer's unfailing curiosity submits another change of subject. "There is one gargantuan elephant in the room."

"What's that?" Traeger asks.

"I imagine there are only a small number of people who know, most of whom are sitting at this table,"

"Know what?" Kovacs urges.

"The source of the Eternals. That's what you're getting at, right Myer?" Chandler adds. Myer nods. "I've thought about that too. It will get out somehow, followed by another upheaval of global proportion," he finishes with concerned eyes looking Kovacs' way.

"It isn't true. My faith is unshakable. Christ was not the product of genetic superiority," the Cardinal declares.

Myer counters, bolstering his own point. "Cardinal, everything Brandt suspected, all she theorized played out just as she described."

"Not exactly," Hamer breaks in.

"Not exactly?" Chandler retorts.

"Since we all were freed, I have been spending more time with her work notes and science. I needed to know the answer to that question myself."

"Wasn't that all confiscated and destroyed, Pat?" Myer asks.

"I saved it off to your cloud site before we were raided at the cabin," she chuckles.

"Pat, you scamp," Myer barbs back playfully with a grin.

"So, what did you find?" Traeger presses, curiosity too much to bear.

"As one might expect, the Christ genes she found were incomplete, damaged," Hamer responds. "After all, it had been two thousand years. She had to make educated guesses about the missing material, so she manufactured some to patch what was missing."

"So, she corrupted the original," Chandler slides in.

"Essentially," Hamer agrees. "Eventually, the final product was more a manufacture of her own design. I think, given her brilliance, talent, and arrogant compulsion, she managed to figure it out on her own and she may not have even been aware of it. She sold her own gifts short, as it turned out. She wanted to believe in her own biblical myth more than her own genius."

"How much did she add?" Myer asks.

"We'll never know, but adding anything changed it from a harvesting project to a makeover. So, to Myer's point, and to the relief of the good Cardinal here, there is no case for Christ simply being a freak of genetics. Further, once she resorted to the Hail Mary pass of impregnating herself,"— she smiles at a wincing Kovacs,—"sorry, Jonas, it's just an expression... Inevitably, her science is too tainted to know what corruptions were introduced. Her lust for success led her astray and her genius was more than even she suspected."

"So, basically, she invented Eternals all on her own," Traeger blurts out, slightly amazed.

"Then there's Kipner's influence," Kovacs adds.

"Right," Chandler nods. "He was working with this stuff every day. He might have manipulated some of it, maybe to pair it better with his own doomsday genes."

"Well put," Myer concedes. "It looks like maybe the world has dodged that theological mess. And I'm glad for it," he finishes with a hand to Kovacs' shoulder. "By the way, Cardinal. What are your plans now?"

"I am going to write and teach. This tribulation has brought many inspirations to me. I feel so blessed by God to have been an instrument of his own hand and to right my wrong from years before," Kovacs robustly replies, carried forth by a new sense of purpose.

"Are you going to return to the monastery?" Hamer asks.

"Briefly. I will say my final farewell, this time a blessed one, to my Buddhist brothers before I am too frail to journey. Then I shall return."

"He is staying with us," Traeger submits to the group's surprised but grateful eyes. "I can think of no greater honor than to have you as an example for my children, in their presence, and mine. You will be cared for in the best fashion I have at my disposal, my brother Jonas." Traeger smiles thoughtfully, a contagious smile to all.

"And what of you, Pat?" Myer questions with added agenda.

"I am going to return to work. Unfortunately, the restoration of the impermanence of the human condition means death and murder are a reality once again," she answers grimly.

"That sounds about right. Can I make a suggestion, though?" Myer begins a new thought.

Hamer prepares for the other shoe to drop and smirks. "Go on... "

"You put a bug in my ear earlier. I think I will reconnect with Christy Raines." Myer's face grows serious. "I think you should join me."

"Join you?" she replies, perplexed.

Myer's face assumes a countenance of resolve. "The world needs to know everything. This must never happen again and the most certain way is for everyone to know every nut and bolt, and you are the only one who should tell it."

"Ivan, I..." she shyly replies while shaking her head. Determined stares from the assembled issue unanimous declaration. She yields. "Okay, I'll do it."

One Hundred Fourteen
Four Years Earlier

"Jonas, my dear friend. Tomorrow it begins. My calculations reveal it as the most opportune event window available. My only regret is that I will not be around to watch it blossom. I will do my part, now you must do yours," reminds William Reader via video camera. Reader's robust form, perched in an armchair in his cozy personal library, amidst billows of cigar smoke and wearing a robe open at the chest, casts him as the Buddha soaring among the clouds.

"Back then we decided the signal would be an empty envelope, but I have decided to send you this message as well. Your return to the city of postmark is one of good fortune. You return to a city with which you are well familiar. I wish I could be the one to greet you."

A brief grin of camaraderie follows, one quickly erased by Reader's next thought. "I had hoped other means less drastic would arise, but it seems a moment of permanence is the only option. Do not despair. I am weary of this life, and my learned understanding of the years to come will be ones of fantastic upheaval for the residents of this planet. Additionally, as we suspected, I sense Carpenter and his henchmen Smith and Jones will not allow my survival much longer. I am surprised they have left me alone this long. I am a loose end that must be tidied up. Brandt is out there somewhere, too. I have no idea where. I have tried to track her down, but she left no trace. If only I could tell you where to look."

Reader puffs again, momentary distraction for a collection of his next thought. Smoke blows past the recorder's lens. Reader's form materializes again.

"There is one change, Jonas. After many attempts, discernment of a *chosen one* has proven a barren result. My method has been exhausted and no individual has emerged. After much thought, I have decided a different way." Reader pauses for effect and to gather the fortitude to issue audible concession to his cardinal friend, the man of belief. "Jonas, I am leaving the matter to faith. I chose a man, just a man. He is a good man, one of pure heart and dedication. He will serve you well, I think. And certainly, with you as his guide, and all the powers you summon, he will succeed. Good luck, my good friend… my best friend… my brother. I think you will need some. Godspeed, Cardinal Jonas Kovacs."

Reader falls back, swallowed in the armchair. He gives another puff into the lens and taps a finger on the remote control's "stop" button. Feeling unusually serene and at peace, he pulls a thumb drive from the camera's side and places it in an envelope. He presses his tongue to the flap and stops. He realizes it cannot be sent. The recording will bias the flow. Faith is faith. If Kovacs views this recording, he will be made aware of Traeger's status, one not *chosen*. Chosen, but not *chosen*. In order for faith to do as faith does, Kovacs must believe the course is the one they decided upon decades ago. Reader pulls the thumb drive from the envelope and snaps it in two.

One Hundred Fifteen
Present Day

"Ivan, it is so good to see you. You look different, somehow," Christy Raines' glee rebounds off the walls of a grand marbled space, the lobby of the World Headline News headquarters.

"It's a long tale, Chris," Myer spills with casual wit. "We can talk about it later. First, I have someone you should meet."

Raines offers a welcoming smile met with a hand extending from the woman standing beside Myer, who says, "I'm Patricia Hamer. I have a story I think you might be interested in."

* * *

Seven stories down, beneath the overgrowth of a United States government-owned swath of the Allegheny Mountains, a rusted screw hatch lies unturned for over thirty orbits of the Earth around the sun. Unknown to any, a menacing history remains entombed. And only for an unlikely series of events, involving a comprehensive audit of long-archived government documents and dark budgets, will it ever be unearthed.

But malicious energies inevitably find their way to culture a new stir of mischief. Seldom do stones remain unturned in perpetuity. Eventually, the creatures of the dark find their release to cast their shadows on the world of light. And if these forces whisper their beguiling words in a fruitful direction, an ear with a curious character would uncover a mystery. For deep in those archives, a paper trail leads to an abandoned bomb shelter. And seven stories below the surface, a cryogenic freezer powered by an uninterrupted source of energy, funded by dark money, holds a bounty of dubious content. Frozen in suspense at negative 150 degrees centigrade lie several vacuum sealed containers marked "471K8D."

Presently, the world has found a new day, one with the full sun gleaming a renewed promise of tomorrow. But the sun always sets and the world will, once again, close its eyes to sleep.